The

CHANGED MAN

The
CHANGED MAN

The Olympic Peninsula series # 4

Cat Treadgold

The Changed Man
ISBN: 979-8-9877363-4-0 (Trade Paperback)
Library of Congress Control Number: 2024903650

Any references to historical events, real people, or real places are used fictitiously. Names of restaurants and companies central to the plot are products of the author's imagination.

Cover design by Gemma Rakia @gemmarakia
Interior design by Cat Treadgold
Anacortes, Washington
cat@cattreadgold.com
www.CatTreadgold.com

Printed in the United States of America

The Olympic Peninsula series

The Silent Woodsman

The Guardsman

The Magic Man

The Changed Man

The Fallen Man

Beyond the Olympic Peninsula series

Mister Movie Star

(Coming Soon)

Miz Country Goddess

Mister Heartbreaker

CONTENTS

PART I

CHAPTER 1

Jake O'Connell's silver BMW bounced over a pothole in the gravel road. He winced, rubbing his stiff neck. *Why not pave the damn thing?* he thought. *It's not like Joe can't afford it.* The rocky road leading to his brother's estate was an apt metaphor for what, most likely, lay ahead. Should Jake have tried to smooth the way for his surprise visit?

He hadn't anticipated the first gate, though the extra security was understandable. A gangly, shaggy young man who reminded him of Scooby-Doo's owner—wasn't the character's name "Shaggy"?—asked him if he was here for the wedding. Wonder of wonders, Jake was on the guest list, though he hadn't RSVP'd. Invite or no, his rash decision to surface in the placid pond of his brother's idyllic new life would be about as welcome as toxic algae.

Though estranged from his twin for years, Jake had kept abreast of the country music star's retreat from fame—if not fortune. Financially, all the O'Connells were rolling in clover, thanks to their father's patents, the family business—Big Paul's Outfitters—and their grandmother's astute investments.

A year after his impressive career as a country music icon had been torpedoed by vocal issues, Joe and Ali had moved here to raise identical twin daughters. Next, Ali's twin brother Liam had essentially risen from the dead and settled in one of the guest cottages. Then the youngest O'Connell and only girl, Teresa, came for a visit and never left. Jake's baby sister had been desperate to escape the clutches of their socialite mother—Jake totally got that. But would marrying Liam—Carrie's worst nightmare—really make her happy? His mother had led him to believe that Liam was essentially a handsome drifter. Finally, strangest of all, their older brother David, a physician with Doctors for Humankind in Africa, had abruptly returned to the States and joined the cult. Or commune. Was there a difference? This afternoon David would marry Maddie—an actress and the daughter of Laurie, Duncan's girlfriend. Ali and Liam's birth father Duncan had only recently reentered their lives. Maddie had hooked up with David while performing in a play at Port Townsend's local theater. All pretty damn incestuous.

Jake grinned, picturing Stephen King's *The Stand*, where the few plague survivors are drawn to Boulder, Colorado, to face the final battle of the Apocalypse. Like Y2K, maybe. Only seven months until the year 2000 dawned, with its computer-induced chaos. The way Jake's own life was going, the prospect of an apocalypse didn't scare him as much as it should.

Sure, he thought, *the Peninsula is nice and all, but why is everyone in my family being sucked into Joe's homestead like it's a magical vortex? And what is it with all these twins? It's positively biblical.*

Thanks to their father's untimely death when Joe and Jake had been nineteen, Jake had turned into *that* guy—the one who trod without question the family-sanctioned path and scheduled everything down to the minute. Not anymore. He might as well have flung all his possessions, including his ID and club cards, off a cliff. Who was he now? He knew who he *had* been or had striven to be: the powerful and respected CEO of Big Paul's Outfitters, wine connoisseur, sophisticated man about town. *Hah.*

"What's it all about … Alfie?" a gruff voice sang in his head. With a dry laugh, it added, "Talk about throwing the baby out with the bathwater."

That would be Rory, who talked like Edward G. Robinson in his gangster mode. Soon after his death, his best friend had taken up residence in Jake's head, his irreverent presence eerily audible—the uninvited and unconventional voice of Jake's conscience. Or was it his id? Jake believed psychoanalysis was hooey. So why was he starting to believe in ghosts?

"What?" he said aloud to Rory. "You think being CEO of BPO was the be-all and end-all?"

"It was to you. Your mom's gotta be so bummed."

Thank god he was alone. Anyone overhearing this bizarre conversation with his dead friend would assume he was nuts. Jake would be the first to agree.

"What makes you think she knows?"

"She's a big shareholder."

Yes, he thought, *she knows*. He was surprised she hadn't confronted him already.

Was this the final gate? According to the directions, yes. You had to be buzzed in. He checked his watch. Noon. Lunchtime for the unfashionable. The wedding wasn't until five. He hadn't thought this through at all. Where would he spend the night? Some B&B, sharing scones and eggs benedict with couples on romantic getaways? He blew out a disgusted puff of air. He'd prefer a seedy motel. For that, he'd have to drive to Port Angeles. Or Forks.

Would his family welcome him or gape in horror at the ultimate wedding crasher?

"Guess you're gonna find out," Rory said.

* * *

Ali was standing at the kitchen sink, gazing fondly at her "clan," all assembled on the flagstone terrace that overlooked the Strait of Juan de Fuca. Her husband Joe, ever the thoughtful brother, had been determined to avoid a last-minute scramble like on the morning of Teresa's wedding, nearly ruined by a freak storm.

Joe and Liam were constructing an African safari tent in the field next to their house. A structure right out of Colonial Africa: built on a wooden platform with an off-white canvas canopy and lots of flowy drapes. It was an odd addition to their ever-expanding compound and hardly practical in this climate. Port Townsend was cornered by the bay and the Strait of Juan de Fuca, so the ocean breezes made it feel cooler than the thermometer indicated. Temperatures rarely rose above 80, even in August. Being located in the Olympic Rain Shadow made it drier than Seattle, but May thirtieth could be on the nippy side.

Not today. Seventy degrees and nary a wisp of cloud. Just enough wind to bathe them all in bracing salty sea air and the pungent, earthy odors of the mossy forest that surrounded the property. The small gathering of friends and family lolled contentedly on their Adirondack chairs, faces raised skyward like sunflowers.

Ali started at the buzzing of the intercom. Who was missing? Becca and Jean-Louis weren't expected until four. She pushed the button, leaned into the speaker, and said, "Hello?"

A brief silence. She was about to alert Joe, worried that the tabloids had breached the first gate, when a male voice replied, "Uh, yeah, hi." A pause. "This is Jake. Here for the wedding?"

At first Ali was too shocked to reply. Her finger shook as it hovered over the button. Seeing no other option, she buzzed Jake in.

Dazed, she drifted out to the terrace. "Joe?"

Her husband looked up, instantly wary. She guessed all the blood had drained from her cheeks. The rest of them stared at her, slack-jawed, as if bracing to hear that a loved one had driven off a bridge.

"It's not bad news," she rushed to explain. "I'd say … just the opposite."

Hands raised in supplication, Joe said, "Sweetie, just tell us."

"Jake's here."

Her little bombshell stopped her husband dead in his tracks. She scanned the faces of her family and friends, which registered bewilderment rather than actual dismay. If anyone should feel dismayed, it was Ali. The last time she and Jake had spoken was in the limo coming home from the fundraiser. She'd confronted him about his motives, having just learned he was dating her to get back at his brother. Far from apologizing, he'd been angry. Incensed, really. Well, she'd been angry too! Not that she'd had any right to be. She'd agreed to go out with him only because of his uncanny resemblance to the man she knew as "JJ." She hadn't realized they were brothers—fraternal twins, in fact—until Joe had resurfaced at the fundraiser. After that, her future husband had blown hot and cold, driving her nuts. Unlike Jake, who had given her the royal treatment, complete with wining and dining and gifts of expensive clothing.

Pulling her back to the present, Joe hooked a reassuring arm around her waist. "Come on, let's freak Jake the hell out by acting like we couldn't be more delighted to see him. He's not here to ruin David's big day. *They* always got along."

Jake was striding down the hill from the parking area. Ali blinked rapidly, as if to refocus the picture. This was not the man she recalled. Tanned and buff, not pallid and male-model thin. He looked … gorgeous. And more like Joe than ever. Same large, soulful brown eyes flecked with gold, same thick, chestnut-brown hair, though longer now and slightly unruly. When they met, she would never have described Jake as "unruly" or even "casual." She'd once compared him to a newscaster. Now he looked like a wealthy lady-killer who played polo and drove racecars. The cut of his bespoke suit would have scandalized Big Paul's board of directors. It was too fitted, too *au courant*, though perfect for his sleek physique. No tie, and his crisp white shirt had enough buttons unfastened to reveal a tanned V of chest. Ali had once read that opening more than two buttons was "unacceptable" in business circles.

Smile tentative, Jake hesitated at the edge of the terrace and gave a small beauty-queen-riding-a-float wave. "Uh, hello … everyone." Carrie rushed forward to embrace him. That was really out of character. The image-conscious, reserved matriarch of the O'Connell clan didn't do hugs or even air kisses. In the right light, you could mistake her for Teresa's sister rather than her mother. Only blonder. Thanks to her team of expensive cosmeticians and plastic surgeons, she was youthening—like Merlin in *The Once and Future King*.

It had originally seemed that Teresa would go the same way. Now, at Liam's urging, she was practically a nature girl. The platinum blonde chignon had been replaced by the strawberry blonde curls she was born with, and she actually had a little meat on her bones. A little. She was still slender as a reed.

David was the next to approach Jake, enfolding his brother in a bearhug and urging him onto the terrace. The vampire now had the necessary human permission to cross the threshold.

Behave, Ali told herself. *He's your brother-in-law now.*

She saw him taking everything in, expression opaque, and tried to see the compound through his eyes. The original structure—the so-called "Sea Captain's House"—was a colonial-style mansion built in 1990. It belonged to David and Maddie now. Ali and Joe's newly constructed dreamhouse stood just beyond, a log-cabin-style mansion with a ski-lodge interior more in tune with Joe's and her tastes. Everyone referred to it as the "Log Palace." The two styles weren't exactly harmonious, and now there was a *safari* tent, for god's sake.

Standing among his brothers, Jake appeared to be the runt of the litter. David, the height of their deceased father—six feet five—towered over them all. With his more rough-hewn features, shock of auburn hair, and stubble of red beard, the guy looked like a distant cousin descended from Vikings rather than an Irish-Catholic O'Connell. Joe was six-two, also powerfully built but more streamlined. He had the same hooked nose and dimpled chain as David; otherwise, his appearance was softer and more boyish, his tanned skin silky smooth. The kind of swoony good looks that elevated you from just another talented musician to a major country music star. Jake was the refined version, a few inches shorter, more like their mother. An aristocratic nose, a less distinctive jawline, a finer boned physique.

David's enthusiastic introductions quickly dispelled the chill in the atmosphere. You'd never know there was bad blood between Jake and Joe—a grudge that predated Ali. Could bygones be bygones, just like that?

* * *

Jake was surprised to see them all playing nice, but really, what choice did they have?

He liked the look of the main house—a variation on modern Greek revival style. A few columns, a covered front porch. Bay windows, cedar siding, rows of small picture windows rather than just a few large ones. Sash windows, they were called. A long flagstone terrace with a killer view of the ocean. According to his mother, Teresa had purchased the place for Joe and Ali during their extended honeymoon in Paris. The newer house, constructed of whole logs, would be more to Joe's liking. He'd always fancied himself a rugged outdoorsman, ridiculous as that was. He was just as much of a pampered Irish Catholic prince as Jake. Jake's own taste ran to clean, modern designs.

Automatically assuming his role as ingratiating CEO, Jake greeted everyone individually, taking the time to register some distinctive aspect of their appearances as a reference point. Remembering names and faces was an important skill for a glorified salesman, which is how he'd come to think of himself.

The man with the short-cropped gray hair, weathered face, and single earring would be the easiest to remember. Duncan Walsh looked like a grizzled version of Ali's brother Liam, only paler, the eyes the same color but not quite so piercing. In his Brooks Brothers suit, he cleaned up nicely for a retired commercial deep-sea diver. Jake appreciated Duncan's plummy Irish accent. The Irish Spring soap guy in middle age. His girlfriend Laurie had a Carol Burnett perkiness, with her blonde pixie cut and amped-up energy—the type who hawked cellphone plans. Liam's relationship to his twin sister was impossible to miss; both were tall, with startlingly blue eyes—cerulean with dark limbal rings—tawny skin, and the kind of shiny, straight jet-black hair beloved of wigmakers. The faint shrapnel scars on Liam's cheek and forehead only underscored his gorgeousness. "Handsome" didn't begin to describe the guy. Small wonder Teresa had overlooked his lack of pedigree. If Jake were gay, he'd definitely go for *that*. He had a man-crush already.

Ali appeared unaltered, despite having given birth to twin girls. From their few dates, Jake had pegged her as an ice goddess, like their mother, not the earth-mama she appeared to be now. His initial physical reaction to her had been surprisingly tepid, knockout that she was. Not his type, somehow. Most men's type, clearly. He'd had his own reasons for pursuing her. Joe wanted her; that was enough. Jake had been eager to stick it to his rockstar brother. Joe's power over women had always been a sore spot. In their college days—Jake had been at Harvard and Joe at Berklee College of Music—Joe's wake was littered with broken hearts and bruised egos. After Joe had let Jake's date hop into his cab, Jake wrote his twin off forever. Then, one day, Ali had stumbled into his path. Joe and Ali, after an intense meeting in the wilderness, had lost track of each other. Ali had been drawn to Jake only because of his close resemblance to a guy named "JJ"—Joe's nickname.

Jake naturally denied knowing any JJs. Rescuing Ali from a rapacious creep should have made bagging her a slam dunk. He'd been making progress, or so he thought, when Joe materialized at their mother's fundraiser. Joe and Ali were clearly destined to be together, everyone said. Jake the cynic didn't buy it. Lust, maybe. Instant "love" was a myth.

Or was it? His gaze lit upon a stunning woman who stood apart, an outsider like him. There was something about her that hit him straight between the eyes. She was doing her best to hide her light under a bushel, but *wowee*.

When David introduced her, she looked up shyly from playing with a young, redheaded boy. *Hold the phone …* David had a *son*? The kid was his spitting image. Why would their mother fail to mention something so earth-shattering as an illegitimate grandson? No wonder she'd clung to him like a life preserver.

The woman's glasses had slipped down her nose to reveal wide, long-lashed eyes—hazel, maybe. Creamy, flawless skin. Very little, if any, cosmetics. Rich brown hair pulled into a tight bun. Full breasts not quite concealed by her loose shirt-waist dress. He'd love to help her remove her protective shell. Outfitting women was one of his greatest pleasures. *Shit*. Was she Lorenzo's mother? If so, why was David marrying Maddie, who was shaking Jake's hand?

Okay, he saw Maddie's appeal. With her large, brilliant green eyes and short, curly blonde hair, she was a Margaret Keane portrait come to life. Nothing childlike about those dangerous curves. She and David made an odd couple. She had to be a foot shorter.

This other woman, Chiara … did he detect a light Italian accent? All she'd said was "I'm so happy to meet you" in a thrilling, lilting voice. When he shook her hand, he caught a whiff of floral perfume. He wanted to glom onto her—get a better handle on that accent and fragrance—but he was still making the rounds. Then David read his mind, or at least the question there. "Chiara is Lorenzo's guardian, along with her husband Arnold. His mother is Chiara's sister Sylvia, an ER doctor in Chicago." Jake heard the hostility in David's tone when he mentioned Sylvia. So, this Sylvia was giving him a hard time. The O'Connell men did like their women docile—not imperious, like their mother. Chiara cowered a little, ill at ease with being the center of attention. A beauty accustomed to being overlooked in favor of her sister? *Damn*. Was she really married?

"The pleasure is mine, Chiara," he said, her name rolling off his tongue a little too fondly.

Rory reasserted himself. "Have I taught you nothing? It's a bad marriage, but *you* should stay out of it."

Jake ignored him.

The twins were Ali clones—only with Joe's wavy hair and a dimple in their chins that hinted at a future cleft—bouncing around in their playpen like puppies. They were doing a half walk/half crawl thing with an occasional roll. He caught the words "May-May" and "Mama," not much else. The rest nonsensical burbling. Little beauties. He pitied their future victims.

Teresa looked surprisingly un-Teresa-like. "Wow," he said when she hugged him. "You look … different." She wasn't as painfully thin as he remembered.

"She's got a bun in the oven, you goof," Rory said.

Startled, Jake cast about to see if anyone had overheard. "You look amazing, actually," he amended. "Sorry, it's a shock, that's all."

"JB, if you're not already checked into a hotel, why don't you stay with Liam and me while you're here?" Teresa said, pulling on his arm like she had when they were children. "We have a Victorian in town. It's a work in progress, but it has a decent guestroom."

CHAPTER 2

Chiara couldn't believe this family, so unlike her own. Calm, reasonable, good-humored …. If they were, in truth, tortured and repressed beneath the façade, like in those Woody Allen films inspired by Ingmar Bergman, they hid it well. *Her* family could have inspired Federico Fellini. Chiara's flamboyant, volatile parents were self-styled aristocrats with a frayed thread of legitimacy. The title was minor and their "estate" run down, its surrounding acreage long since sold off. They called their ancestral villa an *albergo*. The word, which meant "hotel" in English, was too grand. In truth, it barely functioned as a *pensione*. Located on the outskirts of Florence, it had "old-world charm" that required a constant infusion of capital. That was provided by her sister Sylvia, now an emergency room physician at a large Chicago hospital. Their father was a *barone* with no male heirs, which meant the title would go to the eldest male first cousin—unless Sylvia found a way to claim it. Her self-absorbed parents had been happy to see their teenage girls off to school in America. Since then, Chiara had visited them exactly twice, and they never came to the States. Arnold wasn't keen on her parents—neither was she, truth be told—nor did he want to pay airfare to Italy. Her parents didn't care. Sylvia was the blazing success, the one who could subsidize them, Chiara the timid disappointment with the insufficiently respectful husband.

If she did die "young," as the fortuneteller had predicted, would they even mourn her? Thirty was hardly young. Whenever she pictured the hour glass spilling its last grains of sand, she chided herself for taking the word of a young gypsy as gospel. Believing might make it true—a prophecy that fulfills itself. The older gypsy had been incensed by her daughter's arrogance, insisting that no one could predict the hour of death. Brushes with mortality happen all the time, she insisted, often without us knowing it. And, contrary to popular belief, our fates are not set in stone.

And yet … if Lorenzo were taken away from Chiara, remaining with Arnold would be a living death.

Jake … what a *beautiful* man. And so compelling. What role did he play in this household? No one had expected him to attend this wedding. What had happened between Ali and Jake to make them so uneasy together?

The O'Connells had been wonderful to Chiara so far, though they had good reason to view her with suspicion. She was the sister of Sylvia, a crack in the glass of David's happiness. Sylvia and David had been lovers while working together as doctors in Africa. Her sister, who was devoutly Catholic and didn't believe in abortion, had never wanted the child, and David did. If not for Chiara, Lorenzo would live full-time with his birth father. But how could Chiara let the child go? She'd raised him since he was a tiny baby, and now he was almost four—a sweet, solemn child, despite her efforts to bring him out of his shell. Being trapped in her own shell didn't help. She'd wanted a child of her own, but it was not to be. There was nothing wrong with her, the doctor said. Arnold refused to have his sperm tested. With Arnold, the sex act was not only infrequent, but also quick and impersonal. He might have been making a deposit at the sperm bank.

Ali had gone back to the kitchen. Seeing that Lorenzo was occupied with the twins, May Allen the nanny, and May's sister Susan, Chiara rose to join her hostess. Jake's eyes seemed to follow her as she left the terrace. It was as if only he could see her at all. Could he possibly find her attractive? In her experience, men so handsome could not be trusted. Arnold was a "tech guy" and preferred the company of his computer to humans. He'd courted her with presents and dinners at expensive restaurants and a tide of compliments, until finally, she'd agreed to marry him. It had been a novelty to feel wanted. Surely Arnold would never leave her or conduct himself like her father, indiscreet with his mistresses. Marriage offered financial security, a green card to replace her work visa. She could give up her own work as a social worker—not a hardship. That work had left her stewed—"burned out," the Americans said.

Far from secure, she was now more financially vulnerable than ever. Soon enough, she discovered Arnold was not a safe choice. Everything else in his life—his job, his friends—took priority over her. And now, did he miss her at all? He never called.

Her hostess stood at the sink, staring out the window at the ocean.

"Ali?" Chiara said, startling her. "I'm so sorry! I didn't mean to scare you."

"No problem." Ali looked more shaken than the situation warranted. "Don't mind me, Chiara. It's all a little overwhelming."

"All …?" Chiara repeated, moving closer. "It's a beautiful view."

Together they gazed out at the miles of ocean. Ali gave a contented sigh. "You've probably noticed some weirdness. It's just that … we haven't seen Jake for a while. He didn't attend Joe's and my wedding. Or Teresa and Liam's. We don't know why he bothered to show up now."

"He seems nice to me," Chiara said.

Ali didn't confirm or deny. "Your husband couldn't come with you? I hope he knows he was invited."

"Arnold is a busy man," Chiara said in a neutral voice.

"Do you work?" Ali asked.

Chiara shook her head. "I am—I *was*—a clinical social worker with a family therapy specialty. I haven't worked since my marriage."

"Ooh, we could use a therapist here," Ali said, then blushed. "That sounded weird out of context. Joe and I founded a nonprofit called Foster Splash Pad, FOSSP for short. We sponsor boarding houses and offer counseling and support for children who've aged out of foster care. In Port Townsend, Sequim, and Port Angeles. Liam and I were foster children." She took a breath. "That was a lot of information at once. Sorry."

"That's interesting," Chiara said, "about you and Liam. I'm not sure how well I would … adapt."

"Do you mean 'fit in'?"

"Yes." Chiara smiled. "I've lived in the United States since I was a teenager, but the idioms sometimes confuse me."

"We could use a compassionate counselor. The others we've hired haven't worked out."

Chiara shook her head. "Even if I worked for nothing … I'm not certified to practice in Washington State. I don't know the requirements. I have a master's degree, but each state is different."

Ali shrugged. "Oh, well! It's not as if you're going to leave your husband and move here."

Chiara laughed uncomfortably.

"Oregon is full of beautiful places to hike and visit," Ali said.

Chiara continued to stare at the view. "Yes. When Arnold was courting me, we hiked and traveled widely." She didn't have to add that such diversions stopped after the wedding. Judging from Ali's sympathetic expression, she had already arrived at the truth.

"Do you have enough help today?" Chiara looked around the pristine professional kitchen, thinking that workers should be circulating about. "I can cook, clean, whatever is needed."

Ali frowned. "I wouldn't dream of it. We have help, no worries. My friend Becca's husband Jean-Louis is catering the wedding dinner—we had the rehearsal dinner at his restaurant, La Fête Sauvage, last night."

"The Savage Feast?" Chiara translated.

"Yes, it's almost a chain now. Jean-Louis has three restaurants. The others are in North Bend and Bellevue. They feature wild game and fish, farm-fresh produce. I'm sorry you couldn't be there last night. Anyway, Jean-Louis has hired several FOSSP young people as waiters, busboys, and sous-chefs. They'll be arriving with him and Becca just before the ceremony."

"No waitresses?"

"A few," Ali said. "Enough to avoid discrimination claims. Jean-Louis is old school. It's a sticking point. Baby steps. Also, he favors the handsome. The less eye-catching ones need the most help. They might be harder workers too. At least his crew is ethnically diverse. We're working on convincing him that customers who are into luxury dining won't be turned off by female waiters. I did a lot of cater-waiting myself at one point, but we had to wear men's tuxes. I guess that's better than micro-miniskirts and plunging necklines."

"The entire world favors the handsome," Chiara said. "Not to mention that every one of your guests could be cinema stars. Even your father and his girlfriend."

Ali blushed again.

"I'm sorry," she added quickly, "I meant that as a compliment."

A male voice said, "As long as you include yourself." Ali and Chiara both jumped this time. Joe had appeared out of nothing, *whoosh*, as if having emerged, like a genie, as smoke from an open bottle. He kissed Ali's neck with an unconscious intimacy that Chiara envied. Arnold never kissed her like that.

"So," he said, "Jake."

"How's he doing? No bitter outbursts?"

"Nope." Pressing against her back, he wrapped her in his arms. "Sorry for the shock. I know big events like this put you on edge."

Ali closed her eyes, softening into the embrace. "Has he met everyone?"

"Not yet. Rostand is over at the tent, as are Linc and Matthew. Rostand he knows well, of course." To Chiara, Joe said, "Rostand is the family factotum, my mother's manservant. Cooks, cleans, organizes, buttles." He turned to Ali. "How much you wanna bet Jake remembers every name and face after just one meeting? One of the many reasons he's such an effective CEO." He hesitated before continuing, "You won't believe what he brought with him." After a dramatic pause, he added, "The clothing."

Ali's expression was empty. No, the Americans would say *blank*.

"The box," he said, as if that were more specific.

Chiara echoed, "The box?" She didn't see the harm in asking. If it were a secret, he shouldn't mention it in her presence.

Joe looked embarrassed. "When Ali and Jake were … dating, he bought her some clothing. And shoes. Not a lot. When they broke up, she returned it all. One of Jake's quirks. He likes to … *dress* his women."

"I figured it was just me, because I was so hopelessly unfashionable."

"Well, that too," Joe joked.

She gave him a dark look. "Listen, when even Nordstrom Rack is a splurge, you do what you can. BPO wasn't in my budget."

"Big Paul's Outfitters," Joe explained to Chiara. "Our family business. Jake is the CEO. Ali and Jake met when BPO held a client function at Jean-Louis's Fête Sauvage in North Bend." He grew serious. "We don't discuss that."

Chiara's eyes darted from one to the other as she tried to make sense of the conversation.

Noting her confusion, Joe smiled. "In brief, Ali and I met under strange circumstances. She was lost—"

"I wasn't lost," she protested.

"Okay, she was just about to die of hypothermia from getting soaked in a storm when she found my hidey-hole—a log cabin in the Hoh Rain Forest. I was recovering from vocal cord surgery, so I couldn't talk." He paused and cleared his throat as if at the memory.

"We had a good time," Ali took over. Joe's grin caused her to give him a small shove. "Not *that* good. It's not as if we …. Never mind. We both had our reasons, I guess, not to exchange full names. Joe in particular, since he didn't want to reveal that he was a famous country music star. My brother Liam was missing, presumed dead after a terrorist attack. That's what *I* was doing in the woods. Saying goodbye in a place we both loved."

"Long story short," Joe said, "we eventually found each other through a song I wrote about her, but things were still messed up. I was dating another singer—"

"The papers said you were engaged," Ali broke in.

"That's what Rina told them. I never would have married her. Ali was dating Jake."

His wife's eyes held a warning. "Cut to the chase."

"It was painful at times," Joe admitted.

"The ending was not to Jake's liking," Chiara concluded.

Joe gave an airy little wave. "He and I are very different people."

"Jake is … at least I found him to be … calculating," Ali said. She appealed to Joe, "He seems different somehow. Don't you think?"

Joe snorted. "He might have a hidden agenda. You never know with that guy."

"Let's join the others," Ali said, tugging at Joe's sleeve. "If Jake is plotting the fall of the House of O'Connell, he'll reveal himself quickly enough." Ali's eyes fixed on her outfit. "Chiara, don't take this wrong, but would you like to borrow a dress? I think you and Teresa might be the same size."

"Chiara's taller," Joe said. "What about something from the infamous box?"

Ali took his teasing suggestion seriously. "Come to think of it, she might fit into one of those cocktail dresses. If Jake is really as different as he seems, he won't mind. What was he thinking, foisting that stuff back on me so long after the fact?"

Joe huffed a laugh. "You think it's a way of having the last word. I disagree. Knowing Jake, he couldn't stand to trash them or give them to charity. He's a true devotee of fashion."

Ali appeared skeptical.

Chiara looked down at her dress with new eyes. Most of her wardrobe was from Talbot's. Conservatively cut, unrevealing, but not cheaply made. Arnold didn't want her "displaying" herself in public. She was intrigued by the idea of a man who liked to dress women and could do it with taste.

"You look fine," Ali reassured her. "Only … it might be fun for you to let loose a little. The women will all be wearing party dresses. Did you bring anything like that?"

Chiara just shook her head.

"Where is the box?" Ali asked Joe.

"Right inside the door at our place."

She laid a hand on his chest. "Sweetie, will you ask Teresa to join us? We're going to do some girl bonding."

* * *

Jake was a sight for sore eyes. How Teresa had missed him! As young men, her other brothers had done exactly as they pleased, damn the torpedoes. Edward had sowed his wild oats in Europe, then, as if in penance, attended divinity school and joined the Catholic priesthood. David had gone to med school and done a residency to become a surgeon, but instead of accepting a prestigious position in the U.S., had spent four years as an itinerant doctor in Africa. A skilled guitarist, Joe had gone to a music conservatory, followed by a stint as a touring backup musician. His meteoric rise had been as a country music heartthrob. That career crashed to earth—at least the performing part—due to ongoing vocal issues.

While the others pursued their passions, Jake and she had been left to toe the line—perform their filial duties. Jake's youthful efforts at mystery writing had impressed everyone but their parents. So naturally he'd been the one to take over the family business. When it came to Teresa, all that mattered was her school's reputation, not her major. Sarah Lawrence, a small liberal arts college, fit the bill. Ironically, she'd been the one to earn a degree in Creative Writing. What was she supposed to do with that? A swift climb up the social ladder, marriage to the "right" man, and motherhood, naturally. That path got off to a rocky start. Her first and final act of rebellion had been a disastrous elopement with Kilo. An annulment had put a stop to that. But Kilo had the last laugh; he was now on his way to Hollywood stardom. At twenty-eight, Teresa became engaged to Paul, who looked great on paper but proved to be the creepiest of creeps. Thanks to their grandmother's generous bequests, they were all financially set for more than one lifetime. That was how Teresa got roped into supporting her mother's charities. Jake and she had stood on the sidelines of many a tedious benefit dinner privately exchanging snarky remarks and publicly kissing up to donors.

Teresa's escape to Port Townsend, where she'd fallen hard for Liam, had left Jake at the mercy of their mother. No wonder he resented his siblings enough to cut ties with them. Would Jake have become a writer, had there been no family business? Would he even have attended Stanford Business School?

Teresa couldn't put her finger on what had changed about her brother, other than his more relaxed appearance. The Jake she knew didn't do anything without expecting a payoff. That included his attempt to win over Ali—a half-hearted effort if ever there was one. As children, Joe and Jake had been close enough to read each other's minds. Then, in high school, they had pursued the same girl. Joe won. A more serious rift took place in Boston—again over a woman. She still recalled that Christmas dinner when Jake barely gave Joe the time of day. *Brrr*. But the resentment ran deeper than that. Joe's superstardom in such a candy-coated career had rankled.

Had Jake really set his long list of gripes aside? Joe's waning fame might be a factor. He was still in demand as a songwriter, and he'd recently completed a successful tour, but the vocal issues had returned. Chances were slim he'd ever record or tour again. During the height of his career, Joe had racked up the honors, winning Country Music Association's Horizon Award and the Academy of Country Music's Top New Male Vocalist Award. Several of his songs had made it to the Top 40 on the Hot Country Songs charts. Then his break-through hit, "Babe in the Woods"—the song he'd written for Ali—had won a Grammy. It was predicted that two of his songs that had been recorded by other singers would be nominated in January.

Teresa turned her attention back to Maddie, David, and Laurie. She'd paid scant attention to their conversation about the honeymoon and Laurie's ideas for where they might travel after that. *Please, don't let there be a test.* David had quit his job at the clinic in Sequim, and Maddie's movie would premiere at Thanksgiving, though she'd fired her agent and had nothing else in the can. Jake was talking to their mother, whose Botoxed face somehow managed to convey frustration. In fact, the way she was poking him in the chest looked downright painful. What had riled her up? Teresa rose to her feet. "Guys, sorry, I'm just going to—"

Joe saved her from having to invent a pretext. "Teresa, Ali wants you to meet her at the house." Confused, Teresa considered the two buildings.

"*Our* house," he specified, "the Log Palace. Maddie and David bought the Sea Captain's House, remember?"

"You don't need to remind me," Teresa said, casting about for her husband. She was still hurt that they'd chosen to redesign the Art-Deco inspired living room she was responsible for decorating.

"Liam's over at the tent helping with the sound system."

Joe could read her so well.

She walked up the hill toward the affectionately named "Log Palace," a five-bedroom, four-bath behemoth constructed of whole logs. It featured a stone chimney, metal roof, and a large patio raised up on stilts to take advantage of the view. A design better suited to a ski resort. Teresa guessed it was really a nod to their meeting place—the primitive log cabin in the woods she'd never seen. The tall fence that obscured the view on the main floor was meant to keep the deer out but also protect their nearly eleven-month-old twin girls from harm. The decks on the third floor offered the best views. Everyone was nervous about spritely Caryn and Josie, who they imagined were already plotting in their secret language to make a mad dash for freedom.

Teresa rang the bell before entering.

"Come in!" she heard Ali yell through the open window.

Exposed beams, river rock fireplace, cedar floors. Not Teresa's thing. But it was *their* thing, and she respected that. As a newly minted interior decorator, she was determined to take her clients' wishes seriously. She didn't know where her aversion for this style came from. True, she'd never enjoyed those trips to the family ski chalet in Aspen or the sport itself, despite being an advanced skier. Her white jumpsuit was still considered chic, though her skis were outdated. In her circle, you wouldn't be caught dead using any but the latest, greatest equipment. Liam and Ali had never skied and showed no interest in learning. The sport was something that upper middle class and rich people in Seattle learned from a tender age, starting with Saturday classes at Snoqualmie Pass and Alpental and progressing to Stevens Pass and Crystal Mountain.

"Ali?" she called out. "Where are you?"

"Up here!"

Teresa climbed the stairs to the master bedroom with its huge bed, vaulted ceiling, and yet another river-rock fireplace. There was a forty-two-inch plasma TV on the wall, even though Ali and Joe watched only the occasional movie here. She wanted one for Liam's place, but he argued that it was a crime to pay fifteen grand for a television, even when you could well afford it.

Next to the bed was the police sketch of Ali Joe had commissioned when he was searching for her. It looked vaguely like her sister-in-law, she supposed—a gauzy, fantasy version. Teresa could just imagine the flowery language Joe had used to describe her. It sat on Joe's side of the bed next to the thriller he was currently reading. Like Teresa, Ali preferred romances and British-style mysteries.

Ali emerged from the walk-in closet to find Teresa looking at the sketch. "Who *is* that dewy maiden?" She laughed. "It's as if I'd been reimagined as a Breck Girl from one of those early-sixties shampoo ads. I wish Joe would put it away or hang it in his studio." She gestured toward the closet. "I wanted you here for the big reveal."

At the sight of Chiara, Teresa gasped. She was clad in a retro cocktail dress in hot pink that Teresa recognized as Betsy Johnson. She wasn't wearing her glasses, and Ali had applied mascara and lipstick. Her soft brown curls fell to her shoulders.

"Wow," Teresa said, "that is *some* transformation. Not that we didn't already know you were beautiful." *Only, we didn't, not really, not like this,* she added silently.

"I never wore it," Ali said. "Jake picked it out for me when we were dating."

"Just how many dresses did he buy for you?" Teresa asked. She knew JB was in the habit of dressing his women, and she'd always wondered whether it was a question of one or two outfits or an entire wardrobe.

Ali's smile was sheepish. "Only four. Three pairs of dressy sandals and one pair of pumps. See for yourself." The fancy footwear was lined up next to a medium-sized cardboard box.

"What's your shoe size?" Teresa asked Chiara.

"My shoe size? Eight."

Ali frowned. "Hmm. The sandals are open toed, so maybe they would work. These are seven and a half." She rummaged in the box for the hot pink sandals, which fit once she adjusted the straps. "There, take a look."

Chiara squinted at the full-length mirror. "I look a little fuzzy."

Ali handed over her glasses.

The eyes behind the glasses blinked several times. Chiara covered her mouth to stifle a laugh. "Arnold would hate it."

"Humph," Ali muttered, leaving it at that. She tilted her head, regarding Chiara from several angles. "You fill that bodice out a lot better than I ever could have done."

Teresa was impressed. She never would have guessed what Chiara was hiding under that shapeless shirt-waist dress. She checked her watch. "It's four already. Ali, you and I need to get changed."

Ali consulted her own watch. "Shoot. How did it get to be so late? The wedding's in an hour." She shrugged. "It doesn't matter. We're all friends here. The photographer won't like it, but we can push it to five thirty or even six. Becca and Jean-Louis won't arrive much before five, knowing them."

Their guest was casting longing looks toward the exit.

"Chiara, you'll want to freshen up at your cabin, right? Please, go ahead."

After they watched her leave, Teresa said, "You don't think this little stunt is going to piss Jake off? Remember that time we dolled up Maddie to goad Sylvia? Not our finest hour. Just made David's life more difficult. Also, what's the goal here? Jake's already interested, and Chiara's married."

Ali looked stricken. "Joe suggested it." She thumped her forehead with the heel of her hand. "I didn't think it through. Argh! What have I done?"

CHAPTER 3

---·---

Jake sat at the back of the tent. He'd never been on a safari, and this setup didn't make him any more eager to go. It was drafty in here. The day had been clear, but now the sun was going down. They should have held the wedding at noon.

The tent thing …. He knew that was for David, who as a kid had pored over adventure stories set in Colonial Africa. What was Jake's fantasy? Couldn't think of one. In his regimented, disciplined life, he'd devoted his leisure time to easy pickings: expensive wine, top-rated restaurants, and willing females. That last indulgence hadn't gone so well in recent years. Too much trouble. He'd had enough of coy, shallow beauties. During his brief, half-hearted pursuit of Ali, he'd had a comfortable arrangement with a woman in San Francisco, nothing serious. For him. After that ended in a flood of tears, he'd opted for short-term dalliances with free-spirited younger women. Holly Golightly types looking to acquire designer clothes and shoes and enjoy expensive dates on his dime. Most he met through Rory, whose friendship had meant more to him than any romantic fling.

"Me too, bro," Rory said.

This time Jake didn't bother to check if anyone had heard. The voice was in his head alone, a product of his screwed-up psyche. PTSD, maybe.

Most thirty-five-year-olds resisted change, he supposed. Him too, until recently. In high school he'd been in a rock band, played guitar and sung lead vocals. Then Joe knocked everyone out with his talent and stole the girl Jake had set his heart on. *Fuck it*—that was when he'd put his own guitar away. He still had it. Did he even remember how to play?

"You were never passionate about guitar," Rory's voice said. "Whaddya really want?"

Wish I knew, he thought. Other than writing trash under a pen name. That had started as a fun hobby. Then his debut novel had been optioned by a movie studio. A big chunk of change for a real author, the kind who struggled. For him, a drop in the bucket. His agent warned him that more often than not, the movie was never made. He hadn't told a soul about his secret career. While he was in high school, several of his mystery/suspense stories had been published in respected magazines. His parents had not been impressed. Writing "literary trash"—as they put it—was a lowbrow pursuit.

"You're doin' fine, boyo," Rory said. "Play your cards right, and you might get to enjoy yourself for a change."

Jake snuck another peek at Chiara. Ali had lent her one of the dresses Jake had bought for *her*, way back when, and Chiara looked sensational in it. It gave him all sorts of ideas for future outfits to buy her. Not that he'd get the chance.

"You're an idiot," Rory said. "You gonna poach another guy's girl now? Like Joe did to you?"

Those women—girls, actually—were never mine, Jake thought. *You can't put dibs on a woman. She gets to decide. Those girls chose Joe.*

"Well, aren't you the grownup," Rory mocked.

Jake tore his eyes off Chiara, who was shrinking, aware of being an object of curiosity. He was utterly charmed by her modesty. He wondered about her husband, why he was okay with his wife hiding her inner goddess. Or did he force her to dress like a '50s housewife? Probably the jealous type. Just what Jake needed. A duel. Definitely illegal now—even in Uruguay since 1992—but he imagined men still fought them in secret. He could put a duel in his next book. *Yeah. A duel between women.*

How could you tell the difference between the women who really wanted you and the ones in it solely for a free ride? Fantasy … ah. He did have one. Olivia de Havilland as Maid Marian in *Robin Hood*. Come to think of it, Chiara resembled her.

The ceremony began with Joe and Matthew playing a duo-guitar version of "The Call," by Ralph Vaughn Williams. Jake had spoken at some length with Matthew, a backup musician on Joe's last tour. Teresa was decorating his recently purchased Victorian. Jake had gotten the gay vibe from Matthew, however subtle. Was he out or not? With this crowd it wouldn't matter. In the country music world, it probably did. Solidly handsome, not interested in taking center stage. The cuts of the men's monkey suits were conservative, Matthew's even more so than Joe's.

Too bad Maddie, in her role as bride, wasn't on the roster. His mother had told him she had an amazing set of pipes, could give Julie Andrews a run for her money. Maddie wore a simple, full-length white chiffon dress, sleeveless with a nipped-in waist and plunging neckline filled in with lace. Jake might have dressed her that way, given the chance. Did Teresa have a hand in buying it? He guessed Maddie was a Size Four except for the breasts. A veritable Grecian goddess, Hollywood style. David was visibly uncomfortable in his tux, squirming a little as if the material itched. The guy had always hated formal wear. But when you were six feet five with thick auburn hair, broad shoulders, and long legs, you looked good in anything.

Chef Jean-Louis was officiating—one of those internet licenses to marry, some weird church. Jake remembered Becca from that shitstorm of a party at La Fête Sauvage in North Bend. Had she and Jean-Louis already been an item back then—when she was his hostess? Jake had always admired Chef Jean-Louis' flair for fashion. Not many straight men could rock those paisley socks and the fuchsia tie and cummerbund. Becca was a knockout in her own right, with her hour-glass figure and dramatic coloring. Glorious piles of curly brown hair and preternaturally large dark-brown eyes. That pink-floral cocktail dress hugged her in all the right places. Tom Ford for Gucci, he guessed.

Becca darted a glare in his direction. Caught peeking. He recalled *that* about Becca too—not the shrinking violet type.

Matthew and Joe were playing an arrangement of a Bach piece he didn't recognize. But then again, most Bach sounded the same to him—other than the *Brandenburg concertos* and "Jesu, Joy of Man's Desiring." Nah, that was an oversimplification; he was thinking of all those solo cello suites.

Now Maddie was reciting Shakespeare:

> My bounty is as boundless as the sea,
> My love as deep; the more I give to thee,
> The more I have, for both are infinite.

Hmm, Romeo and Juliet. A bad omen for a relationship if you asked Jake. They did die and all. Fortunately no one had … asked him, that is. He would love to see Maddie as Juliet. Or in any part. She was incandescent.

"Yeah," Rory said, "she does have a certain *je ne sais quoi*."

Last winter, Maddie had played Puck in a local production of *A Midsummer Night's Dream*. According to Teresa, she was good, *really* good. Jake was a patron of the Seattle performing arts scene. Had season tickets—best seats in the house—to Seattle Rep, ACT, Seattle Shakespeare, Seattle Opera, and Pacific Northwest Ballet. In general, he wasn't keen on the newer stuff, mostly leadfooted and with an agenda. He never missed a production of Oscar Wilde, Chekhov, August Wilson, Tom Stoppard, or George Bernard Shaw. With regard to opera and ballet, he only genuinely enjoyed the best known. Any Puccini but *Turandot* and *La Fanciulla del West*. *Carmen*. *Nutcracker*, *Swan Lake*, and *Giselle*.

"You're an effin' hedonist. So what?"

Not now, Rory, Jake pleaded silently.

David's turn. Though a middling actor, he *was* a trouper and declaimed his lines with gusto.

> If music be the food of love, play on;
> Give me excess of it, that, surfeiting,
> The appetite may sicken, and so die.

The lines were Orsini's from *Twelfth Night*. This was fun. Shakespeare trivia. Laughter bubbled up in Jake's chest. He covered his mouth with the back of his hand.

"You're a cynical bastard," Rory said in his head, catching him by surprise this time.

"With this ring I thee wed …." David began.

Ah, little Lorenzo, a cherubic ringbearer if ever there was one. He was already tall for his age, his features unfinished versions of David's, his hair the same bright-red color David the toddler had sported. So well-behaved. *Too* well-behaved. Jake hoped there was nothing wrong with him. Or that he wasn't terminally depressed. How old was he? Almost four. Could a kid that age be depressed? Chiara's husband Arnold had to be a complete asshole.

Aaaand … the kiss. *Phew*. Jake needed a cold shower.

Joe was playing again. Bach's *Air on a G String*, a perennial favorite. Jake instantly imagined a woman in a G-string dancing sinuously behind them as the happy couple walked back down the aisle.

"Get your mind out of the gutter," Rory said.

Jake was ashamed of himself. This was a solemn occasion, a beautiful wedding, really. Why couldn't he appreciate it that way?

"Because you're not a saint," Rory told him. "You're jealous. And cynical as hell."

Jake rolled his eyes, then looked around him nervously, hoping no one had seen it. All eyes were on the happy couple.

* * *

Chiara had loved the intimate ceremony and shivered at the obvious chemistry between the bride and groom. She was wearing a cute dress and felt pretty for the first time in a long, long while.

After putting an exhausted Lorenzo to bed, she ventured onto the flagstone terrace, where heat lamps and a gas firepit warmed the cool evening air. Standing on the sidelines, she debated where to go. There was no assigned seating. Then Jake appeared at her side as if he'd been watching for her.

"Chiara, come sit with me." The way her name rolled off his tongue sent a frisson down her spine. "We outsiders need to stick together."

As she followed him, she scanned the bountiful buffet. Smoked goose, salmon, halibut, venison … and that was just the array of meats and fish. All artfully arranged with a fountain in the middle.

"It's sparkling water," Jake explained. "Ali wanted to do something a little special that was non-alcoholic." He filled a glass and took it to the table where Liam and Teresa were seated. When he set it in front of Teresa, he said, "You're not drinking, right?"

She gave him an odd look and pointed to her full glass of red wine.

"Uh, never mind." He filled Chiara's and his glasses from the open bottle.

"To the happy couple," he toasted. He swished it around in his mouth before swallowing. "Château Margaux. Nice."

Arnold liked good wine, and even he would have been impressed by this one. Teresa must have noticed Chiara's approval, because she said, "Joe does have a nice cellar. We enjoyed stocking it."

Ali appeared behind her. "Some of us know nothing about wine. I'm happy to drink it, though."

"What I learned about wine," Chiara admitted, "was mostly for the spectacle … for show, I mean. Sylvia and I came to this country as exchange students in high school. We both attended the University of Washington, and in the summers, I worked at a Chelan winery in the tasting room. The owners schooled us on how to describe the wines—the vocabulary and the theatrics. I could swish it around in the glass, take an appreciative sniff, say it tasted like cherries, chocolate, fruity, buttery, oaky …. But my palate was never really trained." She paused. Why had she admitted that? Because she was a timid mouse!

Ali patted her on the shoulder. "Join the club. Not the club, exactly. Join the elite little group of you and me. Everyone else could go on at some length about wine. It's no disgrace to admit otherwise."

"Hey, I'm a member too," a new voice said. It was Becca, wife of Jean-Louis. Becca reminded Chiara just a bit of her sister Sylvia, in that you couldn't help but admire her flamboyant personal style. Not many women could carry off that ruffled, floral-patterned pink dress, and she balanced on those three-inch heels with such ease, they might have been slippers. "Jean-Louis keeps trying to educate me, but his full-bodied reds give me a headache. I'm hopeless."

Ali and Becca hugged like old, dear friends.

"Here, all you have to be is kind," Ali said.

And beautiful, Chiara thought, taking in the room. *Even the waiters*.

A blue-eyed blond man who reminded her of David Hemmings in *Blow-Up* refilled her glass.

She looked over at Jake, who might appear attentive if you missed the faraway look in his eyes. Everything about this man intrigued her.

"So, Chiara," Teresa said, reclaiming her attention, "we met Sylvia. It did not go well. She might have mentioned it."

Oh, she had. They were *riccaccio*—disgustingly rich—"typical Americans." Naturally her sister would interpret their reluctance to flaunt their wealth as false modesty. Sylvia had scrimped, saved, perhaps even sold her soul to become a doctor, and now that she was finally collecting the fruit of her efforts, she worked too hard to appear more sophisticated than she was. It wasn't as if their own family in Italy was so exalted. As a rule, Europeans thought of Americans as superficial, uninterested in the rest of the world, insensitive, ostentatious, slaves to money and profit. The O'Connells cared about others. They helped foster children to excel in their adult lives. Sylvia had never told David the whole truth, that she'd been in Africa at the behest of her patron, a wealthy Italian American she'd met as a Freshman at university. Their agreement had included sending money to their parents. Chiara wasn't clear about what he got in return, but she had her suspicions. She wondered how he had reacted to the news of Lorenzo's birth. Perhaps leaving the child to be raised by others was part of the bargain.

Teresa laughed. "I see we made a dismal impression."

Chiara rushed to explain. "Sylvia is … insecure. About certain things. She had unrealistic expectations of you that were disappointed."

"She wanted us to be snobs," Liam said, his distaste clear.

"Yes," Chiara said earnestly, "but you must understand … Sylvia is a brilliant physician. In Africa, she … became overwhelmed. The same as your brother, I suspect. It happens to most over time. I was a social worker until I realized my powerlessness against the inadequate laws, the worst of human nature."

She reddened. Her little speech, though received with compassion, had a dampening effect.

"I'm sorry," Chiara said, "this is a party." She forced a smile. "Someone needs to offer up another toast."

"All right then," Jake said. "To new beginnings."

They all drank. Chiara wanted to say, "Who is making a new beginning? Not me." But she wasn't sure that was true. It was already her dearest wish to stay in Port Townsend. In Portland, she was another person. A person afraid to speak up or ask any favors. None of her college friends lived nearby, though they did keep in touch by phone. One of her colleagues from her few years as a social worker, now in private practice, sometimes invited her to go shopping or to the movies. She always accepted but rarely initiated anything. Mostly her time was spent with Lorenzo. When they weren't playing, chatting in Italian, or she wasn't teaching him to read and write, they'd visit the zoo and the parks. Lorenzo preferred her company, making play dates difficult. More and more, she and Arnold led separate lives. A year ago, he'd moved into the spare bedroom without explanation. Chiara couldn't remember the last time she'd been included in one of his company dinners.

"Chiara?" Jake spoke softly, but she returned to the present with a start. "Ah, you're back." He spoke in a soothing, jocular tone. "I thought I must have bored you into a coma."

Oh no, how long had she drifted? "Never," she insisted too passionately. Lowering the intensity, she went on, "It's just that … it's so pleasant here. It's as if their whole life—Ali and Joe's—is a vacation. Or something even more wonderful. My vacations …." She didn't finish the thought.

Oh, *mio Dio*, the way he gazed at her, his eyes warm and questioning. Arnold had never looked at her that way.

"They've cleared away dinner," he said.

David tapped a spoon against a glass and announced, "Dancing in the safari tent! We need to work up an appetite again before dessert. There are several professional musicians here, so let me just say … one"—he held up a finger—"none of Joe's music will be played—sorry, Joe—and two"—another finger—"I had nothing to do with the playlist, other than to ask that it include many cheesy, feel-good songs. Christoff is practicing his wedding-DJ skills."

"He's one of the FOSSP boys," Teresa told Chiara.

Christoff departed for the tent. A few minutes later, Chiara recognized the Bee Gees' "Stayin' Alive." In full John Travolta strut, David led the way, followed by Maddie, who had to run to keep up. Joe took Ali's hand and twirled her to his chest. Liam and Teresa, less exuberant but just as silly, corralled the rest of them.

In contrast, Jake offered Chiara his hand as if they were at a different event altogether—Cinderella's ball perhaps.

She demurred. "My dancing is a poor excuse for the real thing."

The hand remained extended, and she finally took it. "I'm merely competent myself," Jake claimed. "I attended the obligatory dance lessons as a teenager. Cheesy rock songs, however, demand no skills whatsoever. In fact, they might get in the way. The goofier, the better."

Goofy, like the Disney character? Foolish, he meant. Easy for him, maybe. Not for anyone who struggled with acute self-consciousness. Still, she finished off her wine and took his arm. The grass between the terrace and tent was uneven and unfriendly for high heels. Seeing her teeter, Jake put an arm around her waist to steady her. The embrace lasted less than a minute, but the sensations that rippled through her body lingered much longer.

The song seemed to be all about dancing like a fool. She couldn't catch many of the lyrics, other than "You can dance if you want to."

Christoff changed the tempo for David and Maddie's supposed "first dance." The chorus began with "Hold me now." It wasn't really a slow dance, but they treated it that way, holding each other close while the tipsy group hooted appreciatively.

Chiara found herself caught up in a slow swing dance. She needn't have worried about her deficiencies as a dancer. Jake knew what to do as long as she relaxed and followed his lead. Not surprisingly, he'd lied about being a poor dancer. She breathed in his intoxicating scent. She detected notes of moss, lavender, and cedar. Dried herbs and the forest. She nearly swooned.

Christoff moved on to songs even Chiara recognized, Billy Idol's "White Wedding" and David Bowie's "Let's Dance." Sadly, nothing that required contact. Chiara had stopped caring about what the others thought of her behavior. She marveled at Jake's lack of inhibitions. He strutted and gyrated like a man possessed. They began to mirror each other, their movements more and more ridiculous. Eventually no one danced with a specific partner. Everyone, including the Algerian manservant Rostand, was circulating *a caso*, stopping to spontaneously swing whomever they found themselves next to—be it a man or woman.

The most surprising was Carrie, the O'Connell matron. While not entirely sold on all the silliness, she did her best to join in the spirit of things. Becca kicked off her shoes, and soon all the women were either barefoot or in stocking feet. Then the men tossed their shoes aside too. The polished hardwood floor wasn't entirely smooth. Chiara's one pair of pantyhose would be ruined. No matter. Few others wore stockings during the day here. Why should she?

She'd lost any notion of time when the DJ finally played a slow dance. In a heartbeat Jake was there, taking her hands and leading her in another slow swing dance. The song was "Hello, it's me."

She never wanted it to end.

As they drifted reluctantly apart, his eyes held hers. She blinked first.

Behind them, Liam said, "Come on, you two. We're headed back to the Sea Captain's House for dessert."

CHAPTER 4

THE NEXT MORNING, TERESA SAT on a stool at the kitchen island, wearing her pink silk kimono and sipping strong coffee with a generous dose of cream. Liam was still asleep, having crawled into a bottle of particularly fine Bordeaux. Unusual behavior for him. She hoped it was just that Joe's cellar was too tempting, and not that he was looking to drown his doubts about the viability of their marriage. He'd stuck to one glass until Jake offered to drive. In the end, Teresa took the wheel, having stopped drinking at a few sips, her tummy oddly unsettled.

"Good morning!" Jake chirped as he waltzed into the kitchen, freshly showered and dressed as if for casual Friday at a law firm in a polo shirt, chinos, and polished loafers that looked like Ferragamo.

Teresa stared at him in wonder. This was the beloved brother she remembered, always so dapper and energetic as a young man before turning into a bitter and withdrawn adult. "You look chipper this morning," she said, her tone both admiring and accusatory.

He leaned down to kiss her cheek. "And you look a little droopy, though beautiful as ever. Love the hair." As she self-consciously smoothed the unruly strawberry-blonde locks, he slid onto the stool next to hers. "That was some party last night."

"Just think what you've been missing," she said, keeping her tone light.

He raised his eyebrows. "Just think."

She was silent as she served him a mug of black coffee. Too tired to beat around the bush, she blurted out, "Why now, Jake? What happened?"

Jake sipped his coffee, expectant, as if waiting for her to get more specific.

"You know," she said, sounding querulous, "what made you decide to come to the wedding? What got into you?" Her body chose that moment to reject the coffee she'd consumed. She covered her mouth and made a mad dash for the bathroom.

When she returned, Jake said, "Teresa, are you pregnant?"

"No," she sputtered. "You implied that last night. What's up? Do I look fat?"

He chuckled uncomfortably. "Not at all. It's just that … You might consider the possibility. I know you had a bit to drink last night …."

"Only a few sips," she protested.

He raised a finger. "Exactly. Does a taste of wine usually give you a hangover?"

When was the last time she'd had a period? She couldn't recall. Over a month ago. Liam and she hadn't used protection during their extended honeymoon, and she'd wondered why nothing had come of it. Even after they'd returned, when almost every conversation devolved into an argument, they never stopped going at it like rabbits. She suspected she was infertile. Why would Jake, of all people, believe she was pregnant when the thought hadn't occurred to anyone else?

"Okay, I'll pick up a pregnancy test at the store. Can we get back to talking about you?"

Liam came in—*curse his timing*—dressed for work in worn jeans and a ratty T-shirt. He'd been replacing the siding of the Victorian fixer upper. Teresa still didn't think of it as *theirs*. Unbeknown to her, he'd bought it with his own money at the lowest point in their relationship.

"I can't get over how much you look like Duncan," Jake said, shaking his head, "only with the same black hair and honey-colored complexion as Ali."

"Having a real father takes some getting used to," Liam said, scratching his flat stomach through one of the holes in his shirt.

Jake tried not to stare. "I can well imagine."

"Bacon?" Liam asked, already breaking open the package and laying strips in the pan.

"Yeah, great."

Teresa broke in, "Jake was just about to tell us why he showed up out of the blue. JB, you basically shunned us all as if we'd violated your religion."

"Please," Jake said, with an annoyed gesture, "don't confuse me with Edward."

"What did you tell Mom last night?" Teresa persisted. She knew her approach was ham-fisted but couldn't stop herself. Could it be hormones? "She looked as if the plastic surgeon had cut her off."

"Oh that," Jake said, leaning back. "Only that I resigned."

Teresa clutched her churning stomach. "From Big Paul's?" He nodded, placid. "Jeez, why?"

"It was time to move on." He might have been discussing a hobby, such as hang gliding. "I haven't totally abandoned BPO. I'm on the board of directors. A big shareholder."

"But … but there are two headquarters now. The company is huge. It will fall apart without you."

He wrinkled his nose. "It won't. I've groomed my successors well. Both locations are in good hands."

Liam scowled. "Does this have something to do with Ali and Joe?"

"What? No." Jake turned back to Teresa. "You get to run away with the circus, but I have to keep my nose to the grindstone until I have a heart attack?" Far from bitter, he was reasoning with her. "Big Paul's will be fine. More than fine. The people at the helm have their hearts in it."

Teresa couldn't believe her ears. "Then … what will you do?"

"Vegetate, of course."

"Here?"

"Maybe."

Lord he was infuriating.

"Come *on*," he said. "I'm kidding, mostly. As it happens, I have plans."

"I hope they don't include Chiara," Liam said, semi-jocular.

"They didn't until last night," Jake replied, flippant as ever. At Liam's glower, he added, "Don't worry. Sure, we had fun together. Gimme a break, I didn't even kiss her."

Liam was still scowling. "If I hadn't happened along …."

Jake didn't rise to the bait, but his jaw had a stubborn set Teresa knew well. She was fascinated by this streak of puritanism in Liam. Although, come to think of it, he'd rejected April, the fabulous woman who'd cornered him after yoga class, long before he and Teresa got together. Separated from her husband, April had been what most men would consider fair game. Not Liam.

Jake rolled his shoulders as if limbering up for a fight. His exasperation clear, he said, "I *like* her. I'm not *scheming* to steal her from her husband."

Surprisingly, Liam backed off. "Hey, man," he said raising his palms, "I don't mean to sound judgy. Maybe her hubby is a prize A-hole she needs to kick to the curb. Just be careful, that's all. Chiara seems like the type who has no defenses when it comes to … guys like you."

"Pfft." Jake made a face. "Like I'm so irresistible."

"You *are*," Teresa declared. "It's obvious to everyone. But you, I guess."

Jake stared at her like she'd lost her mind. Finally he asked Liam, "Could you use my help today?"

Her husband gave him a mocking once-over, ending with his shoes. "I don't want to scuff you."

Jake barked out a laugh. "I'll change into my grubbies."

Teresa and Ali were en route to the newest location of La Fête Sauvage.

"You're *pregnant*?!" Ali swerved to the shoulder and hit the brakes, causing the trucker behind them to honk and give them the bird.

"Sorry," Teresa said, "that was lousy timing. I should have waited until we arrived." They were minutes away from their lunch date with Becca. Chiara was watching Lorenzo build the LEGO castle David had bought him. Maddie and David were on their honeymoon, and the older generation had returned to Seattle.

"The weird part," Teresa went on, "is that Jake gave me the idea. I thought he was just commenting on the extra pounds I've put on. True, I was feeling punky—but I didn't actually upchuck till this morning. Last night he asked if I should be drinking, like I might not want to, under the circumstances. Maybe as the newcomer he's more observant."

She could see Ali trying to read between the lines. "But it's great, right? You're happy?"

"Yes, of course." Thrilled as she was, Teresa was also afraid. Her relationship with Liam had been fragile as a porcelain tea service ever since the brief but painful separation. She had experienced a too-long season of discontent, debating what to do in the next stage of her life, until Liam was ready to run screaming into the bay. Her passion was for playing piano, but her plans to buy a music school in Port Angeles and teach piano had been met with universal skepticism. Finally she'd realized they were right. She'd never taught, and what if she didn't like it? Then there was the question of students. She didn't need the money, but who really valued what they got for free? People who couldn't afford lessons didn't own pianos. In the end, she had stumbled upon her true calling, interior design. She was not the altruistic type, she supposed. In light of that fact, would she be a good mother?

"How is it, with Jake as your house guest?" Ali asked.

"Great! He's helping Liam put on new siding."

"*Really?*"

Ali's incredulity shouldn't surprise her. "I told you he's a good guy. I know your experience doesn't bear that out. But he's changed." She paused before blurting out her other shocking news, "He's resigned as CEO of Big Paul's."

Ali was momentarily shocked into silence. "Hold on, Becca needs to hear this." She pulled back onto the road, and no words were exchanged as she drove the last few minutes to La Fête Sauvage.

It was a glorious day, and the maître d' had reserved them a table next to a heat lamp at the edge of the blue-tiled courtyard, its periphery of baskets filled with pink, red, and purple fuchsias. Even in summer, it could be chilly in Port Townsend unless you sat in the sun, and none of the women were looking to acquire a tan.

As soon as Teresa announced she wasn't drinking, Becca guessed the reason. She was more surprised to find out who had alerted her to her condition.

"Jake? *Really?*" They were on the early side for lunch, and Jean-Louis had been puttering about nearby. Now he couldn't resist inserting himself into the conversation.

"*Calisse!*" he swore, slipping into Québécois French as he sometimes did when excited. Jean-Louis seemed to be in a perpetual state of excitement. The French adjective *excité*, as Becca pointed out with a broad wink, had more of a sexual connotation. No one doubted that Becca and Jean-Louis enjoyed that kind of excitement in their lives. His frenetic energy could be daunting, leading someone to compare him to the pink cartoon cougar Snagglepuss.

Ali said, "Jean-Louis, there's a fourth chair here. Sit."

Teresa again explained about the conversations with Jake.

"*Là, là*, I always said that Jake was a perfectly nice man," Jean-Louis insisted. "He never forced you, *hein?*" Ali shrugged. "He was a gentleman," Jean-Louis went on. "And his sartorial elegance has never been in dispute. Did you not love the clothes he gave you?"

Another shrug of grudging agreement from Ali.

"Even though you ultimately sent them back, he saved them for you all this time."

"As to his motivation," Ali said, "I think it's clear those 'dates' were about sticking it to Joe. And he bought the clothing because he was so appalled by my lack of style. If you're trying to argue that he was genuinely into me, don't let's forget that I wasn't the only woman he was seeing at the time."

"Ah," Jean-Louis said, nodding sagely, "you believe a man should drop everything and be exclusive with a woman who has not slept with him."

They all appeared chastened.

"A woman he dates sporadically?" Jean-Louis continued. "One who does not light up in his presence? If we look at the facts only, he rescued you from a bad man then spent a small fortune on you."

Hoping to get Ali off the hook, Teresa said, "Of all my brothers, Jake was the nicest. He never teased me, and he was the only one who volunteered to keep me company on shopping trips. He had an uncanny sense of what clothing would suit a woman best, could even guess the correct size." Their expressions made her add, "Okay, that sounds creepy." Jean-Louis shook his head. "To everyone but Jean-Louis," she amended.

Becca wasn't so easily convinced. "What makes you think he's changed? I admit, he was more relaxed last night than I recall, but I only ever talked to him at the restaurant. I always wondered why Ali saw him as a middle-aged lech rather than the incredible catch he is."

Ali finally found her voice. "Give me a break. I already had it bad for Joe."

Teresa patted her on the shoulder. "Of course you did, sweetie. Given a choice, most women preferred Joe. Mind you, Jake had his fans. He was insecure, God knows why. Still is. He's one of those unlucky people who only want what they can't have. Joe had too much self-esteem to chase after anyone who wasn't into him."

"Did Joe ever tell you what caused the bad blood between him and Jake?" Becca asked.

"There was that incident at the school dance in high school," Teresa said.

"He forgave Joe for that," Ali broke in. "When they were in Boston together, Jake's date jumped into Joe's cab. He didn't kick her out."

Ouch, Teresa thought, feeling terrible for college-aged Jake. "I always wondered. After that, Joe and Jake saw each other only at Christmas. A trial for the rest of us. Jake had his knives out for Joe, who just sat there, defenses lowered, like some martyred saint."

Ali nodded grimly. "Joe described one of those dinners to me. Of course, the morning after that night in Boston, he knew how badly he'd blown it. Not that it excuses him, but everyone was three sheets to the wind at the time. Teresa, I thought you knew about that."

"I didn't know the details," Teresa said.

Two waiters arrived, one with a pitcher of iced tea and one with bowls of steaming bouillabaisse and salad, a menu agreed upon in advance.

"I see you've hired all our best-looking FOSSP guys," Ali said wryly.

Jean-Louis's protruding lower lip told Teresa Ali shouldn't push it. She rushed to change the subject. "So … anyway … Jake resigned as CEO of Big Paul's."

Becca whistled. "No kidding. I thought power was his Viagra. *Now* how's he going to impress women?"

"Don't know," Teresa said. "He dodged most of my questions. As far as I can tell, he has no plans to go home, and Liam likes having him around. We'll learn the answer—or answers—yet."

"Speaking of hanging around," Becca said, "how long will Chiara stay?"

"As long as she likes, as far as I'm concerned," Ali declared. "She is the easiest houseguest ever. Always offering to help. Doesn't muddy the floors in her cabin or leave hair in the shower drain. Hangs up her towels. Is fabulous with Lorenzo."

"Can we keep dressing her?" Teresa wanted to know. "I bought her two sundresses."

Jean-Louis blew out a long stream of air. "Shouldn't you stick to decorating houses? She might not appreciate your interference."

Teresa flinched. In Chiara's position, she would have loved the attention. Or would she?

"She liked the pink dress," Ali said. "Why don't you let her decide? I know Jake is just itching to try his hand at it."

They all looked at her askance.

"You know what I mean," Ali protested. "He likes a good fixer upper."

"Hah, a fix-*her*-upper," Jean-Louis said, to general laughter. He aspirated the H, the consonant being silent in French.

Becca raised her palms to the sky. "Who doesn't?"

"I always appreciate your advice when we were roomies," Ali said.

"Well, I knew you better. You didn't look entirely comfortable in Jake's selections, but that was because you believed he was trying to make you fit in with his crowd, and that went against the grain. You've got plenty of clothing Jake would approve of now. I think Joe prefers you in jeans and a T-shirt."

Jean-Louis snorted. "The less clothing, the better."

Becca narrowed her eyes. "*Sois sage!*" she warned him in French. *Behave.*

"Back to Chiara," Teresa said. "Won't her husband miss her?"

Ali blew out a raspberry. "She avoids the subject. I think he's abusive. Otherwise, why is Lorenzo so quiet?"

"That doesn't mean he's been abused," Teresa protested.

Why wouldn't Chiara want to prolong her stay? Ali and Joe were everyone's favorite hosts—generous, amusing, entertaining, and inspiring in their unwavering devotion to each other.

"Children can sense friction between their parents," Ali said. "Our foster parents got on well enough, but I detected no passion. Zero. They were like business partners. With us, they acted like mentors. Strict ones. Overall, Liam and I weren't happy campers."

* * *

It was late morning, and David and Maddie were basking in the hottest soaking pool at Sol Duc Hot Springs Resort, where they'd stay for two nights. As the least spoiled members of what was now affectionately known as "The O'Connell Clan," they were fine with the rustic cabin. David, used to roughing it in tents or shacks in remote African villages, didn't consider any cabin with a bathroom and flush toilet rustic. Maddie was no stranger to couch surfing.

What did require an adjustment was the lack of cellphone reception and Wi-Fi. In general, once you got too far from what could charitably be called a city—even a town—on the Peninsula, you had to search for a signal. Here they'd told them, "Don't bother."

"Your family never wanted to spend the night here?" Maddie said, bumping against David beneath the steaming water. It was all he could do to keep his hands off her in public. He breathed in the sulfuric smell of the hot springs, which evoked happy memories of childhood. The sky was cloudy— no need for hats and sunglasses—and the cold air made the heat of the water all the more welcome. That was the positive way to look at it. In these parts, June was iffy for sun worshippers. For David, weather didn't matter. Or accommodations. He could barely fathom that here he was, at long last, married to the most bewitching, talented, unspoiled, and fun-loving woman he'd ever met. The only cloud on his horizon was his inability to check on Lorenzo. His son wasn't acclimating well, and his father belonged at his side.

"David? Did you hear me? Why didn't your parents want to stay here?"

He heard the laughter in Maddie's voice, the understanding that he was almost too distracted by the sight of her in a swimsuit for normal conversation. He supposed his relentless physical need for her would subside, eventually. At the moment, it was almost debilitating. Everyone should have such problems.

"Sol Duc," David acknowledged, tearing his eyes away from Maddie to take in the majestic setting. The pool area was banked on all sides by moss-covered forest and the inviting colonial-style main lodge, with its dark-stained wood siding and side-gabled, cedar-shingle roof, dormer windows, and long bathhouse. "We kids pushed for it, but Mom and Dad nixed the idea. Too lowbrow. 'You want to visit hot springs?' "—he spoke in falsetto to imitate his mother's imperious voice—" '*Harrison* Hot Springs is the only acceptable choice. Stay at Lake Crescent and make a day trip to Sol Duc.' " He laughed. "Our parents were unrepentant snobs."

"Where is it? Harrison Hot Springs, I mean."

"In Canada."

She chuckled. "All we need is somewhere private to go when the mood strikes."

He laughed too. "Funny expression. What if the mood keeps on striking until we're completely stricken?"

"What, as in old and feeble? Sounds good to me."

"Do you miss acting?" He'd almost said, *Will* you miss acting, which implied she would never act again—his most fervent wish.

Maddie shrugged. "Not at the moment. I'm sure I'll get the itch again. Maybe now that Kilo is rocketing off to super-stardom, I can become a regular at Theatre by the Marina."

Kilo, David thought darkly, picturing the exotically handsome actor, dancer, and yoga teacher. Cast as Oberon, he'd been Maddie's final fling, a guy she'd rejected for David. The thought of her becoming a member of the local repertory theater cheered him. Maybe he could donate enough money to make her a permanent fixture. *Damn it*, he thought, *you can't start buying privilege the way all rich people do*. When you had as much money as the O'Connells, throwing it at problems was a constant temptation—one of the reasons he'd joined Doctors for Humankind. He tried not to think of Maddie's major Hollywood movie, titled *Insanity*, set to premiere on Thanksgiving Day. It was a small but splashy role: she sashayed around semi-clothed, fucked another man, and was killed. All within the opening ten minutes or so. Would he attend the premiere? How could he not? The reality couldn't be worse than what he imagined. What if it had a run at the Rose Theatre? How could he stomach that? In Los Angeles, they probably had support groups for normal guys married to beautiful Hollywood actresses. Unless you were an actor yourself, how could you cope with that crap?

Maddie waved a hand in front of his face. "Sweetie, you look kind of scary, like someone refused to let go of your Eggo. You okay? If we linger much longer, I'm going to look like one of the Weird Sisters in Macbeth. Only from the neck down, of course."

"Hah. I'll still want you. And when you're old enough to be a Weird Sister, directors will stop wanting to see you naked."

She laughed. "You've obviously never seen Polanski's movie version. Yep, they were naked as jaybirds."

David did *not* want to picture it. Pointing to the wall clock, he said, "Okay. Just a few more minutes. By the way, what's next for your friend Jeremy?"

"An industrial. Nothing in the pipeline after that. He plans to return to Port Townsend for a bit. He needs a break from the biz. Do you think he and Matthew might work as a couple? Matthew's such a salt-of-the-earth type— just what Jeremy needs to ground him."

Salt of the earth, David thought. *Doesn't salt destroy crops?* He wondered why his wife was so intent on playing matchmaker. Matthew and Jeremy might be the only gay people she knew in Port Townsend, but the city surely had a thriving community. "Salt of the earth," David repeated out loud. "If we're going with a salt metaphor, Jeremy's Himalayan pink salt and Matthew is good ole Morton's. I don't think Matthew is even 'out.' He tours with country singers, and the fans tend to be homophobic. Jeremy is gloriously gay. I can't picture him with a closeted partner."

"You're probably right." Maddie emerged from the water to perch on the side of the pool, drawing the usual contingent of fascinated onlookers. Ignoring the attention, she kept talking. "If Matthew hosts a soiree to showcase local musicians, I could invite Jeremy."

David plopped his intimidating bulk down next to Maddie. "Does he sing?" he asked, glaring at one of the worst gawkers.

"Does he ever! Though he calls himself an actor who sings."

They went over to the sidelines to fetch their robes and flipflops. David was relieved to be ending another episode of the Maddie Show.

As they were about to part ways to exit through the men's and women's dressing rooms, Maddie stood on tiptoes to give him a quick kiss. "Don't worry, sweetie. I see them stare. I'm resigned to it."

Even if David hadn't been overheated from the water, he'd be blushing. The first time they'd soaked in these pools, he'd been one of those gawkers.

Instead of showering in the changing rooms, they walked the short distance across the parking lot to their cabin. Several deer were grazing placidly on the vast lawn. "Just like home," David said.

Maddie fished the key from the pocket of her robe and said, "Dibs on the shower." Sprinting ahead, she unlocked the door as if pursued by a pack of dogs—he hadn't even picked up his pace—shed her robe and stood in the open door of the bathroom to shimmy out of her swimsuit.

"Need someone to wash your back?" he asked in a husky voice.

"Oh, *definitely*," she purred. She reached in comic consternation for the small of her back, thrusting her breasts forward then laughing as he backed her into the bathroom. After testing the water, he lifted her up so that she straddled his waist and carried her into the shower. Or tried to. The compact Acrylic stall was a tight fit. His hulking figure alone just about filled it.

"Ow," she squeaked, "my knee! This isn't going to work." She giggled. "We'll be so wedged in that only the Jaws of Life can free us."

"Okay," he said, laughing at the absurdity of the situation. She slid down his body. "Your knee okay?"

She rubbed it. "Funny bone. Give it a minute."

Stepping back, he bowed low. "You first, madam."

Behind the shower door, she said, "I bet Harrison Hot Springs has *way* larger showers."

They rinsed off so quickly you'd think the water police were timing them. Five minutes later, they were grappling on the bed. "It's like making love to a squid," he complained, pinning her down so she couldn't move.

"I'll be good. Go ahead, have your way with me." She went limp and solemn, face twitching with suppressed laughter.

He planted light kisses on her mouth, then her neck, moving slowly downward until she couldn't keep up the act any longer.

After lunch in the main dining room, they hiked the loop to Sol Duc Falls and back, always a classic. The mostly flat but uneven path threaded through old growth trees along the river, with various shades and textures of mosses and lichens draped on or sprouting from every surface. A mossy wonderland. It rained intermittently, but not enough to require special gear. At the falls, the sun broke through and made the rushing water and all the rain droplets sparkle. A rainbow bridged the falls.

In a hushed voice, Maddie said, "Oh, that's beautiful. A good omen?"

"Definitely."

CHAPTER 5

———•———

THE NEXT THREE DAYS WERE gloriously sunny, allowing Liam and Jake to finish installing the siding of Liam's Victorian. At five on Friday afternoon, they surveyed their handiwork. Liam noted Jake's arms-akimbo "job well done" stance with amusement. You'd think they'd just finished erecting a pyramid.

"Now we paint?" Jake asked. "What colors did you have in mind?"

Liam was still getting a bead on his new brother-in-law. Jake was nothing like the bitter, fussy man he'd been told to expect. He'd pictured a fop in the British sense. A guy obsessed with superficial crap. Someone who wore Gucci and Brioni and flashed the labels when possible. Who was on a first-name basis with all the local sommeliers and maître ds at the most fashionable restaurants. The American equivalent of Reynard, the French pianist who had tried to steal Teresa away—not that she'd been *his* at the time, though Liam had thought of her that way.

Jake wasn't afraid to get dirt under his fingernails or to tackle challenging or mind-numbing physical labor. Welcomed it, in fact. Like Liam, he wasn't chatty. He never tried to call the shots. In unguarded moments, the man seemed to be mind-traveling down some dark corridor.

At this moment, Jake was beaming like a kid at a toy fair. "Pink?"

"Huh?" Liam laughed. "Oh, the paint job. I was thinking dark gray with burgundy and off-white accents—the window frames and doors."

"What do you call this style of architecture?" Jake was moving about, as if to view the house from different angles.

"Victorian." At Jake's death stare, Liam clarified, "Queen Anne style. Fancier than the folk Victorians you see a lot of in Port Townsend but criminally neglected, which is why it was a steal. Your B and B may be the only Italianate-style place in town. Everything from that period is over the top, but Queen Anne offers the biggest hodgepodge of elements." He pointed to various sections of the house. "You've got your contrasting textures—some stone, some carved wood, some brick. The Disneyesque tower, the pedimented porch—you know, with little triangles on top. In a word, fussy."

Jake was looking at *him*, not the house, as if taking his measure. Men like Jake tended to underestimate Liam, seeing him as no better than a bouncer or a physical trainer, a guy who coasted by on looks and strength alone. No brain, all brawn. No taste for finer things. "I'm surprised you bought such a fussy place," Jake said. "I see you more as a fan of ultra-modern or Prairie Style, like Frank Lloyd Wright."

"You mean some kind of *reaction* to Victorian style. Nothing like that for sale when I was looking. This was a good deal. Besides, I'm not done yet."

"Ah," Jake said, "You're going to risk pissing off your neighbors or the Victorian Society."

I don't want to piss anyone off, Liam thought. "Not really," he said. "I don't think anyone will miss that poufy decorative trim, do you?" He gave Jake a hard look. "Don't you have better things to do than help me with my backbreaking vanity project?"

Jake grinned. "Sick of me yet? I could always check into a hotel."

"Nah. Great deal for me. And Teresa's happy."

"You glad she's pregnant?"

Liam was surprised that his brother-in-law couldn't guess what it meant for a former foster kid to have a child of his own blood. "Hell, yes. I was bracing myself in case Teresa and I … couldn't get pregnant." He'd almost said, "in case Teresa and I split." Jake didn't know about their recent troubles, and he'd prefer to keep it that way.

Startling them into silence, the mailman came right up to hand Liam a package. He'd been watching their progress on the house. "Lookin' good."

"Thanks, Fred." Liam examined the large envelope. "What do we have here?" He tossed it to Jake. "It's for you. From your publisher?"

Jake looked surprised that Liam recognized the name. *Come on, Jake,* Liam thought. *It's a Big-Five publishing house, after all.* "Galley proofs?" He tried to sound casual. Once upon a time, he'd dated a romance novelist fifteen years older. He'd thought, with the age difference—he'd been twenty, she, thirty-five—that things wouldn't get serious. Naïve of him. She'd begged him to pose shirtless for a cover. *As if.* With a mirthless smile, he wondered what she'd think of him now, half his body marred by shrapnel scars.

Damned if Jake didn't look all hot and sweaty, as if he'd just emerged from a steam room. "Uh, yeah, from my publisher."

Why did Jake look embarrassed? *It's not like I caught you wearing a frilly apron or drinking a frozen strawberry margarita*, he thought. *But now we know why you resigned as CEO of Big Paul's.*

"You're a professional writer now," he said. "A guide to corporate success?"

Jake snorted. "Hardly."

"A romance novel?" Liam teased. Jake gave him an "enough already" look. "I can keep guessing. Erotica?"

Jake made a disgusted sound. "Give me a break. You ever hear of Dirk Fartherly?"

Nah ... it couldn't be. "You're serious?

"My alter ego. I write under the pen name Damon Morehouse."

"No kidding." Liam threw back his head and guffawed. "*Kapow* was on the *New York Times* best seller list. Hmm. I can't tell. Most mothers would be proud, but Carrie—"

"Yeah," Jake cut him off, "she doesn't know. She's had a lot to swallow lately. I figured this secret could keep a while longer."

"Oh, she'll come around," Liam said with a broad gesture. "Aren't they making a movie?"

"Early stages," Jake said. "It's not even cast yet. Might not make it off the starting block."

"I thought George Reed Masters was interested in playing Damon."

To Liam, Jake's laughter sounded dry and a little stagey. Liam was still getting used to the man's never-break-a-sweat persona. Like his protagonist Damon—unflappable, impeccably groomed.

"Well, Tom Cruise wasn't available ...." Liam was about to be really impressed when Jake added, "Kidding. The producers floated the rumor about George Reed Masters to see if he was interested. So far, no dice. For his next project, he wants something meatier than an action flick. No one in this film is going to be nominated for an Oscar."

Liam waggled his eyebrows. "Get Maddie to talk to him. He was the star of *Insanity*, that movie she had a small part in."

Jake looked skeptical. "Does she have that kind of access?"

"He did make a pass at her. But probably not."

Fortunately Jake didn't have time to troll for details. Teresa drove up in her powder-blue Miata, parked on the street, and launched herself into Liam's arms. He kissed the top of her head, breathing in her heady fragrance. Until he met Teresa, he'd thought floral scents were for grannies. When he finally experienced Teresa, he got it. Her natural aroma was what made that perfume work, turned it into something delicious. No one could hold a candle to his wife. When they'd met, she'd been a pin-thin bottle blonde, but underneath the intimidating fashion-doll exterior, quirky and vulnerable. He preferred the current version, the softer curves and strawberry-blonde curls.

Jake's smirk was irritating the hell out of him. "*What*?" Liam said.

"You two," he scoffed. "Where did you stash the real Teresa? Sis, I sort of miss the brittle socialite."

Teresa's brow creased adorably. "Brittle, huh? Tell me how you really feel. I'd prefer some other word. 'Arch,' maybe, like Myrna Loy in those *Thin Man* movies."

Behind the playful words, Teresa wanted reassurance. "I like—*love*—both versions," Liam jumped in. After all, he'd fallen hard for the pampered princess.

"If you say so," Jake said.

Liam couldn't help ribbing him. "Okay, Dirk."

Teresa eyed them warily. "Dirk?" she repeated.

"Jake's pen name," Liam said, "Dirk Fartherly."

He waited for her to catch on, but she read mostly tame mysteries and torrid romances. "He's a secret novelist, and he writes thrillers. Best sellers."

"No!" Teresa clapped her hands in delight.

"I've read *Kapow*," Liam said. He pointed to the proofs. "Book Two in the series?"

Jake nodded. "It's called *Thwack*. Another Batman action term. I'll need to take a day off from our work to go through these. They expect a quick turn-around."

"No problem," Liam said. "Joe's been bugging me for a knife-throwing lesson. I thought I'd start on Saturday."

Jake raised his hand and waved it like a grade-school kid with the right answer. "No way. I'm *so* in. That's the perfect skill for Damon to acquire in Book Three. I can pull an all-nighter if necessary."

Jake wanted to learn how to throw knives? Would wonders never cease? Would he be willing to make a fool of himself? *This* Liam had to see.

"Don't bother," Liam said, smiling evilly at the prospect of Jake tossing the knives all which way, like a two-year-old with a ball. "The lesson can wait till Sunday."

* * *

That Sunday, Jake rode over to the compound along with Liam and Teresa, glad to have them as buffers. Joe and Ali still tiptoed around him like he was a snake in the grass. Who could blame them? He'd wasted years gnashing his teeth over his brother's betrayals. Now he saw the folly of that. The only person he'd hurt was himself. Joe's voice, talent, and charisma had once made him the envy of men everywhere, including Jake. He was finally beginning to find joy in his own gifts, as formidable as Joe's in their own way. What if those gifts were taken away? Jake didn't envy his twin now.

"Only because he's down on his luck," Rory said.

Damn. Until now, the day had been Rory free.

He continued the silent argument. *It's more than that. I don't want his career to tank, not anymore.*

"If you say so. I'm rootin' for ya, pal."

Damon's sidekick Mickey was based on Rory.

"Yeah, thanks for that," his buddy said.

Flattered or annoyed? Jake couldn't tell.

"Hey, I'm immortal!"

Flattered, then. God, this was stupid. The only reason Rory was "talking to him" was that Jake was already mentally plotting his third novel. The brain did funny things when it was hashing out a story. Whenever Jake kept a regular writing schedule, he slept poorly. His brain refused to rest. It questioned plot developments, came up with better words, found inconsistencies, suggested twists …."

"Your *brain*? Hell no. That's me."

Stop distracting me, he warned Rory. *I'm already on shaky ground with Joe and Ali. Don't make things worse by making me look like a nutcase.*

The voice was silent as they drove down the final stretch of gravel road, passing the boxy dwelling that housed the FOSSP kids who helped with cooking and cleaning. Had Rory decided to take mercy on Jake just this once?

The dogs greeted Liam and Teresa ecstatically as they exited the car, little Coogan rearing back and dancing on his hind legs, circus-dog style. Harry was the size of a pony but surprisingly decorous. They were well trained, thank God, and didn't jump up on anyone or do embarrassing things with their tongues or snouts. He supposed he'd been grandfathered in. They wagged and grinned for him as well.

Joe and Ali hugged Teresa, and Ali kissed her brother's cheek. When it came to Jake, she was at a loss. So Jake stepped forward for a handshake.

"Ow!" She shook out her hand. "I don't think you realize your own strength."

Jeez, he must be nervous. "Sorry! Next time I'll kiss your hand or something."

"Or something," Joe muttered.

"Off to a super start," Rory interjected.

They convened on the terrace, with its spectacular view of the Strait of Juan de Fuca. Did they realize how much the compound resembled a movie set? A bunch of different sets. You had your safari tent, designed for a gentleman adventurer or tribal chief—Jake knew nothing about bigwigs in Africa—your retired sea captain's retreat, and a hunting "cabin" grand enough for Theodore Roosevelt. Finally, all those private guest "cottages"— more like bungalows. Fun. An adult theme park. The kids were going to love it when they were old enough to roam. They'd have lots of places to hide. Had Joe and David really thought this through? This theme park lacked a unifying concept.

"What do you think?" Joe said as he handed Jake his drink—vodka tonic with lime. He recalled the last Christmas when they'd shared cocktails as a family. Joe had been dating Rina, and Jake had given him a hard time. More than that. He'd been relentless.

"Think of what?" Jake said. He raised his glass. "Cheers!"

Joe's arm swept the compound. "Of Port Townsend. Of this."

"I like it. Just what the doctor ordered. Your place is … like, uh, Westworld, um, in miniature. You know, uh, Fantasy Island." *Huh, that didn't come out right.*

To his relief, everyone laughed.

Joe sat back in one of the Adirondack chairs and swished the ice cubes around in his Scotch. "I'm afraid we have several different, um, styles, represented here. It's eclectic. An architect with any integrity—Howard Roark, for instance—would probably set fire to the whole thing."

"Can we leave Ayn Rand out of this?" Jake said. They all laughed. "Who cares about artistic integrity? Not me, certainly."

Liam wasted no time relaying the news about Jake's new career path. Jake couldn't suppress a smirk at their astonished reactions: like a crowd watching a natural disaster in progress. He knew what they thought of him: the ultimate corporate tool. The shift required a drastic reassessment—he hoped.

"Ah … they're not so bad," Rory said in his head. "That family feud thing was on you."

Turned out Joe was also a thriller fan and had read his book. Liked it, or so he claimed. He couldn't very well say otherwise.

"Hey, it's a good book!" Rory insisted. "Even the *New York Times* said so."

* * *

Liam was second-guessing whether he should subject Jake to possible ridicule. Clearly the family wasn't ready to swallow whole hog that the poor guy's efforts to appease were genuine. He looked conspicuously at his watch. "It's five already. When's dinner?" He pulled two packages out of his leather satchel. "I promised Joe a knife-throwing lesson, and Jake wants in, too."

Alarmed, Ali leaned forward as if ready to spring into action. "Uh, Liam, alcohol and knives?"

Joe was already rubbing his hands in anticipation. "It's okay, darlin', no one's even finished their first drink, and the target's in a spot where even the wildest throw will do no harm. Unless a deer gets too close, and that's on them." He pointed up the hill. "Built according to your specs, Liam. No plywood. Seven feet tall, five feet wide."

"Knives bounce off plywood," Liam explained to Jake.

Joe unwrapped the package of three knives and held one up to the sky in a ridiculous mock-heroic pose. In a hokey British accent, he called out, "I challenge thee to knives at dawn, Moriarty!"

Jake chuckled. "Sherlock Holmes challenging his nemesis to a knife fight, only it's set in Medieval times. I'd see that movie."

Startled laughter all around. Did Jake's family really not know he had a sense of humor?

The men put down their drinks and marched toward the target as if summoned to battle.

"Maybe everyone's a Quaker in this story," Liam suggested, stopping mid-stride to throw his own knife and hitting the target dead center. "They were fond of thee and thouing. Then again, Quakers are all about peace. No knife fights for them." Seeing how everyone gaped at him, he preened theatrically. Knowing he was contributing to the silliness, he settled down. "Okay, enough clowning. This is a serious business. They're special throwing knives. Eight inches, no edges, extra sharp points, and a belt sheath for easy transport."

They walked up to the target, where Joe pulled out Liam's knife, examined it, and shot him a reproachful glare. "*You* use a combat knife."

Liam chuckled. "Baby steps. If you start with a combat knife, you're gonna end up having a tantrum and throwing it out to sea."

He backed them away from the target until they stood at a distance of roughly fifteen feet. "Joe, you go first. Thumb on top of the handle. Keep your grip relaxed and let it slide out of your hand like so … to make it spin."

Joe's first few sorry attempts, accompanied by self-deprecating mugging, had the women on the terrace in stitches. Each time, the spin ended with the handle hitting the target so that it dropped like a stone. With dogged determination and no display of wounded ego, Joe persevered until he started to get the hang of it, adjusting his distance. It took about ten tries before he got a hit.

Jake's turn. Hard to miss the way his gaze drifted toward Chiara, but it didn't affect his performance. Defying everyone's expectations, he managed a hit after two tries. Good for him; he'd learned from Joe's blunders. Joe acted genuinely pleased for Jake, who had to be ecstatic about showing up his brother.

"Bravo Zulu!" Liam called out, giving Jake a military salute.

Jake thrust his forefinger at Liam, aggrieved. "*You* don't use that spin technique. You just throw. That's gotta be a highly advanced move."

Liam tried not to preen. "Well, yeah. The spin technique is easier, but in an actual battle, unless you're a hundred percent sure you're standing *exactly* the right distance away, not the most reliable. A knife thrown with no spin by an expert is gonna hit the target for sure." He threw his combat knife again, another square hit. "I practice a lot. It's meditative."

Joe took a second turn at the target. "I can see that." This go-around he hit the target two out of three times. "You just meditate on your worst enemy."

Liam caught his sly wink and grinned. What enemies did Joe have, other than the relentless tabloid press? Everyone liked the guy. Except Jake. He sensed no ill will between them now. Had there ever been, on Joe's part?

"Enough for one day?" Liam asked.

Joe was already mounting the knives on his belt. "From now on, I'm prepared for anything," he said.

Jake did the same.

"A bunch of jokers," Liam muttered. "You know that saying … 'a little knowledge is a dangerous thing'? Best to leave the knives at home for now."

They marched down the hill as if expecting medals. In the same spirit, Ali and Teresa rushed in to kiss the conquering heroes.

"Hey!" Jake said. "Make a guy jealous, will ya." He searched the terrace. "Where did Chiara go?"

"She promised Lorenzo a story," Ali said. "If she waits till bedtime, she'll have to bail early on our dinner party."

He's got it bad, Liam thought as he registered Jake's disappointment. *I hope Arnold isn't some devoted Ashley Wilkes type, or for that matter, a trigger-happy Othello.*

CHAPTER 6

FRESH DRINKS IN HAND, THEY settled in on the terrace. Jake prodded Liam for anecdotes from his "soldier" days in Israel, but his brother-in-law was a champion deflector. Though never having served in the Israeli army, Liam had gone through basic training in Jerusalem. David had hinted at some private mission he'd carried out to rescue a kidnapping victim. Dirk Fartherly's fictional protagonist, Damon, was ex-military. Jake had interviewed enough veterans that he almost wished he'd fought in the Gulf War—almost. Though technically the country was not at war right now, it appeared all too ready to dive into the fray should tensions in the Mideast escalate. Personally, Jake didn't think oil was worth fighting for, especially in these wars that never seemed to end. Like an invasive weed with roots so deep they couldn't be eradicated. There were lots of ecologically sound alternatives to fossil fuels. Still, he admired the guys who didn't hesitate to serve, who weren't in it for the thrills and the license to kill.

From Teresa, he learned that David and Maddie had gone on to Lake Crescent from Sol Duc and were now staying at Lake Quinault Lodge, though they were expected home soon. So far David had told him next to nothing about why he'd given up on his overseas mission as a doctor for that charity organization—Doctors for Humankind.

"Just you wait," Rory said. "He's been through the wringer."

No one asked you, Jake told him.

"Who else am I gonna talk to?"

Jake soon managed to slip away in search of Chiara.

The first room off the terrace was the kitchen, the air redolent of garlic and roasting meat. A young man was chopping onions with daunting speed. One of the ex-foster kids Joe and Ali had hired, a sous chef from Jean-Louis's restaurant.

"Oh, hi!" Jake said brightly. "Where's the bathroom?"

"There's one downstairs by the rec room and another at the end of the hall," the kid replied in a high-pitched voice. He was on the short side, with a sharply angled fox face. Jake hoped he was also wily like a fox. His own path to success had been smooth and inevitable, given his connections, grooming, and practiced affability. No smooth paths for foster children. He'd never stopped to consider what Ali must have endured, what that encounter in the woods had meant to her at a time when her only blood relative appeared to be dead. And what her unexpected visit had meant to Joe, in the throes of his first vocal crisis.

He followed the voices downstairs.

* * *

Chiara sat on the plush leather couch in the recreation room, Lorenzo nestled at her side. The child thrived away from Arnold. Not that her husband was cruel. He acted bemused and awkward around the boy, sending him sidelong looks as if he were a giant stuffed animal won at the fair who didn't fit the décor. He even spoke to Lor through Chiara: "Chiara, ask Lorenzo if he's had enough to eat. Chiara, Lorenzo looks tired." Much as he craved a father figure, Lorenzo was in awe of David, so dauntingly tall and unfamiliar. The concept of a "honeymoon" wasn't easily explained to a child.

When they were alone, they usually conversed in Italian. "Your *papà* is on a *piccola vacanza*."

No, *vacanza* was wrong. A "vacation" shouldn't exclude children.

"Your *papà* has taken a big step in his life, and he needs time to adjust. Just like when you came here for the first time. It was a shock, yes? But after that, you realized it was a good thing." That one sort of passed muster.

"For us to be together, your *papà* had to leave for a while." Better. But wasn't she overcomplicating things?

The sketchpad Chiara had found on the coffee table in the parlor was filled with images of mythical rain forest creatures helpfully labeled with names. She'd begun to spin a tale featuring those characters, and it had taken on a momentum of its own.

"Shall I tell you more about Mrs. Bigfoot and her friends?"

Lorenzo nodded vigorously, his green eyes huge.

After starting with "*c'era una volta*"—"there was a time," how the

Italian fairytales began—she continued in English, knowing that Lorenzo was comfortable in both languages and proud that he could switch back and forth effortlessly. Unlike her. She tended to think in English now but still stumbled on the idioms.

She always began with the same introduction. Lorenzo, who had endured an upsetting amount of change lately, responded well to routine. *"C'era una volta* .... Deep in the Hoh Rain Forest, a place where no human had visited in so long that they are mythological beings, sits a stump the size of a barn. It is hollowed out and covered with moss so thick, you could bounce on it like a trampoline. This is Moss Manor, the home of Beverly Bigfoot."

"What does Beverly look like?"

What *did* Beverly look like? Lorenzo had never asked this question before. The drawings were in pencil.

"Beverly has silky black hair that covers her entire body, and she wears a frilly blue apron she found in a pile of logs that may be the ruin of a dwelling. She has eyes as blue as a mountain lake, and the apron enhances their color. Beverly doesn't know anyone else like her, and when she sees her reflection in the pond, she is surprised to be so tall. All the other animals are small and sleek. Except for Willy the Leather Bear."

"Where did Willy get his leather outfit? Isn't leather made from animal skins?"

Uh-oh, good question. Because the picture showed Willy dressed in motorcycle leathers with the caption, "Willy the Leather Bear," Chiara was stuck.

"Willy wears a leather outfit he found under a large piece of canvas. It was a tent, but Willy couldn't know that any more than Beverly could know she was wearing an apron."

"Then how did she figure out how to wear it?"

"Trial and error. When she tied it on her head, it kept falling off. If she hung it over her back, she couldn't appreciate the ruffles."

Lorenzo nodded, satisfied. "How did they learn English?"

"They don't communicate like we do. We would hear their speech as grunts and squeaks. You must trust me when I tell you that my translation is accurate, the way foreign people speaking through a translator must trust. I am more reliable than they are because I love you." She mussed his hair, and he giggled. "All the animals understand each other, even those who make other noises. They communicate telepathically. That means their minds send thoughts back and forth in the silence. Gestures and facial expressions help."

Lorenzo blinked rapidly, the way he did when something didn't make sense. Her explanation might be too advanced for a child his age, intelligent as he was.

"You understand that Willy found the leather outfit? That it was left by humans long before these, ah, creatures were born?"

"What did the humans do there?"

"They cut down the trees in that area over a hundred years ago, but it was too difficult to move the logs to market, and they found homes closer to civilization."

He nodded.

"They speak without speaking," she said, in case he was still confused.

"They can hear each other's thoughts?" Lorenzo sounded fearful.

"Only if they wish for the other, ah, *creature* to hear them."

He sighed in relief. "So, the grunts are also kind of 'telepathic.' " He was adding the word to his vocabulary. "They hear the thoughts behind the grunts."

"Their expressions help. The way we understand other people in their presence, rather than on the phone." With every clarification, she dug herself deeper into the hole. The child's IQ had to be formidable.

She heard footsteps on the stairs and looked up, expecting to see May Allen or her sister Susan. May was the twins' nanny, and Susan made herself useful wherever she could, often helping with Lorenzo, who loved her because she was so tall and strong. She still competed occasionally in weightlifting challenges, though she had to be over fifty.

Jake emerged from the stairway. Had he been listening? She felt a frisson of excitement. Physically, he resembled Joe—frighteningly handsome— but he was more refined, as if someone had reimagined Joe for a different audience. He would have made the perfect leading man in a drawing-room comedy of the '30s.

"I'm sorry," he said, "I was just .... I couldn't help but overhear. What do you have there?" He pointed to the sketchpad.

She suddenly wondered if it were like a diary, not for the public. She stammered. "It was s-sitting on a side table in the living room. I hope no one will be angry that I borrowed it."

He sat on a chair opposite them, hands on his knees. "I can't imagine Ali would mind. Hey Lorenzo! 'Member me? I'm Jake."

Clamping his mouth shut, the boy nodded once.

"He's shy," Chiara was quick to explain.

"Are you enjoying the story?"

Lorenzo's eyes lit up. "It's all about Mrs. Bigfoot and her friends."

Jake grinned. "Mrs. Bigfoot bears a strong resemblance to Ali."

Chiara's cheeks felt hot. "Would she feel insulted?"

"Are you kidding? She'd be flattered. Anyone would be."

Lorenzo yawned. "*Tia* Chiara, I'm hungry."

Her watch said six thirty. "Hungry and tired out, I think."

Susan, her timing suspiciously perfect, appeared with arms spread wide. "Lor!" she said. "We're having Beefaroni. Join us?"

He jumped into her arms.

Jake's jaw dropped.

"She's a professional weightlifter," Chiara explained with a laugh. Kissing Lor on the head, she said, "You would never do that with me, right, *caro*? I'd break in half." She tickled him and he giggled.

"Since Lorenzo's going to have some, uh, Beefaroni"—Jake's shudder was intentionally comic—"that means you're free to join the rest of us."

"He's just discovered Beefaroni," she hurried to explain. "At home I feed him spaghetti *al dente* with meatballs. I don't know how he got the taste for that, that ...." She broke off, knowing she shouldn't insult Lorenzo's new favorite dish but also because Jake's disconcertingly hot gaze was making her flustered. Had he noticed her dress? It was a gift from Teresa, tighter than she usually wore. The white sundress with small red flowers had a sweetheart bodice and skimmed her hips before flaring into a swing skirt. Teresa insisted it was "cheerful," not "flirty."

Jake's eyes returned to her face, and although he didn't blush, he appeared less self-assured. She didn't think he was the sort who openly ogled women. *This can't happen*, she reminded herself sternly, but rebellion roiled within her. She couldn't fathom going home to Arnold.

She wanted Jake more fiercely than she'd ever wanted anyone or anything.

She stood and smoothed the nonexistent wrinkles out of her skirt. "I'd love to join the group." Susan and Lor were mounting the stairs to the kitchen. "*Buona notte, caro,*" she called out, though he was already out of sight.

Standing too close, Jake whispered, "Susan and May Allen are really going to eat that unappetizing mush?"

"No." Chiara didn't back away. "And Lorenzo doesn't notice or care. Beefaroni and SpaghettiOs are comfort food. Not many children appreciate pasta *al dente*."

"Is there an Italian word for the opposite of *al dente*?"

It was her turn to wrinkle her nose. "It's not done. Soft pasta is ruined pasta. Lorenzo is growing up to be an American child. I don't think that's bad." She paused. "Usually."

"Usually?"

Her heart was beating faster.

"In many Italian households, several generations live together. The child is surrounded by love and attention. Lorenzo has had only me."

"*You* love him. His father doesn't? Uh, his guardian."

To avoid a lie, she answered obliquely. "Lorenzo needs a real father in his life."

Jake took a tiny step forward, and Chiara had the ridiculous thought that he was volunteering. She'd been about to add that David would now be that man. Reaching for her hand, Jake lifted it to his lips. Something was happening and she didn't want it to stop. He removed her glasses and placed them on the side table, his gentle hand tipping her chin. His eyes roamed her face. She felt her own lids grow heavy as she basked in his hot gaze and breathed in his seductive cologne .... Their lips hovered close enough to touch. His were parted, as if in invitation. She closed the tiny gap and gave him a light, innocent kiss. It didn't remain that way.

* * *

Jake's head was swimming, his body on fire. Hell, if this continued, he was going to bend Chiara over this couch, and he didn't think she'd stop him. What if someone came in? If he paused to lock the door, she might come to her senses. He palmed one of her breasts—God, they were beautiful, so full and lush. His cock leapt like a battering ram desperate to escape the fortress of his slacks.

The image was so ridiculous, the situation so impossible, that he snapped out of his lustful trance and pulled away abruptly. "I'm sorry," he said, hoping she would understand how crazy this was. "I don't know what got into me."

Rory, damn him, was laughing. Could a voice inside your head laugh? At least he didn't verbalize his amusement, or incredulity, or whatever the laughter meant.

Chiara recoiled, mortified, exactly what Jake had feared.

He brushed a chestnut curl away from her sweet face, now deathly pale. "Don't," he whispered. "I don't know what this is ...." He stopped himself. "That's a lie. I *do* know what this is. The question is, is it worth it? To you, I mean. Your marriage ...."

She didn't finish the sentence he'd so helpfully started for her. Her lips were compressed, like a thwarted child's. She drew herself up to her full height—in heels, only a few inches shorter than he—adjusted her bodice and said, "You're right, of course. Let's join the others."

"Chiara …."

"Mixed signals, buddy," Rory said. "You sound as if you're about to burst into song. 'Chiara! I just kissed a girl named Chiara ….'" *Jesus*, could things get any weirder? His subconscious was mocking him with Broadway showtunes.

Chiara raised an open palm. For a hot minute, he thought she might slap him, but then she laid that palm on his chest, where it burned like a branding iron. "Please. As you say, this is not the time or place."

"We've stayed away too long," he said, his voice low and breathless. "I don't want—"

She broke in, "We'll say we stopped to talk to May Allen, Susan, and Lorenzo in the kitchen."

That plan was quickly scuttled. The nanny, her sister, and Lorenzo were not eating at the kitchen counter like they usually did. The fox-faced intern had been joined by a young woman, blandly pretty the way all extremely young people could be, short, with a spray of freckles across her nose, her dark-brown hair pulled into a tight ponytail. The two shot them oddly furtive looks, as though privy to their secret and unsure where their loyalties lay.

"Hello, Steve, Angie," Chiara said with a shy smile. "May I ask where the others are eating dinner? Lorenzo and the others, I mean."

"On the terrace with everyone else," Steve said, gesturing in that direction.

When they were out of earshot of the interns—the catering staff, or whatever they were—Jake whispered, "Let me do the talking. We'll have to brazen this one out."

The party guests were all smiling in that stilted way you did when you were unsure how to react. Hell if he was going to confirm their suspicions. "I heard Chiara telling Lorenzo a story and couldn't drag myself away. Ali, it's based on your sketchbook. I think you'd be pleased! We got to talking and lost track of time."

"Cool," Teresa said, seizing on the excuse. "I wish I could do that. Ali's been bugging me to try my hand at making a story out of her sketches. So much for my Creative Writing degree."

Jake hoped they hadn't speculated aloud about Chiara and him in earshot of Lorenzo. The kid was crazy smart. He might get the full import even if they spoke in adult code.

"They are such clever sketches," Teresa babbled on. "But Mrs. Bigfoot in an apron? A bear dressed in motorcycle leathers? A cute banana slug? The mind boggles."

"That's Beverly Bigfoot," Lorenzo piped up, as if she were a personal friend. "She has blue-blue eyes and silky black hair all over her body." The prospect of an adulterous rendezvous in their circle forgotten, they all gazed at Lorenzo as if he were the Oracle of Delphi. "Her home is called Moss Manor. It's a huuuuge stump. Way huger than this house. She can talk to anyone. It doesn't sound like talking. It's tele—tele-*fonic*." He screwed up his face in concentration. "Uh, *pathic*. Tele*pathic*. They can talk in their heads. But," he was quick to add, "only if they want to. She can't hear them if they think something private."

Eyes bulged and lips twitched as Lorenzo's audience struggled to contain their amusement.

Jake couldn't suppress a wide grin. "What's for dinner?"

CHAPTER 7

Maddie was lounging in an Adirondack chair on the small strip of sandy beach facing Lake Quinault, flipping through a recent *People* magazine. With no cellphone reception, David was checking in with Joe and Ali via the lobby's payphone. The slim stack of mystery novels provided by Teresa was in their suite, and Maddie was too comfortable to fetch one. Besides, others were circling her chair like starlings looking for a vacant nest. There *were* empty chairs on the vast grounds, some near the white gazebo at the base of the hill, but Maddie preferred this one. She could better appreciate the waves lapping against the shore and enjoy an unobstructed view of the wide expanse of lake and the spectacular foothills and forests on the other side.

The pithy articles and plentiful photos in *People* suited Maddie's languor. She couldn't lie naked next to David without getting turned on. Whenever one of them stirred or inadvertently touched the other, they would roll into another round of lovemaking. She could use a night of uninterrupted sleep. So far she had no complaints.

The architectural style of Lake Quinault Lodge was "rustic colonial revival"—two stories topped with an attic under the steep slope of roof. The main floor was the cavernous though still cozy lobby, furnished with overstuffed leather chairs, couches, and game tables that encouraged lingering. The exterior was covered in cedar shingles, and Maddie assumed the walls and flooring were also cedar. A majestic brick fireplace bisected the room, and mounted above it, the obligatory stag head with its impressive rack. Arranged to maximize the view of Lake Quinault, two sides of the three-sectioned building angled downward to frame the hill and preside over a sloping yard the size of a playing field.

David and Maddie occupied the Beverly Suite, which took up the entire top floor of the Boathouse. They didn't require this much space—the two bedrooms or the kitchen—but the setup beat the hell out of their modest cabins at Sol Duc and Lake Crescent. White walls, brown and off-white patterned carpeting, not without charm. Humble as most of David's family might find it, it was the height of luxury for Maddie.

She flipped another page and froze. *Shit.* The pilot hadn't even aired, and here was Kilo in all his beautiful boy-idol glory. She and Kilo had carried on like bonobos during the run of *A Midsummer Night's Dream* (Kilo was Oberon, she was Puck) after she'd concluded David wasn't available. Her agent had come to a performance, and soon after, Hollywood snatched up Kilo and spirited him away. Maddie, happy to have found a graceful exit from that fling, found her way back to David. With a checkered sexual past of his own, David didn't blame her for the Kilo episode.

Of all the men Maddie had "dated," Kilo was the most likely to muck up her future. The guy was a troublemaker. Just by bumping into Teresa, he'd almost managed to sabotage her marriage to Liam—Teresa and he had eloped straight out of high school. Her family had "rescued" her and had the marriage annulled. Now Kilo was "dating" his co-star in the reboot of the '60s TV series *Hawaiian Eye*. Selena was thirty-five with a well-established career; Kilo was twenty-eight. Clearly, they were posing for the photographer. The pose was too perfect, the two of them gallivanting blithely on a beach, he in colorful swim trunks and she with a billowy, transparent caftan over her teeny bikini. A guy like Kilo would welcome a paparazzi invasion at this early point in his fledgling career as a small-screen heartthrob. The caption read, "Selena Lebhart enjoys the beach with main squeeze Kilo Mahelona, her co-star in the much-anticipated reboot of *Hawaiian Eye*." *Hmm,* "main squeeze." Fast work on his part. Made it sound so friendly, when Kilo had to be using Selena to advance his career. Was Maddie jealous? No. Kilo was a graduate from the school of hard knocks, and somewhere along the line he'd sold his soul.

"Huh." David's deep bass-baritone voice startled her. He scowled down at the photo. "True love, do you think?"

They both laughed uncomfortably. "A love match, certainly. Poor Selena."

"Oh, I imagine she'll have a good time while it lasts," David said.

Maddie didn't respond. If her experience was any indication, Selena would have the ride of her life. But nothing compared to what Maddie had with David. Sexual prowess couldn't beat a genuine love connection. And David was no slouch in bed.

She closed the magazine. "Someone left this in the lobby. I was just passing the time. How did he get into *People* so quickly, anyway?" She wished she didn't sound so grumpy.

"He's the ultimate player." David stooped beside her and smoothed her hair as if she were a nervous cat waiting for the vet.

Pointing to a newly vacated empty chair, she switched to the Southern accent she'd used in *A Midsummer Night's Dream* and said, "Set a spell."

He moved the chair closer, settled into it, and let loose a long breath. "Ahhh …. This has got to be the most relaxing spot on the Peninsula."

"As relaxing as Joe and Ali's place?"

"The company, food, and drink are excellent there," he admitted.

" 'Meanwhile, back at the ranch …. Did you talk to Joe or Ali?"

"Joe."

His consternation gave her pause. Not good news, then.

David gazed out at the lake. Maddie had never known a creature as magnificent as her husband. With his thick auburn hair, craggy features, and trace of red beard, he was a lion personified.

Finally he said, "Joe sounded husky."

"Oh." They had dreaded the return of Joe's vocal issues, hoping against hope they were gone for good. One of David's reasons for not pursuing her had been his uncanny ability to heal, a far more problematic gift than one might imagine. As a doctor, he could heal in ways people outside the medical profession might consider miraculous, but occasionally his healings had no medical explanation. He claimed they were not always effective and had insidious unintended consequences. Not to mention that the fallout bit him in the ass. A headache so blinding, he wondered if it might one day prove fatal. He rarely made a rational decision to employ his "gift." He'd healed Maddie twice—mending injuries that were relatively minor but could have derailed her career. She hadn't known about the headaches, hadn't caught on to what he'd done until the second time. His immediate family was in on his secret. There was no hiding it after he'd healed Joe's vocal cords so he could tour again. That didn't mean he could prevent the hoarseness from returning. You couldn't "cure" an Achilles' heel, he'd explained. Then there had been Liam and Ali's mother, now homeless and an inveterate drug addict. David had cured her liver damage, and she'd repaid him by vanishing, along with the thousand dollars Liam had deposited for her.

"Are you going to help Joe again?"

David raked a hand through his hair. "I can try."

"How's Lorenzo?" Maddie asked to distract him.

"Doing well. Chiara's wonderful with him, apparently."

Hmm, not the distraction Maddie had hoped for. If Lorenzo were emotionally attached to Sylvia's sister, wouldn't it be cruel to take him away from her? *Moving right along* …. "Anything new with Jake?"

Finally, a genuine smile. "Get this … Jake is writing thrillers."

"Thrillers, plural? Books? Any published?"

"One. Another's coming out this fall. He writes under a pen name, Dirk Fartherly."

Maddie was impressed. "No kidding? They're casting the movie version of *Kapow*. There was buzz in *People* about that." She raised the magazine above her head and gave it a shake. "Everyone wants to play Damon Morehouse. Except George Reed Masters, their first choice. Actually, the article didn't mention that. That's industry gossip, via Jeremy. They're considering Charlize Theron for Lorelei."

"George Reed Masters … isn't that—"

"The lead in *Insanity*," she confirmed.

"Your movie," he said glumly.

"Yes. Though calling it 'my movie' is a stretch. Blink and you might miss me."

David nodded. She knew what he was thinking. Her ten minutes in the opening was heavy exposure for her. As in, an A-list movie. As in, her near-naked body blown up to Brobdingnagian proportions. Her breasts on full display.

No safe topic this afternoon.

"It's a beautiful day," he said in a determinedly upbeat voice, "and only three in the afternoon. Shall we do the Rain Forest Nature Trail? It's a loop just across from the lodge and only about five miles. Not much elevation gain. We can work up an appetite for dinner." He pulled her to her feet.

She smiled uncertainly, noting her exhausted body's resistance to the effort of standing, let alone hiking. *You'll get a second wind*, she told herself as she gazed longingly at the empty chair.

"Oh, and Teresa's pregnant."

Maddie stared at him, startled into a silence filled by lapping water. Finally, she said, "You saved that tidbit for last?"

He laughed. "It's good news, right? Liam's over the moon."

Maddie thought about Teresa and her obsession with her weight. She already fretted over the few extra pounds she'd gained since marrying Liam.

"I hope she doesn't have twins," Maddie said as they made their way back to the suite to put on their hiking boots. David didn't ask her to explain. He was aware of his sister's insecurities.

* * *

Teresa loved the feel of Liam's soft skin, his hard body curled around her, his hands wandering, only lingering when she squirmed against him. Then she'd spoiled everything by bolting for the bathroom. Liam soaked a washcloth in hot water and bathed her forehead, murmuring endearments and smoothing back her hair while she finished retching. He'd been a perfect angel lately.

"Happy birthday!" Jake said, looking up from his newspaper as she wandered into the kitchen. "Coffee?"

"No thanks." Coffee did *not* sound good. Peppermint tea. Or ginger. She reached for a thick slice of bread from a loaf Liam had baked yesterday, forcing herself to nibble rather than just cram it into her mouth. She could devour the entire loaf. Plain bread, no butter or jam, was the only food that settled her stomach. Reluctantly, she limited herself to one slice. Ali had brought over her pregnancy wardrobe. Her sister-in-law was three inches taller, and everything was too long and shapeless. Teresa didn't own anything loose fitting. *Time for spandex*, she thought with a sigh.

"Are you okay?" Jake said. "Twenty-eight isn't exactly old age."

"I know," Teresa said, unconvinced. "It's the morning sickness." Jake nodded sympathetically. She wished she could get more excited about the pregnancy, but all she could focus on now were the long months ahead, where she would morph into a bloated, funhouse-mirror version of herself. So far she was hardly showing. The one change was that her breasts were fuller and too tender. She vowed to travel to Seattle ASAP in search of maternity clothing she could stand to see herself in.

"Where's Liam?" Jake asked.

"In the shower."

Her brother's hero worship of her husband made her smile. She looked over his shoulder and saw that he was scouring the real estate section. "I thought I'd look at some houses today," he explained.

Teresa perked up. She *loved* looking at houses. "I know a good realtor. I'll call her."

Liam strode in, clad in his work clothes and bursting with vitality. "Sick of us already, are you?" He poured himself coffee and sat down next to Jake.

"It's June fifteenth," Jake said. "You know what they say about guests and fish. I've been here over two weeks, which makes me one stinky fish. I've already decided Port Townsend is a great place to write. Mom can't breathe down my neck, for one." He gave Teresa the hairy eyeball, alerting her to the fact that she was literally breathing down his neck. She backed away.

"Is Carrie even talking to you?" Liam asked.

"We're talking. I have you all to thank for breaking down her resistance. She's gotten the message that we're not her pawns anymore."

Liam raised his eyebrows. "From your lips to God's ears. Can I tag along? On the house hunt, I mean. I'll even dress for the occasion."

Two hours later, they were riding in Jake's silver BMW, Liam in the passenger seat, Teresa in the back, following the agent to the next house. No luck so far. Jake had been ridiculously vague with the agent, only specifying that the place be near town, with updated plumbing and electricity. Price was no object. So, naturally, the agent was showing them the most expensive properties. After an hour, she finally got that "near town" meant "in town." He wasn't interested in the Victorians. Before long, they'd exhausted the available inventory. The agent pulled over at Liam's house, and they all emerged onto the sidewalk.

"I'm afraid that's it," said Martha, a confident forty-something woman in a stylish red pantsuit. "Frankly, I doubt if what you're looking for exists. Not in town, anyway. Closer to Fort Warden, perhaps."

"Is there anything for rent?" Jake asked.

Through gritted teeth, she muttered, "Nothing you'd be interested in."

"Try me."

"All right. Do you see that violet blue, Italianate-style Victorian at the end of the block, the one with the pedimented windows and fussy corbels?" She pointed. "That's the Milford House. Formerly a B and B. The original renters had to break their lease due to a family emergency. It just became available, so long as you commit through Labor Day."

Jake squinted as if trying to make the picture come into focus. "It's quite … blue," he said finally. "Liam, I think it matches your eyes." He fluttered his lashes at his brother-in-law.

"Hah, hah. The retirement villa of the Blue Man Group," Liam suggested.

"Or Violet Beauregard," said Teresa.

"The inventors of Blue Curaçao," Liam countered.

Jake laughed. "You'd think Violet would avoid blue at all costs. And those Blue Men must be sick to death of that makeup. As for the house, it is a bit … extreme."

Liam broke into full-throated laughter. "You think *this* is extreme? You haven't been paying attention. Though I am, on principle, against using a trim color to paint an entire house. At least the trim is white."

Jake cocked his head this way and that. "Nothing else, huh?"

"Not at this time of year," Martha replied crisply.

Jake waved his hand in a devil-may-care fashion. "Let's do it."

Martha's smooth brow furrowed. "Don't you want to see the layout?"

"I'll make it work." He got back in his BMW to follow the agent to her office.

Teresa and Liam remained frozen in place, gaping.

"Weird," Liam said.

Teresa was positively bug-eyed. "No kidding. He didn't even check out the main parlor."

Liam grinned. "How much you wanna bet the house is featured in his next book."

"Could be. The old Jake wouldn't be caught dead in a froufrou house like that. He was the most image-conscious person you could ever meet. Was there a head injury he didn't tell us about, do you think?"

Liam unlocked the door of his house and waited for Teresa to enter first. "Could be. I'd believe almost anything at this point."

CHAPTER 8

———◆———

IIT WAS THE EVENING OF Teresa's birthday. When Jake arrived at the compound along with Teresa and Liam, he had no idea what to expect. He knew his mother was still grumpy about his decision to leave BPO. He and Teresa had always been the "good" children. It wasn't as if he could un-resign. Even so, his mother had tried reasoning with him, then berating him, then laying on the guilt. Lately she'd cut off direct communication, sending him messages through Teresa. Sooner or later she'd accept that it was a fait accompli and move on. Unless he was going to avoid her all evening, he had no choice but to pretend that had already happened. There she was, directly in his path. Her blonde chignon and sleek, chic presence reminded him of what Teresa used to look like before she joined the Cult of the Ryan Twins. He pondered what would happen if his mother ever let her hair down. *Ridiculous*, he thought.

"She might surprise you one day," Rory said, making Jake flinch.

He planted a kiss on her cheek. "How was the car trip?" She and Rostand sometimes traveled to Port Townsend by charter plane. But you still had to begin at SeaTac Airport and fly into the William R. Fairchild Airport in Port Angeles, so it didn't save you that much time. Plus, it was hard to beat the Lincoln Town Car for comfort.

"Pleasant enough." She looked him over with ill-disguised distaste. "I can't get used to you in *casual* clothing." "Casual" translated to "shabby" or "inappropriate." Jake supposed she'd never seen him in jeans. At least his outfit wasn't inspired by grunge or hip hop. She couldn't possibly object to a cashmere sweater over a button-down shirt. His custom-made patina leather shoes were above reproach.

Her mother's manservant was wearing a suit, though with no tie. *He* looked like the executive. "Hello, Rostand. How the heck are you?"

They chatted amiably, mostly about baseball. A big Mariners fan, Rostand was looking forward to the team's move to Safeco Field. To his surprise, his mother too had become an avid baseball fan. To ruffle their feathers a bit, Jake argued that it was a shame to abandon the King Dome after the city had spent so much fixing it. As a CEO, he'd needed to keep up with sports, despite having little genuine interest. He was still in the habit of reading the sports section, in that discussing sports was far safer than politics. You really didn't want to bring up the Clinton impeachment with his mother, scandalized by the very idea of the president having oral sex. Of *anyone* having oral sex. His generation just rolled their eyes.

Jake was saved from further baseball talk by David, just back from his honeymoon. His brother and he would catch up later.

His escape route led him to Becca and Jean-Louis. "Hello, you two! You've had quite a month."

"*Allo, mon chum,*" Jean-Louis said, kissing him on both cheeks. "I thought you would have gone back to North Bend by now."

Rebecca mimed wiping her brow with the back of her hand. "Phew! Let's not do that again. Open another restaurant, I mean. Three is more than enough."

"*Sa coche,*" agreed Jean-Louis. "I should never have let Joe and Liam convince me that the Peninsula was in dire need of a Fête Sauvage."

"Aren't you booked way ahead? And you have loads of help, thanks to the FOSSP crew."

"*Là, là,* that is true, but it is too much."

"There's nothing quite like your place in North Bend," Jake said. "The building is like something Tolkien might have dreamed up."

"Yes, it was the ideal choice," Jean-Louis said. "A former Masonic lodge. I always enjoyed our lunchtime chats. But you are only renting here, yes? How long do you plan to stay?"

"Through Labor Day, at least. That's what I agreed to. I always thought your North Bend Fête Sauvage looked like it was preparing to scuttle away on its wooden stilts like a Millipede." Privately, he pictured Liberace as the ideal customer when he went there. If Liberace had been a hunter. Reams of gilded antlers and fairy lights. Jean-Louis didn't hunt. He was proud of the fact that the animals on his menus had had a fighting chance in life.

"*C'est beau.* I'm glad you're giving Port Townsend a shot, as they say. I believe you belong here."

"Nice threads," Jake said, by way of diversion. The chef was wearing a peacock-blue silk shirt and white linen pants. When it came to his masculinity, he had to be the most confident man Jake had ever met.

"And you," Jean-Louis said. "It is not a sin to be a man who cares for fashion."

One of the FOSSP helpers arrived to whisper something in his ear, and Jean-Louis took off for the kitchen. Seeing Ali, Becca ran over to hug her best friend.

Still no Chiara. Had she returned to Portland? She was constantly on Jake's mind. That one kiss had fanned the sparks he'd felt at their first meeting, and he'd be damned if he was going to bank that fire. He had been charmed by her rapport with Lorenzo and her imaginative take on Ali's drawings. She was fully bilingual—probably knew French too—a social worker, a sophisticated, gorgeous woman who cared about others. What more could a guy ask for? Shame on Arnold for not appreciating her. According to Rory, it was a bad marriage. How bad?

Ali distracted him from his dark thoughts by giving him a peck on the cheek. For a moment he was too stunned by the kiss to speak. She was accompanied by her father Duncan and his fiancée, Laurie—Maddie's mom. "We're heading over to the safari tent," she told him. "The crew is setting up a buffet and a dance floor." One of the interns from their earlier visit—the fox-faced one, Steve was his name—was circulating with an open bottle. Jake grabbed two glasses from the makeshift bar for himself and Liam. As Ali filled Teresa's glass with Pellegrino, he noted his sister's glum expression. *Poor Teresa. No champagne for the birthday girl.*

Amid the hubbub, he managed to slip into the kitchen but drew the line at venturing downstairs to the rec room. Chiara was bound to surface at some point. Unless the crowd was too overwhelming for her. She could be holed up in her cabin.

In the safari tent, Jake found his handsome giant of a brother David standing alone in a cinematic pose—legs spread and hands on hips, gazing out to sea. Maybe he was indulging in an Allan Quatermain adventure fantasy. The H. Merle Haggard novels seemed awfully dated now, but they'd brightened many a dark moment when Jake and David were children. Both had resigned themselves to living in the shadows of their brothers. Edward, the eldest, had a lock on the conspicuous good looks and charm, and Joe, the jaw-dropping talent, teen-idol appeal, and unwavering self-confidence. David was the brilliant geek, the youngest in his class and winner of every science award. Jake was the short guy who won track tournaments and had stories published in magazines, but when it came to the girls, always lost out to Joe.

Recently Jake had tried to re-read H. Merle Haggard's *King Solomon's Mines*. Not good. Rafael Sabatini's stuff had aged better. Wasn't that what thrillers were—adventure novels for grownups? The safari tent had clearly been erected as an incentive for David to buy the Sea Captain's House so Ali and Joe could move into Paul Bunyan's log mansion.

"Hey, Jake," David said, "here to check out the spread?"

Jake hadn't even noticed. He saw raw salmon—seasoned for the grill— fresh crab, shrimp skewered with other vegetables and various exotic-looking side dishes. All under glass and on ice. "Uh, yeah," he said. "No meat?"

"There's a pig roasting on the spit. You don't smell it?"

Jake sniffed the air and felt a hunger pang. Jake couldn't go the whole hog—so to speak—for Jean-Louis's wild game concept. The chef had explained why his cuts of meat never tasted gamy. Something about soaking everything in milk or adulterating it with pig products. If the milk and pork were from domesticated cows and pigs, could the dish still be called wild?

David tapped him on the shoulder. "Jake, have you lost your sense of smell?"

Jesus. He'd been woolgathering again. "No, of course I smell it. Wild boar, no doubt."

"Hey," Rory said in his head, "don't dis Jean-Louis in this crowd."

Jake shook him off but took heed. The others wouldn't understand that Jean-Louis was used to his teasing. "I'm sure it will be delicious." He regarded his imposing brother, five inches taller than his own six feet and blessed with the bulging muscles of their father's people, along with the shock of auburn hair. "How was the honeymoon?"

From David's smug smile, at least one aspect of it had been a success. "Fantastic. How long has it been since I stayed in those old lodges? There have been updates, though the food still leaves something to be desired. It's the ultimate relaxing vacation for a guy used to ramshackle huts and tents in Africa and a girl who's lived under the same roof for too long with a motormouth mother. You can't beat the rain forest for beauty."

"Unless you like heat," Jake said. "Some might prefer the Bahamas."

David laughed. "Next time. I'd love to take Maddie to Europe. She wanted to return here. Says there are few places more beautiful in the summer."

"She might be right," Jake said. "What happens when Maddie gets a role she can't refuse? How do you fit in?"

David scowled. "I'll get back to you on that," he said in a clipped, conversation-ending voice.

Leaving the tent to the catering crew, they ambled up the hill. "What's this I hear about you renting a B and B? You gonna run a rival boarding house?" David indicated the grounds with a broad sweep of his impressive arm.

Jake chuckled. "I have no plans to rent out my guestrooms. Unlike Joe and company, I'm not a people person."

David pointed at the target. "What's that?"

"For knife throwing."

David cocked an eyebrow his way.

"It's for Joe and me," Jake explained. "Liam's teaching us. The man has major survival skills. I want my guy Damon to know what he's doing."

David gave him a brotherly shove that almost knocked him over. "You sly old fox. Writing book candy when you were raised to hold up the family fort. You gonna let Big Paul's go to the dogs?"

Rory weighed in with a "Ruff!"

Jake knew how David felt about the family business—that Jake shouldn't be chained to it simply because he was the only sibling who'd offered up his wrists to be manacled. Until Rory's death, the golden handcuffs had chafed hardly at all.

"I have two successors," Jake insisted, "and they're both whiz kids. BPO will thrive."

"So, your B and B ..." David prompted.

"It was the only decent place available to rent in town. Besides, I'm intrigued by the prospect of knocking around that elegant relic by myself. Maybe I'll encounter some interesting ghosts."

"Hah!" from Rory.

David gave Jake a sidelong glance. "Did you know that Arthur Conan Doyle believed in fairies?"

Jake did recall hearing that somewhere. "Don't worry. I don't believe in fairies. *Although*, if Tinker Bell were dying, I'd definitely shout whatever was necessary to save her life."

Not even a crack of a smile from David. "Saving Tink involved clapping, I believe."

"I've seen the play," Jake said. "Do they even air that Mary Martin musical version on TV anymore? I assume Lorenzo has watched the Disney movie. In the original play or one of the spinoff books, doesn't Tink die anyway? Peter mentions it when he visits Wendy a year later."

This time David's scowl was meant to be comic. "Don't you dare tell Lorenzo."

"Ah," Jake nodded sagely, "we're sticking with Disney versions."

"Give the kid a break. He's just shy of four. Reality will rear its ugly head soon enough. Besides, those Disney versions aren't so tame. They routinely kill off the parents." Just when Jake thought David might raise the taboo subject of their dead father, his brother walked up to the knife target and examined it more closely. "That B and B has got to be crammed with needlepoint cushions and teddy bears. You hate gewgaws."

"Well, yeah," Jake said with a shrug, "but there's a storage area in the basement. I've only had one quick walk-through. Stashing away all that stuff will pass the time when I'm wrestling with writer's block."

"You get much of that?"

"Nah. I just write whatever absurd thing comes into my head. If I'm running dry, I quit for the day and go for a jog. My brain keeps going, and the next time I sit down to write, the words flow again. So far I've had no complaints from my editor."

"Who owns the place?" David asked.

"Not sure, exactly. It wasn't viable as a bed and breakfast. The current owners aren't emotionally attached to the stuff. When I asked, the agent told me I should feel free to box it all up and store it in the basement. No mention of an inventory."

David's eyes sparkled with amusement. "That's because you appear to be so civilized. They can't see the wild man yearning to be free."

"Oh hah-hah," Jake scoffed. "They haven't even met me."

David raised his eyebrows. "They have no doubt heard *of* you."

"Only if the real estate agent told them about my secret identity."

Seeing as how they were the right distance from the target, Jake followed the impulse to reach into the sheath on his belt and cast a knife at the target. *Bullseye.*

David raised his hands, which shook comically, in mock surrender. "I see the wild man is finding his way to the surface."

This time Jake's laugh was genuine.

"Bravo Zulu!" Liam yelled from the terrace.

David wrinkled his nose and looked at Jake. "Huh?"

"It's a soldier thing," Jake explained with a straight face.

"You're here until—"

"Labor Day, at least," Jake replied. "But in the short term, next Friday. They've invited me to Los Angeles because Mr. Action Star—uh, George

Reed Masters—claims he wants to meet me for some unfathomable reason. He's still dead set against playing Damon, believes it's a big step down in his inexorable climb to stardom. I have no clout to sweeten the pot, nor do I have the persuasive powers to change his mind. A short trip, I imagine. I've never been to Hollywood. Might be a hoot."

David nodded in Maddie's direction. "Talk to my wife. According to her, all the star makers in Hollywood are in it to get laid."

Jake regarded Maddie. The simple column of a dress would be modest on anyone else, but only a burka might lessen the impact of that spectacular hourglass figure. "If you look like Maddie," Jake reasoned, "they probably line up to exploit you. Rich, educated white men get the red-carpet treatment wherever they go, sadly for everyone else."

"Amen," he heard Rory say. His friend had volunteered for several equal-rights organizations, and before he died, had been pushing to get Jake involved.

Jake laughed. "Starlets, pool parties, and hundred-year-old bottles, huh." He considered the prospect. He'd never been drawn to trophy blondes with atrophied brains, and he preferred fresh young libations, not whiskey that had been around longer than most living human beings. "I don't have to go to Hollywood for any of that. Well, pool parties. Who would want to hang out by a pool here? Brrr." He shuddered.

"You been seeing anyone?"

Had they been whispering about him and Chiara? He forced a smile. "No one important."

"I heard there's a woman in San Francisco."

"Yes," he said simply and grinned a little wider. It wasn't precisely a lie. There was "a woman in San Francisco," just not *his* woman. She'd emailed him last week, and he hadn't replied. Why bother? He'd broken it off months ago. Not forcefully enough. David didn't need to know that. His brother was strutting around like a giant rooster who'd landed the prize hen. Jake didn't want to admit how pathetic his own love life was, or that he'd fallen hard for the woman determined to keep his brother's son in Portland.

When they rejoined the others, he got stuck chatting with his mother again.

"Joe tells me you're renting a bed and breakfast," she said in that perpetually snippy way of hers. "I thought you couldn't abide Victorian architecture."

Jake pictured the ornate violet villa. It was kind of growing on him. "It's like a living presence …" he began but stopped himself. His mother was not on board with any of his current decisions, so why try to get her there? "It's what was available in town. I'm only committed through Labor Day."

"Then what?"

"Maybe I'll move to Los Angeles," he said, mostly to goad her. David, who'd been listening quietly, waggled his eyebrows. "Future's wide open," Jake added. He'd never seen his mother so visibly perturbed. "Mom, please don't worry about me. It's not like I've joined the foreign legion."

Rory's dry laughter reverberated in his brain.

Ten minutes later, they all stood on the hardwood floor of the safari tent nibbling on appetizers. Hungry for more details about the honeymoon, a small crowd had gathered around David.

Paul Bunyan is throwing a press conference, Jake thought from the perimeter. *He tops even Joe and Liam by three inches.*

"What?" Rory commented wryly. "You got height envy now? I was five seven. And I did jus' fine. You got no complaints. You're six feet tall and look like Roger Moore in *The Saint*."

"We climbed to Colonel Bob Peak in the Quinault Rain Forest," David was saying. "Fourteen miles, five thousand feet elevation gain. Maddie barely broke a sweat."

Joe whistled. They all turned to Maddie, who blurted out, "If you don't count nearly expiring from exhaustion." With a grimace, she went on, "I survived. Not easy on so little sleep." Then she blushed.

Ali clicked her tongue. "I can imagine. You mountain men don't give us mortal women a break. You know, David, there's an easier version of that trail, eight miles with a three-thousand-five-hundred-foot elevation gain. That's the one Joe and I hiked a month back."

Chastened, David took Maddie's hand in his big paw. "You could have said something."

She squeezed his hand. "By then it was too late. I had no choice but to keep going."

"Next time, David, tag along with Liam," Teresa said. "He needs a hiking partner who can keep up with him. Even before this"—she gestured at her nonexistent belly—"I was hopeless as a hiker."

Ali rubbed her back. "You got this, T-Girl. We'll gestate together."

They all stared at Ali, who sighed in defeat. "Yep, pregnant again."

Moving in behind her, Joe gave her a hug. "We didn't want to steal Teresa's birthday thunder, but now that the cat's out of the bag ...." He kissed Ali's neck.

"You guys must be due around the same time," Maddie said.

"I'm supposedly eight weeks along, and Teresa is nine. So yeah, it's close. They could conceivably be born the same day. Sometime in January." Ali looked at Teresa. "I just confirmed it—guess I've been in denial. I'll need to take back some of those maternity clothes."

Teresa gave her a warm hug. "I tell you what—we'll go to Seattle and buy a whole new maternity wardrobe. If I have to look like a Goodyear Blimp, at least I can do it in style."

Joe and Liam were doing an adequate job of keeping their delight under wraps, given that their wives appeared to be contemplating a prison term. Were both pregnancies accidents?

"You guessed it," Rory said. "Hey! Your sweetie pie is here."

Jake turned to see Chiara approaching the tent.

She was in no hurry to arrive, skirting the edges like the most bumbling spy, ever. He met her halfway and held out his hand. "My dancing partner."

She regarded his hand as if it had grown a sixth finger, so he withdrew it, fearing she had changed her mind about him. She was dressed in a pale-yellow dress with a pattern of red flowers and a low neckline that revealed enough creamy cleavage to set his heart racing. The flat-heeled sandals were red, to match the flowers. No glasses. How much did she need them? Perhaps that was the problem, that she couldn't confirm his identity until he stood right before her. Her soft chestnut hair fell in loose curls down her long, slender neck. He was entranced.

Most of the others were already on the dance floor as they joined them, casting speculative glances their way.

"No secrets here," Rory said.

Jake ignored him. But when the DJ played a slow dance, Jake, unsettled by Rory's presence, decided against jumping at this excuse to hold Chiara in his arms. "Let's get you some dinner," he told her and started toward the buffet. She followed. There had been no touching, and Jake wanted to keep it that way, at least in front of the others.

"You rented the house for her," Rory said.

Jake willed him to shut the hell up. Was it true? Had he rented the house so that he could be with Chiara?

Plates filled, they headed for the kitchen. "I hear you moved into your own place," Chiara said as they stood staring at the cluttered kitchen, their least scandalous option for grabbing a private moment. Had the interns gone to sneak a smoke? *Good, take your time.* Jake pulled two barstools up to the counter, which was stacked with dirty plates, and set them a comfortable distance apart. The dishwasher was already running, so he moved the dishes into the oversized double-bowl sink.

"I rented a Victorian near Liam and Teresa's house. It used to be a bed and breakfast, and it's still cluttered with figurines and decorative cushions—Victorian collectables. I'm going to box most of the gewgaws up and store them in the basement. The owners don't seem to care if I chuck the whole lot."

"There might be something valuable," she said.

Jake almost replied, "If there is, I'll know it." He could easily distinguish a treasure from a trinket. Instead he said, "Want to help? It might be fun. A treasure hunt." Several different emotions flitted across her face: joy, reluctance, acknowledgment of the risk. She'd never cheated on her husband, that was clear. Jake was ashamed of trying to tempt her into a possibly ruinous affair. Seeing Chiara push her half-empty plate aside, he added, "Sorry, probably a bad idea. I was being impulsive."

"Are you withdrawing the invitation?" Her mouth was set in a stubborn line.

He touched her arm, briefly. "Not on your life."

She stood and smoothed her dress. "Let's rejoin the others. Perhaps they haven't noticed our absence."

Unlikely, Jake thought. Not that fifteen minutes was long enough to get up to any mischief.

Ali entered the kitchen, her expression merely curious.

"Chiara missed dinner," Jake explained. He picked up her plate and added it to the stack in the sink. "By the way, congratulations!"

"Thanks," she said with warmth if not excitement. He'd heard stories about her first pregnancy, carrying twins. It had been brutal. At least Teresa and she would be bobbing about—equally queasy—in the same boat. That must be some comfort. Nice of everyone else to produce grandchildren for Carrie. That let him off the hook.

"Your children with Chiara would be damn cute," Rory said out of nowhere.

He shook him off. "Shall we dance some more?" he asked Chiara.

"I don't think so. It's been a long day."

"All right," he said gently. "I'll see you around, then." He kept his expression neutral. Would she show up tomorrow or not?

CHAPTER 9

———❖———

After Jake and Chiara parted ways—thank god he hadn't followed her to her cabin!—Ali retreated to the Log Palace. The spectacular "rustic" house she and Joe had dreamed up could easily accommodate a dozen children, though the prospect of even one more was hard to fathom, given the daunting energy of the twins.

In truth, Ali just wanted to catch her breath and have a good cry. Seeing Becca on the pathway, she waited for her to catch up. With Becca, her best friend since high school, she could drop the pretense.

They hugged. "I'm so sorry, sweetie."

Her friend's sympathy broke the dam. "No one else would understand," Ali sobbed. For a while they just stood there at the door until Ali sniffed back the last few tears. She drew in a ragged breath.

"Better?" Becca asked.

"Yeah." Ali hoped her smile appeared genuine rather than brave. What the hell did she have to be brave about? Just because the last pregnancy had been godawful, that didn't mean she was in for another eight months of misery. She was fairly sure she wasn't carrying twins. "Check on the girls with me? If we're super quiet, we won't wake them. It doesn't take much."

They found May Allen and Susan in the upstairs playroom, knitting next to the baby monitor. The nursery was on the other side of the wall. Becca tiptoed in as Ali held the door open. Caryn and Josie slept soundly, arms touching. Their sooty lashes and black curls stood out against the creaminess of their plump cheeks.

"They're gorgeous," Becca marveled once they were settled in the living room on the black leather couch that faced the river-rock fireplace. "They'd just started to stand the last time I was here. Are they walking yet?" She reached over to the coffee table and handed Ali the box of tissues.

"Oh, yeah"—Ali blew her nose—"*too* well. Their first birthday is in a few weeks. We can't leave them alone for a second. They're also talking a blue streak, most of it unintelligible. To us, anyway. We've been hiring extra help from among the FOSSP crew we've housed down the road." Over at the safari tent, visible through the picture window, the party guests were beginning to disperse. Ali nodded in that direction. "Do you think the compound has turned into an adult theme park?"

Becca chuckled, and in a moment they were both wiping away tears of laughter.

"Who cares?" Becca said, blotting her eyes with a tissue. She kicked off her dancing shoes and tucked her feet under her. Not many women could carry off that red-ruffled gypsy dress. It suited her olive skin, dramatic black curls, and sparkling brown eyes. "If you were hoping for a feature in *House Beautiful*, don't hold your breath, and you might get called out by some tabloid, but I doubt it. It's fun, and that's what counts." She slapped the arm of the couch to signal a change in topic. "So … Jake's renting a B and B? I haven't seen it yet, but Jean-Louis heard it's more up *his* alley. Almost as bright a blue as the silk shirt he's wearing tonight."

Ali pictured the elaborately detailed design. "Not at all. It's kind of cool. The color is … bright—sapphire blue—and it has a lot of fussy details. I've never seen Jake's North Bend place, but according to Teresa, it's the polar opposite. You know, clean lines, pristine, uncluttered. An architect's showplace. You'd think Jake would avoid Victorian style like the plague. He's making a lot of contrarian decisions these days, as if his goal is just to shock the hell out of us all. Particularly Carrie."

"Nah." Becca waved the theory away with a grand sweep of her long red nails. "After following the prescribed path for so long, he's randomly taking on new challenges, kind of like George Plimpton. But it *is* true that his mom is an A-number-one control freak."

Ali thought of Chiara and the way her eyes always seemed to follow Jake. "I wonder, is Chiara going to become a casualty of his experimentation?"

Becca shrugged. "She's an adult, right? None of our beeswax."

"She brings out my protective side," Ali admitted.

Becca broke into more peals of musical laughter. "Okay, 'Sister of Liam.' I don't think *you* appreciated your brother meddling in your love life.

You aren't anyone's keeper, not your house guest's or your brother-in-law's, AKA your ex-boyfriend. We're all consenting adults with the right to screw up our own lives."

Ali shifted uncomfortably. "Says the woman who once excoriated me for sleeping with Joe when he was in the throes of his second vocal crisis. Jean-Louis told *you* to lighten up—don't think I've forgotten. Besides, Jake hardly qualifies as an ex-boyfriend."

Becca wrinkled her nose. "I'm sorry I judged Joe so harshly. You have to admit, for a while there, it did look like he deserved my poor opinion. As for Jake, for a casual date, he spent some major moolah on you. And don't forget that he rescued you when you were attacked by that poor excuse for a human being. I know you deny having any chemistry with Jake, but if not for those few days in the cabin with Joe …. Well, I wonder, that's all."

Ali tried not to follow trails of logic that stemmed from "what ifs." What if Joe hadn't resurfaced when she and Jake were on their third date? What if Jake had pushed for sex? She thought about the sex act, how it seemed unimaginably awful when you first heard the schoolyard whispers as a kid. As she'd once told a friend, "If I'm ever willing to do *that*, I'll *have* to be in love." Growing up, Ali had no inkling of the danger a young girl/woman faced from unscrupulous men. Liam had. He had told Teresa about a few of his first "girlfriends"—all older women. Had he ever stopped to consider that those women were predators, too? Liam matured freakishly early—they had a name for it, "precocious puberty." He must have appeared ready for anything. Maybe that was true, maybe not.

"Where did you go just now?" Becca asked.

"Oh … just thinking that while I may not have appreciated Liam's overprotectiveness, it was justified, under the circumstances."

Of course, she thought, *you don't have to be a foster child to be exploited sexually*.

Becca must have been reading her mind. "Mr. Fortman," was all she needed to say to revive Ali's memories of that high school English teacher. He'd had the kind of harmless surfer-boy looks that appealed to young women and had seduced several girls in the class, including Becca. Becca had told no one but Ali, and not until months later. Another of his underage victims did come forward. So began his downfall. He'd never been prosecuted. In those days, they simply ran you out of town. Shortly before he disappeared, he'd cornered Ali after school. Liam had materialized out of the ether and punched him in the stomach, where the bruises wouldn't show.

Becca threaded her fingers through her unruly curls. "What a scumbag. I wonder where he is now."

"In prison, I hope. Or dead."

Becca spread her arms, closed her eyes, and took in a cleansing breath. "Talking about him just gives him power. Back to Chiara. Do you think she's too innocent to know what she's getting into? She's gotta be at least thirty."

Ali shrugged. "I'd bet good money she's never slept with anyone but her husband."

"So? You and I get what it means to be with someone who doesn't value you. Not every marriage is worth saving."

Her comment put Ali on high alert. "Are you and Jean-Louis okay?"

Becca snorted. "No worries there. You and Joe?"

Ali nodded. "He's thrilled about the baby. I hope he gets a boy this time."

Becca gave a dramatic sniff. "*He*? What about you?"

"I'd like a boy too." She smiled, acknowledging her friend's real concern. "You know, same old. On the days when Joe is noticeably hoarse, he hides in his studio. For a while now, we've been hiking once a week—just day hikes close by. Sometimes Liam comes along. Teresa is too busy with the interior design business, but then again, she never was much of a hiker. I told her she could keep using the gym here, but she's joined one on Lawrence Street. I don't know how much composing Joe's doing. He claims there's enough for a new album. Only, I don't think he's in any shape to tour. Vocally, I mean."

"I thought he didn't enjoy the last tour so much."

"That's what he says. I see something else. He's restless."

Becca touched her arm. "What about you? Don't you get a break from baby-making?" Her brow furrowed. "This is an 'oops' baby, isn't it?"

Ali made a vague gesture. "We wanted another child—Joe *really* did. And I'm sure I'll be happy about it … ultimately. I was using a cervical cap. I guess I didn't use enough spermicide. If it were up to Joe, the entire place would be overrun with children." Seeing Becca tense up, she added, "That's not gonna happen. If it's a boy, he might not press me for more."

That "if" hung in the air between them. Becca shifted gears. "How's your rock-star dad?"

It had only been a few years since Ali's birth-dad Duncan had come into her life. He did look a bit like a middle-aged Billy Idol with his rangy build, spiky gray hair, and single earring.

"We caught up some. Not like B.L., I mean 'Before Laurie.' They might move here when Laurie retires, so there's that. Real estate people never really retire, do they? I can't picture Laurie sitting on her hands." She paused and put on a broad smile. "How's the apartment above the restaurant?"

Becca made a face. "It's noisy as hell. Traffic, plates clattering, patrons and waitstaff yucking it up. Jean-Louis keeps the cooking smells bearable, but I'd prefer to live farther away so I can breathe in the ocean or the forest in the morning instead."

Ali wanted to shake her. "I wish you'd stay with us while you're here. Ever since we built the new cabins, several are always vacant, and I'd love to see you more often. Who's going to dress me when I bust out of my regular wardrobe again?"

Becca laughed. "Teresa, that's who. When I dress you, you look like you're costumed for Mardi Gras."

Not for the first time, Ali wondered if self-absorption had turned her into a bad friend. "Do you regret the Port Townsend location?" Without Ali and Joe's encouragement, Jean-Louis never would have opened the third restaurant.

Becca appeared distracted by the chipped polish on her fingernail. "Darn, when did that happen?" She looked up. "Three is too many. I wish we could get out of Bellevue—it's the least successful. We're stuck with Port Townsend for now. This town isn't my thing the way it is yours. I *do* like to hike, but there's little time for that. Everyone *here* is cool, but if you venture far beyond the town, the politics get scary. Jean-Louis is part-Indigenous and I'm Jewish."

Ali nodded. "Liam and I don't know our ethnicity, but we're clearly not lily-white. What you're describing is true of any place in the boonies. The Peninsula is better than most. People are kind to Joe and me wherever we go."

"Well, Joe …."

"You think they recognize him? Most people aren't good at hiding that. They get all excited. That's only happened once. The guy politely asked for an autograph and said he was a fan. That's all."

Throwing off that serious moment, Becca leaned forward confidentially. "So … Jake is writing thrillers?"

"Wild, right? Get this: his first novel has been optioned for the movies. I haven't read it, but Teresa tells me the hero is a dead ringer for Liam."

Becca frowned. "He can't be based on Liam, unless your stories about your missing brother fired up his imagination."

"No way," Ali was quick to say. "I didn't tell him much, and all Liam's superhero skills date from his mysterious stay in Israel. It's a weird coincidence, that's all."

Becca raised her eyebrows. "Liam may not have had superhero skills, but he has always been fearless. And big for his age. Stronger than the others. Did Jake see a photo of Liam at our place in North Bend?"

Ali shook her head. "He never got beyond the threshold. Besides, there are so few—school photos and some blurry Polaroids."

"What about your sketchbook? I seem to recall one of him on his Harley. Jake might have seen that."

"I never showed Jake my sketchbook."

Becca stood to stretch her legs and straighten the ruffles on her dress. "You guys never did much more than scratch the surface. On the basis of nothing, we just wrote him off." It smarted to hear Becca put Ali's own thoughts into words. "Sweetie," she went on, "I did too. We dismissed him as nothing but a slick businessman. Jean-Louis alone kept insisting he was a normal guy who couldn't compete with the memory of the legendary 'JJ.' Now it seems like he has all these facets no one guessed at. I think that's interesting."

Ali smiled. "It's a huge relief for Joe. The estrangement was never his idea." Her smile broadened. "Jake's about to make it up to us."

"Huh?"

"Now that the 'Maddie and David Show' appears to have reached a satisfactory conclusion, you're swamped with all the restaurants, and Teresa and I are transitioning into ungainly human incubators, maybe we can live vicariously through Jake and Chiara."

Becca grinned. "You said it, I didn't."

CHAPTER 10

———————

SHORTLY AFTER MIDNIGHT, JAKE WAS driving Liam and Teresa home in his BMW, his brother-in-law riding shotgun, his sister in the backseat. Another fabulous party with surprisingly congenial company, considering their initial reservations about him. He had to contain his joy at the prospect of seeing Chiara tomorrow. Because rejoicing would be premature. The logistics were complicated. Chiara wouldn't be able to sneak out of the compound for a few hours without having an accomplice. What had Liam called it? The Hotel California. You could check out but never leave. No wonder Liam bought the Victorian house in town without consulting Teresa. Joe and Ali's cozy retreat sucked you in, zapped your ambition, and robbed you of your free will. According to Liam, anyway.

Jake hoped his sister's marriage was on more solid ground. Their sex life was going strong—another reason for Jake to skedaddle. Morning, noon, and night. Middle of the night …. Didn't they realize you could hear a pin drop in their bedroom, much less creaking bedsprings? More and more, when he pictured Damon, he saw Liam. The guy could be a movie star, but his needs were simple. The space to brood, build, and fix things. And shtup Teresa.

"Can't blame him for that," Rory said, as if just now waking up.

She's my sister, Jake silently told Rory. *Give me a break.*

"She's hot," Rory said.

* * *

Holding Lorenzo's small hand, Chiara wandered into the kitchen as Maddie stood at the industrial-grade machine making lattes for herself and

David. Lorenzo could have stayed with Chiara in her cabin as he had initially, but when his father returned from his honeymoon, the child had been given a room at the Sea Captain's House. The dogs, self-appointed guardians, followed him everywhere and slept next to him at night. They all welcomed the greater peace of mind. The house stood uncomfortably close to the bluff and rocky cliffs below.

Chiara ignored Maddie and David's mostly idle chit-chat until the name "Jake" jangled her nerves like a poorly tuned violin in a string section. Lorenzo and the dogs had convened in the basement, and she'd filled a small plate with scrambled eggs and toast. Now she was making an espresso, and the machine was asking her to refill the water and beans—tasks made more complicated by eavesdropping.

"Did you have a good talk with Jake?" Maddie asked.

"Yeah. It's great to see him so relaxed. The old Jake was so image conscious and driven."

"What's he up to?"

"He's going to Los Angeles next week to check on the progress of the *Kapow* movie deal. Said his presence isn't really required, but he's interested in how Hollywood works. Might consider moving there. Then there are the starlets. A major draw, knowing Jake."

They both laughed. Chiara's espresso stood untouched as she stared into the cup.

"Is he seeing anyone?" Maddie asked.

"Jake's not interested in settling down. Remember, he was supposedly dating Ali but actually seeing someone else in the Oakland office. Implied that he still is. The guy's a player."

"So were you," Maddie said. "People change."

David answered too quickly. "Not men. Not often, anyway."

When Chiara picked up the cup, her hand shook, and the espresso spilled onto the saucer. As the newlyweds wandered onto the terrace, Chiara sat heavily, nearly falling off the stool. Why hadn't Jake told her about the trip to Los Angeles? Would he move there? Did he really have a girlfriend in Oakland? She'd flattered herself that she was special to him. But no, she was deceiving herself. Would any woman with an ounce of self-respect keep a rendezvous with such a man? She wanted him with all her heart. That was the problem. He wasn't interested in her heart.

* * *

The next morning, after a relaxed breakfast with Teresa and Liam, Jake packed up and "moved" the one block to his rental. Leaving his luggage in the foyer, he drove to the natural foods store and loaded up his cart. He looked forward to cooking in his own kitchen. The state-of-the-art refrigerator, with space sufficient to store food for a houseful of guests, was still mostly empty after he'd finished shelving his purchases. He should have inventoried the larder first. The former owners had left every spice imaginable, rice, canned goods, and several types of flour. Though for all Jake knew, those supplies were purchased along with the first edition of *Joy of Cooking*. If he couldn't find an expiration date, he tossed it.

He scouted out the fanciest bedroom, located on the second floor—there were three stories, plus a basement—and took a moment to sit on the loveseat overlooking the bay. Sun streamed through the window, which looked out on a colorful though straggly rose garden. The vast expanse of water and the few sailboats and fishing trawlers just setting out filled him with well-being. He loved to sail and considered purchasing a smallish yacht to keep at the marina. With his handkerchief, he dusted off the nightstand. A pottery vase, primitive enough to have been a child's art project, held one dried rose.

His thoughts drifted to his home in North Bend—a modern "green" building designed for Jake by a celebrated architect. The walk-in closets contained a small fortune in suits, dress shirts, and neckties. An Armani tux. Here even a sportscoat and slacks got the side-eye. Lately he'd favored shorts, golf shirts, and sandals, buying them off the rack without even checking the labels. He'd packed a few of his nattier outfits, which might come in handy if Teresa ever got her soiree idea off the ground. Once he'd dressed to impress and might want to do so again someday. But also, he liked nice things.

He imagined donating the suits to a charity for executives down on their luck. That made him smile. As if such charities existed. He pictured all the overpaid, smug board members and executives he knew. Their qualifications? Ivy League degrees, the proper pedigrees, slick exteriors, and the ability to butter up clients and investors. If they failed to yield results, they were released with golden parachutes. Rory had been a refreshing change from that world. But then, his dead friend hadn't been part of that world. Now he was otherworldly.

Cue sarcastic comment by Rory …. *Nope, nothing*. Did Jake really believe that a spectral presence resided in his head? At first he'd nearly driven himself around the bend worrying about his mental health. But Jake was a sensible guy, and it was ridiculous to be crazy with worry about going crazy. Sane or not, as long as Jake could function in the world without endangering himself or others, his mental health was nobody's business.

As with all the rooms in the B&B—other than the dust and vases of dead flowers—the master bedroom appeared immaculate and ready for guests. It reminded Jake of that merchant brigantine the *Mary Celeste*, where everyone disappeared mid-activity. What had prompted the latest renters to abandon ship? For all he knew, they'd left behind a half-eaten meal. The cleaners would have dispensed with that. He could ask the owners, but it was more fun to speculate. Maybe the explanation was as pedestrian as sudden poverty or an ailing loved one in another state. After he finished *Zwap*, the latest entry in the Damon Morehouse series, Jake might try a horror/suspense type thing set in this house. His agent would squawk, but he'd only signed a contract for three Damon Morehouse Thrillers. If they wanted too many more, he'd run out of titles. *Kapow*, *Thwack*, and *Zwap* were all onomatopoeic bat-fight words from the '60s *Batman* TV series starring Adam West. "Wham" was the name of George Michael's original pop duo. "Bang," "Bonk," and "Pow" didn't have the right ring to them. Besides, "Bonk" sounded sexual. He'd started writing thrillers on a lark then found himself caught in a trap of his own making.

Back in the kitchen, he made himself an espresso from a machine built to service a full contingent of guests. He vacuumed and dusted, wiping down the miscellaneous "collectables" he intended to pack up after Chiara and Teresa got a look. He sifted through candelabras, porcelain figurines, decorative boxes, needlepoint pillows, and porcelain dolls with creepy glass eyes. The statuettes of nymphs and deities in various stages of undress could stay.

Finally he cleaned and sanitized all the bathrooms. Borderline OCD. Still no snarky comments from Rory. *Weird*.

The grandfather clock chimed eleven. Jake wished he'd pinned Chiara down for a specific time. The idiom "pinned down" got him thinking about Victorians and their butterfly collections pinned to boards and framed. Had he rushed things with Chiara? His life was a mess. With Rory forever intruding on his thoughts—except for right now, oddly—should he really be plunging into a love affair? It was like one head of a two-headed man trying to exclude the other. Or a conjoined twin.

Jake hadn't been with a woman since soon after Rory's death. Initially, hoping to dull the pain, he'd had a few reckless flings. Then, one day, Rory appeared in a dream and was still there when Jake woke up. The dream had been simple. They sat next to a stream scattered with clumps of pink Monkeyflowers, staring at the glacier—Mystic Lake, the spot where Rory died.

"You can't keep this up," his friend said. "I won't let you."

"You and what ghost army?" Jake quipped.

Other than being semi-transparent, his friend appeared hale and hearty. "No army required," he replied. "Call me a one-ghost occupying force for change."

"What kind of change?"

"Hey, man, everything. Different work, different women. Throw off the chains. You're like Jacob Marley, only you don't know it."

"*You're* like Jacob Marley," Jake replied in the spirit of this surreal conversation. "That makes me Scrooge. And I think that's a little harsh, don't you?"

"I got no chains," Rory said with his gap-toothed grin. "Not alive, not dead. I 'forged' no chains in life. I was a free spirit, always. Now I'm freer. You, my friend, are trussed up tighter than King Kong after his capture." With that, Rory grew more transparent until only his grin remained. Knowing Jake's fondness for *Alice in Wonderland*, he was probably doing the Cheshire Cat thing to amuse him. Instead it creeped him out. "Not goin' anywhere," the grin said before disappearing.

Jake woke up next to a woman he'd picked up at the bar the night before, surprised to find her more attractive than he might have expected, given his killer hangover. How had they even gotten here? He looked around. Where was "here"? Not his own place. Her apartment? Had to be. Seriously cluttered, and not just with their clothing from the night before. His eyes fixed on a stuffed koala bear, then a pile of magazines with a *Playgirl* on the top. He couldn't recall a single detail of what went down after he sat at the bar. Very disturbing. Before Rory's death, he'd been a light drinker, had certainly never blacked out.

The woman looked like a platinum-blonde Betty Boop, with childishly plump cheeks and flawless skin. Lushly naked. He hoped she was legal. On the floor next to the bed were two used condoms. *Ugh.* How had he managed that, under the circumstances? At least he wouldn't be atoning for last night's activities with childcare payments or an STD. As long as she wasn't jailbait …. She snuggled against him and opened her big, round eyes. Yep, definitely Betty Boop.

She blinked sleepily. "Jake?"

She knew his first name. Hopefully not his last. Not knowing hers, he said, "Good morning. Sleep well?" He sounded like a hotel concierge.

"Oh, you bet," she said, reaching for his cock.

He gently pried her hand loose. "I could use some coffee," he said, scrupulously polite. "How about you?"

"At least part of you is already stimulated," she commented, reaching for his erection again.

"Uh, what time is it?" He spied a clock on the wall. Twenty after eight. What day was it? He groped the heap of clothing on the floor, hoping to find his cellphone. That's when he had heard it for the first time—Rory's voice, singing.

" 'Monday mornin', it was all I hoped it would be ....' "

The woman's baby-blue eyes grew even rounder. "Jake? Are you okay?"

Uh-oh. She looked as shocked as he felt. *Jesus. That voice ....*

"You're at Sally's place," an amused Rory informed him. "I'd say 'go for it,' but you already did that. It's time to vamoose and get a leg up on your new life. Sally's old enough," he added, "and she's been around. But be nice."

How far am I from work? Jake wondered.

"You're in downtown Bellevue," Rory said. "You'll be late, but not too late. Traffic ain't bad."

How would you know?

A chuckle. "I know *all*."

Jake kissed Sally to make her feel good about the night before and was tempted to stay and re-experience what he'd blanked out. "I have a nine o'clock meeting," he lied, "or I'd love to stick around."

"Another time then," she said. "This was good. We both miss Rory." She stood up, comfortable in her beautiful birthday suit. Writing her number on a slip of paper, she stuffed it in the pocket of his sportscoat. When he rose from the bed, she let loose a startlingly loud wolf whistle. "Hey, gorgeous!"

He couldn't get into his boxer briefs fast enough.

That was in December, six months ago. Rory had died in August. He suspected his dead buddy had engineered the whole one-night stand so *he* could be with Sally one last time. Rory hadn't denied it.

One chime from the grandfather clock brought him back to the present. Eleven thirty. Jake had been reliving that surreal morning for half an hour, and still no Chiara. The phone rang.

"Miss you already!" his sister said. "What are you up to?"

"I'm on a roll with the writing," Jake lied, knowing that otherwise Teresa was going to invite him on some errand, either buying furniture for a client or shopping for clothing. Normally he'd enjoy that. *Jesus.* He'd be stuck here all day like a lovesick teenager waiting for the phone to ring. It was then he knew for sure—no telling how—that Chiara was a no-show. He sighed.

"JB? You still there?"

"Uh, yeah. Can you come over tomorrow? I need someone with a good eye to help me catalogue and pack up all the stuff gathering dust in this place. We'll have a good laugh over the junk people collect."

"Ooh, I'd love to. What time?"

"I'm an early riser. Come when you feel like it. After breakfast, before breakfast, whenever."

"Feeling lonely?"

"A little," he admitted.

After he hung up, he listened to the silence, deafening in its profundity. "You picked a weird time to check out, buddy," he said aloud.

He brewed another espresso. Would extra caffeine cheer him up or bring on a panic attack? He'd been feeling fantastic this morning when he'd believed Chiara would fill the Rory-sized chasm in his life. "She's married," he said out loud, talking to himself in Rory's absence. "For a truly fresh start, you'll need to find an unattached woman."

"Screw that," he said in reply, proof positive that he'd become a two-headed monster. "I want Chiara, no matter how messy that gets."

"You can't have her." He was still talking to himself.

Sipping the espresso, he opened his laptop. The only way to stop this ridiculous internal debate was to escape into the world of Damon Morehouse, a guy's guy who wasted no time or energy on personal reflection or ethical dilemmas.

He'd just finished revising the last section when his cell rang. He was about to get excited until he recalled that Chiara didn't have his number. The Caller ID listed a 213-area code. L.A. calling.

"Hello?"

"Jake O'Connell?" the woman's voice said.

"Speaking."

"Please hold for Ralph Goldfarb."

A man's voice came on. "Ralph here. Hey, Jake, how ya doin'?" It was the producer who'd floated the idea of the Los Angeles trip. Not waiting for an answer, he said, "No need to fly south right now. George Reed Masters is on location in Vancouver B.C. for the next couple of weeks."

CHAPTER 11

———•———

Teresa arrived at Jake's place promptly at ten the next morning, knowing her brother was sure to be up and about by then. She was temporarily struck dumb by his casual getup: khaki shorts, a T-shirt covered by an open flannel shirt, Birkenstock sandals. It was as if he'd helped himself to Liam's closet, though two Jakes could fit into one of her husband's tees. His new man crush, Liam.

"You look comfortable," she said with a grin. *Don't tease him,* she told herself.

He surprised her by not rising to the bait. "When in Rome …. Espresso? Tea?"

"No thanks. I can't handle adult beverages right now. Maybe a glass of water?"

She followed him into the kitchen, admiring all the contemporary touches. "Someone cared enough to buy the very best," she commented.

"Yes indeed." He poured two glasses from the spigot on the refrigerator door. "I rented this place sight unseen, so it was a pleasant surprise."

Water in hand, Teresa exited the French doors in the parlor to find herself in the rose garden. Next to the fence was a target identical to the one Joe had built. "Practicing your knife-throwing, I see."

He came up beside her and gave her a little nudge. "What's with 'the cat who caught the canary' smile?" he said in all good humor. "Okay, so I'm in awe of Liam. You of all people should understand. He's right about knife-throwing. It's meditative. You should try it."

Now she laughed outright. "In my spare time, maybe. All right. Show me your stuff."

She suppressed a laugh at the sight of the sheath mounted on his belt. Ready for action, just like her husband. Hardly pausing to aim, he threw each knife in turn. Only the second one missed, and the others hit close to the bull's eye. He barely broke a sweat.

Teresa's anemic attempt at a whistle got the point across. "I'm impressed. Great view, by the way."

Back inside, they climbed the stairs to tour the bedrooms. "It's so neat and clean," she marveled, "and ready for guests."

"Weird, right? Not my doing, most of it. I cleaned some. Dusted, sanitized the bathrooms. I'd love to know what happened—why it closed. Martha said there were prior renters. If so, they were disciples of Mr. Clean. Or practiced criminals. Left no trace of DNA."

When they reached the third floor, Teresa flopped down on a bed, closed her eyes, and flailed about as if making a snow angel. "Ooh, nice mattress. Just firm enough. Do you suppose the B and B competition was just too fierce?"

Jake shrugged.

Teresa hopped to her feet, smoothed her sundress, and put the mussed bed back to rights. "Is it haunted?"

Jake weighed his words before answering. "I heard a few creaks, nothing that can't be explained by the house settling—as houses do."

Hmm. Was he editing himself? Teresa had never experienced supernatural phenomena firsthand, though she now believed such things existed. Liam's spotty telepathy and David's healings were all the evidence she needed. Jake had dropped his customary sardonic air—the snarky smile too—when she'd asked about ghosts. She wouldn't push him … this time. She didn't want to spoil their renewed rapport.

"Shall we?" he said, leading the way toward the staircase. "All the curios are on the main floor. Could be that we'll find some vintage Meissen figurines or that rare Hummel that sells for eight thousand dollars."

Teresa rubbed her hands together. "It's virgin territory? You haven't done a preliminary assessment?"

He raised his eyebrows. The crooked smile was back. "And deprive you of that pleasure? Perish the thought. I'm your favorite brother, and don't you forget it."

He was, hands down, her favorite brother, mostly because he'd read aloud to her regularly during her childhood. Ignoring her requests for fairytales, he'd stuck to books *he* enjoyed, such as *Treasure Island*, and later on, the John D. MacDonald Travis McGee mysteries that weren't geared toward women and certainly weren't "appropriate" for kids. Unlike her other brothers, Jake shared her taste for finer things. He was the only straight guy she'd ever met whose passion for window shopping equaled hers. His enthusiasm extended to evaluating antiques.

With no real job, their mother was a know-it-all when it came to heirlooms—furniture, art, jewelry … a common esoteric hobby among the idle rich. In June of 1982—Teresa turned eleven on the 15th of that month—Carrie treated her to a full six weeks of antiquing on the East Coast, renting a car and staying in quaint country inns. Da, still alive then, begged off, but Jake was eager to come along. He was fresh out of high school, with no summer job, and back in his parents' good graces for ostensibly giving up thriller writing for serious studies at Harvard. They paid close attention to Carrie's appraisals. Imaginations fired up, they pored over their mother's coffee-table books. Both had memories that glommed onto minutia. For the rest of the summer, Jake drove them to antique malls on the outskirts of Seattle, where they'd show off their "expertise" and mock items they deemed "inferior." *Jeez, we must have been obnoxious*, Teresa thought.

Jake had purchased a bundle of medium-sized boxes, three rolls of tape, and a raft of packing sheets at the local UPS Store. Now, with four of the boxes already assembled, he stood poised with a notepad and pen to do inventory. Surprisingly dust-free items were crowded together on every possible surface—the fireplace mantel, the side tables, the spaces between the bookends on the shelves—often atop lace runners. The walls were crowded with decorative plates.

"Why do people collect perfume bottles?" Teresa wondered aloud, holding a blue cut-glass bottle with a bejeweled stopper. It sat on one of the taller bookshelves, which also contained a complete set of Alexandre Dumas bound in blue cloth with the title and author's name in gilded letters. She put the bottle down and drew a volume off the shelf, finding Roman numerals indicating that it had been published in 1898. The pages had been hand cut with a letter opener. "Who would read the complete works of Alexandre Dumas?"

"*I* might," Jake said as he scanned a page of one of the books and flipped through the rest. "These illustrations are gorgeous, and the translation seems lively. I read *The Three Musketeers* aloud for you, remember? These are the sequels." He pointed to the two volumes of *Twenty Years After* and the six volumes of *The Vicomte de Bragelonne*. "There are only fifty volumes. I could get through most of the set by Labor Day."

They both laughed.

"You'll be too busy with writing your books and fending off women," she predicted.

Ignoring her comment, Jake addressed her earlier question. "Perfume bottles," he said, examining another bottle. He separated the much larger stopper from its base and held it out to Teresa—a tiny female dancer in a diaphanous gown. "I like this one. I've decided to keep all the naked and semi-naked figures on display as inspiration. The Czechs do make beautiful crystal. This one must be worth a pretty penny."

Teresa turned it over in her palm. "Aren't you afraid of scaring off your dates with the figurine equivalent of etchings?" In her best imitation of a lascivious male, she said, "Come up and see my perfume bottles?"

He blew out a derisive breath. "Do I really sound like Snidely Whiplash? Give me a break. I may not be Joe, but I do okay with women. However, I'm currently taking a break."

Teresa placed the perfume bottle back in its prominent position on the bookcase. "You do realize that we old married people depend on you singletons to provide us with vicarious thrills, right?"

"A singleton is an only child," Jake said. "There are five of us O'Connell siblings. And you haven't been married long enough to get bored. Obviously."

Oh no. She pictured Jake covering his ears with a pillow as Liam and she made love, and she felt a blush spread to the roots of her hair. "You obviously haven't read *Bridget Jones Diary*," she said, avoiding his eyes.

"Should I?"

"It might help you understand how women think." Right away she wanted to take it back. She didn't wish to imply that Jake didn't understand women. Besides, Bridget Jones wasn't his type. What was his type? Not Ali. Chiara, obviously. Was dating a married woman really on the table?

Jake pointed to a pink crystal bottle. "I can put her away, right? And this one ...." He indicated a porcelain shepherdess. "She's probably worth something, but she ... annoys me."

Teresa checked the stamp on its base. "It's Dresden, so yes, expensive. Still ... I agree with you. The proportions are off. Her head is too large for her body. I don't think she'll 'inspire' you." She wrapped it in paper and laid it in the box.

He shot her a reproving glance. "I'm not interested in *that* kind of 'inspiration.' "

She blinked, feigning confusion.

"The kind you get from dirty postcards," he clarified.

"You *did* say you're not interested in dating …."

He shook his head as he carefully packed away another shepherdess. "You're incorrigible."

She considered a statue of an amorous shepherd and his shepherdess, cradling it in her hands for different perspectives. *Hmm.* The girl was rearing back, her breasts nearly bare. The boy loomed. Was she willing or not? A suggestion of a smile. *Depends on the sex of the artist,* Teresa thought. She was definitely overthinking this.

"Keep? She's much prettier. Louis the Fifteenth porcelain, quite valuable."

He regarded it critically. "No, pack it away. They're a little too innocent."

"Ah." She reached for the stack of packing paper. "We're banning all innocents. *He's* not so innocent. I *could* argue she's about to be ruined. Does that mean the teddy bears are out?"

Jake zeroed in on a stuffed bear perched on the bottom shelf of a bookcase. He crouched down to pick it up, feeling its fur and registering the details. "The identifying button is missing, but the fur seems to be mohair. It has black shoe-button eyes and five claws. This could be an authentic Steiff, circa 1905. Built to last. The arms and legs are long, and they're attached with metal rods and joints." He handed it to Teresa. "I like him. I'll enjoy his company."

"He looks sad," Teresa said, "and his nose is threadbare from all the nuzzling. The child who loved it has got to be dead. This thing would depress the hell out of me."

Jake put it back on the shelf. "He's a kindred spirit."

"Are you sad?"

"Hardly." He didn't sound convincing. Teresa should know better than to try a "gotcha" with Jake.

"You know, you can talk to me, or David. Even Joe, though I realize it might be early days for that. David experienced some bad juju in Africa."

Ah, that got his attention. "Like what?"

"Not my place to say. Ask *him.*"

Jake laid a lesser teddy bear in the box. "Predictable," he said. "The disease, the poverty, the corrupt governments. What a nightmare. It's a wonder he lasted as long as he did."

"There's more to it than that." Teresa couldn't stop herself, though she was close to spilling the beans. "You can tell him stuff, too. Why you upended your entire life, for instance."

He gave her a long, unreadable look. Worried that he was questioning her own tenuous hold on happiness, she averted her eyes. "I hear you're headed to Los Angeles."

"Nope. Change of plans." He checked his watch. "Lunch?"

"Definitely! Liam's favorite haunt is Kelpies."

"Of course. Let's stop by your house. Maybe he'll join us."

She almost corrected him. *Liam's* house.

"Are we done here? It still looks like an estate sale. I see tasteless figurines, too many clocks, some truly unfortunate lamps, and many, *many* corny needlepoint cushions."

"To be continued after lunch. It's twelve fifteen. We might still nab a place on the balcony."

"So, Los Angeles ..." she said as he locked the main door. They both filled their lungs with briny air, making Teresa realize the house could use a good airing out.

Jake replied, "I might still go at some point. The main reason for the trip was to meet George Reed Masters and charm him into playing Damon. Turns out he's on location."

"Why should *you* be the one to charm him? You can't offer him more money." They crossed the street, arm in arm. "Shoo!" she said to a large buck posed in the yard next door. He didn't budge. "Isn't that *their* job?"

"Apparently he wants to meet *me*. 'What?!' you say. Who wants to meet the boring author?' "

"Lots of people would enjoy meeting you." Teresa gave his arm an affectionate squeeze. "I could round up half of Port Townsend for you—the female half, anyway. The ones who like men. Hmm, that might be a quarter of Port Townsend. Or, alternatively, you could go to yoga with me."

He laughed. "Liam told me about that yoga class. So, weird coincidence, huh? Kilo, the owner of a yoga studio? I gather he still had feelings for you."

She stared straight ahead. "*Feelings*. That's too nice a word for it. *Feelings* for me, *feelings* for Maddie. 'Feelings, nothing more than feelings ...' " she sang in her husky little voice. "For a while there, he was a nasty fly in the ointment here. He's in Hawaii now, filming a TV show. According to *People* magazine—Maddie saw a captioned photo in the latest issue—he's dating his co-star. For all I know, he sold the yoga studio. I can't see him teaching again. I do like the teachers who've replaced him. They're all women. Seriously, you should go with me."

"Yoga." He made a face. "I tried it a few times. Boring."

"Only at first. You get into a rhythm. I find it restful. Keeps you flexible."

"If you say so."

Liam was working on a side gate when they approached. "Kelpies?" he asked.

"So, what do you think, should I go to a yoga class with Teresa?" Jake asked as they walked down the Terrace Steps toward the downtown tourist area.

Liam laughed long and hard. "The teacher might object to the disruption. It *is* a great way to meet women."

Their neighbor and Joe's bandmate Matthew approached as they arrived at the landing, the location of the Haller Fountain, presided over by a stone nymph and cherubs.

Teresa stepped forward to give him a hug. "Join us for lunch?"

Matthew shook his head a little too vigorously, as if certain he'd be *de trop*. Before Teresa could reassure him, he said, "Rain check?" With a big smile, he added, "Hey, I'm throwing a Summer Solstice party this Sunday at four. Will you let the rest of the crew know they're invited? Teresa, I'm hoping you'll play for us."

CHAPTER 12

———◆———

IN THE COOL MORNING AIR, Chiara sat by herself on the terrace, warmed by an Icelandic-wool sweater and a lap blanket. She didn't know how to dress herself anymore. All of her usual outfits looked like what a guilty person would wear to a court of law. Plain Talbot dresses and sensible pumps. Thanks to Teresa's skilled eye, she now owned the basics of a more casual wardrobe—jeans, T-shirts, shorts, cotton skirts, and a few sundresses. This was the first morning she'd worn jeans. She'd been afraid to own the new life she was trying on, a life where she fit in with this privileged family. That would presume too much. Clothing spoke its own language.

When Ali joined her—coffee in one hand, an espresso for her in the other—she braced herself. So far no one had raised the delicate subject of her houseguest status. It was time to take the bull by the horns.

Accepting the coffee with a broad smile, she said, "Thank you! But I wish you wouldn't wait on me. In Italy, we say, 'corpses and guests stink after three days.' It's been two weeks. I don't wish to wear out my welcome."

Ali wrinkled her nose. "I prefer the 'fish' idiom."

Chiara laughed. "We say that too."

Ali remained serious. "Stay, please. You are the perfect houseguest. If you *need* to go home, that's something else, but we would miss you terribly. Then there's Lorenzo." Chiara was all too aware that the issue of custody hung in the air like smoke on a windless day. Ali took small sips of her coffee as if buying time to think. Finally she said, "Lorenzo reminds me more and more of that precocious kid in *Lost in Space*. A little genius. You're so great with him." She paused. "Do you *need* to go home?"

Chiara wondered what Ali really meant. *Is being here too much temptation, considering your obvious attraction to Jake?* Or, *does your husband miss you?* Yes, she was running from Jake—but like a small girl who really wants the boy to catch her. Arnold did *not* miss her.

"Ah … no." Her reply was too long in coming.

"If you go back to Portland," Ali said, "Maddie, David, Joe, and I are never going to find out what happens to Beverly Bigfoot and friends. I thought we could try one of her special dishes of sautéed greens. I seem to recall they included mushrooms and plants with strange names like cattails, bitterroot, and pigweed. Lorenzo didn't think that sounded so great, but the rest of us are game. Unless they're poisonous."

Chiara giggled at the absurdity of the idea. "I confess, I have no idea. But you should know that Lorenzo was not enthusiastic about my meal plan. I think he wanted the menu to include Beefaroni or SpaghettiOs, which, I confess, I never fed him in Portland."

"Oh, no! Are we spoiling him? I'll speak to May Allen and Susan right away."

Wishing she'd kept her mouth shut, Chiara rushed to say, "Perhaps you could ask him to try one bite of everything on the adult menu—"

"Of course," Ali broke in. "I'm sorry … After our first foster mother fed us nothing but cheap junk food, George and Emily took the opposite tack. Liam and I were both eight years old. Everything they served was under-spiced and undercooked—health food from the co-op. A lot of grains and weird greens, rice and beans. A step-up nutrition-wise, no doubt, but a brutal about-face for a kid. We were always hungry, especially Liam. That's why I didn't see any harm in occasionally serving Lorenzo fun food."

"Please don't worry." Chiara was eager to get back to discussing her stories. "About the menu … I try to be true to the rules I set at the start: none of the creatures has ever interacted with humans."

"I loved your explanation of why Beverly didn't have spices or sugar or chocolate or all the things we think we can't do without. Lor's answer was priceless: 'I like Beverly and all her friends, but if they invite me to dinner, I would prefer to sit that one out.' "

"That comes from Arnold. Whenever I propose dinner with my friends or an evening at the opera or ballet, he says he'll 'sit that one out.' "

"Arnold sounds like a killjoy," Ali muttered. "Would he let you go, I hope? I mean, to the opera or ballet."

"Would he let you go" echoed in the room—with regard to divorce, not an evening out. *Would he?* Chiara wondered. *Could I leave anyway? Could I afford to go? Perhaps the real question should be, do I really want to waste the rest of my life with Arnold?*

"Arnold doesn't usually object," Chiara told Ali. "I attend most cultural events without him." She didn't add that he discouraged dinners with her friends and their husbands, not wanting her to go without him but refusing to accompany her.

Thankfully, Ali let the subject drop. Chiara preferred to pretend Arnold no longer existed. She could hardly confess to her hosts that all communication between them had ceased. Her phone message that she and Lorenzo had arrived safely went unanswered. For all she knew, Arnold's corpse was decomposing somewhere in their townhome. But because she'd been gone much longer than three days, his body would stink like a latrine, and the neighbors would surely notice. Anyway, his employers would sound the alarm if he didn't show up for work. She was still his emergency contact.

Ali was back to talking about story time. "I hope you don't mind that it's turned into our nightly entertainment."

Their presence *had* raised the stakes, forcing Chiara to think through the continuing plot line in advance.

"Uh, Chiara, is it a problem that I've been writing everything down? Joe and I together, before bed. We missed the first installments, so perhaps you could fill in the blanks?"

Chiara hadn't forgotten Teresa's comment that Ali was looking for someone to invent a story for her illustrations. She'd hoped against hope that person might be her.

"*Certo*, I mean certainly," she said with a broad smile.

Ali waved both hands in the air. "Yay! I'll just keep my fingers crossed that Arnold doesn't for—, uh, *encourage* you to come home anytime soon."

Ali had almost said "force." No one was fooled. They understood that her marriage was a disaster.

* * *

Joe was soaking alone in the hot tub, feeling guilty. Ali couldn't use the jacuzzi while pregnant, especially in the first trimester. If only *he* could do the heavy lifting this time. He was the one who wanted a house full of kids. She had to be bummed to be pregnant again so soon.

At least this time she had company. If anyone could cheer Ali up, it was Teresa. Usually. Liam and Teresa seemed to be on firmer ground, thanks to Jake. He got along great with Liam, and Teresa was thrilled to have another missing brother back in the fold. Joe couldn't get over Jake's transformation from slick, vengeful business guy to laid-back thriller writer. What the hell had happened? Sooner or later one of their crew—not Joe—would wheedle it out of him. Ali joked that they were like the Kravitzes in *Bewitched*—her peeking out the window at other peoples' dramas and imagining all sorts of fantastical things Joe couldn't see. The difference was, he'd believe just about anything at this point.

David and Maddie were having dinner in town with her friend Jeremy, who had stolen the show as Titania in last winter's production of *A Midsummer Night's Dream*. Joe had struggled not to laugh in every scene where Jeremy appeared. Not because he'd camped it up. Joe had been incredulous rather than amused. The performance was so damned uncanny. The rest of the audience was riveted by Maddie and Kilo as Puck and Oberon. Well, yeah, their chemistry had been off the charts. When you knew what was really going on behind the scenes, more embarrassing than anything else. Kilo, an obvious horndog, had worn Maddie down, though she'd never admit it. In any other field, that would constitute sexual harassment. It seemed the theater world lagged behind even corporate culture in acknowledging shit like that. Now Kilo was on the cusp of Hollywood stardom. For the sake of all Joe's loved ones, he hoped the guy's star kept on rising until Port Townsend was just a wee speck on the horizon, too insignificant to bother with. Kilo was probably done messing with the heads, hearts, and bodies of Teresa and Maddie, but Joe wouldn't put it past him to hit on the twins once they came of age.

"Wow, what's up?" Ali said as she shut the gate. "You look so fierce, I wouldn't trust you with a weapon right now, not even a throwing knife." Joe didn't mind that his knife skills lagged behind Liam's and Jake's. Let Jake show him up for a change.

His beautiful wife was wearing jeans and a turtleneck Irish-wool sweater against the chill of the evening. She was still slender but shapelier, even more stunning now than when they'd first met in that little cabin in the woods. With the twins, she'd gained enough weight to do a serious number on her self-esteem, but it hadn't dimmed her beauty one iota in his eyes.

She leaned down to plant a soft kiss that whooshed all the tension out of him. Or at least focused it in one spot. "Don't get out," she said when he moved toward the stairs, "unless you want to." She stood up again, kicked off her sandals and rolled up her jeans. "Now, explain that murderous expression."

"Kilo, seducing the twins."

She barked out a laugh. "*What?*"

He grinned, seeing the humor in it. Sort of. "I wouldn't put it past him to waltz back into town fifteen years from now and seduce one of the twins. Or both. They're going to be gorgeous."

She dangled her feet in the water. "No way. Look on the bright side: they'll have way too many guys their own age panting after them to be bowled over by some middle-aged actor."

Joe frowned. "That's the bright side? In fifteen years, Kilo will be forty-three, but he'll probably still be able to pass for thirty."

"You worry too much." She closed her eyes and wiggled her toes in the steaming water.

"I'm surprised he didn't have a go at you."

She reached down and splashed him. "Hah. Not everyone finds me irresistible. I'm glad you do."

Wiping the water from his eyes, he said, "I've never stopped wanting you and I never will."

She didn't answer immediately, her look speculative.

"What?" he said.

"Your voice ...."

"Yeah ...." He felt a rush of guilt. She'd noticed that the hoarseness was gone.

"David?" she said lightly.

"Yeah." He'd tried to refuse David's offer. Having his brother heal him felt like cheating, and David spent the entire next day in bed with a migraine.

"Will you tour again?" she asked, her tone slightly frosty.

He held her gaze. "Not anytime soon. I'm with you all the way through this pregnancy and beyond. But eventually ...." He couldn't promise not to tour. Surely she knew that.

"There's a Solstice party at Matthew's this weekend," she said, bringing them back to the immediate future. "Teresa asked if you'd perform. I'd love to hear one of the classical Spanish guitar pieces you played for me that first time. It's my most erotic memory, ever." She exaggerated her sigh for his benefit.

He laughed. "For me too."

"You used to serenade me in Paris. How come you never do that now?"

He thought about how much time he spent in the studio and vowed to practice over at the house more often. "I should," he admitted. "For professional musicians, it's not practicing if you have an audience. But I do want the girls to grow up loving music. I'll make more of an effort, I promise."

Her smile had a twist to it. "I could bring the girls over to the studio ...."

"Now you're scaring me. Imagine the destruction …. All right, sure. I'll play guitar at the house at least once a week."

To distract her from his deficiencies as a husband, Joe climbed out of the jacuzzi, stark naked. With deliberate slowness, he fetched his robe from the hook next to the gate and slipped it on, tying the sash. Then he turned the deadbolt to lock them in. His actions had the desired effect. "Gate's shut," he said, reading her mind. "Chiara's not going to wander in without an invite, and Lorenzo's too young for hot tubs. Or to worry about naked bodies. Besides, Chiara's not *that* much of a prude."

"I don't think Chiara's a prude," Ali protested as she smilingly tracked his moves.

He sauntered back over and stood directly in front of her. "She dresses like one."

"You haven't noticed the new additions to her wardrobe? She's working them in gradually, so as not to seem too obvious. I don't think she's shy about her body. Just afraid."

"Of what?" When his hand grazed her hip, she caught and held it.

"Of Jake. Of her husband. Of life."

She let his hand remain on her hip.

"Wait. Come on! She told you all this?"

"She dropped a few telling details about Arnold. I can read between the lines. Anyone with eyes can see she's got a thing for Jake. She's more afraid of wearing out her welcome with us."

"That's ridicul—"

"I know," she broke in. "Her husband is obviously an abusive prick. He neglects her, tries to keep her from socializing on her own, and now that she's here, he's completely out of touch."

"For all you know they talk every night."

"Nope. I'd bet the farm."

"It's a good thing we don't have a farm."

"Didn't that tabloid article call you a 'gentleman farmer'?" She made a playful grab for the sash of his robe, and he took a teasing step backward.

"Behave, you shameless woman. All right, say you've read her correctly. We're just going to keep her here? What if Arnold turns up to pry his wayward wife from our clutches?"

Ali's eyes had a mischievous glint. "I fully expect that to happen."

Joe moved in and grasped her hips with both hands this time. "You're scaring me. What are you gonna do about it?"

"I have no idea … yet."

His hands strayed to her breasts. This time she didn't stop him. "I have an idea. Moving right along …."

Her eyes widened. "You've got to be kidding. Here? What, up against the fence?"

Damn. He hadn't thought this through. His eyes darted around the space, settling on the changing room.

Following his gaze, she shook her head. "No, no, no! That looks really uncomfortable."

He grinned. "We'll see."

He gently backed her up against the wall, staring into her eyes all the while. She was trying to keep a straight face. Then he let his robe fall open and pressed his naked body against her.

"You'll need to stay very, very still," he whispered as he unzipped her jeans and pulled them down.

CHAPTER 13

EVER SINCE THE HONEYMOON, MADDIE had been squirming in her most ill-fitting role to date: idle rich lady. She felt like a boxer, fists raised, protective equipment in place, who is suddenly told, "No, you're good, the match is over. Your opponent conceded, and you've won the lottery. You'll never need to fight again."

Talk about a letdown.

No artificial high could top acting on stage, the feeling of dancing away from yourself in a new character's shoes. No matter that the offstage experience could be problematic—one or more rotten-egg cast or crew members, budget constraints …. David had given up practicing medicine and clearly expected Maddie to retire as well. Why couldn't he see the difference? David's uncanny gift was also his curse. Sticking to cures that could be affected with science alone had proved too frustrating. For Maddie, the equivalent might be discovering she could psychically channel her characters, making acting unnecessary—as long as she could handle the blowback of blinding headaches.

No fun in that.

Even the movie had been a worthwhile, if not ideal experience, thanks to the gratuitous nudity. You couldn't build a film career based on physical assets. Those would be leached away in the next fifteen years unless taken in one fell swoop by accident or illness.

Maddie was getting dressed for the first non-family-centric social event any of them had attended since the original four—Joe, Ali, Teresa, and Liam—had settled in Port Townsend. That had been June 1998, just over a year ago.

Liam and Teresa had befriended a few locals—Liam due to his handyman skills and Teresa in yoga classes. Joe had a business to run—keeping his alter ego Joe Bob Blade in the public consciousness, which involved occasional trips to Nashville to consult with his manager Linc, submit to interviews, and offer "impromptu" performances when his vocal cords allowed. Ali was more introverted, but she and Joe did go for the occasional dinner in town and attend performances locally. Friendly as they were, they were busy with the twins and still wary of being exposed to another hitjob by the tabloids, so they hadn't made any real effort to widen their social circle. Matthew, the session guitarist who toured with Joe last spring, had already cozied up to enough Port Townsenders in his brief residency to host a party. Though not particularly sociable, Maddie enjoyed the parties Ali hosted at the compound. This was different. It had been a few years since she'd partied with a roomful of strangers.

Fortunately, Maddie's castmate from *A Midsummer Night's Dream* would attend. Jeremy had stayed on after the final curtain, not only because his sister had asked for his help with her new baby, but also because he needed a breather from pounding the pavement. At thirty-one, he hoped to start transitioning from romantic leads to roles that required actual skill. His popular character on a soap opera had been killed off after he'd gone afoul of the powers-that-be. He'd told Maddie only the scantest details, but she assumed he'd slept with the boyfriend of some bigwig. To find his way back to the real money—TV or movies—he needed a breakthrough role that would force casting directors to see beyond his angelic blondness.

David rapped on the open door. "Hey! Are you ready?" He gave her a wolf whistle. "Nice outfit!" She was wearing white jeans and a flowy light-blue and pink silk crop top that bared a few inches of tummy. The style had run its course, but it was one of the few dressy blouses she owned that downplayed her breasts.

David spanned her waist with icy fingers. "Yow!" she cried out in protest.

"God, you're tiny," he whispered, kissing her neck.

She couldn't share his playful mood. She ran her fingers through her short, honey-blonde curls. "I miss having Teresa at the compound. These jeans are so last year. Make that, year before last. I didn't want to look too fancy or too, too … *sexy.*"

David wrapped her in his arms. "Don't worry. We're old hat. Jake's the new kid on the block. Matt may well be the least pretentious professional musician ever—other than Joe. He'd have no patience with the kind of judgmental snobs who care whether your outfit is too revealing or on the cutting edge of fashion." His gaze fixed on her feet. "Won't those sandals hurt after about a minute?"

"Otherwise I'm freakishly short next to you."

His brow furrowed. "They're your arches, not mine. Just don't expect me to heal you if you fall off those platforms and break an ankle."

Maddie was surprised to hear him joke about that ill-fated hike with Jeremy. If he hadn't "fixed" her ankle, her Hollywood career would have been over before it started. Now it was over anyway, and she had only herself to blame.

"I wish I knew what Ali was wearing." Standing in front of the full-length mirror, she gave herself one last critical once-over, almost surrendering to the urge to ask if the white pants made her butt look fat, a classic relationship misstep.

David scoffed, "You're *way* more confident than she is, especially about fashion." Somehow he managed to look both casual and elegant in his black jeans and Polo shirt. Temperatures were in the high seventies, but the ocean breeze made it feel cooler.

Ali and Joe were waiting next to Joe's Subaru Outback. No flashy Ferrari for him. In another life, he might have been a hot park ranger. Pointing at his guitar, she asked, "You going to play something?"

Unsmiling, he nodded. "At Matthew's request. You should also be prepared."

Her mind raced. *What? Ah.* Of course this would be an "impromptu" soiree. These supposedly off-the-cuff performances were the worst. "Oh Maddie, could you do a song for us?" Singers were supposed to welcome any opportunity to perform, as if life really were a musical comedy where people randomly burst into song when the mood struck. Never mind that an optimum performance required warming up the voice, testing your memory of the lyrics, and abstaining from alcohol.

Joe gave her shoulder a squeeze. "I don't like it any better than you. But when we choose entertainment as a profession, that's the price of success. Then people speak of you as a 'gracious' celebrity rather than one who insists on privacy and is forever labeled an asshole."

"I know," she said with a sigh.

Ali, with her crossed arms and air of resignation, didn't radiate excitement either. Hard to believe she was really pregnant, especially in that body-hugging sheath. When you had exaggerated hips and breasts like Maddie, getting dressed was a trial. Women with her sister-in-law's gazelle-like physique could pull off anything.

Ali gave her a hug. "We're in this together, Maddie. Matthew believes the exposure is for our own good. That it will help to normalize his presence—and ours—in Port Townsend."

"He *is* single," Maddie said, "and I doubt he's the type to go clubbing—not that I know of any gay clubs on the Peninsula. They must exist. I bet Jeremy would know."

Crossing the threshold of Matthew's house was like stepping out of a time machine into pre-World-War-I Paris. It should have been a costume party, with men in summer suits and straw hats and women in corsets and long dresses, their hats crowned with birds and flowers. Many of the key pieces in the living room such as the mirrors with their fancy frames and the graceful side tables had been repurposed from the Sea Captain's House. Why not? David had taken the parlor in a different direction, with vibrant colors, massive leather furniture, and African art and textiles. Not Maddie's taste, but she didn't think of the house as hers, having contributed nothing toward its purchase. Matthew's cream floral damask couch was new, also the poster art from the nightclubs, which did not appear to be reprints. None of those ubiquitous *Tournée du Chat Noir* posters here. Teresa had wisely relaxed her taste enough to allow for comfort.

Matthew had seemed so low key and yes, closeted, when she'd met him earlier. Maddie no longer believed he was in the closet, just not looking to lead the rainbow parade. It was a good-looking bunch. Matthew told her many of them were accomplished artists or musicians, mostly retired. She hadn't thought of her outfit as trendy, but compared to the elegant casual clothing she observed here, it stood out, and not in a good way.

Gradually, as Matthew introduced them, the O'Connell clan began to venture outside their clump. Maddie was dismayed by the sea of faces she was unlikely to recognize out of context. She had to meet people at least twice before their identities truly registered and their names stuck. Part of the reason she'd always dreaded parties was that people would ask those wince-inducing questions about her acting career, starting with "What have I seen you in?" Not a problem here. Most of them had seen her as Puck.

One older man in a white linen suit with gelled, wiry gray hair introduced himself in a vaguely British accent. "I'm Colin." He shook her hand. "We saw you at the Theatre by the Marina. You were quite good. *Quite.*" He owned the folk-art gallery on Water Street and had a show of his own work coming up in the fall.

"You were Puck," a pretty though intense fiftyish woman said. She was wearing black slacks and a button-down blue striped blouse. Her nose was imposing, but somehow her wide eyes and full lips made it work. *A pleasant, Carol Burnett-type face*, Maddie thought, *though not as friendly*. "Great fun," the woman went on. "I'm Emily Davis." She gave Maddie a teeth-rattling handshake as she checked out her body with curiosity rather than sexual interest. "We've all been wondering about you."

"How long have you lived here?" Maddie asked.

"Five years?" the woman said as if it were a question. "We aren't here full-time. My husband and I own a vacation place. He's retired, but I still practice law in Seattle part-time. I'm a divorce attorney." She handed Maddie a card. "You never know. I'm a Rottweiler when it comes to getting you what you deserve." Maddie's dismay had to be evident, because she quickly added, "I didn't mean *you*, of course. You may, uh, run across someone else who needs my services." Maddie put the card in her purse. She thought of introducing the woman to Chiara.

She looked over to see Joe and Ali wearing attentive smiles as a young man droned on. When she passed them, she understood that the droner was talking about his novel and bulged her eyes comically at Ali. But then she heard him mention the title of his award-winning novel and felt ashamed for jumping to conclusions. Other than Joe and Ali, Maddie was used to hobnobbing with *aspiring* artists, not the real thing.

She shuffled sideways into another room, right into the path of a bounding golden retriever intent on her crotch. She wobbled on her stacked sandals then began to topple backward, unable to stop the momentum.

She was caught by a pair of strong male arms.

"Charlie!" Matthew scolded. "Maddie, I'm so sorry. Charlie's just a puppy. He was shut in for everyone's safety. Somehow he got out."

Full grown or not, the dog was a monster. The man helped her to her feet. "I'm sorry," she said, a little dazed, "I'm not usually such a klutz."

His grin drew attention to his sharp teeth. "Not at all," he said in a light French accent. "I'd give you a nine point seven." *Ah.* Reynard. Maddie had met him only once—at Ali's birthday party, where he'd made a play for Teresa that led to a couple of dates. "You know, the Olympics? But really, it was a foul on the part of the dog." He gave the panting, squirming animal a comically stern look and told him, "*Mauvais chien!*" Charlie whimpered.

In no time David towered over them both. Reynard released her and stood back. He was close to Jake in height and somewhere in the range of forty. His fine-boned handsomeness, etched by age, suffered in comparison with David's rough-hewn masculinity and conspicuous vitality.

"I warned you about those shoes," David grumbled as he led Maddie away, giving Reynard a terse nod.

The embarrassing diversion was quickly eclipsed by Jeremy's grand entrance. Charlie the dog had been safely locked away, and someone had posted a sign on the door saying CHIEN MÉCHANT, literally, "mean dog." If Charlie hadn't chosen to plow Maddie down in such an undignified fashion, she might have been amused. She brushed at the scuff marks on her white jeans.

Although Jeremy's linen trousers were a cut above most of the guests', his color choices were generally brighter—particularly the sunflowers on his coral Hawaiian shirt, worn open over a turquoise tee that made his blue eyes blaze. In handsomeness, with his strong features and streaked-blond hair, he was hard to beat. Though Jeremy couldn't help but attract attention, Maddie thought he had attempted to dial down his usual high spirits. In this setting, he didn't want to be the only Mexican jumping bean in the bowl. Matthew, an inch or so shorter than Jeremy's six feet one, had subtler good looks. His face and nose were on the long side, which some might describe as horsey, though with nice teeth and arresting deep-set brown eyes. Not for the first time, Maddie pondered the concept of charisma. Was it a quality you chose to radiate? Jeremy sparkled with mischief and vitality. Could people with such different energy work as a couple? Not if their stiff body language was any indication.

"Jeremy Fisher!" she cried out, forgetting her vow not to attract undue attention.

Predictably, her friend's banked energy blazed forth. Wrapping her in a bone-crushing hug, he gushed, "Maddie May!"

Matthew's smile was polite but puzzled. "Jeremy Fisher? Maddie May?"

"Oh," Maddie sputtered. Why-oh-why had she introduced the stupid in-joke when Matthew and Jeremy were behaving like nine-year-olds on the first day of school? She didn't want to embarrass her buddy by explaining the nickname. Jeremy saved her the trouble.

"You know the Beatrix Potter book, *Jeremy Fisher*?" Matthew didn't. "Doesn't matter. It's just the frog part. I, uh ...."

He stopped, only now understanding that the story didn't work out of context.

"You know, the frog prince," Maddie said, coming to his rescue. "Jeremy's an unusual name, and it just kind of flew out of my mouth at one point." The nickname was ironic. Jeremy didn't require a kiss by the right man to achieve a princely form.

"And Maddie May," Jeremy rushed to say, "that's from the Rod Stewart song, you know, '*Maggie* May.' Maddie was complaining about being too old for the business. That song is about—"

"A man berating an older woman for making him fall for her then rejecting him," Matthew broke in, smirking. "I get it."

Maddie, wiping away flop sweat, admitted, "Both are a little random. That's private jokes for you … they lose something in the translation. Maybe that's true of most humor." *Jeez*, she was usually comfortable around Matthew, but now she'd inadvertently embarked on a treatise on humor. She really wanted him to like Jeremy.

Unable to stop herself, she kept going on in that runaway-mouth way of her mother's, "How many people really listen to lyrics, do you suppose? I'm surprised you know what that song is about, Matthew."

He shrugged. "Musicians listen to music differently. I also see chord structures and modulations visually. With songs, it depends. People paid attention to the lyrics of 'Fire and Rain' because James Taylor was writing about something intensely personal—same with Joe and 'Babe in the Woods.' "

Jeremy clearly didn't get the reference.

"Joe and Ali met in the Hoh Rain Forest," Maddie explained. "He was hiding out in a cabin, protecting his voice, and she got lost in the rain. He saved her life. After they went their separate ways, he kept thinking about her. They hadn't exchanged last names or even their full first names, so he didn't know how to find her. That's why he wrote the song. He hoped she'd hear it."

Jeremy waggled his eyebrows. "She obviously did. I don't follow country or pop music. Sounds like a great story."

Matthew's laugh was a single mellow "hah." "Just don't ask Joe about it. After it won a Grammy, everyone thought he'd be another Garth Brooks."

"So … what …?" Jeremy began, open palms egging her on.

"Vocal nodes," Maddie said in a low voice, not wishing to elaborate here. "He was forced into partial retirement."

"Will you excuse me?" Matthew said. "I need to check on the kitchen and the bar."

Once he was gone, Maddie blew out a frustrated breath. "Sorry, Jeremy. That was awkward."

Jeremy snorted. "God. Women and their apologies! No need. No bolt from the blue there for me. Not for him, either."

"It's hard to tell with Matthew. He's a laid-back guy."

"Any more laid back and he might just topple over, head first in the crab dip," Jeremy said with a sniff of disgust. "Now, *that* guy …." He pointed his noble jaw at Jake, surrounded by a small group of men hanging on his every word. "That is one smokin' stick of dynamite."

Maddie chuckled. "Jake? That's Joe's brother. He's straight."

"Oh well! Coulda fooled me. Coulda fooled *them*."

Maddie was surprised to see Jake holding court with men. Chiara stood in the corner, listening attentively to two older women who illustrated their speech with exaggerated hand gestures. Their house guest had never looked better. Her soft brown hair was swept into a fetching updo, little tendrils framing her rosy cheeks. The low-cut lavender cotton dress with its flouncy skirt might as well be labeled, "Style by Teresa." That did it. Maddie was going to ask her sister-in-law for a complete wardrobe makeover.

Joe came into view, checking his watch. "Let's get the show rolling. Shall we do 'Our Love Is Here to Stay'?" It was the song she and Joe had performed at Teresa's wedding.

He turned to Jeremy, who now that he knew Joe's story, was a little starstruck. "Jeremy, Could you sing something?"

"Uh … I suppose. If someone can accompany me."

They all whirled about in surprise at the sound of classical piano coming from the main parlor. "A Rachmaninoff prelude," Joe said. He listened some more. "Reynard," he concluded. "Teresa's good, but not that good."

Uh-oh, Maddie thought.

* * *

David had been itching to leave ever since Maddie had fallen into Reynard's arms. He'd had enough "circulating," fielding the questions people felt free to ask doctors at cocktail parties, seizing the chance for a free consultation. After four-plus years in Africa, he was woefully out of practice in society. Ali, who obviously felt the same way, clung to him like a buoy in a riptide.

"Can we leave now?" she said out of the corner of her mouth. "I'm fresh out of chitchat. Chiara is way better at this than I am. Maybe it's because she's a therapist."

"She's also a great storyteller," David said. "When will Beverly Bigfoot meet her soul mate? And will Joe Bigfoot serenade her with an instrument made of moss?"

It was impossible not to respond to Ali's merry laughter. Leave it to Joe to fall hard for the nicest woman on the West Coast.

"It's a *children's* story," she protested.

David continued, undeterred. "So what? The adults reading it to their kids might appreciate a romantic subplot. But for the instrument, you're stuck with percussion or wind. Strings are made of animal guts."

Ali scrunched up her face. "Yeah … no."

"Have you talked to Chiara about doing the book?"

"I have! I confessed that Joe and I have been writing down her stories. She seems psyched."

At the sound of loud, complicated piano music, they turned to face the main parlor. It was as if someone had flipped a switch and slowed time to a crawl. Ali's sapphire eyes widened. "Uh, David? That's Reynard, isn't it?"

"Yeah. Isn't he the guy Teresa dated? The film score composer?"

"Briefly," Ali said. "This could be awkward. I had the impression he basically tried to rape her on their last date."

"Huh. Are you sure?" *I knew I had a reason to dislike him*, David thought.

Ali shook her head. "Well, no. Liam made like Zorro and leapt to her rescue before it came to that."

They walked over to the arch leading into the parlor to get a better look.

"Who's *that*?" As subtly as possible, David indicated the statuesque woman with the sumptuous curly black hair, striking green eyes, and long, muscular legs encased in tight black jeans. It was difficult not to fixate on the deep cleavage revealed by her diaphanous green blouse.

"Ooh, she's gorgeous," Ali said. "She definitely works out. Or teaches aerobics."

"That must be Reynard's girlfriend. The way she's hovering, she's clearly staking a claim." He looked over at Liam, Joe, and Teresa, who had clumped together again, noting his sister's glum expression. "Does Teresa know that woman?"

Ali was already heading toward the others. "Let's find out."

"It's Lisette," Teresa replied as they approached.

"Ah," Ali said. "I get it."

David frowned. "Get what?" These women could be so maddening.

"It's a long story," Ali said. "Teresa believes Lisette and Liam have a history."

"Based on …." He waited.

"A business card she found in his leather jacket."

David stared at his sister in disbelief. "You went through Liam's pockets? That's a violation of privacy. Plus, it's common knowledge that snooping never pays."

She stood a little straighter, indignant. "I wasn't snooping, I was fondling his jacket."

David snorted. He could just imagine his sister fondling and nuzzling Liam's buttery leather jacket when he wasn't around. "How do you know the card was from that woman?"

"When I was in Port Angeles, I just happened to stop by her bistro. It's called Café Lisette, and it's hard to miss. Downtown Port Angeles is mostly a few main streets."

"Uh-huh." In David's experience, the stores and restaurants on the side streets were easy to miss unless you were looking for them.

"Liam was on a hike, and I found his jacket hanging there in the open—"

"—just begging to be fondled," he finished with a grin.

Maddie had given David the Haiku version of Teresa and Liam's love story. *At last he gave in. As different as they were. Love does conquer all.*

"Speak of the devil, where's your husband?"

Reynard had moved on to a different piano solo. David recognized it as one of Liszt's few genuine crowd pleasers, and he suspected Ali did too.

"*Liebestraum,*" Teresa whispered.

"You've been talking about this soiree idea for a while," David said, hoping to reason his sister out of her foul mood. "You must have known Reynard would jump at the chance to show off."

No answer, but her look skewered him.

"Did you warn Matthew?"

"No."

As the final chord resonated, Reynard rose and said, "I apologize. I saw this magnificent instrument and could not contain myself." He patted the piano as if it were a well-trained pet of excellent pedigree. Locking eyes with Teresa, he added, "Perhaps Teresa would like to go next."

Two red spots appeared on his sister's pale cheeks. Joe acted quickly. "You're a tough act to follow, Reynard," he said. "Let's take a little breather from classical music." David recognized the jovial air and the light Southern lilt that accompanied it and wanted to laugh. Consciously or not, Joe had assumed the folksy, aw-shucks persona of Joe Bob Blade. It was a funny role for a gently raised Pacific Northwest Catholic boy.

Joe and Matthew acted swiftly, pulling two chairs in front of the piano. They tuned their instruments, and with no verbal preliminaries, launched into a guitar duet, a bluegrass number David didn't recognize and thought might sound better on banjos. That was Joe in a nutshell—a classical guitar masquerading as a banjo. It was his looks and charm that sold the illusion.

With her usual aplomb, Maddie took center stage, accompanied by Joe on the guitar. David did *not* appreciate the way Reynard salivated over her. One of those guys who never appreciated the woman he was with. Always looking for the next shiny object.

When the song ended, Maddie passed the baton. "Jeremy?"

Jeremy placed an oversized volume on the piano. It didn't surprise David that Matthew would own musical theater scores, but he doubted Jeremy had expected it. To Reynard, he said, "It's 'Being Alive' from Sondheim's *Company*. Does that work for you?"

"Of course," he replied as if asked to play the birthday song.

Maddie, who had returned to David's side, whispered, "It's his go-to audition piece. We were in *Company* together ages ago before Jeremy's career took off."

David wanted to ask, *Then why is he gathering moss in Port Townsend?* But then, you might ask the same question of Maddie. Except that he knew the answer. She was here for him. How long would that be enough?

Jeremy's star power turned the parlor into a theater. You could almost see the spotlight. With no need of a microphone, he belted out "Being Alive," nailing every note, including the lung-busting climax. The words and soaring melody amounted to a serious cry for emotional connection, the last thing you'd expect to hear from a lightweight like Maddie's friend.

Maddie grinned as she led the applause.

Much to Teresa's relief, it was a literal showstopper. She breathed much more easily when David and Maddie joined her. To Maddie, she whispered, "Let's work something up for next time; I *never* want to find myself in this position again. Not if Reynard's around." Maddie readily agreed.

"Okay, that's weird," David said, jutting a thumb in Reynard's direction. Liam was standing with the composer and Lisette, joking around as if they were buddies. Feeling his sister stiffen, he said, "Relax. No doubt Liam has an ulterior motive. And just because a man has a woman's business card doesn't mean he does anything with it. Women are a ballsier than they used to be." Maddie narrowed her eyes. "I, uh, *personally*, haven't collected any phone numbers in a long time."

"Nice save," she said as Matthew joined them.

"I was just about to wrap things up," he said. "Most of my guests figured the party was over after Jeremy's performance. We have a last-minute arrival I think you'll want to talk to."

Perhaps Maddie and David had forged some kind of psychic connection. Before he observed it, he sensed the tension in his wife, who might have been staring at a ghost. The newcomer was on the short side, with sharp, striking features, dramatic eyebrows, and thick, dark-brown hair. Flashing a killer smile, he said, "Hey, Maddie, how're ya doin'?" He leaned in. "You okay?"

Reaching out to shake the man's hand, Maddie said in a studiously bland voice, "George, I'm doing great. Thanks so much for asking." She did a sweep of the room with her left hand, blinding them all with the oversized diamond of her wedding ring. "Fancy meeting you here." In her stage voice, she announced, "Everyone, this is George Reed Masters. Though he needs no introduction." Interrupting the murmurs of greeting, she said to George, "What brings you to our small town?"

George was so relaxed that he might have been in his own living room. "I was in Vancouver—you know, the one across the border. After they were finished with me, I thought, 'Hey! This is my chance to see the Olympic Peninsula.' Damon Morehouse seems to be a prime role for someone, so why not meet the author? Especially after I found out he was *your* brother-in-law, Maddie. Is he here?" He scanned the room.

Damn it, where was Jake? Where was Chiara, for that matter?

Ali, also searching in vain for Jake, said, "Where are you staying?"

George gave a careless shrug. "I dunno. Some hotel?"

"How did you find us?" Ali said.

"Sorry to crash the party. I bought a coffee and heard the barista mention a shindig all the town celebs were attending. She said the host was a guitarist and owned the Victorian on the corner of Washington and Harrison. I decided to check it out. Who was that guy who was just singing? He's got a fricken' awesome set of pipes."

"That was Jeremy," Joe said. "He's a fabulous actor, too. You should have seen him as Titania in *A Midsummer Night's Dream*."

George looked taken aback. "Titania? Isn't she a woman?"

"You can't stay at a hotel," Joe went on, not bothering to explain. "You'd be mobbed."

"You should know," George said with a wink.

Matthew stepped forward. "Stay in one of my guestrooms."

Ali broke in, "Jake would want you to stay with him. He's renting an entire B and B just for himself." Then, David noted, she froze. So the truth had dawned on her, too. "But," she backpedaled, "that might not work tonight."

David came to her rescue. "Earlier, Jake told me he felt a migraine coming on."

"Shouldn't someone check on him then?" Matthew said with genuine concern.

"No, no," Joe said, too jolly. "Jake'll be *fine*. He gets these headaches sometimes and needs to sleep them off. I wouldn't want to spring any houseguests on him—even one he's been dying to meet—without talking to him first."

Liam and Teresa had reappeared, and Liam said, "The answer's obvious. Stay with us. We're just a few houses away."

Starry eyed, George extended a hand. "We haven't met."

"I'm the brother-in-law, Liam Ryan." Slipping a possessive arm around Teresa's waist, he added, "This is my wife, Teresa."

George grinned. "You're the model for Damon Morehouse," he said, jabbing finger guns in the air.

Liam's supercilious expression said the very notion was absurd. "Hardly," he scoffed.

PART II

CHAPTER 14

———•———

JAKE FELT LIKE A SHOWGIRL who had just jumped out of a cake at a bachelor party. The guests the kind of pre-gay liberation "bachelors" who "never married." Served him right for writing a book that reeked of testosterone. Now all his fans were male. That was okay. Fans were fans. All he needed to do was be attentive and gracious. His years as CEO of Big Paul's Outfitters had prepared him well for such situations.

Meanwhile he had not lost track of Chiara, who—he was pleased to see—was also keeping tabs on him. He hadn't seen her since the day she was supposed to help him sort through the Victorian gewgaws—the day he'd told himself to move on. Not that he had.

"*Please.*" Rory sounded disgusted. First word from his ghostly friend in days. Why now? Jake resolved to ignore him.

One of the younger men—a fortyish, tall, and very pale blond who somehow reminded Jake of a white pipe cleaner—was telling him about the best night life in Port Angeles. By "night life," he meant gay clubs. He pretended to listen closely, letting the names evaporate the minute they hit his eardrums like raindrops on hot pavement. Then someone mentioned restaurants, which *did* interest him, or would, once the novelty of eating his own cooking wore off. Enthusiasm was high for La Fête Sauvage, and talk turned to Chef Jean-Louis—his original style and joie de vivre. Apparently the flamboyant chef also had a local gay following.

"Too bad he's back in North Bend," one of them pouted. "The experience is entirely more delicious when he's around."

"He does hire some tasty young people," said another.

Jake's lips began to twitch. He'd heard Ali complain that Jean-Louis favored only the best-looking male members of their crew of former foster children. Did she realize how much the chef's most devoted customers appreciated his preferences?

They were deep into a debate about the best actor to play Damon Morehouse, including many ridiculous candidates who were far too macho to qualify, when he heard piano playing impressive enough to grace a concert hall. "You gentleman will have to excuse me," he said, knowing his own ideas regarding the casting of Damon were beside the point. "I don't want to miss the entertainment. It's been a treat." He shook their hands as he backed away, grinning hard enough for his jaw to crack.

Walking backward like that, he smacked right into Chiara, who immediately flushed crimson. *Lord, she's a vision*, he thought. He almost forgot to breathe. Seeing that her hands were empty, he said, "Can I get you a glass of wine?"

No sound emerged from her open mouth. He fetched the beverages anyway—an innocuous merlot for him and a pinot grigio for her. She followed him outside through the French doors onto the terrace, where they found two chairs in the shade of a tulip tree. All the windows and doors were open, and the music wafted to them on the breeze.

"He's a marvelous pianist," Jake remarked unnecessarily.

Still silent, Chiara nodded. Her flush made him wonder if she'd reached her limit already and regretted bringing her what might be the proverbial last straw—the glass that made the camel black out. Too late. She'd already consumed most of it. Dutch courage?

"She's fine," Rory said. "She's drunk on you."

"I'm sorry …" Chiara began. He waited. "I'm sorry I didn't …."

"There's nothing to apologize for," Jake said preemptively. He didn't want her excuses.

"I heard David say …" she began and stopped herself.

Oh, Jeez. It all came down to that stupid conversation he'd had with his brother about Los Angeles and the woman in San Francisco. "Please tell me."

"You have a girlfriend …." She waited.

"I don't. My brother was acting nosy and I implied I was still seeing that woman. We broke up ages ago."

"But you wish to move—"

"I don't," he broke in. "Are you kidding? I would hate LA. Bunch of phonies."

"I wish …."

He leaned forward. This he *did* want to hear.

Joe and Matthew were finishing their duo guitar piece. Jake and Chiara sat in silence while Maddie sang. "She has the voice of an angel," she sighed when the song ended.

Jake impulsively took her hand and gave it a light squeeze. What was he doing?

Jeremy was singing "Being Alive" from Sondheim's *Company*. The man belonged on Broadway. Who would have guessed?

"Chiara," he blurted out, "that sounds like a grand finale." He stood abruptly, and so did she. "Let's go." All rational thought had fled. He waited for a sarcastic comment from Rory that didn't come. "Do you have a coat?"

She shook her head, still at a loss for words.

As Jeremy's final notes rent the air, Jake took Chiara's hand and led her along the narrow path to the sidewalk, where they headed toward his home.

As he unlocked the main door, Jake scanned the area to see if they'd been observed. It was just after seven, still daylight, and the street was eerily quiet. Not even a dog walker in sight.

Once inside, Chiara did a slow pivot, taking in the details of the spacious parlor before running a fingertip along the top of the white marble fireplace mantel. Regarding him in wide-eyed wonder, she said, "Not even a speck of dust."

She sounded neither impressed nor turned off, so he simply replied, "Literal dust, no. Metaphorical dust, maybe." *Jeez*, what the hell did that mean? *Moving right along* …. "Can I take you on a tour?"

She nodded and stepped forward to follow him up the stairs. When he turned around, she nearly ran into him. He could just reach out and …. *Stop it*, he told himself. *Patience*. "Teresa helped me pack up some of the clutter. You know …." He stopped himself. He didn't want to address Chiara's no-show again. No sense in reminding her of the *valid* reasons she'd stayed away. He went on, "I spend most of my time in the downstairs office, writing, or outside, throwing knives." He hesitated. That sounded weird. "I'm practicing the techniques Liam taught us." She was watching him, but his words were just noise to her now, like she was in a trance. Was she afraid? Paralyzed with indecision? Poised to run? "I've also been experimenting in the kitchen. I never had time for cooking in real life." If BPO had been his real life, what was this, his fantasy life? "I've mostly stayed away from the guestrooms. Other than the master, um, *bedroom* … naturally." He stumbled over the word. "Rather than a 'tour,' we'll call it an 'exploration.' "

Jesus, he sounded like a blithering idiot. Or a really inept museum docent.

Through French doors, they emerged into a yard surrounded by tall lattice fencing. It hadn't stopped a young buck with impressive antlers from leaping in. Jake yelled at it to "git!" and they both watched, gaping, as it sailed over the fence. "Guess I'll be adding barbed wire on top," he said. "Maybe he's Superbuck—you know, able to leap tall fences in a single bound." The lame joke elicited a startled giggle and a blush from Chiara. She was just as off-balance as he.

The side yard featured a substantial rose garden in need of deadheading and several stone benches positioned to take advantage of the ocean view. He made a mental note to buy pruning shears and add a porch swing for two.

"Shall we continue the tour?"

She gave a jerky nod.

Another exit led to a sunroom converted from an open patio. The long row of vintage wicker rocking chairs faced a different view of the ocean.

"I can almost imagine the guests occupying them." It was Chiara's first complete sentence. She blinked several times, visibly disoriented.

"Are you all right?" He touched her arm, and the light contact delivered a zing of pleasure.

"Oh yes. It's just that … never mind." She smiled. "The house and the grounds have been designed to profit from the view. I could sit here for hours."

Fluent as her English was, she had a charmingly quaint turn of phrase, as if translating from Italian. He steered her by the elbow back into the house. "Once we've finished exploring, *you* can decide on the spot where I'll serve dinner. Onward."

They entered the dining room, with its red and gold patterned damask wallpaper and five round tables covered by lace cloths. The mahogany sideboard dominated an entire wall. Artwork in various shapes and sizes was hung on another wall in a cleverly organized patchwork. Many of the landscapes featured the B&B's view of the bay.

Chiara pointed to the few portraits in oil—all unsigned but similar enough in style to be painted by the same artist. "They don't look happy," she said, echoing his thoughts. "Do you think these might have been relatives of the original owners? I believe I …."

When the sentence petered out, he prompted her, "Yes?"

She shivered. "Nothing. Second floor?"

As they ascended the winding staircase, Jake said, "In France, the ground floor is the *rez-de-chaussée*. That means we're headed for the first floor."

"Yes, also known as *pianoterra* and *primo piano* in Italian," she said, her smile indulgent.

His cheeks grew hot. *Like she wouldn't know.*

As he followed her up the stairs, he hung back to better appreciate the view of her swaying hips. They were about to enter dangerous territory, as in bedrooms. He was waging an inner debate. They could still rejoin the others, stroll over to Liam's house as if all they'd done was embark on an evening constitutional. His current plan was to keep his grubby hands to himself. Unlike Joe—he suspected—Jake had always erred on the side of caution when it came to initiating sex. He and Ali had never done much more than kiss, thank god. Their sexual chemistry had been tepid, mostly due to her reluctance. What kind of satisfaction could you get—physical or otherwise—from seducing a woman who didn't want you?

Chiara *did* want him, which complicated things. The steam between them had fogged up his moral compass.

There were several bedrooms on the second floor, and all appeared to be ready for guests. Most were smallish with a shared bathroom in the hallway. Some of the lamps were interesting. With their elaborate bronze bases, they could be genuine Tiffany. He'd have to examine them more closely—do the nail varnish test to see if the color held. The upstairs was basically clutter free. You didn't want to tempt your guests with easily pocketed souvenirs.

At long last, they arrived at the master bedroom. Chiara's eyes lit up. "Oh! This is beautiful." They went to stand in front of the sash windows divided by mullions and gaze out at the waterfront and the bay.

"I believe they're the original panes. It would be more practical to put in storm windows."

She grabbed his hand impulsively, her wide hazel eyes sparkling beneath her glasses. "Nothing is practical about this place. And that's how it should remain. How fun to reside in a house with so much history!"

He was ready to ask her to move in with him right then and there. He loved that she loved it. Had he sensed she would—even rented the house to please her? He'd always preferred places with no history, like his custom-built home in North Bend. Chiara herself had the kind of old-fashioned prettiness that inspired artists to draw milkmaids. The same fresh, unworldly quality that had attracted Joe to Ali.

They faced each other now, so close he could smell her sweet breath. He temporarily forgot to be self-conscious, captivated as he was by the maple streaks in her rich brown hair, her heart-shaped face, sun-kissed skin, and rosebud lips. Which were parted. She removed her glasses with trembling fingers and placed them on the side table. Then she took the final step, closing the space between them. With her soft body pressed against his, his cock pulsed. He didn't kiss her. *She* kissed *him*.

Not many women surprised him. He kissed her back, but lightly, enjoying the novelty of ceding control. Then he shut his eyes and enjoyed the exquisite sensation of her soft, nibbling lips on his mouth, face, and neck. Unbuttoning his shirt, she glided her fingertips over his hard nipples and along his quivering torso. Then she started in on the buttons of his trousers. A light breeze traveled through the open window, bathing the room in the scent of roses and the even more intoxicating essence of Chiara. He couldn't stay passive much longer. He wanted to snarl like an animal and burrow into her. His cock was painfully hard, and when she fell to her knees, he gasped.

With a low moan, he pulled her to her feet.

* * *

Chiara felt as if her soul had left her body and now hovered on the ceiling, watching her. Who was this shameless woman? In bed, her husband Arnold was a disaster. His nakedness disgusted her. The man was hairy as an ape. Strong as he was, his muscles were buried in flesh that reminded her of bread dough. This man was the opposite—like a Greek statue come to life— only much better endowed. She had never cuckolded her husband, but night after night of erotic dreams had broken down her resistance.

Jake tore off his clothing and tossed it onto a chair, his lean body glistening with perspiration. Chiara stared in wonder at the sight of him. He tried to set her on her feet, but her legs wouldn't bear the weight, so he laid her gently on the bed. The skirt of her dress trapped her legs, and she felt deliciously helpless as she struggled to catch her breath. First Jake freed her legs, spreading the skirt like a fan. With slow, deliberate movements, he unbuckled the straps of her sandals. Then he rocked her sideways and unzipped her dress carefully, as if worried the mechanism might jam. She smiled. She could tell he liked the sight of her pink-lace bra and panties.

After a long moment of caressing her with his eyes, he unhooked the bra and eased it off her shoulders. He cradled her breasts then stroked her nipples with his thumbs, sending rushes of pleasure to her core. He hadn't touched her down there yet, and she quaked at the promise of what was to come.

"Please," she said, the first words spoken since this delicious disrobing had begun.

His smile was remarkably boyish as his hands traveled back down to cup her buttocks, pulling her forward so that his erection strained against her. She shut her eyes, stupid with desire. Tentatively, he touched her sex, began to probe and twirl. She nearly levitated with pleasure, gripped by an unfamiliar tension. The startling burst of ecstasy that followed left her exhausted and full of wonder.

"This is what you want?" His voice was husky. She opened her eyes to find him fumbling with a condom. *Oh*, he hadn't even entered her yet.

"Yes, *yes* ...."

He eased his beautiful erection inside her, and she met him halfway, gasping with need. Jake tried to move slowly, but she urged him on until he lost control. She rode the wave along with him, caught up in his animalistic fervor. As he took her, he murmured against her neck, "My god, Chiara, *darling*, you feel so good, so tight ...."

Speech was beyond her, or so she thought, until she heard herself rambling in Italian, things like *"incredibile, amore mio,"* that she would surely regret. It was far too early to speak of love.

Then she was lost, drowning in sensation. The exquisite tension claimed her again, and she gratefully surrendered to its delightful tyranny.

Afterward they lay together, limbs entwined, like the lovers Philemon and Baucis turned into enjoined trees. Should she tell him she'd never found release with her husband? Or for that matter, by herself ....

CHAPTER 15

———•———

"HUNGRY? I CAN MAKE US supper."

He inwardly rolled his eyes. *Jake, you smooth talker.* After that—dare he say it—*transcendent* experience, he was seriously at a loss for words.

When you were easy on the eyes, well-behaved, but most of all, wealthy, willing women swarmed you like flies. Big Paul's female employees were off limits. Even if the number hadn't been so small, dating them was against company policy, not to mention tacky. Rory, a software engineer whose stock options had allowed him to retire at thirty-five with a bulging portfolio, loved playing Jake's wingman. An admitted extrovert, he had met women wherever he hung out—at bars, restaurants, the gym, the post office ... *heck,* the licensing bureau. Unlike Jake, Rory was easygoing and good-looking in an approachable way—a boy-next-door type with dark brown eyes, a stocky but solid build, and a thick shock of prematurely white hair. He enjoyed talking up strangers of any age and from all walks of life. Beautiful women especially, but not exclusively. The women Jake met through Rory were enthusiastic, but none held his interest for long. Most were okay with these casual encounters. But then Jake felt as if he were servicing them, or vice versa. One night of satisfying sex didn't seem worth the hassle.

With Chiara—an intelligent, creative, and educated woman he genuinely liked and respected—he felt dangerously vulnerable.

Jake gave her another light kiss, then held her flush against him, eyes shut as he breathed in her intoxicating essence. "Stay here," he whispered against her soft chestnut curls. "Shower, if you like, but not on my account.

You smell like heaven. There's a guest robe in the closet. Join me when you're ready."

He put on his own robe and headed downstairs, wishing he'd asked for her food preferences. In the end he opted for simple—smoked salmon with a lemon-butter-caper sauce, a green salad, and fresh angel-hair pasta with parmesan on the side. When she joined him a short while later at the kitchen counter, she was freshly showered and wearing the terrycloth guest robe. He observed, rather smugly, how her cheeks glowed.

"Our exploration was interrupted," she said. She giggled adorably, fingers covering her lips. "Of the house, I mean. I still haven't seen the attic."

"I hope you don't expect me to reveal everything all at once," he said. It was meant to sound playful, but then he thought of Rory and bit his tongue.

Fortunately she took his words in the flirty spirit they were offered. "*Bene. What you've shown me so far is very exciting.*" She ran her fingers down his back, and he closed his eyes, instantly responding to the light contact.

His male ego would have appreciated a few more strokes. *Give it time,* he thought.

There was a more pressing subject to discuss. He wanted assurance that he hadn't just cuckolded a candidate for sainthood—he didn't know whether to take Rory's snide remarks seriously. "Your husband …" he began, then stopped, waiting for her to pick up the thread.

"Arnold," she said, sitting heavily on a kitchen stool, shoulders slumped in defeat. The name didn't exactly roll off the tongue, and the way she uttered it put it on a par with "Adolf" or "Attila." As he poured the cooked pasta into the colander, she went on, "Our marriage is, how do I put this … to speak frankly … bad."

He exhaled with relief as he joined her at the counter.

"You may have noticed that he doesn't pressure me to return."

"I wondered."

"To be truthful, I haven't spoken to him since I left a message to say we arrived safely. He didn't call me back. I assume he is alive or I would have heard from his office. Unless I am no longer his emergency contact." She forced a smile.

Jake mixed the pasta with olive oil. "Parmesan?"

"Please."

He grated cheese over the top. Filling her wine glass, he said, "Have you discussed divorce?"

She looked down at her hands, clasped tightly before her on the counter. "Only in my head. We have separate bedrooms, and sometimes he visits mine. The arrangement suits him. He works long hours and supports us both. I maintain the household and raise Lorenzo. I believe he has another woman. He never stays out all night, but two or three in the morning is suspicious enough. I don't search his pockets. What purpose would that serve?" She raised her eyes to his. "Do I scare you?"

"Not at all. I don't want to appear unsympathetic, but you're telling me good news. Not the part about you being neglected. I'm just glad to confirm that Arnold doesn't deserve you and you don't feel beholden to him. Is Oregon a community-property state?"

"No, common law. I signed a prenuptial agreement, and Arnold is unkind to those who cross him. He would behave badly and make sure I walked away with as little as possible. He might even fight for custody of Lorenzo simply to punish me."

"Legally, he wouldn't have a leg to stand on. Lorenzo is your sister's son. Unless Arnold formally adopted him."

"No, he didn't. I am a trained therapist and social worker, but I haven't worked in some time. I let my certification expire. Arnold loses no sleep over me leaving."

"In our family, money is not a problem." It sounded like bragging. Jake had only meant that they could help. What, he was going to offer to support her after one session of mind-blowing sex? He really *was* losing his mind.

She regarded him gravely. "We won't discuss money. We are little more than strangers."

God, how he *hated* the idea that financial insecurity had trapped her in a stinker of a marriage.

They were both silent as they ate their supper. She dabbed at her lips and looked around. "This place …" she didn't finish.

"Yes?"

"Do you think it's haunted?"

"Yes," he said, matching her serious tone, "but then, you shouldn't listen to me."

"Why not?" She took another sip of wine.

If he held back the story of Rory's death much longer, he would turn blue in the face. He could just out with it and let the chips fall where they may. His family was panting to hear what had prompted him to upend his life and start over. But would they understand? Somehow he was sure Chiara would. And yet, he didn't want to break the spell of this magical evening. Also, where *was* Rory? The voice in his head rarely left him alone for so long.

"That's a subject for another time," he said. "Are you finished?" Removing her glasses, he leaned in for a deep kiss, then released her and headed toward the stairs. He turned to say, "You haven't seen all the bedrooms."

She giggled. "What, all of them?" In an instant, she was behind him, planting a kiss on his bare shoulder blade.

"Every single one. I need to prove my theory that no expense was spared in this place. Testing the mattresses is a good start. Admittedly, it's an ambitious undertaking. I need a second opinion."

She feigned gravity. "It's important for a hotelier to provide comfortable mattresses for his guests."

He laughed. "Is that what I am?"

"In my fantasy," she whispered, "I am the only guest, and this accommodation offers unique services. *Boutique* services. Very exclusive."

Jake swept her into his arms and carried her toward the first bedroom. This time there was no shyness, no hesitancy. He had opened the condom in advance and managed to slip it on, though they didn't make it to a bed, just the rug in the hallway. Giddily, he reflected that he was floored—*hah!*—by her sexual hunger. Still waters and all that. He could make love to her all night.

"What just happened?" he said as they lay panting in the hallway, naked limbs tangled together. He rolled to one side and brushed damp tendrils from her cheeks. "Are you okay?"

She winced a little. "I have an abrasion from the friction."

"Rug burn," he said, apologetic. "I tried to make it to the bed, but you had other ideas." He brushed her lips with his.

The grandfather clock struck eleven.

He squeezed his eyes shut, the full import of their actions finally sinking in.

"You have to go home," he said, helping her to her feet. "We'll need an excuse …. We decided to take a long walk and then grabbed dinner at, uh, what's that bistro called, the one by the theater?" He snapped his fingers, then remembered. "The Silver Bay Café. We ate at the bistro, then walked back here, and I gave you a tour. See? Partly true."

"What did I have for dinner?"

"Salmon," he said. "All the restaurants serve salmon. They'll suspect the truth, but they will *pretend* to believe you. That's the key. As long as you go home tonight. If you spend the night, they'll have no choice but to draw the correct conclusions."

"But I want to stay," she pouted. "Why pretend?"

He raked a hand through his hair. *Good question*, he thought. Mainly, because it was messy. Sleeping with someone's unhappy spouse was so … *sordid*. Not that Jake didn't know several marriages that had started that way. Marriages that ended when the cheater went on to cheat again. In those cases, the cheaters were men. He barely knew Chiara. But her inexperience was obvious. And he could swear that her climax had startled and delighted her, like a child with her first taste of cake.

Knowing the night had come to an end, they found their clothing and dressed.

"Jake?"

The fabric of her dress was seriously rumpled. "Can I iron that for you? You definitely look like you've had a roll in the hay."

Chiara laughed. "We have the same expression, *rotolare nel fieno*." With an impatient gesture at her dress, she said, "The wrinkles don't matter. I'll go straight to my cabin. You will drive me? They'll see me come in. The lies can wait until tomorrow."

He moved in for a kiss.

"Don't smudge my lipstick," she said, turning away abruptly so that the kiss landed on her neck.

"Regrets?" he said, pulling back.

"None. You?"

"Definitely not."

Her smile was brave, like Anne Boleyn anticipating the chopping block. He chided himself for being too dramatic. More like a teenager who had overstayed her curfew.

They drove to the compound in silence. He wanted to normalize the situation with small talk but drew a blank. When they reached the gate, it opened: they'd been watching for them. He didn't drive in, just let Chiara out, first grabbing her hand and kissing her palm. In the darkness, he couldn't read her expression. He idled the car until the lights came on in her cabin. It was midnight.

He should have told her not to bother with the lie. He suspected she was a terrible liar.

"Whaddya care, anyway?" Rory said, startling Jake as he backed up to turn around.

The car lurched as he hit a pothole. Rattled, he grumbled, "Where have you been?".

"Miss me?" Rory's dry laughter set Jake's teeth on edge. "Just givin' ya space. Don't want to bring on performance anxiety or anything. Couldn't have stopped you anyhow."

"She's in an unhappy marriage," Jake said in his own defense.

"Sure," Rory said, " 'cause that guy Arnold is one nasty sonovabitch."

"What do you know about it?"

"Ask her next time."

"Maybe there won't be a next time."

A noise like a Bronx cheer. "Are you kidding?"

Back at the house, Rory was silent again, and it occurred to Jake that his ghost had never spoken to him behind the closed doors of the sprawling Victorian. He couldn't begin to fathom what this, or any of it, meant. Would he and Chiara continue their furtive affair, knowing they weren't fooling anyone? How would that work, given that it would be up to her to initiate further contact? He couldn't just show up and park his car conspicuously outside the gate. She didn't have access to a car. Thanks to Lorenzo—her reason for being here—she felt compelled to account for her whereabouts. She could hardly claim to be shopping. Teresa had already overseen the purchase of a complete wardrobe. She also couldn't claim to be lunching with friends. What friends?

The next morning, the doorbell rang—an elaborate ditty like church bells—as the grandfather clock struck ten. Ever since the clocks had started chiming the hour and the half-hour again on their own, Jake had left them to it. At all the Victorian clanging, he half expected a visit from Sherlock Holmes.

He peered through the peephole at Liam, vital enough for three strapping young men. Played by Liam, Sherlock Holmes would have a whole new following.

"Hey," Jake said, throwing open the door. "Welcome to the *fin de siècle* according to Disney."

Liam scratched his head. "You mean like, uh, *Mary Poppins*? Wasn't *that* Disney? Now that you mention it …." He took in the front parlor as he wiped his feet on the welcome mat.

Liam was dressed more nattily than usual in cream-colored linen slacks and an unbuttoned black-linen shirt over his signature black T-shirt. Perhaps it wasn't a workday, even though the weather was sunny and mild. The guy rarely took a day off.

His brother-in-law was still assessing the interior, his gaze lingering on the array of naked and semi-naked statuettes. "I hear Teresa helped pack up some of the crap. I do like this one." His eyes lit on a slender ceramic nymph, pink nipples and all, holding a cut-crystal ball above her head. He chuckled. "I sense a theme here."

"A man gets inspiration where he can," Jake admitted with an unconcerned shrug. "Coffee?"

"Always." In the kitchen, Liam remarked, "Nothing Victorian about this room. Puts *my* kitchen to shame."

Once again Jake noted how Teresa's husband still referred to the house as "his" rather than "ours," but he let it slide. "Was Teresa disappointed that she didn't get to perform last night?"

"You know about that?" Liam grinned. "I thought you'd left by then."

"I was sitting outside. The grand finale was 'Being Alive,' right?"

"Yes. If it hadn't been for Jeremy's tour de force, the entertainment might have continued a bit longer. Teresa was relieved. She did *not* relish being compared to Reynard."

"I hear they dated."

Liam glowered. "If you can call it that."

"No love lost there, I see."

"The guy's a popinjay," Liam growled.

Jake considered the word. Did it really apply to Reynard? Was it conceited to volunteer to perform when you were a master of your craft? Some might call it magnanimous. Reynard didn't exactly preen, and his sartorial style was conservative and expensive, like Jake's. Once again he was being too literal.

Carrying their espressos on a tray along with a few Petit Beurre biscuits, Jake led them through the French doors into the garden, where they sat in the padded but uncomfortable wrought-iron chairs at the matching glass-topped table. A dining set from an old-fashioned ice cream parlor, maybe.

Jake wished Liam would get to the point. "Were you interested in a house tour, or did you have another reason for visiting?"

"She didn't stay over?" Liam asked.

"No. We took a walk, got some dinner, had a nightcap, then I drove her home."

Liam nodded. "Good to know the official story. Do you expect anyone to believe it?"

"No." Jake sipped his espresso.

"Great coffee, by the way."

"Only the best," Jake quipped.

Liam cleared his throat. "I'm not here to chew you out. Only to let you know we had a house guest last night."

Jake's mind was racing, though he remained outwardly calm. *Not Arnold, surely?*

Liam put him out of his misery. "George Reed Masters."

Jake released his breath in a *whoosh*. "No kidding? I thought he was on location."

"In Vancouver, B.C., not far away. Says he wanted to see the Peninsula … and meet you, of course."

Jake rubbed his throbbing temples. "How did you explain my absence?"

"Ali and Joe improvised. Said you had a migraine. He couldn't just check into a motel or a B and B, so he spent the night in our guestroom. He expects to stay with you tonight."

So much for finding a way to have Chiara back here …. "I was *not* expecting that," he admitted.

"Disappointed? I thought you wanted him to play Damon."

"I don't object to casting him. His presence alone could make the movie a smash hit." He paused. "Was that weird for Maddie? Weren't they naked together in that movie, *Insanity*?"

Liam shrugged. "Virtually … or so I'm told. I suppose we'll all find out when it's released in November."

"Wouldn't that be weird for you—if Teresa were naked in a movie with someone else?"

Liam bristled. "Hell, yes! I'd want to rip the guy's throat out. David didn't welcome him with open arms, but he didn't overreact, either. Hey, it's not like anything real happened between them."

"Must be confusing, though, being naked with a guy on a set. Or *pretending* to make love to a woman who looks like Maddie. So, what about Reynard? It didn't escape anyone's notice that you went over to talk to him. You're the only one who did."

The grin was back. "Reynard isn't going to make a second play for Teresa. She treated the famous, sophisticated Reynard like some greaser who expected her to put out after he covered her movie ticket. Anyway, he's got Lisette."

"The black-haired beauty? I kept thinking of that children's book, *The Black Stallion*. The long, muscular legs, the curly mane, the tossing head."

Liam gratified him with a hearty laugh. "I met her in Port Angeles, when I was prowling around trying to forget Teresa."

Jake arched his eyebrows. " 'Met' her?"

"Mae West's come-ons were subtler. If not for Teresa, I might have gone for it. I have a hunch she was a pro once."

"A 'pro,' as in call girl? Really? What does she do now?"

"Owns and manages Café Lisette—it features Cajun cuisine. Told me she's opening another one here. Or maybe relocating."

"She and Reynard must be serious. How did Teresa react to that news?"

"Didn't tell her. Teresa doesn't know I ever met Lisette, and I'd like to keep it that way."

Jake wondered if that was possible in a town this small. He'd seen the way Lisette looked at Liam, more like Bagheera the panther than Black Beauty the horse. Though, come to think of it, both those fictional animals were male. She exhibited the kind of straightforward, steely energy he tended to associate with men. He'd like to get to know her, if only as material for a character. Hard experience had taught him to avoid getting involved with such women. Was Lisette done trying to seduce Liam? Did a woman like that care if you were married? Men with pregnant wives could be especially vulnerable. Not Liam, naturally. On the other hand, Teresa was hardly showing yet, so how would Lisette know? At least Liam wore a wedding band. Not all men did.

Liam stood up. "You done brooding? We shouldn't keep Teresa waiting. It can't be easy to keep ol' George entertained."

"I hear he's charming," Jake said, still seated. "Aren't you afraid to leave her alone with him?"

"What? No." Liam's expression said the very idea was preposterous.

Jake suspected Liam had Teresa wrapped around his little finger. The guy had already hurt his sister enough. For their marriage to survive, a power shift might be in order.

CHAPTER 16

———•———

TERESA FUSSED ABOUT IN THE kitchen while George Reed Masters lounged on the back porch, skimming the Port Townsend *Herald* and glancing up every so often to take in the view of the bay.

"Not much news here," he remarked as Teresa joined him. She'd like to slap that sly grin off his face.

"We like it that way," she said, unaccountably offended. "Not that we aren't well informed. We read *Newsweek* and all. The Sunday *New York Times*." She didn't know why she felt compelled to defend their laid-back lifestyle to this guy. She guessed he avoided newspapers and magazines altogether, other than the ones that wrote about him.

The way he zeroed in on her was unnerving. Like he was delving into his mental bag of tricks for the most effective strategy to win her over. He was an actor, after all. Charm was an essential tool. He wasn't physically impressive to her—on the short side—but his looks were distinctive and unsettling. It was the eyes, the limbal rim of his irises so dark blue that the color rivaled Liam and Ali's. Then there was the shock of coarse black hair, the slash of dark brows, the winning grin. She'd seen several of his movies, enough to know how well those sharp features transferred to the big screen, and he had the kind of sleek, perfectly proportioned physique of a gymnast or a dancer. The hungry smile reminded her of Reynard; the body, of Kilo. She didn't trust either man as far as she could throw them.

He cocked his head, reminding her of a curious fox. "You don't seem like you belong in the sticks to me. I see you as more of a penthouse woman."

She was working up to an indignant sputter when he added, "You know, as in 'I just *adore* a penthouse view.' " She didn't appreciate suggestive banter from virtual strangers. Misinterpreting her silence, he said, "*Green Acres*, not the magazine."

Teresa closed her eyes briefly in a "give me strength" moment before saying, "Yeah, thanks, but I'm not *that* dense. I'm just trying to figure out why you think it's okay to be so cocky with me." *Jeez*, unfortunate word choice. She wished she'd said, "forward" instead.

"I apologize," he said with a smile that was both sheepish and wolfish. Or maybe foxy.

Teresa was suddenly hyperaware of how snugly her sundress fit her swollen breasts. She *really* needed to make that trip to Seattle to buy a maternity wardrobe. "Uh, I'm pregnant," she confessed, as if that would shut down the *Penthouse* thing.

"Yeah," he said. "I was pretty sure. Okay, maybe *Cosmopolitan*."

He was incorrigible. She summoned her frostiest tone. "You're on thin ice."

He leaned in. "So, what's your story?" When she took a step back, he finally got a clue. "Sorry," he said, hands raised in surrender. "I didn't mean to pry. I know I'm supposed to follow all these unwritten social rules, but I wasn't raised like that. Working class, all the way. Still and all, I recognize quality when I see it." His frankly admiring gaze remained fixed on her as he relaxed in the deck chair, fingers tapping the armrests. "I love this place," he said, shifting his laser-like focus to the bay. "I needed a break. That last movie made me want to check into an ashram … or maybe a psych ward."

It was then that she noted the shadows beneath his eyes, the fatigue that might be about more than physical exhaustion. And felt a twinge of pity. "What kind of movie is it?"

"A serial killer thing set in Seattle though filmed in Vancouver. It's cheaper that way."

"Are you the killer or the detective?"

"Oh, I'm *always* the good guy." His aw-shucks expression turned hard and cynical. "I'm told I have to wait until I 'age' a bit before they let me stop being the pretty boy romantic interest. I keep picturing a wheel of underripe camembert. The mirror tells me I'm getting riper by the day." Now he was frowning outright. "At least that role called for some real acting. Something more than swinging around like George of the Jungle, shooting people, jumping off buildings, and dangling by ropes from helicopters. This movie is more *noir*—you know, my character drinks and broods a lot. Wife murdered a year after they married."

To Teresa, it sounded like dozens of other movie plots. She resisted the urge to ask what was original about it—if anything. "Sounds kind of grim."

"Yeah." He sighed. "I'm still trying to throw it off. Sometimes I get too deep into character."

Teresa warned herself not to let her guard down. "Port Townsend is a good place to recover. That's why Liam and I got together. We were both licking our wounds."

"I don't see *your* wounds, but I do see evidence of your husband's. He's still one of the best-looking dudes, ever."

"He was in an explosion."

"I know the story," George confessed. "The gist of it, anyway. From the tabloids. He survived a terrorist attack in Jerusalem. Killed that guy who was stalking you."

Teresa flinched. "He didn't kill him. He was with us at the compound when that happened. All he did was scare the guy, rough him up a little."

George laughed. "My version makes for a better story. Wasn't he protecting you?"

"Yes."

"God, that's hot." George fanned himself. "Now *that* would make a great movie."

"*What* would make a great movie?" Liam said, looking from Teresa to George with a vaguely hostile air. Liam had this uncanny way of sneaking up on a person. She expected that of Liam, but Jake, who stood by his side, had been equally stealthy.

"Your love story," George Reed told him, gripping the arms of his chair like a jet plane passenger encountering unexpected turbulence. "Yours and Teresa's."

Teresa wasn't sure why her handsome husband had his hackles up. Did he really think this famous movie star was making a play for his bloated, pregnant wife?

* * *

Liam drew in a slow, calming breath. *You're not going to pound this guy. He wouldn't dare hit on Teresa, would he? Just let him try* …. He squared his shoulders and rolled his neck, then said in a deceptively calm voice, "Jake, meet George Reed Masters. George Reed, Jake O'Connell, AKA Dirk Fartherly, the elusive creator of Damon Morehouse."

The actor leapt to his feet, agile as a cheetah. "Call me George. Jake, I hope you're feeling better?"

Jake went blank but recovered quickly. For a minute Liam thought he'd forgotten his cover story. "Uh, yeah," he said, shaking George's hand with—Liam was pleased to observe—none of his usual bone-shifting firmness. Maybe he was getting over the corporate version of my-dick-is-bigger-than-yours. Jake flashed his formal, meet-the-public smile. "It's so great to meet you. I do get these weird migraines sometimes. Fortunately, they happen, uh, infrequently. Not sure what triggers them."

Liam smirked. *Raging lust. I know it well.* George's dark slash of brows, sharp features, and full lips reminded him of some B-list actor whose career started in the '50s .... *Ah,* George Hamilton in *All the Fine Young Cannibals,* one of the films Maya introduced him to.

The pregnancy had given Teresa the most glorious breasts Liam had ever seen—and they were pretty glorious to begin with. The dress barely contained them. He wanted to throw a blanket over her and force her to wear nothing but muumuus until she gave birth.

"I hear you met the rest of the clan," Jake said.

George bared a predicably flawless set of pearly whites. "All you studs would be shoo-ins for the remake of *Spartacus,*" he said with a snicker, "and your women would even turn heads at Cannes. That is some weird coincidence, Maddie being married to David. No mention of him when we were making *Insanity.* Wait till you see her in that movie. She will blow your socks off."

Liam exchanged a look with Jake that made him wonder if their thoughts were running along the same lines. Not the brightest star in the Hollywood firmament, but street smart, with a certain guy's-guy appeal. *Shit,* this was going to be Kilo all over again. Another Loki, a mischief maker, a fox in the henhouse. Still, didn't George have his own beautiful wife waiting in the wings?

Jake produced a semi-convincing chuckle. Liam could just picture him kissing up to some client he was pretending to like. "Maddie's a pistol," he said. "You should hear her sing."

George all but licked his lips. "Can't wait."

"Hey," Jake said, "why don't you bring your stuff over to my place and get settled in? Then the three of us guys can go to Kelpies for a late lunch. Best pub in town with a great view of the bay." He looked at his watch. "If we show up around two, we can sit on the deck."

George frowned. "Won't people recognize me?"

Liam laughed. "Nah, people here are cool."

Teresa raised a hand in warning. "I don't know. It took them a while to get used to Joe. Jake, it's hard for nobodies like us to fathom what it means to be a celebrity at the peak of popularity. Wouldn't it be safer if no one knew George was in town?"

Liam recalled his own annoying fortnight of notoriety, following the death of Teresa's stalker. Part of the reason no one hassled Liam was the fear factor. You didn't mess with a guy his size. George was a medium-height guy who appeared larger than life onscreen.

"George is super recognizable," Teresa went on, "with a large teenybopper fanbase. All I ask is that he tone it down a notch. A weird hat. Dark glasses at the very least."

George shrugged. "I have stuff like that. I'll be mellow as a manatee."

Liam frowned. *Mellow* was the last word you'd use to describe George. More like peppy as a porpoise. The guy had to be ninety percent fast-twitch muscles. From Teresa's expression, she didn't buy it either. "All right," she said, "it's your funeral. Don't forget that Joe and Ali expect us around six thirty for dinner. Jean-Louis is in town, and his restaurant is catering."

"Becca too?" Liam asked.

George shuffled his feet. "That sounds like a crowd."

"It'll be fun, you'll see," Jake said. "Their place is a hoot. Like an adult theme park. Teresa, want to come with us to lunch?"

She summoned a tight-lipped smile. "I'll pass. George, it's been, uh, real."

"Likewise." The guy had the gall to kiss her hand. Liam had to bite his tongue to keep from ordering her to change for dinner.

* * *

Jake watched, amused, as George blinked at the ornate electric blue exterior of the rental Victorian. "Jeez, I'm wearing shades, and that place still hurts my eyes," he joked, briefly shielding the lenses of his sunglasses.

"No kidding," Jake said with a smile.

"I never would have pegged you for—"

"Stop right there," Jake interrupted him. "It wasn't my first choice. I wanted a place in town, and this was all that was available. Although I have to admit, it's growing on me. I sleep really well here." *No Rory*, he added silently. His friend had been plaguing him with a running commentary while they were at Liam's. Rory had a few choice words to describe George Reed Masters, among them "putz," "dickhead," and "weasel."

As they crossed the threshold, George lost his footing and had to steady himself on Jake's shoulder. "Uh, sorry. Damn! Tripped on something." He looked around, searching for the culprit. Then he rubbed his arms. "Is it me, or is it cold in here? He pointed to a lamp with two bare-breasted shepherdesses standing back-to-back. "This is a B and B? For couples only, maybe. You wouldn't want Junior to be exposed to stuff like that."

Jake laughed. "I can turn up the heat. As for the décor, when I first moved in, this room was cluttered with collectables. I packed everything up and left only the nude and semi-nude figurines. They were originally hiding behind teddy bears and needlepoint cushions."

George smirked at him. "Nice."

"You can have the third floor to yourself," Jake said as they climbed the stairs.

When they reached the attic room, George whistled. "Great view." He took his time studying the two portraits. "Who are these guys? They look like someone put salt in their tea."

Jake squinted at the portraits. "Funny, they looked less dyspeptic this morning. And their eyes only move occasionally." Seeing that George appeared genuinely freaked, he rushed to reassure him. "Uh, just kidding. You don't believe in ghosts, do you?"

"Not generally," George hedged.

Sun beamed through the sash windows, casting flickering quadrilateral shadows on the sloped wall. *What a great painter's studio this attic would make*, Jake thought. He imagined the light would be special whether cast by the sun or a kerosine lamp. Aside from the master bedroom where Jake slept, the attic suite had probably been the most expensive to rent. The king-size canopy bed was draped with royal-blue velvet curtains, and the overstuffed, black velvet upholstered chair with claw feet was positioned to take in the view. Other than the two small portraits of the stern ancestors who appeared to be posing under protest, two large landscapes were the perfect size to fill the non-sloping wall adjacent to the row of windows. They were unsigned. The one on top depicted a stormy ocean with a ship battling the waves. Directly beneath was a painting of a busy American Indian village. Neither was the work of amateurs. Jake wondered if they'd been appraised. When he'd tried calling the owners the other day, he'd reached an answering machine message saying they were traveling in Europe. He opened the adjoining door to find a smaller room with a single bed and nightstand. A servant's room? Didn't really make sense. He would have expected three small attic bedrooms for servants, not a luxurious one next to a cubbyhole the size of a walk-in closet.

In the nineteenth century, closets were tiny and a novelty. Jake was no expert, but he imagined most people stored their clothing in armoires and their small clothes—otherwise known as underwear—and linens in chests and dressers.

His guest startled him by asking in a stagy whisper, "Whaddya think that's all about?" as he jutted his chin toward the single bed that took up most of the tiny room.

Jake scratched his head. "I was wondering the same thing. I'd love to know the history of this place. I haven't been able to reach the owners. My imagination runs wild."

"Any guesses?"

"A few, but you have to sleep here, so I'll keep them to myself." He couldn't resist poking fun at George. His famous houseguest was weirdly jittery, as if already convinced he was going to meet George C. Scott's character's fate in *The Changeling*. He checked his watch. "We'll meet Liam and walk down to lunch around two. That gives you a few hours to rest."

"Uh, what will you do while I, uh, *rest*?"

"Thought I'd go for a run."

An audibly breathless George asked, "Can I come along?"

Jake gave him a surprised double take. It might be a trick of the light, but the guy had paled a shade or two.

"Uh, sure. As long as you don't mind hills. I like to jog to Fort Warden and back. My usual route is about six miles."

"Whatever," George muttered, gazing around the room as if the walls had eyes.

He'd wager George would swim a mile in the bay to avoid being left alone here. Should Jake move him down a floor? *Okay, George,* he thought wickedly, *admit that the attic is freaking you the hell out, and I'll let you off the hook. Otherwise ....*

"Meet you downstairs in ten minutes," Jake said aloud.

Smiling to himself, he loped down to his bedroom to change. Was he a bad person for wanting to see how George's night in the attic played out? Nah, he was just taking a page out of Liam's book.

CHAPTER 17

JAKE DROVE THEM ALL TO the compound in his BMW. Matthew, no Jeremy in tow, sat in the passenger seat. The matchup must have been a bust—no surprise.

Teresa was wedged between Liam and George in the back seat. Liam looked like a prisoner in transport. Teresa—pregnancy forcing her to abstain from alcohol—would take the wheel going home. The alcohol did tend to flow at Joe and Ali's parties, and Jake was looking forward to sampling more amazing wines from their incredible cellar—stocked by Teresa, an expert on California varietals. With five people in the car, it was a tight fit, and he could just imagine that George was enjoying the enforced proximity with his lovely sister, still wearing the same too-snug-in-a-delightful-way sundress. She'd explained to Jake that her clothing options were limited until she had a chance to shop for a maternity wardrobe. He hoped Liam understood that. Judging from her husband's thunderous expression—George appeared clueless— Teresa had to be aware of the divisive impact of her exposed cleavage.

"Georgie Porgie," Rory grumbled in his head, "kissed the girls and made them cry."

Rory, please *let me concentrate on my driving. I get it—you don't like him. But while I have your attention, why can't you talk to me in the house?*

No response.

George had been a pleasant companion on their run, keeping pace without getting winded and limiting the chitchat. He'd also been on best behavior at Kelpies. Baseball cap and sunglasses notwithstanding, he'd attracted a few speculative looks from patrons, maybe because everyone noticed Liam, and they'd never seen him with this guy. No one commented on the resemblance to George Reed Masters.

The actor was in high spirits, oblivious to Liam's dark mood and dominating the conversation. That was good because Jake wasn't up to playing host. He couldn't simultaneously drive, keep the conversation flowing, and field his dead buddy's snarky comments.

"I love this town," an amped-up George was saying. "The Victorian houses, the waterfront, the boatyard … all the cool history. It must be so great at Christmas."

"The weather might get to you," Liam remarked in a flat voice. "It's not warm like in L.A. Not cold, either, but a lot of cloudy days."

"I've only been based in L.A. for five years," George said, unperturbed by Liam's sullenness. "I grew up in Southern Washington on the coast. Weather's similar."

When Liam didn't reply, Matthew asked with friendly interest, "Which town?" From what Jake had observed, Matthew was ever the peacemaker.

"Seaview," George replied.

"Near Fort Canby," Matthew said. "My family used to camp there every summer."

"Yeah, my dad ran a motel," George said. With a sardonic edge, he added, "Good times."

Was it a bid for sympathy? Jake thought so. Matthew chatted about the beach, and how they'd fished on the jetty and collected Japanese fishing floats. The light conversation filled the time until they reached the compound.

* * *

Maddie had been dreading this evening. She wore one of her more modest sundresses, wishing she could borrow something from Chiara's shapeless Portland wardrobe for maximum coverage. Only, that would be a dead giveaway. Might as well scream, "Something happened with George in Hollywood!" It didn't, but not for lack of effort on his part. He'd suggested that the half-naked kissing and theatrical humping would be a lot easier if they did it for real first. At the time, he'd been newly married to Helena Richards, a blonde beauty and a star in her own right, the daughter of Oscar-winning director Harrison Richards. Thank God he'd taken no for an answer.

She didn't detest George. He'd helped her dodge Henry Makos, a notoriously sleezy but powerful producer. In the end, even though George had pretended they were an item, Henry had cornered her. She figured her rejection had doomed her movie career. Surprisingly, it hadn't. She'd been offered other parts, all involving maximum nudity and minimal dialogue. So she fired her agent. David had also quit his job as a general practitioner at the clinic in Sequim, and now they were both … what … on a permanent honeymoon? Oh well, only a month had passed since their wedding day, and they hadn't been home for long. There would be time enough to plot the future. Money was no object. David and each of the O'Connells had personal fortunes that could finance the whims of several generations. David had bought the Sea Captain's House from Joe without batting an eyelash.

As the contingent from town drove up, Maddie stood at her husband's side, smiling and silent. Matthew …. Would he be irked when Jeremy arrived? Matthew was just what Jeremy needed, a grounded lover to pull the flighty actor down to earth. Liam looked pissed off, and Maddie could guess why. She should have warned them about George's compulsive flirting. Why would Liam waste energy on such an obvious lightweight? If anyone should feel unsteady in their relationship, it was Teresa. Liam had been the one to leave *her*, if only for a short time. Jake had his usual air of distraction. Ali had pronounced him "calculating." Not that Maddie could see. He seemed comfortable enough in his own skin, just preoccupied, as if weighing the effectiveness of some plot point in one of his thrillers. She did see him scan the crowd—for Chiara, no doubt. Their mysterious visitor was still in her cabin. Chiara had not confided in the rest of them as to her whereabouts following Matthew's party, forcing them to swallow her indigestible story of "taking a walk with Jake and going to dinner."

Jean-Louis emerged from the kitchen, where he'd been overseeing his minions from FOSSP, and made his usual splashy entrance, crackling with energy, gesturing broadly, *delighted* to meet George. Becca wore a frilly, hot-pink number with matching pumps. She looked vibrant and festive, ready to dance the samba on a hilltop in Rio de Janeiro. George, in turn, was *enchanted* to meet them … or had the grace to appear enchanted. Nothing any actor worth his salt couldn't pull off.

She joined Matthew at the terrace bar, where he was helping himself to a drink. "No Jeremy tonight?" he asked, surprising her.

"I did invite him," she confessed. "He said he'd try to make it. He's been babysitting his new nephew. That's his gig until something better comes up."

"With his talent," Matthew said, "he must have other options."

Maddie scanned the group to make sure Jeremy hadn't arrived without her noticing. "He's enjoying a hard-earned rest."

"You guys are close?" Matthew asked.

"Yes. Granted, he can be a bit much until you get to know him. Even after. But I adore him. He's brilliant and hysterically funny. I think, if he weren't so beautiful, he'd be a huge star. He's got the personality of a comic sidekick and the looks of a leading man. And in Hollywood, being 'out' definitely makes it more difficult to get hired as the romantic lead. It's easier in musical theater. Sure, he could do another national tour of some Broadway show. He wants to do a TV series where he can stay put. Pilot season didn't work out."

Matthew gazed up the hill where the guys were gathering around the target. "First the pilot would have to be picked up, then it would need to last more than one season. Seems like an unrealistic goal." He paused. "Listen, I'm going to watch the knife-throwing contest. See you later?"

Hmm, maybe he and Jeremy had a chance after all.

She was just about to follow when she heard, "Hey, Maddie" behind her and jumped. George had sneaked up on her.

"Uh, hi, George. Enjoying your stay in Port Townsend?"

She might as well say, "Welcome to Fantasy Island."

"Uh, yeah. What's with the safari tent?" He pointed. "I was just heading over to investigate." In an amusing accent, he added, "Come weeth me to za Kasbah?"

Maddie managed a tight smile. No way was she following him into a closed tent. She pointed at the gathering of men on the hill. "You don't want a knife-throwing lesson?"

He laughed. "I don't do my own stunts. The insurance company wouldn't let me even if I wanted to." He was already starting toward the tent, crooking a finger for her to follow like a molester luring a child to his car. Still, what was he going to do, make a pass at her in shouting distance of the house? David could take him out with one punch.

Reluctantly, she followed. "My husband spent five years with Doctors for Humankind in Africa," she explained. "He's also a fan of adventure stories set in Colonial Africa."

George grinned knowingly. "Ah! That's what Jake meant by the 'adult theme park' quip."

Maddie frowned. Had Jake been making fun of David?

"So … you and David. That was quick."

They entered the tent and stood two feet apart as the gauzy curtains floated in the ocean breeze. One inch closer and she might have slapped him.

"Or were you already engaged when we were filming and just didn't mention it?"

"Something like that," she lied. At the time she and David had been circling each other warily, neither willing to take a definitive step toward declaring their feelings. "I didn't think my personal life was relevant."

George made no attempt to close the gap. He'd assumed a sexy-cowboy stance, like James Dean in *Giant*, one knee bent and thumbs hooked in the pockets of his expensive jeans. The light blue Western shirt, cowboy boots, and leather belt with big silver buckle added to the illusion.

"Is David the reason we didn't make it?"

"Make it? As in, 'go all the way'?" She didn't bother to hide the mocking subtext. *Jesus*, they weren't horny teenagers. "Uh, you were married … *are* married."

He snorted. "You must not keep up on industry gossip."

She took a reflexive step backward. "You're divorced *already*?" She hadn't meant to sound shocked.

"Marry in haste …" he quoted from the proverb, implying that she'd also married hastily and must regret it. "You're not pregnant?"

She planted her feet. She was done being polite. "Uh, George, that's a rather personal question *on such short acquaintance*. No, I am *not* pregnant."

Undaunted, he asked, "What about your career? Are you gonna chuck a chance at superstardom for your Indiana Jones wannabe over there?"

"That film took place in Egypt."

"Among other locations. Northern Africa, Southern Africa, whatever." He looped his forefinger in the air, trying to get her up to speed.

"I'll have you know that David is a highly skilled doctor." *Jeez*, he'd goaded her into full high dudgeon. She'd never, *ever* used the phrase "I'll have you know" before.

"Who's not doctoring."

"*At the moment.*" The words were shards of ice.

"Now that I have you spitting toads and snakes"—his reference to the obscure fairytale startled her out of her fit of pique—"give it a rest and allow me to make it clear just how much I respect you as an actress. Your screen presence is, well, explosive. I've seen a rough cut of *Insanity*, and the movie just barely survives your character's murder. They've used every bit of footage of you, sprinkled it throughout as flashbacks. If they could, they'd call us all back and expand your role. But the other actors have moved on, including me."

He might as well have doused her with his drink. Every last bit of footage? Maddie's magnified naked body parts peeking through in every scene of the movie? How would she ever live that down?

"It would be a crime for you to retire now. David isn't the prince of Monaco. You could still have a career."

Becca and Ali appeared out of nowhere, and Maddie hoped she didn't look guilty. "Hey, guys," she said with a big smile. At least she and George were now several feet apart. He'd known better than to counter her retreat.

Ever the actor, George quickly hid his annoyance at the interruption.

Maddie introduced George to Becca, who greeted him warmly. "Becca is married to Jean-Louis," Maddie explained, "the owner of the wild-game restaurant here in town and two more, in Bellevue and North Bend, uh, a suburb of Seattle."

"You're talking about La Fête Sauvage." George was just full of surprises. "My movie *The Last River Game* was filmed partly in North Bend, so I spent a few weeks there once."

"Where did you grow up?" Ali asked.

"In Seaview, on the Pacific Coast."

"Seaview," Ali repeated. "Do you know Tokeland? Joe and I were married at the hotel there."

"Sure," he said. "My dad owned and managed a motel. Isn't the Tokeland Hotel a little, uh, *modest* for a celebrity wedding?"

"Ali and Joe aren't your typical celebrities," Becca explained.

"Obviously not." George spread his arms wide. "I love this place. It's got a great feeling. Peaceful."

Becca laughed. "Careful. Rumor has it that it's the Hotel California. You know, you can never leave."

George screwed up his nose. "What was that song about? Like, why couldn't they leave? I always thought it was some haunted house thing. Like in *Poltergeist*. Was this place built on a sacred burial ground?"

"I think *Hotel California* was about drug addiction," Becca said.

"Or maybe an addictive woman," George tossed an admiring glance Becca's way, then fixed his gaze on Ali with the same masculine appreciation. "You all are just so easy on the eyes. I can see why no one wants to leave."

Ali cleared her throat, and in the polite but formal tone of a nurse summoning a patient to the doctor's office, said, "We actually came over to tell you that dinner is served."

Maddie smiled at the way Ali had managed to wipe the grin off the cheeky actor's face.

But George was hard to resist. By the time they reached the flagstone terrace, even Maddie had realized the futility of trying to hold him to recognized standards of adult behavior.

CHAPTER 18

———•———

WHEN CHIARA SLUNK OUT AT breakfast, they were all lounging on the terrace as if trying to hide the fact that they were staging an intervention. *So silly*, she thought. *They don't care. Guilt has made you paranoid.* She couldn't meet their eyes, much less blow smoke in them. She might as well be wearing a hair shirt. They were dressed in sweaters and jeans against the morning chill and stiff ocean breeze. Another gloriously blue sky dotted by a few wispy clouds.

They greeted her cheerfully, as if nothing had changed. They had guessed the truth and weren't inviting her to lie. She did anyway.

"I'm sorry about last night," Chiara began, the loudness of her voice startling in the attentive silence as if she'd wandered into an acoustic shell. "Jake and I needed to take some air, and then it was dinnertime, and we found ourselves next to Silverwater Café. We got to talking, and our time flew by so fast." *Uff, that was a tongue twister*, she thought, wishing she'd let them ignore her indiscretion.

"I'm glad you're getting to know Jake," Ali said, forcefully cheerful. "He obviously has depths I never guessed at."

"Or he experienced some life-changing event," Joe commented from behind the Book Review section of yesterday's Sunday *New York Times*. He put the paper down and took off his reading glasses. "I'm confident that David will get him to open up."

David, nose buried in *Newsweek*, blew a raspberry. "Don't hold your breath."

To Chiara's ears, their delivery had a staged quality. They might have

144

been reciting lines in a drawing room comedy. But she had worried for nothing. The subject was closed.

Joe headed for his studio, Ali and Maddie went to the nursery to play with the twins, and David came to help Chiara and Lorenzo construct his Legos pirate ship—a new fixation, ever since his father had started reading him *Treasure Island*. After lunch, Chiara resumed the saga of Beverly Bigfoot, knowing that tonight's dinner party would preempt their bedtime ritual. Her audience consisted of Maddie and David and Joe and Ali, each cuddling a toddler. Chiara still couldn't tell the twins apart.

Lorenzo often challenged her when she altered a detail. Sometimes he objected to a plot development that violated his child's sense of logic or justice. The adults enjoyed Lor's interruptions almost as much as the story. They laughed so heartily that the twins gurgled and smiled too.

The current chapter featured Slinky the Deer Mouse, who had written a play. Her leading actor was Orson the River Otter, and rehearsals were not going well. " 'How can I set up a show with you darting this way and that?' " she said in Slinky's squeaky voice. " 'You are terrible at taking direction.' But Orson was a bad listener. He kept sliding around in the mud, chasing his tail. Squeaky pointed the second of the four toes of her front paw in Orson's face and cried, 'Pay attention!' "

"Do you mean 'put on' a show?" Ali suggested in her kind way.

"Yes, of course," Chiara said with an apologetic smile. With creatures who communicated mostly through telepathy, it would have to be one very strange play.

"Why is Slinky pointing with her toes?" Lorenzo asked. "Doesn't she have fingers?"

"She has only toes," Chiara explained, "though on her front paws, they look like fingers. Only four, with claws instead of nails. No thumbs."

Ali smiled. "Someone's done her homework."

From the coffee table, Chiara picked up an oversized book called *Animals of the Olympic National Park*. "Your library is an excellent resource."

"I'm glad," Ali said. "I can't wait to draw Slinky pointing a threatening claw at Orson."

"They are short claws," Chiara said, "for gripping food and climbing. Mice don't threaten. Mostly they run away."

"What kind of play is it?" Joe asked with a sly smile. "Slinky's a girl, right? If they're doing some cheesy rom-com, you can hardly blame Orson for getting bored."

"Joe ...." Ali drew out his name and rolled her eyes. "If you want to get technical, we'll have to question how a squeaking mouse can communicate with a grunting otter."

"Actually," Chiara said, "otters squeak too. But mostly they make a sound like 'ha-ha-ha-ha-ha-ha-ha.'"

Everyone began to imitate her, including Lorenzo. "We sound like the Beavis and Butt-Head Appreciation Society," Ali laughed.

Chiara tilted her head at them, mystified. *Who, or what, are Beavis and Butt-Head?* she thought. *Such strange names.*

"I'm just saying," Ali went on, "that it all demands a certain suspension of disbelief. If Lor's okay with it, we should be too. And Orson's an enlightened otter. He'd be totally fine with a cheesy rom-com."

"But what if Orson doesn't like cheese?" Lorenzo asked with genuine concern. "I can see that Slinky would like cheese, 'cause she's a mouse."

"Everyone likes cheese," David said. "Though unless Beverly Bigfoot knows an obliging cow or a goat, cheese is bound to be scarce in those parts."

"You can probably milk a black-tailed doe," Ali said, "especially if you're a female bigfoot. In Finland they milk reindeer."

"What's a rom-com?" Lorenzo persisted.

"A romantic comedy," Ali told him. "It's a funny story where two people fall in love."

"Two people," Lorenzo repeated. "Can they be men?"

Joe and David almost choked. "Why, yes," Joe said, grinning. Ali and Maddie were wiping away tears of laughter. Chiara wasn't sure what to tell him. Wasn't Lorenzo too young to hear an explanation of same-sex relationships? But Lorenzo accepted the answer with a simple nod.

"Anyway," Chiara continued, smiling, "the play is *not* a cheesy rom-com. It's an adventure story about buried treasure."

"Who buried it?" Lorenzo asked. A smile crept across his face. "Pirates?!"

"Ah, Charlie Chipmunk," Chiara improvised. There was no Charlie Chipmunk, but she hoped Ali wouldn't mind drawing him. "He's good at burying things."

"What did he bury? Nuts aren't valuable," Lorenzo reasoned.

"I don't know," Ali said. "Last I checked, pine nuts cost a pretty penny."

"These are not pine nuts," Chiara said, narrowing her eyes at Ali. "Those pine trees don't grow in the rain forest. These are special nuts, very rare."

"What kind is that?" The child was relentless.

"I have to save something for next time." Chiara sighed. She was not in good form today, her brain still muddled by fevered memories of warm lips and roaming hands.

"Won't Charlie be mad if someone else claims his treasure?" Lorenzo asked.

"He doesn't remember where he put it either," Chiara said. "And if they find it first, he's happy to share. He's an unusually magnanimous fellow."

Lorenzo's brows flew together. "Mag-nan-i-*mouse*? But he's the chipmunk, not the mouse."

"Magnani*mous*," Chiara said. "It means generous. His mother taught him it is better to give than receive. A lesson you know already."

Uff. Chiara was exhausted. "I think this chapter could use some work," she told Ali.

Ali chuckled. "A few tweaks, maybe. But we're enjoying every minute of it."

Fortunately, after story time, David took Lorenzo and the dogs to Fort Warden, allowing Chiara to escape to her cabin for a nap. She quickly fell into a deep sleep.

It was past six, time for Chiara to come out of hiding. She took a deep breath, squared her shoulders, and walked down the hill. The men, along with Teresa, were gathered around the knife target again. No sign of Ali, Maddie, or Becca.

Only one man looked up as she approached. And kept looking. Jake's avid stare was at once disconcerting and reassuring. She breathed a sigh of relief. Clearly he wanted more than one night's adventure. She'd worried that once he'd had her, he'd move on, considering her complicated life.

She wandered into the Sea Captain's House—they still prepared big feasts in the kitchen there—to find Jean-Louis shouting orders to the small crew of sous-chefs. Seeing that she would be *in mezzo*—underfoot?—she returned to the terrace. Jake was waiting for her.

"Where are the other women?" She tried to appear calm and tranquil, but as he handed her a glass of white wine, her hand shook and the wine spilled.

Jake pretended not to notice. In a low, urgent voice, he said, "We won't be alone for long, and I need to clarify something. George Reed Masters—the movie star—is staying at my house, I'm not sure for how long." She nodded. "After he leaves, I want you to join me. If that's what you want, too, of course."

"How would I get there?" she whispered.

"I'd come for you," he whispered back, "any time of day or night."

"The others—"

His gesture dismissed her objection. "—are not fooled. They aren't going to intervene or do something rash like contact Arnold."

A silky male voice interrupted them. "I haven't had the pleasure." It had to be the movie star, because he was the only person Chiara hadn't met, and he looked like someone who would magnify nicely on a big screen. In person he suffered by comparison to the other men—she'd never seen a more robust group. He was more beautiful than handsome, and distinctive: full lips, deep-set eyes, strong eyebrows, and a long, somewhat pointed nose.

"I'm Chiara," she said.

"Chiara. Just one name, like Madonna?"

She smiled, mostly to be polite. "Exactly. Only, I'm not famous or talented."

He laughed. She didn't know where that impudent comment had come from.

"I do have a last name. It's Conti, I mean Jeffreys. Chiara Conti Jeffreys."

Why had she given him her maiden name first? Was she already thinking of herself as divorced?

"Are you Italian? I hear an accent."

"Yes," she said, hoping short answers would make him go away.

"How do *you* fit in here?" George persisted.

Ali came to the rescue. "Chiara is a family friend, visiting from Portland. She's sister to the mother of Lorenzo, David's son."

George looked flummoxed, as if Ali had given him a complicated equation to solve. Given only *that* explanation, Chiara might have been confused too. But George didn't ask for clarification. "How long are you staying?" he asked Chiara. "I hear this place has the gravitational pull of a black hole." At Ali's reproving look—mild, as if he were a naughty child—he added, "Just kidding. Make that Shangri-La."

"Better."

"Camelot?"

"Not if that makes me Guinevere." Ali was smiling now.

"Ooh, I'd love to play Guinevere," Maddie jumped in. "In the musical. It's a great role."

"I could totally see you in that part," George said. He was looking at Maddie as if imagining her naked, not dressed as King Arthur's queen. This George was *un Lotario*, a lady killer, annoying to all the men, not only David. Now that his attention was back on Maddie, Chiara saw Jake's shoulders relax.

The arrival of Maddie's friend Jeremy created a welcome diversion.

Apparently he had played a surprisingly convincing, if unusually tall, Titania in Shakespeare's *A Midsummer Night's Dream.*

For the rest of the evening, Chiara and Jake were never alone. George regaled them all with funny stories from his movie career. She noticed that he was careful not to mock his fellow actors. He spoke of on-set mishaps, poorly trained animals, and a storm they "weathered" in the Bahamas. He shared an amusing anecdote about an older actor who gave him advice. "I won't name names," George said, "but this one really famous guy told me, 'It's not musical theater, son. Keep a lid on it.' That was hilarious, coming from him, a notorious mumbler. I didn't bother to tell him I'd never done musical theater."

She committed to memory "keep a lid on it," which seemed to mean maintain control. She liked adding new idioms to her repertoire.

"So," Jean-Louis said, "how did you find your way to Hollywood? Did they discover you in an ice cream shop like Lana Turner?"

"I was twelve," George replied. "A crew came to town to film *The Rumble*—maybe you've heard of it? The movie based on that hit young-adult novel? I was an extra. The director saw me and gave me a few lines. In his next film, he cast me as one of the leads. From then on, it was one movie after another. I had to be home-schooled. But come on, enough about me."

"Not at all," Jean-Louis said. "We are starved for the company of someone who is out in the world. Especially someone as talented and famous as you."

George did appear to be modest, for such a big star. He laughed. "Ah, come on. It's all luck. I'm certainly not the handsomest guy in Hollywood or even in this place"—they all joined in on the laughter—"but the camera does seem to like me."

"Uh, George," Maddie intervened here, "you must have an entire mantel stacked with industry awards that have little to do with luck." The actor must know that his everyman act fooled no one.

Chiara watched Jeremy and Matthew drift to the far side of the terrace and become absorbed in a private conversation, wishing she and Jake could do the same. She smiled, recalling Lorenzo's question about two men falling in love. Becca and Ali also stood apart, whispering back and forth with a conspiratorial air. The rest of them gave George their full attention, laughing in all the right places. Jean-Louis and Maddie kept the questions coming. It was like an episode of *Inside the Actors Studio.*

Joe and George commiserated about the tabloids, Joe assuring him that they had an effective security system. The dogs, lying on cushioned beds nearby, lifted their heads and whined at the mention of "security," which made everyone laugh.

"Don't worry," George insisted. "No one even knows I'm in the area."

Joe raised a skeptical eyebrow. "Don't jinx it. That's like saying, 'I haven't been sick for months.' You'll definitely wake up tomorrow with a fever."

* * *

Jake enjoyed George's showbiz talk, even though Rory said, "Gimme a break! It's well-rehearsed schtick. You all are easy enough to read. He assumed the role most likely to win you over."

No point in contradicting Rory—it only encouraged him.

Jake kept stealing glances at Chiara, also content to listen. *Patience, man*, he told himself. *You've already told her that after George leaves, you'll be at her disposal day and night. But damn, she's so well mannered. She might be afraid to inconvenience you or something.*

At lunch that day, Jake suspected the crowd at Kelpies had caught on. Why else the surreptitious glances and the woman photographing the view just behind George?

The party was breaking up. Jean-Louis headed to the kitchen to supervise the cleanup, and Ali and Becca went to the nursery to check on the twins and Lorenzo, who tonight would stay at the Log Palace so May and Susan could watch him.

Earlier, puffed up with paternal pride, David had shown Jake Lorenzo's newly remodeled bedroom—a young pirate's dream. *Nothing like that in any of our childhoods*, Jake thought. A jolly roger flag, a vintage wooden foot locker with a domed lid, a hammock, and a pirate ship preassembled from a model. It looked handcrafted. Jake kept expecting the dogs' tails to knock it over. But those dogs were surprisingly graceful, like dancers in dog suits. Chiara had told him that in Portland, Lor lived simply. David was doing his utmost to change that. Was that wise? David wouldn't hear boo from Jake.

David has also purchased two lightweight digital video cameras so he and Joe could document their kids' childhoods. They were latecomers to the camcorder craze. But then, their family had always been slow to embrace technology.

Teresa jingled the car keys in his face. "Wanna leave? I'm pooped."

Her pallor worried Jake. "Of course."

Liam immediately rose to join them. "George, Matthew? Our caravan awaits."

On the way home, the conversation was patchy. Everyone but Teresa and Jake seemed to be in a wine-induced stupor.

Back at the house, George collapsed on the couch in the main parlor and fixated on a particular figurine of a semi-nude water nymph leaning over a pool. "Is that a bud vase?" he asked. Then, "Got anything to drink?" He looked totally drained, like someone had stuck a pin in him.

"Espresso?" Jake said helpfully.

George gave him the hairy eyeball.

Although George needed more alcohol like a fish needed air, Jake held up a bottle of very expensive cognac—Hine Antique XO Premier Cru. His guest perked up when he handed the bottle over for his approval. "It's not Louis-the-Thirteenth," Jake added with a careless shrug, "but *I* like it."

George barked out a laugh. "Hah! Wasted on me. I wouldn't know 'cru' from 'crude.' "

Jake took back the snifter. "In that case, I'll get the cheap stuff."

George made a gimme gesture. "Come on, hand it over. It's not like the good stuff was mother's milk to me, but even I know rotgut when I taste it."

Jake sat in the chair opposite. "No rotgut here."

Assuming a posh British accent, George said, "Perish the thought." In his own voice, he added, "You'd make a great character, ya know. You're good at hiding what's going on in that noggin of yours. Your family … not so much. I figured out a few things."

Jake raised his eyebrows as he took a sip.

George smacked his lips in appreciation. Mirroring Jake's nonchalant body language, ankle resting on his knee, he said, "You and Chiara have got something going, all very hush hush but obvious to one and all." Jake's jaw clenched, and George reacted with a defensive palm up. "Why not? She's a peach. No judgment. Liam and Teresa have been through some rough shit, and my presence in 'his' home wasn't helping. David and Maddie know each other only slightly better than contestants on a dating show, and Joe is nuts about Ali, but he'd like a little of his old life back."

Jake was surprised and unaccountably miffed by George's simplistic assessment of their family's couple dynamics. He lurched to his feet, drunker than he'd realized. "You'll have to excuse me, George. I'm gonna turn in." He put aside his unfinished drink. "Stay put as long as you like. Help yourself to whatever appeals." Though a little bleary himself, Jake noticed that George appeared pale and hollow-eyed. "Everything okay?"

George wrinkled his nose in distaste. "This place gives me the creeps."

"Don't worry," Jake assured him. "No malevolent spirits, cross my heart."

"What about the other kind? I'd kind of like to avoid them too."

"Ever seen a ghost?"

"You?" George countered. "Wanna tell me what's eating you alive?"

What was it with this guy? It was a ballsy question coming from a shallow movie star Jake had known for about a minute.

"When I was sixteen," George went on, "they used to let me into nightclubs even though I was underage. 'Cause I was famous. They'd sneak us in, give us a private suite. In one of those rooms, a buddy overdosed right in front of me. I didn't even know he'd popped any pills. He had nothing to do with the movie biz. Just a guy I'd known since I was five. It didn't even make the news." He paused as if expecting a response. But Jake waited, already guessing what came next. "He died in the hospital—never woke from his coma. I didn't get to say goodbye."

Jake sat back down on the couch with a thud.

"So," George went on, "am I getting warm? Someone died in front of you." Jake was too flabbergasted to reply. "No need to explain"—George gave a careless wave of his hand—"I'm just sayin', you have that look."

"It's a *look*?"

"Yeah, it kind of is. Haunted." Jake narrowed his eyes. "Not literally. Or do I mean *literally*? There was something in your expression just now .... To me, it's written all over your face. The others might not see it. Or they're waiting for you to come clean. You could, you know. They've got their troubles too. Everyone does." He stood up. "Sorry to stick my nose in it. See you in the morning." Eyeing the stairs as a pirate might a gangplank, George began a slow, heavy ascent to the third floor.

Despite his annoyance with the actor, Jake smiled to himself. Lorenzo's preoccupation with pirates was rubbing off.

Jake snapped out of a deep sleep and sat bolt upright. The house shook. It sounded like a herd of cattle was stampeding down the staircase. Heart in his throat, Jake confronted the wraith who had flung open his bedroom door and trembled there, silvered in moonlight from the hall windows.

Not a ghost. Only George, bug-eyed with terror.

"Jesus!" Jake clutched his chest. "Do you have hooves instead of feet? I think my heart stopped." He hopped out of bed, glad for the pajama bottoms. Normally he slept in the buff, but with a houseguest, anything could happen.

As in, the guest might see a ghost and burst in. Had Jake planted the seeds of this nightmare in George's overactive imagination?

The white grandmother clock in his room began to chime, along with all the downstairs clocks. Jake had silenced them the night before and they'd stayed that way … until now. Midnight. Jake had been asleep for less than an hour. Neither man spoke or moved till the last chime stopped resonating. It was as if they expected some horrific vision to appear in the ensuing silence.

George bounced into the room, shut the door, and leaned flat against it, as if his middleweight body could fend off a supernatural being. "Sorry, I'm sorry …" he muttered. His black hair bristled. Jake had never seen hair stand on end before. Wearing only boxer briefs, George was as ripped and sleek as an Olympic swimmer. Made sense. When you were a heartthrob, your physique was part of what the studios paid for.

Jake grabbed the two terrycloth robes from the back of the closet and tossed one to George. "Don't apologize," he said, pulling on the other robe. "Have a seat." He pointed to the chair by the window. "All right. Tell me what happened."

George raked a hand through his hair. "I wasn't even asleep. I was reading a script. First the lights dimmed. I figured the bulb was burning out because it flickered. When I tightened it in the socket, it died. Then I saw *him*."

"Him?" *Damn! Had Rory materialized for George?*

"A young man, skinny, transparent. Like he was sickly. Though it doesn't get any sicklier than dead. That *thing* started floating toward the bed." George made a surfing motion with his hand. "Skimmed across the ground. I upped and ran. Right on through him."

Jake felt energized. Proof of the afterlife! "Did he look familiar?"

"Huh?"

"Like any of the portraits?"

George's teeth were chattering. "I d-dunno. I haven't checked out all the portraits."

"Let's go downstairs. I'll lead the way." Jake opened the door, stuck his head into the corridor, and scanned the area.

"You think I'm crazy," George sulked.

"No, I don't." Jake crooked his finger as if beckoning a stray dog. "Come on, George. There's nothing out there … now. I think another glass of cognac is in order. Or a valium."

George followed so closely on Jake's heels that Jake held on tight to the banister in case the other man tripped and sent them both ass over teakettle down the staircase.

Jake lit the fire. Seated once again in the parlor, George gulped down the cognac. "I'm not a lunatic," he whispered.

Jake kept his voice low and smooth. "I haven't seen anything like what you're describing myself, but I've often wondered what went on in the attic room. Or maybe I should say, 'goes on.' " George's eyes were closed as he concentrated on his breathing. Jake continued, "Did you get a good look at the landscapes? They're fantastic. I believe a resident of this house painted them. Maybe a shut-in. That room would make the perfect artist's studio, don't you think? The light is incredible."

George opened his eyes and gazed up at Jake with the pathetic hopefulness of a rescued street urchin. "You believe me?"

"Why not?" Jake said. "Ever since … let's just say that some odd shit has been going on with me for a while now."

"Ever since …" George leaned in, all ears.

Jake sighed. "Ever since my friend Rory died in front of me."

George smiled for the first time, a little smug. "Thought so."

Might as well come clean, Jake thought. *It's not like he hasn't guessed it already.*

"We were hiking the Wonderland Trail. Do you know it?"

George shrugged. "Who doesn't?"

Most Washingtonians were aware of the Wonderland Trail, which encircled the state's most spectacular still-active volcano—in Seattle, they just called it "The Mountain"—leading hikers through valleys and forests, up from the subalpine to the alpine and through glaciers, all gloriously lorded over by magnificent Mount Rainer. The hike took about ten days and required rigorous conditioning. Its campgrounds offered shelters, pit toilets, and bear poles.

Jake went on, "About halfway through, approaching the Mystic Camp, Rory grabbed his shoulder and gasped for breath. Then he just … keeled over. I know CPR. It didn't work. He was only forty-three."

"Christ on a cracker!" was all George could say.

Jake took a deep breath. "I was gutted. Four months later, I woke up in bed with one of Rory's girlfriends, not knowing how I got there. He started talking to me, like *he'd* orchestrated it. Now I hear him in my head. Most of the time." He looked around the parlor. "Except in this house. That's why it's so restful for me. I used to think I was going crazy. Now I believe he's actually *in* my head. I figure there's gotta be something here that keeps him out of this place. Competition, maybe. So, you see, I do believe in ghosts."

George poured himself another glass and sipped this time. "Until tonight, I might have thought you were nuts."

"Yeah. That's why I don't go around telling people."

"I can't sleep here," George declared in a flat voice that brooked no argument.

"Sure you can," said Jake, in his soft, dog-trainer voice. "You'll sleep in my room. Not in my bed," he was quick to add, recalling the gay fan club at Matthew's party and realizing George might leap to that conclusion, despite his comment about Chiara. "Because this used to be a B and B, there are at least two cots in the hallway closets. I'll haul one of them into my room."

CHAPTER 19

THE DARK CIRCLES BENEATH GEORGE'S eyes told Jake he hadn't slept much, if at all. Hearing his groan when Jake got out of bed, he left him in the cot and went downstairs to turn on the espresso machine and pull breakfast together. The clocks all began to strike nine. They hadn't chimed since midnight. Jake didn't bat an eyelash.

Soon after, he heard the thud of boots on the staircase. They seemed to belong to a heavier, less fleet-footed man. Several minutes passed before George appeared and leaned against the kitchen doorframe.

"Found him."

"Who?" Jake handed over a mug containing a latte with three shots.

George accepted the drink with piteous desperation. "The ghost. The portrait, I mean. It's the one next to the fireplace in the parlor."

Exactly as Jake had expected. "The only portrait of a young man," he said. *Young, except for his eyes,* he thought.

George slumped onto a stool at the counter.

"Bacon and eggs, coming right up," he said.

"Thanks." George guzzled the coffee. As he dug into breakfast, he said, "You're a mensch. I'm sorry I got you to spill the beans about your buddy. It's not like *I'm* gonna tell anyone, but *you* should."

Jake regarded him wearily. How did you confess to your family that you had a dead guy besieging your brain like some occupying army?

George read his mind. "Not about the ghost. Tell them about your friend—how he died in front of you. That explains a lot right there. The rest, uh, would be too weird for most people." He cocked an ear. "Wait a minute …. Did you hear that? Some kind of commotion outside."

Jake strolled to the main entrance and peered out the peephole. "Shit!" he muttered to himself.

The crowd was composed of restless young women, a few older ones with cameras, and one camera-toting man. The paparazzi. Fans. Joe had called it correctly. Jake called David on his cell.

"Jake!" David said, sounding pleased. "How's it going?"

"Not so well. My houseguest is unlikely to give my accommodations a good rating."

"Huh?"

"For one, the house gives him bad vibes. He barely slept. Then there's the little matter of the screaming banshees gathering outside for autographs and photos."

David groaned. "Oh, man, here we go! What now?"

Jake rubbed his forehead. "I have an idea. I'll call you right back." He returned to the kitchen. "George, your fans await."

The actor sighed heavily and pushed his empty plate away. "Fuck it all. I should've known better. I can't *ever* travel incognito."

Jake gave him a big, encouraging smile. "Hey, buck up! I have a plan. Pack up your stuff. We're going to transport you to the compound. Way better security there."

"Won't they see me go?"

Jake gave a low chuckle. "Leave that to me."

* * *

Teresa caught a glimpse of Liam's red pickup truck as it rolled at a snail's pace toward Jake's back door. Aiming for devil-may-care casual, she sauntered down the sidewalk toward the three-paned stained-glass front door of the former B&B. She scanned the crowd for familiar faces. This was not going to work if she was recognized. But no … she saw no one a bartender wouldn't card. The women her age all carried cameras. Female paparazzi. None of the women in her yoga class was shameless enough to chase after a movie star. Granted, Joe had a lower profile than last year, but although he was gorgeous as ever and a major star in his own right, the tabloids left him alone now. Mostly.

News of George's presence had traveled quickly—not quite at the speed of light, more like the speed of an express letter. Teresa sighed. *No shit, Sherlock.* George Reed Masters was a red-hot movie star with an especially large following among girls and young women.

"Where are *you* from?" Teresa asked a Pretty-Baby type who might have been wearing springs on her shoes. Her face was so plastered with makeup that she resembled a Kabuki actor.

"Forks!" she said, bopping up and down.

Teresa nodded. Not much happened in Forks, the rainiest town in the Pacific Northwest. "Ah. What's this all about, then?"

Another girl said, "George Reed Masters is in there!"

Teresa widened her eyes theatrically. "Is that so? How can you be so sure?"

"He had lunch at Kelpies yesterday," the leggy brunette replied in a high, childish voice. "He's here to talk to that author about his thriller."

They were surprisingly well informed.

"I live right over there," Teresa pointed, "and I saw someone leave real early this morning in a great big black limousine."

"Really?" the lone male said. Teresa almost held her breath. Her photo had appeared in the tabloids a time or two, but her hair was different now. She told herself not to worry. If he had recognized her, he'd have taken her picture.

"*Really*," Teresa repeated. "He must be headed to Port Angeles to catch a chartered plane."

The man eyed her with suspicion.

"Where else would he go?" Teresa asked reasonably. "He's hardly going to drive across the Hood Canal Bridge and catch a ferry."

Out of the corner of her eye, she saw Liam's truck round the corner and disappear. He and George were on their way to the compound. She wanted to pump her fist in the air. *Too bad, assholes*, she thought.

The front door swung open and Jake appeared on the stoop. "My, my," he said, hands on hips. "What do we have here?"

The female photographers started snapping away. The fans hung back, unsure whether to request Jake's autograph. "Did George Reed Masters stay here last night?" one of them called out.

"Why, yes … he did." Jake beamed at them with an open-mouthed grin. "I'm so sorry you missed him. He's a busy man. Back to Vancouver for more filming, I'm afraid."

The reporters lobbed a lot more questions at Jake, about the movie, George's role if he had one. Jake told them it was in preproduction and nothing had been decided. He was all charm and affability. Then his smile turned smarmy. "Girls, *girls*," he said. "I realize I'm a poor substitute, but I'd be happy to give you my John HanCOCK."

Teresa snorted. The girls began to back away, like in the horror movies when the vampire shows its fangs. Jake was cute enough—cuter than George, to be honest, at least in person—but his vaguely predatory turn had done the trick. They were looking for a reluctant pretty boy, not a mature seducer. She heard one of them say, "Did he say something about his *hand* and his *cock*?"

The lone man stepped forward. "How do we know you're on the level?"

"About my John HandCOCK?" he said, adding a D and then stressing the last syllable. The way he swished his hand in the air might have had something to do with a hand and a cock. Then again ….

"Not about your no-doubt-impressive John HanCOCK," the man remarked through gritted teeth. "About your houseguest."

"Come with me," Jake said, beckoning him into the house. Halting the rest of them with an open palm, he added, "Only him. This is for verification purposes only. No photos inside the house." He reached for the camera. "I won't damage it, I promise. You can search to your heart's content."

They both disappeared for several minutes, with the man reclaiming his camera upon their return. "Come on," he told the others. "He got away. Should've kept an eye on the back door."

"Oh, he was gone long before you arrived," Jake lied.

The man made a disgusted sound. "Gimme a break. I saw the breakfast dishes. You don't seem the type to leave them for the maid."

When they had finally cleared out, Teresa joined Jake on the stoop. She'd retreated behind a neighbor's fence during the house search. "Is it possible that none of those kids knows a John Hancock is a signature?"

Jake shrugged. "They were babies. I wonder where they all came from."

"The girls I spoke to came from Forks. Cell phone service on the Peninsula is spotty at best. Word must have spread the old-fashioned way, over the telephone wires."

Jake grinned. "I'm glad I'm not their type."

Teresa laughed. "You made sure of that. Even I wondered if you were into jailbait. Darn. Now the crew at the compound are stuck with George. For how long, I wonder? Until he's wanted on a set somewhere, most likely."

"He's not so bad," Jake said. "I'll admit, he's a terrible flirt. You can hardly blame him. You ladies are all so beautiful."

She pulled him in for a quick hug. "Ah, JB, you're so nice! Well, he's going to have to settle for manly company for at least a day or two. I'm going to drag the 'ladies,' including Becca, to Seattle. Ali and I need to shop for maternity clothes, and Maddie asked for wardrobe help—something about no clothing appropriate for garden parties. Chiara insists she's all set after our last shopping trip to Port Angeles, but I'll drag her along anyway." Seeing his wistful face, she added, "Cheer up, JB. You'll get your chance to dress Chiara."

Jake gave her a sharp look. "Do you know something I don't?"

Teresa shook her head. "Not yet. But I'm working on it." She called Ali's cell, and her sister-in-law answered immediately.

"What the f—*fudge* …?" Ali began.

"I gather he arrived."

"How did he end up as *our* guest?" Ali said in a furious whisper.

"Shhh, it's for the best, you'll see. I'll explain later. Remember that trip to Seattle we talked about? No time like the present. Jake says George is decent company when no women are around." She winked at her brother.

"How long will we be gone?" Ali asked. "I'll have to okay it with May Allen and Susan. The twins have required all hands on deck lately. Who's going to watch Lorenzo?"

Teresa scratched her head. "Couldn't some of the Port Townsend or Sequim FOSSP kids use the work? Pay them overtime. The house down the lane has extra space. I'm sure they'd be thrilled. Lor adores Xenia, right?"

"He gets lost in her enormous eyes," Ali said with a chuckle. "He's definitely his daddy's son. I'll see if she's free."

"Remind Becca that she promised to come. Maddie and Chiara too. No arguments. We can all crash at Mom's—she's on a Caribbean cruise. Tell the guys to take George on a backpacking trip or something."

CHAPTER 20

———•———

JOE WAS IN THE KITCHEN making lattes for David and Liam—a decaf for George, who insisted he'd had enough stimulation for one morning. The three men were lined up in Adirondack chairs on the terrace facing the Strait of Juan de Fuca as if waiting for the next show to start … or the AA meeting to begin. Ali had told him to get George the hell out of Dodge, which Joe thought was an excellent idea. He knew the paparazzi were likely to stay hot on their trail. They'd figure out George was here, if they hadn't already, and then their group would be under siege until it was time to scuttle him off to the airport. If it were up to Joe, that would be their next move. However, George had another week to kill before he was due on set, and he didn't seem inclined to cut his visit short, not with such entertaining company to impinge on.

Joe chuckled as he thought how uncomfortable George must be at this moment, with only David and Liam to shoot the breeze with. Neither was feeling kindly toward him, considering how blatantly the actor had flirted with their wives. Ali had been on guard from the start, bless her, so he personally had nothing against the guy—yet. He hoped Jake was right that he was better behaved in the company of men. Ali and Maddie had fled to join Teresa shortly after George arrived with Liam. And Jake was on his way. Jake and George shared a shoe size, so he was bringing a spare pair of hiking boots—Big Paul's, naturally.

"So, George …" Joe said in a jovial voice as he handed him the decaf latte, "do you hike?"

"I *have* hiked," George rephrased, "and I work out a lot."

161

The men exchanged amused glances. It wasn't the same thing. Hiking engaged all your leg and butt muscles and tested your balance, especially on trails with lots of roots, shale, rocks, and streams.

"It's so relaxing here," George said. "Can't we just hang out?"

"You mean until the paparazzi show up," Joe said. "Unless you want to be confined here until it's time to leave, I propose heading out for an adventure. Nothing too challenging. I was thinking lunch at Lake Crescent Lodge then a hike up Mount Storm King. The lodge had a cancelation. I've reserved us a large cabin for the night."

"Mount Storm King," George repeated, frown lines forming. "It's a *mountain*? A stormy one?" Then his aspect brightened. "Does Lake Crescent have Jacuzzis?"

"Nah," Joe said, "it's not that kind of resort. Sol Duc Hot Springs is nearby. I got us the large cabin there for the next day." He regarded George critically. "I'm worried about you being recognized wherever we go."

"What about you?" George sounded defensive. "People must recognize you all the time."

"Nah, I really don't have one of those faces," Joe said, "especially when I'm sporting facial hair." He smoothed a hand over his short beard. "I'm a musician, not a movie star. It's a different kind of celebrity. At least here. And I'm not a teenybopper magnet." He sipped his own espresso, weighing the possibilities. "I can disguise you enough to throw people off the scent. We should hurry, though. I'm guessing the hounds are already sniffing around."

"I don't have hiking boots or gear with me," George argued, as if hoping that would allow him to stay put. "No swimsuit for the hot springs."

Joe was glad George didn't know about the hot tub at the compound. He'd be even more likely to dig in his heels. "We've got extra gear, and Jake has boots for you. Our family business is Big Paul's Outfitters. You know it?"

"Sure," George said, impressed. "I love their stuff."

"We always have first shot at the new line, and I keep extra gear here for guests. The swimsuit isn't exactly camera-ready, but that's for the best." His lips twitched as he pictured the long, baggy swim trunks they kept for male guests of all sizes. "The point is to keep a low profile. David, why don't you help George take his bags up to the African-themed cabin? He can get settled in while we wait for Jake to arrive and Liam and me to throw our gear together."

David shot him a whip-quick look of annoyance. Joe smiled. David and Liam had become thoroughly spoiled, free of unpleasant duties and obligations. Joe thought of all the press conferences and ass-licking on his own schedule whenever he'd promoted an album or a tour. Now was their chance to do something nice for Jake, like not spoil his chances of nabbing George for *Kapow*. After throwing a bunch of clothing into a duffle bag and loading up a few backpacks with gear, energy bars, emergency supplies, and water bottles, he and Liam dragged the stuff onto the terrace, where David was waiting with his own overnight bag and backpack.

His older brother stood on the terrace, arms crossed, petulant. "How long are we going to be gone?" David whined like a child who'd been called into dinner too soon. "What about Lorenzo and the twins?"

"At least two nights," Joe replied. "Xenia's coming over to take charge of Lorenzo. The girls will be back Thursday. I'll give Ali a call at that point and find out if any photographers are attempting to camp nearby. If not, or they've given up, it should be safe for George to stay here for the rest of his time off."

"Won't he be pissed once he realizes his cell doesn't get reception on most of the Peninsula? Also, when you talk about 'resorts,' you don't convey the real flavor of Lake Crescent or Sol Duc. The accommodations are pretty rustic for a guy like that."

"He doesn't come from money," Joe argued. "His father ran a motel in Seaview, for pity's sake. He knows the Olympic National Park lodges aren't like the Ritz."

"He did mention Jacuzzis."

"He was just being optimistic," Liam said with a grin. "Or sarcastic. It's hard to tell with George."

"Let me get this straight …" David said. "We're trying to *help* our brother, not *harm* him, right? You're not settling an old grudge with Jake by purposely giving George a hard time?"

"No, nothing like that. This will hardly be roughing it."

"Mount Storm King, *really*? Don't you think Marymere Falls is more his speed?"

Joe and Liam exchanged an evil grin. "Probably. But he's hardly gonna complain. I'd think you'd welcome a little payback after the way he's drooled over Maddie."

Now David was grinning.

"It's innocent fun," Joe said with a careless wave. "He'll be hurting … a little. Jake can chat him up while the three of us forge ahead. Other than the hike, it'll be a breeze. We'll pack a good supply of single malt to ease the pain at the end of the day."

Jake's BMW pulled up, and he emerged, looking more relaxed than Joe could recall. Nothing seemed to faze the guy now. He couldn't believe this was his brother, so tense and calculating in his former life.

"How'd you handle the paparazzi?" Liam asked.

Jake's smile had a devilish twist. "There were only a few reporters with cameras, and the fans weren't from around here—all teenagers, too young to be anyone Teresa recognized. I told them George was on his way to the airport. No one thought to stake out the back door." He scanned the yard. "Is George ready? They're bound to catch on that he's here. How are you going to keep some random fan on the Peninsula from recognizing him?"

Joe waggled his eyebrows. "Hang on. I'll be right back."

When he emerged from the cabin with George, the actor sported a baseball cap and had a ridiculously long mustache with waxed points, like Salvador Dali's. He doffed his cap to reveal a purple streak and grinned to show that one of his teeth had been blacked out.

Jake snorted. "Won't people wonder why three classy guys like us would hang out with this trailer trash punk?"

"Hey!" George said, wounded. Knowing the guy's upbringing, Joe hoped Jake hadn't hit too close to home. But no, George looked pleased with himself. Joe knew from painful experience that a semi-demented guise was worth it if it kept the nuttier fans at bay.

* * *

Ali, Teresa, Maddie, Chiara, and Becca were sitting in a booth on the passenger deck of the Kingston Ferry, en route to Edmonds. Becca had needed time to clear her schedule, so it was three in the afternoon by the time they boarded the ferry.

"Becca, what are you looking at?" Ali asked. Her best friend had been staring intently out the window for the last fifteen minutes.

"Just enjoying the ocean. You never know what you might see. A sea lion, an orca. A harbor seal. The seagulls drifting alongside, riding our air currents. Neptune, even." She chortled to herself. "You know, the god of the sea? Even if nothing special appears, it's meditative. I'm a regular on this route. All the back and forth is exhausting." She clicked her tongue. "*Three* damn restaurants. Enough already."

Now she had Chiara staring out the window too. "You see harbor seals this far from the harbor?"

"Well, no," Becca admitted. "You see them in the harbor. And you probably have to go to Italy to see Neptune, which I'll never do because Jean-Louis doesn't believe in vacations."

"You don't see any of *us* going to Italy," Ali said, hoping to cheer her up. "Joe never wants to leave the Peninsula unless it's about business." Not for the first time, she wondered if her husband was borderline depressed. He always acted cheerful, but that was Joe. She knew he didn't miss the fox-hunt part of being a celebrity, but he was too young and vital to retire. He missed the creative parts of his old life—collaborating with other musicians, the feeling that he mattered as an artist. He was a new man when Matthew was in town. Matthew had talked to Joe about approaching other musicians to record albums in his Port Townsend studio, and they were discussing upgrades.

"Where did you just go just now?" Becca asked. "Traveling to Italy in your mind?"

"Nah," Ali said, "I don't see the wisdom of traveling while pregnant. Paris would have been a lot more fun without the twins kicking inside me every few minutes."

"We'll do Paris again," Teresa promised. "We can leave the men behind. Do girly things."

They all looked at her.

"When we're fifty," she amended with a rueful sigh, "and our children are in college."

"David wants me to go *now*," Maddie said. "He wants to take me on a grand tour of England, France, Italy, and Germany."

"You mean like in *Room with a View*?" Becca asked. "My family did something like that, a few times. I'd love to see Europe with Jean-Louis. You'd think he'd want to check out the Michelin-starred restaurants."

Ali could see that Maddie wasn't jazzed by the prospect. Should she keep digging? Just as she'd decided against it, Becca said, "Why don't you look more excited? You have no children, you have no obligations, you have a gorgeous hunk of a husband with pockets as deep as Crater Lake. Seize the day!"

Ali got it. "You'd rather be acting."

Maddie smiled. "Yes, I miss it. Last year I had taken this giant step forward in my career. Then David came along, and I got swept up in the whirlwind. I'm back to Square One. Things are so … calm. I wasn't ready for"—she waved her arms around as if searching for a different word—"*calm*." She frowned. To her, "Calm" clearly meant "stagnant."

"Things aren't good with David?" Teresa asked, worried.

"I adore David," Maddie said without hesitation. "I just wish he were open to my having *some* sort of career. We should have discussed it before we got married."

In the awkward silence that followed, the unspoken words, "Yes, you should have" rang in the air.

Becca turned to Teresa. "Where will we stay in Seattle—your townhome?"

Ali broke in, "At Carrie's, right? My dad and Laurie are renting Teresa's townhome," she explained to Becca. They'd had to force her to let them pay rent, but it was way below market value.

Becca scrunched up her face. "You're keeping it as an investment?"

Teresa blurted out, "It still has all my stuff in it—the furniture and artwork, anyway, extra clothing, books, knickknacks. I don't feel like dealing with it all right now. It was perfect that Duncan and Laurie wanted to live there."

"Why don't you bring your stuff to Port Townsend?" Becca asked.

Teresa threw up her hands. "Where would I put it? Liam's house?"

"It's your house too, isn't it?" Becca didn't bother to hide her annoyance. "That man! I could just smack him. Whatever's yours is his, but whatever's his is his."

"It's not like that," Teresa insisted in a small voice.

Becca patted her leg in a conciliatory manner. "I'm sorry, Teresa, but you're *pregnant*. It's about time he started looking after *your* needs."

"That was the problem before," Teresa said. "It was *all* about me. He got fed up. These are the new terms."

Ali looked at her sister-in-law with alarm. Did Liam understand that he was being a prick? "Teresa, why don't *you* buy a place?"

Teresa looked startled.

"If you feel like his place is his, then you buy a place in Port Townsend too, one where you can put your stuff. You can use it as an office—or something. Or just a room of your own. I'm worried that, with the baby, he'll have too much power. He's my brother but … he's still a mystery. I agree with Becca: I'm worried. Have you talked to him about the whole 'his' house deal?"

Teresa gazed mournfully out to sea. "Not really. I wanted to get that all straight, but then I got pregnant …. You know how much I wanted a baby … yet the timing, with his leaving and all …."

Chiara, who'd also been staring out the window, looked at Teresa in alarm. "He *left you*?"

They had all assumed the separation was common knowledge. "Uh … briefly. I was trying to figure out what to do with my life, and he thought I was interested in a"—she scrambled for words—"an ex. It was all a misunderstanding."

"I'm sorry," Chiara said, "I don't mean to stick my nose in your business. It's just that you are so … special. Why would any man discount you, I mean, take you for granted?"

The way she spoke, she didn't include herself in the "special" category. If Ali ever met this Arnold character, she'd be tempted to give him a piece of her mind.

Becca, who had been mulling something over, finally spoke. "Don't you think Liam is restless too? All the odd jobs around town, the work on the Victorian … It's like he's casting about for his next gig. Port Townsend …. I know you all love it, but it's a vacation destination, a retirement town, a place to recuperate. Is being the idle rich really a life? Excuse me, Ali and Teresa, I don't mean to criticize. I don't think of *you* that way, but Liam …. I know he loves it there too, but he's a big, dynamic man with so much to offer. These guys need challenges, adventure. We can't expect them to settle down and behave like … like lap dogs."

Ali palmed her tummy, which was just starting to protrude, and sighed. That did it; she was overdue for a talk with Joe. If he wanted to tour again, she wouldn't stand in his way. She'd also like to give her brother the what-for. Liam had no inkling how much the separation had chipped away at Teresa's confidence. She was positive he adored his wife, but her brother was stubborn as a mule.

She glanced at Chiara, who seemed happier than the rest of them. Now *here* was someone who appreciated the recuperative powers of their home. Had she and Arnold formally separated? Why did she never raise the subject of returning to Portland?

CHAPTER 21

------·------

AN HOUR INTO THE HIKE, Jake could tell that George was hurting. He kept stopping to clutch his chest as if to keep his heart from bursting forth. A sheen of sweat coated his ruddy face and neck.

"Water break!" Jake called ahead to the others, who were almost out of earshot. They'd gladly leave George in their dust with Jake to pick up the pieces. George had initially bubbled over with enthusiasm for the beauty of crystal-clear, turquoise-tinted Lake Crescent and the sun filtering through the towering evergreens coated with sparkling moss and frilly lichen. Now he seemed to be on his last legs. Jake sat beside him on the log and reached over to collect the fake mustache, hanging from his lip like a crushed caterpillar. "I'll keep this for you." He placed it in a plastic baggie where he kept extra tissue. "You'll need it later at the lodge. If anyone passes us, pull your baseball cap down. Here." He rubbed some dirt on George's upper lip and chin. "That'll help."

George swiped at his face in irritation, smearing the dirt around. But he didn't complain. He reached inside his backpack and pulled out a square, silver object.

"What kind of camera is that?" Jake asked as George snapped several shots of the lake.

"A Sony Digital Mavica MVC-FD7."

"It looks kind of heavy." Poor George didn't need the extra weight in his backpack.

"It's compact," George insisted. "Only a pound or so, and it's cool.

Digital, and the shots are really easy to download. That's why it's so big—there's a floppy disk in it."

"Expensive?" Jake asked.

"Nah, less than a thousand. My wife, uh, ex-wife, gave it to me last year—the 1998 model. I wanna get something more compact." He took another picture of the lake.

"Trail mix?" Jake handed the package to George, whose breathing was still labored. "If the pace is too fast, we can slow down. Liam, David, and Joe can go on ahead."

"I think they already did—go on ahead, I mean. How long is this hike, again?"

"Five point three miles."

"Oh, man! You didn't warn me it was straight up all the way."

"There are switchbacks."

"Steep ones."

Jake's laugh was rueful. "Yeah, sorry. The elevation gain is about two thousand feet."

"And how far have we gone?" George fixed his doleful gaze on the place where the mountain met the sky.

"Well, we're doing good," Jake assured him. "We just passed the 'end of maintained trail' sign, which means we're a little more than halfway."

George groaned. "Is that *all*?"

"We can turn around now," Jake said reasonably. "I'll go with you."

"You've hardly broken a sweat," George grumbled.

"We've been hiking a lot since I arrived here for David's wedding," he explained.

George looked ahead. "Those ropes … they freak me the hell out."

"They're sturdy. Don't worry so much. You can skip the scramble at the top."

"*Scramble?*"

"Personally, I don't care for heights," Jake lied. "So if you want to stick with me, that's cool."

They took it slow, finishing the last part of the trail in heavy silence and taking frequent snack and water breaks. Jake hoped George didn't have an undiagnosed heart condition, because he had sweated through his T-shirt to the point where it clung to his beautifully sculpted muscles like plastic wrap—more decorative than functional, it seemed.

When they finally reached the goat trail, it had an actual goat on it. A mountain goat. It was the size of a smallish adult moose, awkward like that animal, with sharp horns, a shaggy coat, and a deceptively lovable face. Except for the eyes, which glittered malevolently.

Joe, David, and Liam sat together on a log, tracking the animal's every move. Liam had his hunting knife out.

"We're waiting for it to leave," David explained. "It's standing its ground. No scramble for us."

"Oh, *darn*," George said with obvious sarcasm.

"The view's spectacular, right?" Joe waggled his brows. "Worth the effort?"

Their guest was clearly wise to their little scheme to bring him down a notch. He silently cursed his brothers and brother-in-law and admired George for not rising to the bait.

George set down the pack and pulled out his camera. Too late, it dawned on Jake and the others he was angling for the best shot of Mr. Goat.

"George!" Liam said in an urgent whisper, so as not to startle the volatile animal. "Keep your distance. These beasts are dangerous."

The goat charged. A split second later, Liam threw his knife, hitting it squarely in the throat. George lay on the ground, moaning, blood spurting from his inner thigh.

In no time, Joe yanked off his T-shirt and passed it to David, who ripped it into strips to fashion a makeshift tourniquet.

"That looks bad," Joe said in a shaky, horrified whisper.

Jake couldn't believe his eyes. *Jesus*, was *another* man going to die on his watch? Come to think of it, where had Rory been all day? Not a peep. Had he known this was going to happen? Probably. He didn't care for George, so why warn Jake? The thought infuriated him. The goat didn't look so great either. It wasn't dead, but its breathing was shallow, and blood bubbled from its mouth. Liam pulled the hunting knife out of its neck, sending blood gushing everywhere, and wiped it on his own shirt. He didn't speak, didn't panic, just kept a careful watch on his physician brother-in-law.

David's eyes were closed as he pressed on George's wound. Wouldn't his dirty, germy hand contaminate it? Was this some weird voodoo trick he'd picked up in Africa? George had passed out. Several minutes later, David rose slowly to his feet. He was breathing hard, his face nearly as ashen as his patient's. Curious, Jake knelt down to examine the wound. It was barely visible, a pink circle with a shallow dent, as if the horn hadn't penetrated at all, just left a bruise. Shocked, he gazed up at his brother. "David?"

David was looking at Liam. "The goat?"

"Not worth it," Liam said. That's when Jake saw that he had quietly slit its throat. "They're not native to the Olympic National Park, and when people pee in their vicinity, they're attracted to the salt. This one was especially aggressive and might have wounded other hikers if you, uh, had opted to, um, care for it."

What did he mean, "care for it"? Jake thought. They were speaking in code.

"Will George be able to hike back down?" Joe asked. Jake couldn't help but notice that David's actions had surprised the other two men not a whit.

David stood and shook out his hands. "George will be fine. He'll need to eat something. He's lost a lot of blood."

"Anything else?" Jake said, digging in his pack for an energy bar and a Gatorade. "Sounds like a breeze."

Joe ignored his sarcasm. "What about you?" he asked David in a hushed voice. "Can you make it down?" He raked his hands through his hair. "Jesus, how do we explain this to him?"

"You can start with me," Jake said. "I'm all ears."

George's eyelids fluttered open. "Wha— what happened?" His head lolled from side to side as he took in his surroundings. "Am I dead?"

"Nope," Joe said, lips drawn back in an unnerving grin. "You'll live to climb another day."

George surveyed the scene of carnage: the glassy-eyed mountain goat, its fur matted with blood, his own shredded, red-streaked hiking pants. He touched the wound, where only a faint mark remained. "That thing gored me," he said flatly as he pulled himself up against a tree. "I didn't imagine it."

"Just a scratch," Liam said with a genuine smile.

Damn it, Jake thought, *this isn't a Monty Python sketch.*

George wasn't smiling. "That's not even a scratch." He pointed at his non-wound, the gory hole in his pants revealing a pink circle with a small dent. "Where did all the blood come from? The pain was excruciating, and it was *not* caused by *that*."

Liam and David exchanged carefully neutral glances.

"Uh, bad bruise?" Joe offered. "Goat blood?"

George glared at them, unconvinced.

"Here," Jake said, crouching down beside him. He handed over the open Gatorade and the unwrapped energy bar.

Still eyeing them warily, George munched and sipped. They all sat patiently, still as statues. The silence was deafening.

When the color returned to George's cheeks and his shivering subsided,

Joe stood and checked his watch. "Let's go. It's already past four. It's hairy enough navigating this trail in full daylight. Any minute now, David is going to have a helluva headache, and we might have to give him an assist."

David began, "I can—"

"No, you can't spend the night here," Joe broke in.

Clearly now was not the time for Jake to demand an explanation. "Come on," he said to George. "We'll sort this out later, once we're safely back at the lodge."

They descended in grim silence. For the first hour, the focus was on keeping George steady. Then David leaned against a tree, holding his head. "Liam," Joe said, "why don't the three of us hang back? You guys, keep going. Jake, can you get the car and meet us at the parking lot?"

"Sounds like a plan," Jake said. He and George forged ahead, the normally chatty actor glum and taciturn.

In the silence, Rory resumed his role as constant and unwelcome companion. "Don't blame me, boyo. I couldn't have warned you. That's not how it works."

How what works?

"He's okay, right? No harm done."

Physical harm. Otherwise, it's a shitstorm.

"Is it?" Rory said. After that, nothing.

When they finally reached the trailhead, Jake told George, "Stay with our packs while I get my car. Shouldn't take long." Not waiting for a reply, he set off at a run.

It was after seven, and they were sitting in the dining room of Lake Crescent Lodge, staring at their menus. George was hatless, his purple streak on display. He wore a fresh mustache with a goatee plus clear glasses with thick black frames. Seemed like overkill to Jake—like a wacky guest on *Pee-Wee's Playhouse*. At least Joe hadn't blacked out one of his teeth. David was asleep in the cabin.

After the waitress took their orders—pointedly ignoring George in favor of the rest of them—George adjusted the glasses and said, "Amazing. No one recognizes me."

"Told ya," Joe said. "As long as you're willing to look ridiculous, everyone will leave you alone."

"Like if you pick your nose on public transit," George said.

"Or floss on a plane," Liam chimed in. "Your seatmate won't talk to you."

Jake made a face. "You guys *do* stuff like that?"

"Well, no," said Liam. "No one talks to me anyway. I'm scary. Joe, how do you put them off?"

"A blacked-out tooth is the most effective," Joe said. "No one can look at anything but that." He jabbed a thumb at George. "No point in that if you're eating. It gets rubbed off."

Jake was surprised at how quickly George had rallied. A hot shower and a few drinks and he seemed positively jolly. Small wonder. He'd had a genuine adventure.

Once their steaks arrived—rare for everyone but George, who liked his medium—they ate quickly and silently. For David, they ordered a ham and cheese sandwich with extra fries. "I imagine their kitchen staff moves on when the lodge closes for the winter," Joe said as he handed the waiter his credit card. "Next summer I'll push for some of the FOSSP kids."

"So they're not just your servants," Jake said, belatedly realizing it was a remark worthy of his old snarky self.

Joe didn't take it that way. "We make them all come up with a plan. Some are getting their GEDs and many are applying for universities or technical colleges. We provide breathing space."

"Of course you do," Jake said, his tone apologetic.

Back at the cabin, David sat on the porch, watching the sunset. He was freshly showered, but his face was drawn, the smudges beneath his eyes pronounced. Reaching for the open bottle of single malt next to him on the side table, he poured everyone a glass. "I'm starving," he said, devouring the sandwich in a few bites. "Sorry, but I raided your backpacks for anything edible. Down to the last stray cashew."

Conversation over dinner had been casual and teasing, never touching on the afternoon's near-cataclysmic event. Jake didn't want to be the one to raise the subject. He hoped George wasn't going to go home with PTSD, despite his current devil-may-care attitude.

"What is this shtuff?" George asked in a slurred voice. "It's shmooth."

"Maccallan single Highland malt Scotch whiskey," David said, in a poor attempt at a Scottish brogue.

"How old?" Joe asked.

"Sixty years."

Joe whistled. "That must have cost you."

David finished off his glass. "What else am I going to spend my money on?"

"So, all you guys are loaded?" George asked, some of the precious liquid splashing out of his glass. At this point in the evening, "loaded" didn't just refer to wealth. They were all the worse for wear. George's tongue had loosened to the point where Jake anticipated a confrontation. He was looking forward to it, in fact. Rory was leaving them to it.

The other three looked at George as if floored by his rudeness.

George didn't apologize. Making a big effort to enunciate, he said, "I wasn't the first to raise the subject of money."

"No one's hurting," Joe said.

"*You* I get," George pointed at Joe. "You had a *huge* career. Jake too. He was a big CEO and now he's a bestselling author with a movie deal. But David? You were a doctor for poor people. And Liam, what's your story?"

They all exchanged amused glances.

Joe said, "Liam was blown up in a terrorist attack in Israel then became a mercenary. He had one mission in particular that paid quite well."

George's index finger was unsteady but relentless. "You think I'm gonna conclude you're putting me on, but I *believe* you. I knew about the terrorist attack—the scars and all are a dead giveaway even if I hadn't read the story online. Not the mercenary thing. It makes sense. He flings that knife like a medieval warrior."

Liam automatically touched the side of his face.

"Oh, they look good on you," George said. "You're the best-looking guy I ever saw. Even in Hollywood, where everyone's looks get a lotta help." He turned to David and jabbed the annoying finger in his shoulder. "You?"

"All the O'Connells are set for life," David said, scooting his chair out of George's reach. "It's family money from wise investments a generation back. I thought *genteel* people didn't discuss such things." Jocular tone notwithstanding, he was decidedly ill at ease.

And now George will get to the crux of the matter, Jake thought.

"Yeah, and asides, besides"—he stumbled over the words—"you're like Ellen Burstyn in that movie *Resurrection*. You can *heal*. That's gotta be worth a chunk of change. I was a goner, and you know it."

Aaaand ... here it is, Jake thought with a secret smile. Their features were barely discernable in the darkness, but David's clenched jaw was impossible to miss.

"You don't have to say anything," George said, draining his glass. "I know what I shaw ... saw. Jake?"

Jake aimed for nonchalance. "What?" He held out his glass for more whiskey. He really didn't want to get pulled into this truth-or-dare thing.

"Tell 'em what happened to you," George demanded, leaning in close enough to give him a contact high.

Jake thought, *Why not?* He'd spilled the beans to George, who wasn't even family. *And if I show David mine, he'll have to show me his.*

He blurted out the truth as succinctly as possible. "I was hiking the Wonderland Trail. With my best friend Rory. He had a heart attack. I couldn't revive him." *I wish I could heal*, he thought. *Such a nice skill to have when your family and friends are on the verge of death.*

Joe leaned in. "There's more to it than that. That's traumatic, sure, but Jake ...." He sat back, shut his mouth.

"Okay, there's more." He looked at David, who might have been the model for Rodin's *Thinker*. "After that, Rory started to, uh, *talk* to me."

George was chuckling to himself like an inmate in an insane asylum. They all turned to stare at him until he stopped, chastened, and hiccupped.

David said, "He talks to you ... in your head?" They might have been discussing symptoms of a virus.

Jake nodded. Then, realizing a nod would be missed in the darkness, he said, "Yes, in my head. But it's real. I believe it's real, anyway."

No one spoke for a while.

"Why did you tell George first?" David asked.

"The circumstances, uh, warranted it."

"Circumstances?" Joe asked.

"The place where I'm staying is haunted. Apparently."

"It sure is," George said, lifting his empty glass in a salute then waving it in David's face for a refill. David ignored him.

"David?" Jake said. "I'd love to hear what happened to you. Last I heard, your healing was more of the medically proven variety."

"*Jake ...*" Joe said.

A loud snore from George.

Jake fluttered his fingers at their guest. "You're going to have to figure out a way to silence him."

"Are you kidding?" Joe said. "If he told that story to anyone, they'd assume he was crazy. He's got no proof."

"What about his camera?" Jake said.

"*If* he managed to snap the photo," David said, "all it'll show is a mountain goat charging him. That doesn't mean the goat found its target."

"By the way, how *did* you handle that?" Jake asked. "The dead goat, I mean."

Joe replied, "We reported it at the ranger station. They knew about the aggressive goat harassing hikers. Apparently there were notices at the trailhead. That's why the trail was so sparsely populated. The ranger was relieved to hear it was dead."

"Okay," Jake said. "Now, David? I told you my story, to be continued."

"Yes," David sighed, drinking more whiskey. "I can heal. It's not altogether reliable, and the aftermath is almost always a ghastly headache. That's why I gave up practicing medicine entirely."

"How did it happen?"

They paused to confirm that George was still passed out.

"Car accident," David said. "They drive like maniacs over there. Head injury. Like in that movie George mentioned, *Resurrection*, only I believe the car *she* was in drove off a cliff and her healings were more reliable. We might have escaped with minor injuries if the car had had working seatbelts. The nurse with me was thrown clear but, uh, miraculously, only sustained bruises and cuts. When I recovered, I had a new skill. Speaking of miracles. Damned inconvenient."

"Is that what allowed Joe to tour again?" Jake asked.

David paused before replying, "It helped."

"Ah."

"We need to get George to bed," Joe said. "He's had a long day."

CHAPTER 22

—◆—

THE NEXT MORNING, LIAM COULD tell that George wasn't feeling so hot. After they ordered him a big, greasy breakfast and many refills of bitter but strong drip coffee, he revived, only to fall asleep in the car on the way to Sol Duc Hot Springs, his head lolling on Joe's shoulder. David was the largest of them, so he sat in front with Jake, leaving the other three to squeeze into the back seat. Joe sat in the middle, partly out of deference for their movie star guest, but mostly because Liam—the same height as Joe but more muscular—was too big to be wedged between them.

"Let him sleep," Jake said from the driver's seat. "We just about killed him yesterday. And that was *before* the goat came along."

"I think we should do the hike to the falls before lunch," Joe said.

"What if George doesn't want to?" Jake asked. "I don't think he trusts us anymore. I wouldn't."

"He doesn't have to go. He can doze in the car, or maybe we can check in early."

"Wh-what?" George said from his semi-conscious stupor. "You guys talkin' about me again?"

"We'd like to hike to the falls before lunch," Joe said. "We can soak in the pools after."

George heaved a longsuffering sigh. "How far?"

"Six miles, but flat as the Kansas prairie, I promise," Jake said.

"*You* I believe," George said, rubbing his neck. "The rest of you can go to hell."

"It's worth it," Jake went on. "Sol Duc Falls are spectacular."

"Yeah, I heard that." He dozed off again.

Liam was fully conscious of all the curious stares once they were settled in the hottest pool. If they'd thought they were going to avoid attention here, they had another think coming. Whether or not anyone recognized George—and they didn't appear to, given the floppy hat and sun goggles that hid the famously blue eyes and dark brows and the baggy swim trunks that almost covered his knees—they were gawking at the rest of them. They did make for an impressive, if intimidating, group. Despite the furtive looks, no one dared to initiate conversation.

George had become positively ebullient during the hike, realizing it really was just a walk in the woods with an impressive waterfall at the halfway point. Now he was enjoying the long, healing soak. Liam was glad to see him happy. He still didn't exactly *like* the guy, but it was hard to *dislike* him. Jake had recounted the story of George's own run-in with death, how his friend had OD'd at the nightclub.

Ghosts, for Christ's sake. And yet … if you were prepared to accept David's power to heal, believing in ghosts shouldn't be a stretch. Liam and Ali had this strange nonverbal communication system that had reached across the ocean. Anyone who had never experienced strange subjective phenomena would find that psychic connection implausible enough. He'd had that connection with Teresa too. Was it still there? He loved his wife, but did he trust her? She'd insisted she felt nothing for Kilo, but he still recalled the wistful way she'd looked at the man as they sat at the bar, unaware that Liam was watching them from the sidewalk outside, through the window.

"You're quiet," Joe said, startling him out of his dark thoughts.

"I'm always quiet," Liam said easily.

"You're quiet and broody," David clarified.

"I'm always—"

"No, you aren't," Joe broke in.

"George was just telling us about the ghost at Jake's house," David said. "Huh?"

"He was reading a script when he heard the floor creaking and looked up …" Joe began. "Take it away, George …."

"Yeah." George drew in a sharp breath. "I saw someone walking toward the bed. He was super skinny, young."

"Transparent?" Liam asked.

"Yeah, but other than that, he might've been an actual person. Like a hologram. Freaked me the hell out. Somehow I managed to leap out of the bed and run right through him. Later on, I recognized his face in one of the portraits. In the parlor, next to the lamp with the naked nymphs on it."

Liam was amused by the interest the naked-nymph detail sparked in Joe and David. Having never toured the house, they didn't know about Jake's collection of nude and scantily clad figurines.

"What do you know about the history of the house?" Liam asked Jake.

He shrugged. "Nothing, I'm afraid. I've had no luck contacting the owners. When I moved in, it was downright eerie, as if the entire place was prepped for a houseful of guests. All the beds made and festooned with frilly pillows, the larder fully stocked. Some amazing landscapes are on display in the attic room where I put George. I'd love to know their provenance."

"Have *you* seen any ghosts?" Joe asked.

Jake's laugh was brittle. "No. I *hear* Rory, but I don't *see* him. I've always felt weirdly at ease in that house. If there *are* ghosts, they're fine with my presence. And it's the only place where Rory leaves me alone."

"Is he with you now?" David asked, looking into Jake's eyes as if Rory might be reflected there.

"No," Jake said. "Or if he is, he's not letting on. He's kept to himself lately, which is fine by me."

After their soak, they passed through the lobby, where George lingered in the gift shop to buy a couple of postcards. Liam examined some of the American Indian jewelry, wishing he could buy stuff like this for Teresa, whose taste was too refined for turquoise bangles. Maybe they'd have a daughter who could enjoy simple things. How would he keep Teresa from spoiling her rotten? He wouldn't wish his own upbringing on anyone, but it had been a character builder.

At the cash register, George was flirting with a college-age girl, a wholesome blonde with a full face, pert nose, and cornflower-blue eyes. Like Betty in the *Archie* comics. Perfect for a jaded guy like George.

"Full-time job for you?" George asked as he counted out his cash.

"Just in the summer," she said with a girlish giggle. "I'm a student at Seattle Pacific."

"Fun here?"

"Not much to do, so far from the city. They house us in a big dormitory past the cabins. This your friend?" Her eyes flicked over Liam and widened.

"Uh, yeah. I'm here with several friends. This is just a stop between hikes."

Liam smiled to himself. Like George was some big hiker.

The girl cocked her head. "You look an awful lot like that actor."

"Which actor is that?" George asked, unworried.

"George Reed Masters. I read that he's been …." She gasped. "Omigod. You *are* him."

"I'm *not*," he insisted, alarmed.

Liam sneered. Like that floppy hat was enough to fool anyone now that he'd shed the rest of his disguise. The guy was an idiot.

"Okay, well, have a nice day!" George tipped his floppy hat and speed-walked to the exit. Once outside, he made a mad dash for the cabin. *Way to confirm her suspicions*, Liam thought with disgust.

"He gets that a lot," Liam said in a flat voice to the dazzled girl. "Uh, if anyone else decides that's him, we'll know who told them, yes?" Liam smirked in a vaguely threatening way.

She gave him a shaky nod and pretended to occupy herself with straightening the postcards in the rotating display.

That evening at dinner, George wore the horn-rimmed clear glasses, mustache, and goatee, and no one approached the table but a poker-faced, tremulous waiter. *Word has gotten around*, Liam thought. *Damn it.*

"What's up with the waiter?" Joe said after he'd taken their orders.

"George got careless," Liam grumbled. "The girl at the gift shop recognized him."

"Careless?" David said, sipping his drink. He didn't sound surprised.

"She's cute. He flirted."

Joe clicked his tongue and said with an exasperated laugh, "Now you're in for it. Or should I say, *we're* in for it."

"I basically threatened the girl," Liam admitted. "I'm surprised she told the rest of the staff."

David clinked his ice cubes around. "So what now, you give her a spanking?"

Liam scowled. "Good point." He hadn't thought it through. He should have told her they'd get her fired if word got out. No doubt she'd *love* a spanking.

Their food came, and no one hassled them while they ate. But the room was crowded, and rather than the usual animated conversations, there was a low hiss of whispering. *Great*. Now word was spreading among the other diners.

Skipping dessert, they headed back to their cabin, the largest available, with a full kitchen and four bedrooms. Liam had volunteered to sleep on the couch, even though his bulky body would spill over the sides, like a big cat in a shoebox. He figured that, other than him, David was the only one used to sleeping rough, even though they'd all done their fair share of tent camping. Why hadn't he thought to bring a sleeping bag? Convincing George to play Damon was worth the discomfort. Secretly he found it all hilarious. For a famous movie star, George was such a putz.

Once again, they settled into the chairs on the porch with glasses of single malt, Joe having opened the bottle he'd packed. They shined a flashlight into the grassy field surrounding them, lighting up the eyes of the deer grazing near the cabins.

George was goading Liam into telling him about his adventures in Israel when a tight group approached. There were five young women, led by the girl from the gift shop, less wholesome now. They were all heavily made up and wearing tight jeans and skimpy T-shirts. Curiously, Liam glanced at their feet, expecting to see stilettos. But no, only tennis shoes. Difficult to walk on grass in spiked heels—any heels, for that matter.

"Hi, girls," David said in a booming voice that set them back a step. "What's up?"

Ah-ha, Liam thought, *that's how we're going to play it. We'll scare them away*.

The gift-shop girl was the spokeswoman. "We wondered if you'd like some company."

He saw George assess them as if they were cattle at an auction. They were all young—that was in their favor—but none of their gang had been into "young" per se even when single, and this group was trying too hard. Pretty enough for an evening's entertainment, he supposed. At their age, he might have been willing to kill a few hours that way.

Joe rocked back in his chair, legs spread. "Do you all work here? How do you know we're not ax murderers or just garden-variety rapists?"

A cascade of giggles.

"No, seriously," Joe said, unsmiling.

The gift-shop girl jutted a thumb at George. "We know *him*."

"Do you?" Joe said. "Say you did know his name; do you really *know* him? Like what he prefers in bed? Who do you think *we* are?"

"I dunno," she said, her confidence waning, "his bodyguards?"

Liam threw back his head and guffawed. The rest of them burst into laughter too. The girls backed up as if blown by a strong gust of wind.

"Listen," George said, "we're honored, we truly are. It's a trip when people think I'm … *that guy*. But sadly, I'm not. And we're all married. Tempted as we are, we're not going to be bad boys tonight. Right, guys?"

"Pity," David said.

"Can we at least get your autograph?" the gift-shop girl said. Her eyes glistened in the porch lights, and her friends were all slump-shouldered in disappointment.

"Sam," Joe thumped George on the back, so the actor knew he referred to him, "why don't you sign *that guy's* name and send them away happy?"

George breathed out a sigh that Liam interpreted as faux disappointment, as if finally accepting there would be no partying with the locals tonight. "Do you have anything to write on?" he asked the gift-shop girl, and they whipped out paper and pens. Two of them had journals decorated with flower decals.

George signed his name five times in a fast, illegible scrawl, turning on the movie-star charisma to stare into each pair of eyes. They would go away happy enough.

"No calling your friends, right?" Liam said. "Otherwise, you'll be finding other jobs for the rest of the season. And we expect to have a nice, quiet breakfast tomorrow with no tails on the road back to 101."

They nodded like a collection of bobbleheads, each no doubt convinced that if George had been alone, she would have gotten lucky. They backed away, tittering, then shoving each other, exchanging excited whispers as they headed toward the dormitory.

"That was a close one," Jake said.

Joe laughed. "Sorry if you and George were interested."

Jake slitted his eyes, but George chuckled. "Are you kidding? We're trapped here. There's only one road out, and it's not a highway. Give me some credit. Even *I'm* not that stupid or reckless. Plus, they probably have a housemistress or a curfew. We'd end up out on our asses or worse."

"Maddie says you just got divorced," David said, "from some gorgeous actress."

"Yeah," George said with obvious regret. "It's not easy being me."

Liam locked eyes with Joe, and they clinked glasses.

"I imagine you all know what I'm talking about," George said.

"Girls don't throw themselves at me," Jake said.

"Then you're oblivious," George said without hesitation. "Because, seriously, what's not to like? Wait till the movie of *Kapow* comes out. You'll have so many choices your head will spin."

Liam grinned. Did that mean George was going to do the movie?

CHAPTER 23

———•———

Chiara was in the rec room of the Sea Captain's House with Lorenzo, playing a not-so-rousing game of Chutes and Ladders. It was recommended for "ages three and up," but Lorenzo's bored expression told her they might as well be playing Peekaboo. He'd probably graduate directly to chess. When the game was over, he said in Italian, "I'm tired, *Zia* Chiara."

She ruffled his hair. "Tired of the game or just tired?"

"The game. I want the story."

"I'm sorry, *cucciolo*, that will have to wait. *Zia* Ali and *Zio* Joe are giving a party tonight. They have an important houseguest."

He crossed his arms and stuck out his lower lip. "There are too many parties here. Couldn't *Papà* and Aunt Maddie come instead?"

"Everyone's busy tonight, *cucciolo*. I have to go soon too. You could have Beefaroni for dinner again." The offer felt like a bribe, but what could she do? She wanted to dress up before Jake arrived. She was still wearing her new jeans and tight T-shirt.

Susan arrived and spread her arms, inviting a hug. *Grazie a Dio!* Chiara thought. *He has so many mothers here, he almost doesn't need me. And David is more father than Arnold ever was.* She felt guilty for putting her own wants and needs first. She thought back to her life in Portland, perpetually ignored by Arnold and clung to by Lorenzo. She hadn't minded Lorenzo's stickiness until now—had cherished it—but then Jake had come along and she couldn't help it, she wanted more time with him. She hugged Lorenzo and kissed his cheek, saying she'd see him in the morning, which drew more protests. Tonight she would go home with Jake. Her hosts would look the other way.

The others were already on the terrace, sipping cocktails, looking so beautiful and fashionable, every last one of them, like models posing as real people. They waved and toasted her, calling for her to join them. Waving back, she replied, "In a moment!" A moment could be short or long.

Ali's father Duncan and his girlfriend Laurie were visiting from Seattle for the weekend and occupied the cabin next to hers. George the actor was staying in the cabin closest to the house, putting him a comfortable distance away. She didn't think he wished to try her—to "make a pass" was the English idiom—but as the only woman without the obvious protection of a man, Chiara didn't trust him not to probe the ground, uh, *test the waters*. The idioms were so similar yet not. Maybe it was because most Italians thought in terms of solid earth rather than water. Though that didn't make sense. There were many lakes in Italy, and of course, *lo stivale*, the boot, had sea on all sides. It was a peninsula, after all, like the Olympic Peninsula.

Becca, Ali, and Teresa sat together. She was grateful that this close-knit group of friends had made room for her. Never for a moment had she felt like the last wheel of the wagon. In Seattle Teresa had constantly prodded her to add to her wardrobe at Teresa's expense, possibly out of guilt because they were on a shopping *sfrenato* themselves. Chiara had rarely dressed casually in her former life. Now, along with sundresses, she owned sandals, designer jeans, filmy blouses, and close-fitting T-shirts that made her feel—dare she say it—*sexy*. She smiled. The Italians used that word too.

In her cabin, standing before the bathroom mirror, she sifted through her purchases, holding them up to her body one by one. There was no full-length mirror here. Everyone was dressed casually. She didn't want to appear to be trying too hard. *Basta*. She would change only her shoes and blouse and freshen her makeup. She liked the way she looked in these jeans, and she did *not* regret sleeping with Jake. Her sister would say, "You wanted the bicycle, now ride it." The American idiom was more apt, "You've made your bed, now lie in it." But that sounded so negative, as if she would face consequences. She had heard nothing from Arnold since her arrival. He might as well have vanished into thin air. She would claim her freedom, no matter what destiny intended for her and Jake. If she stayed away, Arnold could say she deserted him. Fine. She would find a job here. She'd expected her husband to mention the thousand dollars she'd withdrawn the day after Maddie and David's wedding. She had spent only a few hundred; no one let her pay for anything here, no matter how much she protested. She felt like a freeloader. But they needed her for Lorenzo. Or did they? What if she tried to withdraw more money and found that Arnold had canceled her bank card? That wouldn't be fair. Her savings from her social worker days had been deposited in their joint account at his suggestion. She had trusted him, let him convince her to quit working when Lorenzo joined them rather than hire a helper.

On her way back down the hill, she took geisha steps for fear of tripping in her heels. Her heart beat faster when she saw Jake standing at the bar, gazing at her as if she were a heavenly vision.

* * *

Ali couldn't wait to catch up with her father. It had been less than two weeks since his last visit, but they'd barely exchanged two words at Teresa's birthday party.

"When will you find out if it's a boy or a girl?" he asked her.

She knew how badly he wanted a grandson. "Teresa and I will go together to get a first-trimester ultrasound. She's only a week ahead of me. That means … about a month from now."

"In Seattle, not here?"

"A concession to Carrie," Ali admitted. *We could just let David touch it,* she thought with irritation.

"Did you have a good time in Seattle? Sorry we missed you. The trip to B.C. was already in the works."

"No problem," she said, though it was. Laurie's plans often interfered with her "Dad time." "We were on a mission, so it was just as well. I'm going to be much more fashionably pregnant this time around, thanks to Teresa. As long as I don't turn into a sea lioness like last time."

Duncan chortled. "I believe they're called cows." Then he blushed.

She grinned at his discomfort. There was no way to win on this subject. "Are you saying I looked like a cow?"

"Of course not, you impossible woman. You had twins. How could you help bein', uh, large?"

She sighed, her hand spanning her round belly. It was the size of salad bowl—nothing like last time … so far.

"How *is* Carrie, by the way?" Duncan asked.

"Great," Ali said, wishing she could warm to the subject of her mother-in-law. "She's thrilled at the prospect of more grandchildren. The more children we have, the better her chances of having a pint-sized comrade in arms—you know, a player on 'Team Carrie.' Like we're all bent on thwarting her at every turn."

Duncan chuckled. "Give her some slack. She's endured *three* impromptu marriages in the past few years—none of them to socially appropriate people, and none of them in the Catholic Church. As to wanting a child who is the closest thing possible to her clone, maybe we all feel that way. I'd love a little Joe-Duncan combo. Or in Teresa's case, Liam-Duncan."

She laughed. "If the baby looks like Liam, he'll also look like you."

She tried not to dwell on Joe's dreams of being the patriarch of a large brood. Too bad they couldn't be like the Dionnes and have five children at once. Then maybe Joe would call it good. Of course, that could only happen if they put her in an induced coma for the entire pregnancy.

Duncan broke into her thoughts. "Is Carrie warming to you at all?"

Ali debated how to answer. "Somewhat. I'm not sure what 'warm' looks like with Carrie. If 'warm' is the way she is with Teresa, the adjective I'd use is 'intrusive.' I'm better off without it."

"What are we discussing?" Joe said, kissing her cheek. He'd snuck up on her again. She had to watch her mouth when it came to talking about Carrie.

"Oh, *stuff*," Duncan replied, radiating his usual warmth. "We've had precious little time to chat lately. How are you, Joe? Planning another tour? Your voice sounds nice and clear."

An involuntary shudder ran through Ali. *Like someone walked over my grave*, she thought. They were both staring, meaning that her reaction had been noted. "A little chilly out here," she said, a lame excuse in that she was warmly dressed in long sleeves and jeans with an elastic waistband.

Joe held her in the circle of his arms, his hands on her belly. "No tours in the works yet," he told Duncan. "I'm trying something new. With all the improvements I've made in the studio, I'm inviting other performers and bands to record here. Matthew is learning to be a sound engineer so the two of us can multitask." Joe gave Ali a gentle squeeze and added, "Matthew and I are both looking for a way to stick around and still keep a toehold in the biz. He has a solo album in mind and I'm almost ready to record another myself. Now we just need a really great drummer to move here. Don Henley, maybe."

Duncan laughed. "I doubt he's ready to retire. It was only a few years ago when The Eagles got back together."

"The Hotel California," George said in a stage whisper, making everyone jump. "Just invite him to stay here for a week, and he'll never leave. You've got spare housing." He pointed to the cabins.

Giving George the side-eye, Joe said, "David and I have a bet as to when the paparazzi will make camp outside our gates."

"Why now?" Duncan asked. "I thought you convinced them he'd returned to L.A. Did something happen while you were on your trip?"

The actor started playing with the zipper of his hoodie. At least he had the grace to look embarrassed.

"At Sol Duc, George flirted with the receptionist. He wasn't wearing his disguise." Joe sounded more amused than reproachful. "There's no cell service or internet at Sol Duc, so she'll only be calling her friends for now. The press is bound to figure out that George is staying with us, and they know all too well where we live."

"They didn't ask for *your* autograph?" Duncan asked Joe.

He snorted. "They thought we were his bodyguards."

Their laughter drew the others, who wanted in on the joke.

Ali felt as if a weight had been lifted from her shoulders. Joe would stay home for now, at least through her pregnancy. All was right with the world.

* * *

Rory was back with a vengeance. Commenting on Jake's every move, like an omniscient narrator in an eighteenth-century novel, with Jake as its unfortunate subject. Fielding's *Tom Jones*, for instance. Annoying and impossible to block out.

Liam, George, and his brothers now knew his secret. That meant the wives would soon know it too—if they didn't already. The others, including Chiara, might just assume he had his mind on his work. Jake didn't consciously work out what would come next in his novels. Plot holes and incongruities would occur to him out of the blue, and he'd jot them down in notes to be dealt with later. When, early in the morning, he settled in to write, he would usually find that his subconscious was two steps ahead of him. The key was not to force it.

Back in his BPO days, he'd heard whispers that he was "calculating." Didn't they know that being a CEO demanded the cold-blooded strategizing of a Roman general—a charming one, naturally. Though even he realized it wasn't cool to use those tactics on women. Was his pursuit of Chiara a serious lack of judgment? Too late to turn back now.

He finished off a second vodka tonic and vowed to stop with that. He wanted nothing to prevent him from carrying Chiara off to his now empty house, where he would be blessedly free of Rory.

"I heard that," Rory said.

Buddy, let me get this straight, he said in his head, *are you good or bad? 'Cause I'm pretty sure you're real.*

"I can prove I'm real. Ali's having a boy, and Teresa's having a girl."

Shit, don't tell me stuff like that! I don't want to foresee the future.

"All right, I'll stop there. Anyway, they'll know soon enough. They're having ultrasounds in a month."

How did you know that?

"All seeing," Rory huffed.

"Jake?" Chiara broke into his warring thoughts. "Are you all right?"

God, she looked incredible. In her tight jeans, semi-transparent blouse, heels—chestnut curls falling past her shoulders—she embodied all his fantasies of innocent carnality.

"Fantastic, now that you're here."

Rory blew a Bronx cheer in his head.

"They're about to serve dinner," Jake said. Lowering his voice, he added, "Are you prepared to slip away with me?"

"Yes," she said, avoiding his eyes.

A thrill passed through him.

Rory remained silent.

Dinner was a casual affair of burgers with blue cheese, sweet potato fries, a large green salad, and watermelon, all prepared, served, and cleared away by the FOSSP kids Jake referred to privately as Foxface Steve and Cutiepie Angie.

Jake ate sparingly, fixated as he was on seizing the moment. Rory seemed to know there was no point in reasoning with him.

CHAPTER 24

—◆—

It was wonderfully mild out—the most pleasant weather Chiara had experienced here. Near the coast, it always cooled in the evenings, even in summer, and at the end of June, it was still early in the season. The days didn't grow truly warm until late July. Still, with less wind than usual, a sweater was enough. The heat lamps were on, the tiki torches blazed, and the wine flowed. Chiara let the FOSSP young people keep her glass filled. She was enjoying the salty sea air and lazy feeling of unreality that claimed her as she sat on the sidelines. The sun was just disappearing over the horizon as the last of the orange glow on the water receded.

With so many theater people present, the spectacle was ongoing. George had, surprisingly, yielded the spotlight to Maddie and Jeremy, who had been colleagues in a large number of shows. It was a strange world where you could be extremely talented and yet barely earn a living. If Maddie hadn't married David, she would still be residing with her mother and Duncan— Ali and Liam's father. Or perhaps not. She'd had a part in a very important movie, one that might lead to great things if she chose to let it. Wouldn't David have a say in that? *There's always a man to consider*, she thought with a sigh. Not that she'd considered Arnold at all since coming to stay here. She wasn't about to start now. She took another sip of wine.

To everyone's relief, it was George's last night here; he would depart before dawn the next day. Not long after darkness fell, he began to press Maddie for a song. Jake sat with his brother David on the other side of the terrace. Like Chiara, he'd been content to let the others shine, and although they hadn't conversed since agreeing to leave together, their rare glances were all the reassurance she needed. The evening couldn't pass quickly enough for them. When they all rose to gather around the piano with Teresa at the keyboard, Jake drifted over and whispered in her ear, "Ready to sneak off?"

"Yes!" She hated to miss seeing Maddie perform, but they'd have no better opportunity to leave undetected.

"Don't worry," Ali had assured her earlier, after she'd confessed their plans. "We'll take good care of Lorenzo. I'll tell him you … uh, what should I tell him?"

Chiara winced. "That I'm visiting a friend in Port Angeles?"

Ali nodded. "That way he won't worry if you don't return for a few days."

Chiara blushed. She hadn't thought beyond tomorrow. Lorenzo had been perfectly fine during his solo visit with Maddie and David in the spring. Sylvia only asked after her son as an afterthought when she sent updates from Chicago, where she was an emergency room doctor in one of the larger Catholic hospitals.

No one appeared to notice as Chiara and Jake hurried up the hill toward the cars.

* * *

George was reminding Maddie of the annoying little brother she'd never had. He was even dressed like a kid—albeit a rich one—in tight jeans, white T-shirt, and a red hoodie. His bulky high-top sneakers had a chessboard black and white pattern with red panels—probably one-off Air Jordans costing hundreds. What was it with men and big shoes? Women always wanted their feet to appear smaller. Until recently, some ladies in China had still bound their feet, crippling themselves for fashion.

Well, *duh*, of course *men* wanted their feet to look big. There was supposed to be a correlation with dick size. Some men—like her giant husband—had nothing to prove on that account.

Maddie almost longed for a catering job, *any* excuse to leave the compound. The closest thing she had to a "duty" was caring for Lorenzo, and since the men had returned, George was making like those irritating mimes who mimicked your every move. Finally she'd called him on it. She had asked Lorenzo if he'd like to go down the path to the beach. It was a low-tide morning so they could search for starfish and poke—gently—at sea anemones, watching them retract their tentacles. David was off with Joe on some errand. When, uninvited, George had moved to follow, she'd said, "Uh, George, do you have any drag roles in your future?"

Ignoring her sarcasm, he'd said, "What, drag racing?" He was strolling just behind them, hands in his pockets.

"No, as in dressing in drag. Otherwise, why the hell are you shadowing me?"

He didn't rise to the bait. Instead he started whistling. The tune was easy to recognize.

" 'Me and my Shadow,' really?" she said with undisguised annoyance.

He just laughed and … *no*.

She swiveled to face him. "Did you just pinch me?"

He continued to whistle, bugged eyes darting every which way but at her in a parody of innocence.

"You!" She thrust an accusing finger. "Stay in front where I can see you."

Lorenzo picked up the sharpness in her tone. "Aunt Maddie, are you mad at Uncle George?"

Hands on her hips, she repeated, " '*Uncle*?' " She couldn't very well say, "Don't call him that" and had to settle for giving George the stink-eye.

She moved on in stony silence until they reached a tide pool.

"Can you ask *Zia* Chiara to add a starfish character?" Lorenzo said as they observed the purple and orange starfish clinging to the rocks, sometimes in layers. He pointed to a cluster. "They like each other."

Maddie crouched down beside him. "I don't think a starfish could survive in the rain forest. There are no tide pools, and starfish move so slowly we don't even see it happen."

"They can outrun a snail if they need to." George leaned down until he was level with Lorenzo. "Under those arms, there are hundreds of little tubular feet. And do you know what happens if they lose an arm? They can grow another. And that arm? It can grow into another starfish."

Lorenzo gazed up at him, fascinated. "Are they really fish?"

"Nope. They're sea stars. They don't have brains. Fish do."

Lorenzo turned to Maddie. "If they can move, they can go into the rain forest."

"Not without salt water, they can't," Maddie said, "at least according to our expert." She flicked a few fingers in George's direction. To George, she said, "How come you know so much about starfish—excuse me, sea stars?"

"Grew up in a resort town, remember? Nah, just kidding. Not a lot of time for beachcombing. I learned it from the script of a movie that never got made."

On the way back, as Maddie held Lorenzo's hand, George whispered in her ear, "You like me, you know you do."

"Do not," she shot back. "You annoy the hell out of me."

"Maybe a little," he conceded, "but *deep* down …" he trailed off.

"Deep down, you annoy the hell out of me," she insisted with a steely stare.

"You said 'hell,' " Lorenzo remarked gravely.

"That's okay, Lor," George said, tousling his hair. "She didn't mean it."

"Then why did she say it?"

"Because she really likes me a lot," George said in a stage whisper.

"You have to stop flirting," Maddie said in her own furious whisper.

George grinned. "Tempted?"

Realizing she couldn't win, Maddie stalked ahead in silence, making sure she and Lorenzo took up the entire path so George couldn't walk alongside. Silence, that is, except for George's disconcertingly skillful whistling. The tune was "Pretty Woman."

At dinner that evening, David's presence did nothing to deter George from his ongoing harassment, which just grew stealthier. Whenever they were unobserved, he went for it. Flirting was as essential for him as breathing. He'd brush by her on the way to the bar, stopping ever so briefly to sniff her neck and drag a finger along her thigh or sneak a not-so-subtle peek into her cleavage. David never caught him in the act, though he had to sense something was going on. It wasn't as if George was targeting any of the other women. She couldn't tell if he genuinely thought he had a chance with her or if he was simply amusing himself. She suspected the latter. She couldn't wait for him to leave. When was that going to be, anyway? He hadn't committed to a date.

Then … sweet relief. "I'm sad to be leaving so soon," George whispered in her ear. She couldn't help it. She let out a long sigh, which he willfully misinterpreted. "I know, I'll miss you too."

There was no time to set him straight. Duncan stood at her side, telling her how eager he was to hear her sing. "Teresa told me you've been working on an act."

"Sort of," Maddie said, knowing that George was listening. "She doesn't want to be caught unawares next time she's asked to play piano, and she'd prefer not to be the center of attention. I'm more used to the performing-seal thing."

George broke in, "Personally, I love a good performing seal, especially one who sings."

Soon they were all urging Maddie and Teresa to entertain them.

"It's my final wish," George said, hand over his heart, "before I am ejected from the mothership into Outer Space."

Maddie narrowed her eyes at him. He ought to be ashamed of that metaphor, if nothing else. Arm in arm, she and Teresa headed for the living room with its marvelous Bösendorfer grand piano.

They agreed on a set of Cole Porter, beginning with "I Get a Kick Out of You," which she pointedly sang to David.

As she took an ironic bow, she noted that Jake and Chiara had vanished. She hoped Chiara knew what she was doing.

* * *

On the road back to the house, Jake felt like the driver of a getaway car. He had escaped with a fortune, but would he get to keep it? Rory had no comment. One of these days they were going to have a frank talk, starting with what the hell this was all about. If Rory's goal was to ease the trauma of his sudden death, it wasn't working. Jake felt like more of a head case than ever.

He wished Chiara would say something. He didn't want to feel as if he'd lured her away against her better judgment. At the light touch of his hand on her thigh, she relaxed. The air between them began to grow thick with desire. Then his fingers grazed her forearm, finding her palm and lifting it to his lips.

The car stopped in front of the Victorian. He turned off the engine, and they sat in silence. A hard rain had begun to fall, enveloping them in a cocoon of privacy.

"It's raining," he said.

"Yes," she whispered. When she kissed him on the cheek, he turned so that the next kiss found his mouth. They started to devour each other with kisses, leaning in as close as the gearshift would allow. He savored her sweet, wine-tinged breath and drew in a heady draught of her floral scent. His hands cupped her breasts, and he felt the hammering of her heart.

The rain had let up. Jumping out of the car, Jake raced over to throw open the passenger door. He lifted Chiara out of the seat with such care that she might have been a porcelain figurine. Heat flooded him as he pictured her naked, posed like one of the nymphs and goddesses gracing the parlor. She stumbled as he set her on her feet, and he instinctively curled an arm about her waist as they fled to the porch.

Once inside, they came together in a tangle of limbs. Laughing at their mutual clumsiness, they staggered over to the couch and collapsed in a heap.

He brushed a soft curl away from her face. "Would you like a nightcap … tea? A roaring fire in the fireplace?"

She gazed at him adoringly. "Ooh, the complete treatment, like in the movies." Her eyes sparkled with mischief. "I appreciate the gesture." She touched his lips. "Maybe after …?"

She stood and headed for the stairs, walking backward, beckoning him, shedding clothing as she went. She tripped and almost fell, catching herself on the banister, but she quickly shrugged off the awkward moment. At the first few steps, she kicked off her sandals, then she threw her cashmere sweater at him, although it only made it to the bottom of the stairs. He kicked off his Birkenstocks. Next came her filmy blouse, which she slid off slowly, and he did the same with his Izod shirt. Sitting on the stairs, she pulled off her jeans, bunched them up in a ball, and tossed them over the banister. He unbuttoned his jeans and stepped out of them. If she wanted to strip professionally, her act needed work, but for Jake, its enthusiastic, inexpert quality was the most erotic thing he'd ever witnessed. When she was down to her lace bra and panties and he wore only boxer briefs, he playfully chased her the rest of the way up the stairs, like she was one of those scantily clad nymphs, and he was a satyr. She gasped in delight as he hoisted her over his shoulder.

Once she lay on his bed, Jake quickly dispensed with her bra and panties. He paused, intending to admire every inch of her soft, pliant, long-limbed perfection. But Chiara had other ideas. Far from shrinking from his gaze, she arched her back so that her round breasts with their erect rosy-brown nipples lifted to meet his tongue. She was pulling ineffectually at his boxer briefs, so he obliged her by wriggling out of them. And just like that, he was inside her. She'd managed it almost without his participation. Gritting his teeth, he forced himself to pull out and put on a condom. She could hardly be more ready, so he surrendered, giving Chiara the frantic sex she seemed to crave.

It was over too soon. No matter, he was fully charged, hopped up on the drug of her soft skin, floral scent, and exquisite curves. It could be hours before they slept, maybe days.

CHAPTER 25

IN THE WEE HOURS OF the morning, Jake drifted off into a blissful, exhausted sleep. When he opened his eyes at dawn, Chiara faced him, fully awake, smiling, the covers pulled down to her waist. His cock responded instantly to her lush nakedness. When she reached for it, he caught her hand and held it to his heart.

"Let's talk for a bit, shall we?" Jake said, amused by her impatience. "I realize my body has other plans. We have time, right? I, for one, could use sustenance."

He slid off the bed and walked over to the closet, preening a little for her benefit. Slipping into one of the guest robes, he laid the other at the foot of the bed. "Don't shower unless you want to," he whispered. "I love to smell myself on you." He pressed his nose into her slender neck and drew in a long breath. "Ahhh." His voice grew husky as he asked, "Do you wanna stay here and let me wait on you or accompany me downstairs?"

"I'll come with you," she said.

After a light breakfast of scrambled eggs and toast, they lingered at the counter over espresso, speaking in low voices, their rambling conversation frequently interrupted by kisses that derailed their train of thought.

"Were you always so beautiful?" she asked in a voice full of wonder.

"Hey, that's my line," he said. Then he laughed, a dry and joyless sound. "I was the runt of the litter. And maybe too pretty for a man. Having a twin like Joe was a constant lesson in humility. After Edward, so handsome it almost hurt to look at him, Joe was the golden child. Confident, insanely talented, big for his age, built, even at sixteen. David and I were the nerdy kids, but at least he was a physically impressive nerdy kid. I escaped into my imagination, wrote stories that turned me into some invincible hero. Somewhere along the line, Da got it into his head that I should take over the family business. I had a few stories accepted into magazines that published professional writers. I was strutting like a peacock. Until my parents hosed me down. The stories weren't literary enough, they said. At least they bothered to read them. They told me, gently, I was wasting my time, that my writing was 'cartoonish.' " He sighed. "So, after my father died—Joe and I were nineteen—Big Paul's was my only hill to climb. Da had ordained it in his will. He might as well have hung a yoke around my neck. I stopped writing and turned myself into who, I imagined, he'd wanted me to be." He shook his head. "Hah. Come to think of it, Da was nothing like who I became. I was James Bond without the skills."

"What does that mean?" Chiara asked, her eyes shining with sympathy.

"Listen," he said, "don't cry for me. I never had to worry for a moment about money or how much I spent on suits or my house, or skis, or trips abroad, or Scotch, any other luxury I could imagine. I was the boss's son, and leadership came easily to me. But weirdly, none of it was anywhere near as fun as it should have been." He made a face. "I'm not sure what I expected. That someone would throw me a parade? That my brothers would slap me on the back and thank me for my service? None of that happened, of course. Freed from any responsibility to Big Paul's, they struck out on their own quests. Joe was flying pretty high for a while there. David's math and science brain seemed ideal for a career in medicine. We all just assumed Teresa was going to marry someone fabulous, though no one was particularly keen on Paul, her erstwhile fiancé. I don't what happened to Edward. Speaking of yokes, I can't think of a heavier one than becoming a Catholic priest." He stopped to give her a light kiss. "Listen to me, running off at the mouth. If any one of us O'Connells is unhappy, we have only ourselves to blame. We made our own damn beds."

Chiara was smiling now, though her eyes were still shiny. "Or chose our own bicycles."

He cocked his head, waiting for an explanation.

"An Italian version of the idiom. 'You wanted the bicycle, now ride on it.' "

"Did you get the bicycle you wanted?"

"Bah." Chiara shrugged. "Shall we move to the living room? These chairs have hard seats."

"Of course," he said, "thinking she hoped to avoid talking about herself.

He wasn't going to let her off that easily. He poured them glasses of water and lit the fire. Chiara folded her legs beneath her and her robe gaped open. She didn't pull it back together. Now *that* was a distraction. "Please," he said, "I want to know everything about you. It's as if you don't believe you're interesting. You are to me."

She sat with her hands on her knees, staring into the fire. "I know how it feels to be lost in the shadow of a fearless sibling. Sylvia was the smart one, like David, good at figures, the one they called Sophia Loren with a brain. With no son to take the family name, my parents looked to her to save them from their spendthrift ways. The brighter she shined, the more I faded into the wall. When she found a way for us to receive a high school education in the United States, my parents made sure I went along. They didn't wish to be burdened with me. They thought I would come to nothing. And like you, I felt so … plain and stupid in comparison."

Parents, he thought with a wave of disgust. "I can't imagine that," he said. "You'd have to be blind to see you as anything but a beauty."

She chuckled. "I'm glad *you* think so."

She stood then, done talking for now, and let her robe fall to the floor. He smiled, wanting to hear more but helpless against the surge of lust the sight of her inspired.

Two more glorious hours were whiled away in bed before they showered and dressed. Finally, sipping wine and nibbling on smoked salmon, cheese, and crackers, they cuddled on the porch swing to enjoy the afternoon sun and gaze out at the bay.

"I hate to be a buzzkill … uh, a spoilsport," Jake said, "but I've got something pressing on my mind." He also had "something pressing" in his jeans, but he refused to get sidetracked. "What about Arnold?"

She screwed up her face. "Pfft! Do you know he has not contacted me in any way since I arrived in Port Townsend? I may never hear from him again."

Jake was taken aback. "He'll just put you out of his mind?"

Her smile was sad. "I've been expecting divorce papers. Hoping for them, in fact." She touched his cheek. "I have a 'buzzkill' question too."

He grinned. "Ask away."

"Why are you so distracted?" After a thoughtful pause, she added, "Except for in this house. *Here* I have your full attention."

"*He* leaves me alone here." No need to hide his secret any longer. After what they'd shared, he trusted her to understand. If she didn't, better that he find out now.

She cocked her head. "He?"

"My friend, Rory."

She regarded him for a long moment. "This friend is dead?"

"Yes."

"How did he die?" Her fingers brushed his cheek. "Only tell me if you want to. I can see it's a difficult subject."

He was certain she'd been an excellent therapist. He didn't beat around the bush. "We were on a ten-day hiking trip. The Wonderland Trail, the one that loops around Mount Rainer."

She nodded. "I know it."

"Rory had a heart attack. There was no reviving him."

"Oh, Jake …." She gave him a heartfelt hug. "And now you hear him in your head?"

"Yes."

"Is it horrible?"

He didn't hesitate. "No, not at all. Only, I wish I understood the reason for it. Is it guilt? Do I believe I might have saved him? Maybe I botched the CPR. Is Rory a real ghost who can't let go of life? He won't tell me. If indeed he's not some aural hallucination. He *did* tell me some stuff about the future that pretty much disproves that theory. If you think I'm nuts, I get it. Crazy, I mean."

"Nuts," she repeated with a delighted smile. Then turned serious again. "No, it was a terribly traumatic event in your life. Everything was going smoothly, yes? You were a successful businessman with everything a man could want."

He laid a hand against her cheek. "Not everything."

She smiled shyly. "You didn't know I existed."

"I felt the lack of you. As if someone like you must exist. But I believed that if I did meet you—someone *like* you—you be too good for me. Or you wouldn't want me."

She was silent for too long.

"Please," he said in a rush, "if you're not as crazy about me as I am about you, tell me now. Because I'm in too deep."

A fat tear rolled down her cheek. "It's not that. It was hard enough for you to lose Rory to the other side. I'm not long for this world either, I'm afraid."

IT WAS LATE MORNING, AND Maddie was in the rec room, playing quietly with Lorenzo while Ali attempted to cajole the twins out of their foul mood. Food and clean diapers weren't enough. At least their screams had turned into whimpers. Ali adjusted her ponytail and blew a strand of straight black hair out of her face, which looked more drawn than usual. More than once this morning, she'd gone running for the bathroom. It made Maddie want to get her tubes tied.

"They sound so sorry for themselves," Maddie said. Making googly eyes at the teary babies, she sang in a silly voice, "You poor things, you poor things, you poor, poor things!" The twins' reaction was more gratifying than a round of applause. They appeared riveted.

Ali's jaw dropped. "Wow. I'm impressed! Next time they're out of control, we'll try this first. Is that from a musical?"

"*Juno,*" Maddie replied. "The musical version of the play *Juno and the Paycock.*"

" 'Juno and the Peacock,' the Aesop fable? Something about a peacock asking the goddess Juno for a nicer voice but having to settle for being beautiful?"

Maddie hadn't considered that the play was based on a fable. Though the plot didn't sound similar. Joe and his vocal issues came to mind, but she pushed that thought away. "I don't know the fable. The play is by an Irishman, Seán O'Casey. A vain man thinks he's inherited a fortune and goes on a spending spree. Then, no fortune. His family is ruined, his son is killed by soldiers, and his unwed daughter gets pregnant and is disgraced. At the end he goes off to get drunk and his wife and daughter leave him."

Ali looked horrified. "Who's Juno and who's the peacock?"

"The man is the peacock; Juno is his wife."

Lying side by side in their bassinet, the babies stared up at the two women. In a baby-friendly voice, Ali said, "Remind me to skip that one if it comes to Theatre by the Marina."

Maddie laughed and both babies giggled. "We did a concert version of the musical. The score by Marc Blitzstein is gorgeous. There's a little comic relief where the women all vie for the dubious distinction of whose lot in life is the hardest."

Ali was bouncing Josie. "Sounds grim for a musical."

"Musical *theater*, not musical comedy." Maddie turned to Lorenzo, who was also observing them in wide-eyed wonder. "Hey, Lor, what do you think?" He often watched them as if they were animals in a zoo.

"I don't like to hear people complain … or argue," Lorenzo said. Maddie assumed the "people" in question were Chiara and Arnold. Who else would argue in front of him?

To Ali, Maddie said, "They keep trying to outdo each other—you know, this one says, my husband doesn't want me, another says, my son was a soldier killed in battle—and the others respond in a chorus of 'You poor thing.' But enough. My point is, I like the way you are with the twins. You don't say, 'Poor things!' You stay upbeat. Does anyone ever really want to be pitied? It's either annoying or it makes you feel more sorry for yourself."

The smiling babies started babbling to each other, taking turns as if engaged in a serious discussion.

"If only I spoke baby," Ali said. "They clearly have a lot to say." She gave Maddie a long look. "You miss acting."

Maddie couldn't deny it. "Yes, I don't know what to do with myself. You can only read and exercise so much."

"What are you reading?"

Maddie made a face. "*King Solomon's Mines*."

"What?"

"You know, Allan Quatermain. David loves that story."

"They read those books as kids. Not everything holds up when you look back as an adult."

Maddie nodded. "I can see the appeal for a boy. The old movie with Deborah Kerr and Stewart Granger is way better. In the book, Allan is short and dark with grizzled hair. At one point they slaughter an entire herd of elephants and crow over it. There are no women."

Ali chuckled. "Boys probably prefer 'no women.' Lorenzo, what do you think?"

"That would be like Moss Manor with no Mrs. Bigfoot," Lorenzo said reasonably. "And it's bad to kill animals."

Maddie regretted mentioning that part.

"Yes, it is," Ali said, her face solemn, "and your papa and uncles don't approve of killing elephants one little bit. Still, I think you'd prefer a story with no romance."

They laughed at Lorenzo's "icky" face. Maddie had to bite her tongue to keep from asking what "romance" meant to him. Nothing good.

They both turned at the clomping on the stairs. Teresa strode in on a rush of fresh air, accompanied by happy dogs. The twins had gone back to looking angelic.

"Time for their naps," Ali said. "Shall we take them back to the Log Palace? Teresa, I wanted to quiz you about some photos."

"I'll stay behind with Lorenzo," Maddie said easily. Ali was awfully perceptive, and Maddie wasn't ready to discuss a future she was fairly sure had nothing but clouds on the horizon.

* * *

Ali carried Josie and Teresa, Caryn, as they entered the Log Palace and settled in on the living room couch. The babies were enjoying a rare moment of calm and contentment, cooing on their shoulders. The black leather couch, large enough to accommodate Mrs. Bigfoot and her gang, faced a similarly oversized river-rock hearth.

"Poor Maddie," Ali began. "She keeps searching for common ground with David."

"Oh, yeah? How many men and women really share much common ground, do you think? Straight men and women, that is. Jeremy and Maddie have loads in common."

Boom, that topic was dead on arrival. So much for getting Teresa to open up about Liam. In truth, they were all odd couples. Even if Ali and Joe had attended high school at the same time, chances are they'd never have crossed paths. Not in math club, drama club, book club, or even show choir. Ali and Liam hadn't gone to school dances. Everyone dressed up, and they owned nothing vaguely appropriate.

Ali watched her sister-in-law as she assessed the exposed beams of the ceiling and the cedar-paneled walls of the cavernous living room. "No artwork? Maybe a TV? It's a beautiful room. It seems ... underutilized."

Completing the room hadn't been a priority. Ali couldn't very well tell Teresa that Joe wanted to make those decisions himself. She'd think Ali was spineless. Perhaps her metaphorical spine was too burdened by her unborn child to function properly. A topic for a therapist, not Teresa. "Joe dictated the basic design, and I was okay with whatever he decided. Then he just … didn't decide." Suddenly conscious of how her voice boomed in the resonant space, she lowered it a notch. "It's the opposite of cozy in here. A car showroom is cozier. Artwork would help, but what kind? Somehow a big reproduction of Monet's water lilies just wouldn't cut it, though that might be *my* choice. American Indian art, I suppose. A herd of buffalo. A large moose head."

Teresa gave her a dubious look.

"Forget the moose head, obviously," Ali said. "What do you picture here?"

Teresa planted a kiss on Caryn's head. "I wouldn't presume. My efforts at the Sea Captain's House were not appreciated."

"I liked it," Ali said with excessive ardor. "The Art Deco living room was amazing. But it was so … pristine. A house for a childless couple."

Teresa grimaced. "Maddie and David didn't care for it either, and they're childless. Or baby-less, anyway. Lorenzo isn't your average child. I can't picture him tramping dirt into the house."

A moment passed as they stared at each other's bellies. Both were showing, though Ali had gained more weight, and she worried about the effect of the pregnancy on her health.

"Will they survive, do you think?" Teresa asked. Ali froze, as if Teresa referred to their fetuses. Her sister-in-law hastened to add, "Their marriage, I mean. Maddie and David's. David is such a wonderful guy. And I love Maddie too. But her career … his lack of direction … I'm afraid …." Without finishing the thought, she blurted out, "Jake agrees with you about buying a house. He doesn't like that Liam refers to the Victorian as 'his' and makes all the decisions."

Ali didn't second Jake's concern—aloud, anyway. "You can't move out right now. That might have worked before the pregnancy …."

"I wasn't saying I would *live* there."

"Let's put the girls down for a nap, okay?"

Ali led the way to the nursery on the second floor, where they laid the girls in their cradle. Teresa did need more breathing space, Ali thought. If she owned a house that reflected her own taste, perhaps she could view the growing fetus as a shared joy rather than a pending burden. If only Teresa would call Liam on his BS. Ali knew he loved and desired her. Thanks to

Kilo, he no longer trusted her. *Damn that troublemaker*. They say you never get over your first love, and he had certainly been Teresa's, enough that she'd run away with him straight out of high school.

Who in their right mind would choose Kilo over Liam? Ali hoped he was gone from their lives forever.

"May Allen will be back around five," Ali whispered. "I think we can sneak away to my studio for a bit. If they wake, we'll hear them on the monitor." As they climbed the final flight of stairs leading to the attic, she said, "You could buy a house and call it an office."

Instead of answering, Teresa asked, "You have a 'studio,' really?"

"A room of my own," Ali said wryly. "The best natural lighting in the house."

The attic room had a sloped ceiling, and a hardwood bench stood by the window overlooking the bay. Its colorful cushions were illustrated with seals, clams, and river otters—all manner of sea creatures native to the area. The warm cedar paneling of the walls was the backdrop for several other drawings, mostly pastels. Sunlight streamed in through the windows.

"They're your designs," Teresa said in a hushed voice. "I love them." She gazed around in wonder. "Your amazing artwork is everywhere! I didn't know you'd started working in pastels. The twins are going to love this room when they're old enough to appreciate it. It's so … whimsical."

Ali beamed. "The next children's book I illustrate takes place in Puget Sound. I'm hoping Chiara will want to write the story once she sees how the first book turned out. Meanwhile, we're having these pillow shams manufactured in Port Angeles and sold in several area boutiques, a few in Seattle. Also sheets, duvet covers, and tea towels."

"I've seen them for sale on Water Street," Teresa marveled, picking up a cushion. "I should have known they were yours. Chiara, huh? The story is that good?"

"I've been transcribing it rather than having her write it down. She's got a little of that 'English as a second language' vibe on the page." Ali had initially asked Teresa, who'd majored in Creative Writing at Sarah Lawrence College, to come up with a story. She'd passed. Now that Chiara had accepted the challenge, Ali hoped Teresa wasn't having second thoughts.

Teresa did another slow pivot. "Was there something in particular you wanted to show me? You mentioned photographs."

Ali went over to a cardboard box and pulled out an album. "This is it. I have to admit, this task bums me out. The retrospective of Joe's career is downright painful. So many publicity shots of Rina and screaming fans."

"Rina's a bigger star than ever," Teresa said. "The tabloids called her his fiancée, but she and Joe were never really engaged, you know. And she's still married to that guy."

Ali looked up. "Amazing, right? He's four years younger and a good Christian boy, or so Joe says. I guess she likes having the upper hand. I know she tried to lead Joe around by the nose."

Teresa scrunched up her face in disgust. "Having a child may have given her a reality check. Thank God she's not *your* problem anymore. The biological father is some roadie, right? Weird that she thought she could pass it off as Joe's."

"Yes." Ali flipped to the first page. "This particular album features Joe's childhood."

Teresa peered over her shoulder. "Mom made one for each of us. The first several pages, those dating back to Mom and Da's wedding, are duplicates. Some of the photos of our older siblings are included in our books, but once we're born, we become the focus."

"That was thoughtful of Carrie," Ali said, looking at her mother-in-law's wedding photos—the elegantly slim bottle blonde with the big blue eyes and the towering hunk of a husband—the spitting image of Joe, only with David's extreme height and more powerful proportions. "What a pair they made! She's hardly changed at all."

"Yes," Teresa said. "If anything, age has improved her."

Ali's smile was a little crooked. "Age?" They both laughed. "Your dad was a handsome devil. Like Mr. Universe."

Teresa nodded. "Joe, David, and Eddy have his cleft chin. David has his height. Eddy's an inch taller than Joe, but with Jake's refined features and more streamlined physique. Objectively speaking, he's the best looking."

"Really? I would have said Joe. Your mom agrees with you."

"Joe's more muscular. Ruggeder. Physically, David takes the rugged to extremes, though he has the sweetest nature. Edward is a little"—she cast about for the word—"cold. It's so strange that he was the one with the religious calling. I always wondered how he managed the celibacy thing after such a wild youth. Mom worried he'd end up with a 'bevy of bastards.'"

Ali winced. The word "bastard" never failed to punch her squarely in the solar plexus. "Is that the collective noun?" she tried to joke. "Like a 'murder' of crows?"

Teresa caught her reaction and immediately started backpedaling. "Her words, not mine." Realizing she was putting salt on the wound, she went on, "Bastard is a terrible word. I hope no one called you or Liam that."

"Please," Ali said, knowing Teresa didn't mean to be insensitive. "They did, but they also called us worse things. Now, with Lorenzo in the fold, I hope Carrie has banished that word from her vocabulary."

"One can only hope so," Teresa said with a frown.

"Moving right along …" Ali said. "I gather Edward used something other than the rhythm method and managed to avoid contributing to the population explosion."

"As far as I know, he didn't, uh, sow any wild oats that found fertile ground."

"Why become a priest?"

"Your guess is as good as mine. He had a Damascene moment? Like in the Gospels, when Saul had a vision, became Paul, and turned into a holier-than-thou jerk. That's Edward, unfortunately. Perhaps his calling was a delayed reaction to Da's death; he entered divinity school two years later. He didn't exactly break with the family, just distanced himself. After he graduated with a degree in Philosophy from Harvard, he spent a year in Rome doing God knows what." She laughed. "Presumably, God *does* know, but the rest of us are unlikely to find out. None of us kids have seen him since 1987. Only Mom, and her short visits to Philadelphia have been unsatisfying, judging from the time it takes her to throw off her bad mood after she returns."

"We invited him to our wedding," Ali said, settling in on the turquoise-blue couch. "He wrote back that he'd come for the religious ceremony."

"Ha!" Teresa flopped down beside her on the couch. "Only because he was confident there wouldn't be one."

"What? You all are too ungodly?"

Teresa shrugged. "Guess so. It was the height of hypocrisy—or do I mean irony?—that *he* was the one who felt duty bound to 'rescue' me from Kilo."

For a long moment, they sat in companionable silence. Teresa gave her shoulder a squeeze. "You look sad. What's up?"

"My own photo 'album' wouldn't fill a page. There are a few formal school portraits of Liam and me. Other than that, some blurry Polaroids. What will I say when my children ask to see photos of my parents?"

"Duncan could make copies of photos from various points in his life."

Ali wished she hadn't brought the subject up. She was hardly the only one with an undocumented childhood. Maybe it was better that way. If there *had* been photos, she wouldn't care to pore over them.

She put the album down on the side table. "Maybe I should have taken a picture of my mother while I could. Then I could say, 'Look, Josie and Caryn, here's your grandma. Sorry, the only photo I have of her was when she was homeless and dying. She dropped into our lives to con some money out of us for drugs, then disappeared again."

"It wasn't that simple," Teresa said softly. "I think she wanted to connect with you, but after David healed her liver and Liam put that money into an account for her, the temptation to resume her old life was too great."

"I'm sure you're right." Ali patted her arm. "I wonder if we'll ever see her again."

"That money isn't going to last long," Teresa said.

Ali stared at the ceiling, thinking she should paint a night sky there—stars, a crescent moon. "I wonder, will we even know when she dies?"

"Best not to think about it," Teresa said. "I, for one, would hate to be able to foretell the future. What's that Bible saying? 'Sufficient unto the day is the evil thereof.' " She pointed at the pastel drawing on the easel. "Is that a starfish?" The creature in the drawing had exaggerated suction-cup feet. Its scampering was indicated by motion lines. "What are those red mounds at the end of each arm?"

Ali gave a snort of self-deprecating laughter. "Eyes. A work in progress. Accuracy versus cuteness, my personal bugaboo. Starfish—excuse me, 'sea stars' is what Lorenzo insists I call them because they are *not* fish—have an eye at the end of each arm. They don't look like eyes—more like red dots. So I raised them some. I'm thinking of putting them on the end of antennae or giving them irises and eyelashes. I have to take some liberties. Sea creatures are not warm and fuzzy. Making them cute is a challenge."

"What's his—or her—name?"

"If I go with the alliteration thing, Sally or Sammy, depending on how he or she ultimately turns out."

"Can't he-she be sexually ambiguous?"

Ali gave it some thought. "Isn't Sam one of those names that goes either way? Technically starfish have distinct sexes, though some are hermaphrodites. You can't tell by looking at them, but they know ... somehow."

Teresa gave her an affectionate nudge. "You're overthinking this."

Ali grinned. "I fully expect Lorenzo to factcheck me. That kid keeps us all on our toes."

Teresa rubbed her belly. "This is so strange, isn't it? I hope it's a girl."

Because you need her to be on your *side*, Ali thought with regret. *Which means she'll probably be a daddy's girl.*

Ali massaged her own belly. "If Joe his way, we'd just be getting started.

Ever see those stray cats who've had litter after litter? That will be me in ten years, everything sagging."

Teresa looked perplexed. "Can't you call it quits after this one? Pregnancy is hard on you." Avoiding Ali's eyes, she added, "It isn't all about pleasing Joe, you know."

Said the pot to the kettle, Ali thought, aware that saying it out loud might drive a wedge between them without solving anything.

A wail rose up from the monitor. *Saved by the wail.* "Yes," Ali said with a tense smile, "it's also about pleasing the little ladies of the house."

Teresa walked over to the door, listening. "Someone's coming up the stairs."

"Must be Joe, checking on lunch. Or maybe he heard the girls crying from the music studio."

Joe stood at the door, wearing a deadly serious expression.

"Arnold's here," he said, as if announcing the arrival of the Four Horsemen of the Apocalypse.

Ali might have preferred the Horsemen. If possible, the wail of the twins rose a decibel or two.

"First things first," Ali declared in a firm voice, determined not to give in to rising panic. "Teresa, can you greet our guest while Joe and I tend to the twins?"

Of all the times for May Allen and Susan to have a day off ...."

CHAPTER 27

———◆———

"Do you have a fatal disease?"

Jake thought his heart might give out. It was racing, and he could hardly breathe, as if all the oxygen had been sucked from the room. Chiara wouldn't meet his eyes. *Damn it, tell me what's wrong so I can find a way to fix it*, he silently urged her.

"No, no disease. I will tell you a story. Please do not comment until I am done."

Clearly, it wasn't a bedtime story on a par with "Moss Manor." He ordered himself to keep his cool. If she weren't ill—if, say, mobsters had put a hit on her—there had to be a solution. Besides, that was the kind of thing that happened to Damon's girlfriends and former mobsters and their molls, not real people. "Let's move to the parlor," he said, his voice remarkably calm. "Might as well be comfortable."

While he stoked the fire, Chiara sat with her hands in her lap, her face bleached of color. The dread that gripped Jake was more effective than a cold shower—or a hefty dose of saltpeter. Metaphorical saltpeter. It turned out that chemical compound did *not* suppress sex drive. *Damn it*, his brain was misfiring, going off on a tangent, trying to deflect with humor as it always did. He did *not* want to hear that he had found Chiara only to lose her again.

Stay present, he told himself as he numbly joined Chiara on the couch.

She stared into the fire, but her gaze had turned inward. "You may recall I worked in the tasting room in a winery in Chelan—the summer of my freshman year at the University of Oregon. The next year, I found a similar job in the Southern Willamette Valley, not far from Eugene. My sister Sylvia's summer jobs were in laboratories. On my day off, I went into Eugene with Emily, the daughter of the owner, to get a haircut. Next to the salon was a fortune-telling place. It was run by gypsies, and the business had no identifying sign. I don't know how much they enforce the laws, but in Oregon, predicting the future for money is a misdemeanor. If there are permits, this place didn't have one."

Chiara was wringing her hands. Jake wanted to still them, massage her shoulders, reassure her somehow. Instead, he concentrated on appearing receptive as he willed her to get to the point.

She went on, "During my haircut, Emily visited the psychic. She was so impressed, she bought me a session. I thought it might be fun, but I was also apprehensive. In Italy, there are still many gypsies living in encampments. They're believed to be kidnappers, pickpockets. My parents used them to scare us when we misbehaved. The little shop was badly neglected. I walked through a beaded door curtain, many of the beads broken or missing. It reeked of stale cigarette smoke. A girl greeted me, maybe ten years old. She was too thin and might have been much older. She sat at the table for two and invited me to join her. After shuffling the cards several times, she told me to cut them and choose three.

" 'This card is the past, the middle one is the present, and this one is the future,' she said, pointing them out. 'Tell me what questions you want answered.' I suppose she meant questions such as 'will I find my true love?' 'Whatever the cards tell you,' I said. Almost no time passed before she put the cards aside and told me three things. First, that my sister would go to Africa. Second: I would help raise a child not my own. Finally: I would die young, not of an illness."

Jake itched to call bullshit on this so-called "fortune." For once he wished Rory were around to act as the voice of reason. *Focus*, he warned his errant brain.

"Her mother arrived, furious. She slapped the child, right in front of me. The girl was defiant, shaking her fist. I shrank back. The older gypsy asked what the child had said. I didn't wish to make things worse. 'Nothing,' I told her. She hastened to do a more conventional session, telling me positive things—such as, I would marry and have a child. I dismissed the entire reading as absurd." Tears glistened in Chiara's eyes. "You can guess the rest. When Sylvia told me she was going to Africa, the girl's predictions replayed in my head, word for word. Then, two years later, Sylvia brought Lorenzo home and asked if Arnold and I would care for him. Arnold objected until

Sylvia agreed to send money for his care. She still sends money—money we don't need. I don't know where it goes because Arnold refuses to discuss it with me. He manages our finances and comments on everything I buy."

Jake wrapped Chiara in his arms as she cried herself out. Handing her his handkerchief, he said, "I don't believe in such twaddle. What matters is, you do. It doesn't scare me. In fact, I want to get to the bottom of it."

She looked even more beautiful after her crying jag. Luminous.

Blotting her eyes, she said, "What will you do, find another fortune teller?"

"I have a live-in fortune teller. Rory. He's got to be good for something. For some reason, he won't talk to me here."

Jake's cell phone rang. The Caller ID told him it was David.

"Hello?"

"Hey, Jake. Weirdness here. We have a houseguest."

"Let me guess." He looked up at Chiara, whose ghostly pallor told him she already expected the worst. "Arnold."

"Yep."

"Does he know where Chiara is?"

"No. He tried to call her, but she's not answering her cell phone. She's with you, right? When his car was blocked at the entrance to the gravel road, he parked along Hastings and walked in. The dogs alerted us to an intruder. We made him wait, assuming he was the one paparazzo who didn't get the message George went home. By then the guy was super pissed off, convinced we were hiding Chiara. Ali told him she was on a day hike and that cell service is spotty outside of Port Townsend."

"That's true enough," Jake said. "Did he believe her?"

"He said Chiara doesn't hike."

"Do you hike?" Jake asked Chiara.

"I could have started."

"What did you tell him?" he asked David.

"Ali told him everyone here hikes. She was surprisingly convincing."

That made sense. Once upon a time, Ali had led Jake on a merry chase. He imagined that she excelled in the art of the white lie. He checked his watch. Three fifteen. "Okay, we have a few hours to make the lie plausible."

"Will you come with her?"

"No, what I have in mind involves Teresa."

"Think again. Teresa is here."

"Liam's not, is he?"

"What, you want Arnold to think his wife hiked with Liam? Arnold would never buy that it was platonic."

"Okay, I'll try Matthew. Tell Arnold she went hiking with our gay friend."

David didn't reply immediately.

"Who did you say she hiked with?" Jake persisted.

"Just 'a friend.'"

Ending the call, Jake said to Chiara, "Let's go talk to Matthew. The story is that you went on a day hike with your gay friend. We'll find you tennis shoes and a T-shirt."

Chiara was blinking rapidly. She was clearly a rotten liar, no matter how much was at stake. Normally that would please him. "If I buy shoes, they will look too new."

"We'll try the secondhand store. But first, let's call Matthew."

"What if he isn't home?"

The phone rang again. Damn it—his agent. William was an older gay man who represented several of the best-selling thriller writers. It had been a coup to sign with someone of his caliber. The call had to be important.

"Hey, William, how's it going?"

"How about you?" William said. "You sound tense."

"I do? Oh, yeah, there's some craziness going on here. But we have it under control."

"That's good, I guess. My news should cheer you up."

His dramatic pause was long enough for a train to pass through. "Uh, William? We're a little pressed for time here."

"Tada! George Reed Masters agreed to play Damon Morehouse."

Jake tried to summon the expected enthusiasm. "That's fantastic."

"Under one condition, and I think you'll agree this is also good news. He wants your sister-in-law Maddie Leftwood to play Holly Relish ...." Jake was momentarily dumbstruck. "Uh, Jake?"

"Still here."

"But less thrilled apparently."

"It's not that. It's … complicated."

"Isn't this just the lucky break Maddie needs right now?" William asked.

"Can we talk tomorrow?"

"They'll want an answer."

"Tell them I'm psyched but I'll need a private moment to talk to Maddie. She's between agents."

"I can find her one, on the basis of this offer alone."

"Still, I'd appreciate it if you put them off till tomorrow."

"Of course."

"Uh, William? In a nutshell, here's my problem: George has the hots for Maddie. If she takes this role, my brother David will blow a gasket."

William cleared his throat. "This is the doctor? The one who was in Africa?"

"Yes, and they've only been married a month. It's awkward as hell."

"I get it. That's rough. Would he really stand in the way of an opportunity like this?"

"No, but the marriage is … young. I don't like the odds of it surviving if, well … you know."

"Okay, let's talk tomorrow."

Jake closed his phone. He felt overwhelmed, his muscles bunched up in knots and his brain muddled. He looked over at Chiara, who in contrast, appeared almost preternaturally calm. "George wants Maddie to play Holly," she said.

"Yep. Holly is the romantic interest. She wins Damon's heart after some torrid sex scenes but dies at the end of the book."

"Oh. David will not be pleased."

He squeezed her hand. "One crisis at a time." How would Damon handle this? he thought. Crazy shit happened to him all the time. Jake prided himself on his ability to write Damon out of seemingly impossible binds.

He helped Chiara to her feet.

"Wait a minute." Sitting down again, he pulled her onto his lap.

"What is it, Jake?"

"What are we doing?" he said, giving her a squeeze. "Staging some elaborate ruse for Arnold's sake? Even if Matthew *is* home and we manage to find some used but not-too-used tennis shoes …. *I'm* the friend you've been quote/unquote hiking with, and *I'm* taking you back to the compound."

"We should still buy the shoes." Chiara wiggled her bare toes. Her sandals lay beside them on the parlor floor. "I couldn't walk a mile in these sandals, even on pavement."

"If he asks, we'll say you were wearing tennis shoes and they're still in my car."

"What if Arnold does something rash?"

The man Jake pictured would have no physical courage. "If he challenges me to a duel, I'll choose knives."

"*Pfft.*" She blew out an impatient breath. "Be serious."

"Do you intend to go back to Portland with him?"

Her eyes flashed. "No!"

"So, let's face the music. We'll go with the hiking story. On Dungeness Spit in Sequim. It's nothing but miles and miles of beach. You could totally do it in tennis shoes. We'll say we didn't make it to the lighthouse. The one time I attempted that hike, I gave up out of boredom. I don't want Ali to be caught in a lie, no matter how well intentioned."

CHAPTER 28

BOTH TWINS SMELLED PUNGENT—THEY SEEMED even to soil their diapers as a team—so Ali changed Caryn while Joe attended to Josie. The two were using real words mixed up with made-up language. It sounded like gobbledygook to Ali but made perfect sense to the tiny co-conspirators. At this point they had few real words. About fifty percent of their coherent conversation consisted of "Mama" and "Dada." The rest was "No!" "Me!" "Mine!" "Oops!" "Up!" "Down!" and "Uh-oh." "Bad" but not "good." Ever since David had brought home the camcorders, Ali and Joe had been filming their every move. Soon they'd need to dedicate an entire cabin toward storing the videotapes.

"What do you think of Arnold?" Ali asked Joe, hearing the bleakness in her own voice.

"I can't get a read." Joe sounded bemused rather than irritated. "Seems like an ordinary guy. Not some arch villain like Dr. No. I'd call him grouchy rather than angry. Naturally he was pissed off that our security system forced him to walk in. I guess no one responded to his call on the intercom."

"Some advance notice would have been appreciated," Ali muttered.

"Yeah." Joe sighed. "Believe it or not, he apologized for that. Said he didn't know how long it would take him to get here. Whenever he pulled over to make a call, he didn't have cell reception, and by the time he'd arrived in Port Townsend, his phone was out of juice."

Ali bounced Josie, who gurgled in appreciation. "We can't leave the others holding the bag. Let's take the girls. Arnold might be easier on us if we arrive looking like the harried parents we are."

Joe spoke in a baby voice to Josie, as if addressing her directly. "What else would we do with them?"

Ali rolled her eyes. "He probably thinks his wayward wife has sought our protection. It's true that if I'd believed their marriage was happy, I'd have urged her to invite him to join us. Instead, we all chose to pretend he didn't exist."

A squirming Josie pleaded, "Dada, Dada, Dada! Up, up, up!"

He lifted her in the air and she merrily flailed about. Caryn immediately reached out with her plump arms, crying, "Me!"

"They're not going to settle down anytime soon," Joe said.

Each trying to hold a thrashing baby without getting kicked in the face, they made their way down to the terrace.

Ali didn't know what she'd expected Arnold to look like—just not like this guy. Fortyish, receding hairline, gray mixed in with the black. If he'd been on *What's My Line?*, she would have guessed "insurance salesman" rather than "software engineer." He had a bit of the salesman's slickness to him as he confidently reached out to shake her hand—only she didn't have a free one. Joe, who could balance Josie on his hip with one arm, managed a handshake. Chiara's description had Ali picturing a nerdy, socially awkward guy who had trouble making eye contact. Arnold wasn't tall or short, maybe five feet ten, with the slight paunch and thick backside of a middle-aged man who sat too much. All in all, not one to inspire fear or repulsion. He was no Jake, however. Should she pity him?

Arnold responded well to their hospitality, appearing marginally less harassed. His trip had been plagued with mishaps. He'd waited in line for hours to board a ferry in Edmonds and got a speeding ticket in Port Gamble, where the limit was twenty-five. They all commiserated, though to Ali, the worst dullard could guess that the stretch of road passing through that charming little hamlet was a speed trap.

Joe set up the bar for cocktails, leaving the job of entertaining Arnold to Ali, Teresa, and Maddie. They led him downstairs—where David was helping Lorenzo assemble his Lego pirate ship—and placed Josie and Caryn in their playpen. Mercifully, their fussing soon turned into happy babbling.

"Hello, Uncle Arnold," Lorenzo said in a formal voice, as if he were a seldom-seen benefactor in a Dickens novel rather than a father figure.

Chiara's husband barely spared him a second glance. "Yeah, hiya, Lorenzo. Nice ship. Both of 'em." The realistic pirate ship model stood atop the small bookcase. Ali made a mental note to move it to higher ground once the twins could reach that high.

Arnold bombarded them with questions, mostly about Port Townsend, carefully avoiding the subject of Chiara. The dogs didn't snarl the way they did when facing down paparazzi. In fact, they appeared almost as blasé as Lorenzo. "Who is this colorless human?" their eyes seemed to say.

Ali's breath caught in her throat when she heard Jake's and Chiara's voices in the kitchen. Footsteps on the stairs. He couldn't have dropped her off? Once they stood before them in the rec room, Ali noted that Chiara wore her party outfit from the night before, including the strappy sandals. She did *not* look like she'd been hiking. She wore her hair in a loose ponytail. Only vaguely did she resemble the tightly wound wallflower who had arrived a month ago in a severely tailored dress and unflattering glasses, her soft curls tamed in a severe ballerina bun. Her new glasses complemented her large hazel eyes and heart-shaped face.

Had Chiara misled them? They'd all assumed Arnold was a creep of the first order. Ali felt like she was viewing a picture upside down while her corneas struggled to adjust the perspective.

The surreal moment spun out. Arnold shook hands with Jake as if they were cordial business associates at a company meeting. When he kissed Chiara on the cheek, she couldn't summon a smile. "Hi, babe, how's it going?" His eyes bugged out and his jaw dropped as he took in her appearance. Ali steeled herself for his outrage over her lack of hiking gear. Instead he appeared unruffled. "Never saw you in jeans like that before. You look about eighteen." Said with a sneer, it was more dig than compliment. He didn't question whether the outfit was appropriate. "Where'd you hike?"

Jake replied, "It's an easy one near Sequim, Dungeness Spit. About an hour's drive from here."

Suddenly Ali understood. Without altering his voice or demeanor, Jake had counted on Arnold to assume he was gay.

"Sort of an interpretive trail then," Chiara's husband said, not the least bit threatened.

Arnold clamped a possessive hand on Chiara's arm. "Uh, babe, I need to get my car. It's at the end of the road. Come with me?"

Chiara stole a quick glance at her sandals. Ali knew what she was thinking—that she'd like to change into tennis shoes. She couldn't do that without copping to her cover story being a lie. Arnold, if he truly hadn't caught onto her subterfuge, must assume her tennis shoes were in her gay friend Jake's car. If she fetched them from the cottage, the jig was up.

Chiara shook Arnold off and swiped at her arm, as if his hand had left a nasty residue. "All right." She nodded to the group. "We'll be back soon."

"It's almost dinnertime," Ali said cheerily, "and cocktails await." She dearly wished she could have one. Or two.

She watched as they trudged up the hill, separated by several feet, toward the main entrance. The dogs, who normally accompanied guests to and from the gate, didn't budge. They returned her gaze, strangely solemn. "Do you guys know something we don't?" she asked them. The big dog Harry whined, and little Coogan gave a single high-pitched yip.

"I may not speak dog," Jake said, "but I could swear they're worried that's not going to be a pleasant conversation."

"I don't know," Joe said, massaging his temples. "He seems perfectly normal to me."

"*Too* normal," David said. He looked over at Lorenzo, vastly relieved, like a boy who'd narrowly escaped a spanking. Lor had greeted Chiara with the same puzzling formality he did Arnold, as if worried about causing trouble for his beloved aunt.

"Let's take a load off," Joe said. "Why do I feel like we're in the waiting room of a hospital, holding our breaths to see how the surgery went?"

Amen, Ali thought.

David stared at Jake in disbelief. "I thought you were going to play the part of her gay friend."

Jake made a face. "What, mince around the room like the Scarlet Pimpernel or Robin Williams in *The Birdcage*? Apparently other men assume I'm gay anyway, no theatrics required."

"Gay men aren't the only sharp dressers," Teresa said.

Jake wiped his brow with a handkerchief. "The last thing I need is a duel."

Joe stopped pacing. "Surely no one duels anymore."

Jake raised his eyebrows. "In Damon Morehouse's world, they do."

David slapped him on the back. "Good thing you've been practicing with those knives."

Jake glared. "You could just challenge him to a slapping match at dawn. Arnold wouldn't have a chance in hell."

* * *

As Chiara walked beside Arnold down the gravel road, keeping her distance, she thought of the expression, "I wouldn't touch him with a ten-foot pole," which also existed in Italian. Perhaps the idiom dated back to before Europe adopted the metric system. In any case, she wanted nothing to do with this man. To avoid putting words in his mouth, she waited for him to speak first.

"You been enjoying yourself?" he asked, like some divorced father visiting his daughter for the first time in a month. "What do you do all day besides hiking with your gay friend?"

She gave him a long, measuring look. "I take care of Lorenzo."

He nodded. Did he expect her to confront him over their lack of contact? She wouldn't give him the satisfaction. She imagined him testing and discarding approaches. Presumably he'd had ample time to rehearse what he wished to say to her.

When they reached the rental car, Arnold stopped walking and thrust his hands into the back pockets of his chinos. "You're probably wondering why I haven't called."

She folded her arms across her chest. "Not really."

He appeared mystified by her hostility. Unlocking the car, he said, "Let's go for a ride. They're not expecting us back immediately. We need to talk."

Chiara reluctantly slid into the passenger seat. Nothing good came of "We need to talk," but sometimes you had to endure it. If he asked her for a divorce, that would be worth the discomfort.

The seatbelt indicator flashed as he took off. She quickly clicked on her own. "Arnold, please, put on your seatbelt," she said, but he continued to stare straight ahead as he turned the car around with dizzying speed, screeching tires, and a spray of gravel, heading toward town. You'd think he was escaping a crime scene. "Slow down. You aren't familiar with the area." When he still didn't reply, she pleaded, "Can't we just park by the side of the road?" Her heart thumped in her chest like a panicked animal. He was exceeding the speed limit by quite a bit, the way many did on this road. It wasn't a highway. "There are deer everywhere," she warned him. She held the strap in an iron grip. "Slow down!" she yelled. "Listen, if you have a lover, that's fine. I want a divorce too."

He gave her a sharp look. "That's not why I—"

The tires screeched and the car swerved before it slammed to a halt with a piercing squeal of brakes. She felt a jolt and heard a *bang* as the airbags deployed, shoving her head hard against the window. An acrid smell filled her nostrils as her vision dimmed.

* * *

Jake's apprehension had reached a fever pitch. The vigil on the terrace dragged on as they morosely sipped their drinks and made weak attempts at conversation. Liam was on his way. Jake's futile attempts to summon Rory made him doubt his friend had ever truly resided in his head.

Maddie stood alone by the bluff, gazing out to sea. Might as well get *that* conversation over with.

"Hey, Maddie." She turned to look at him with weary impatience. This lack of animation was *so* not Maddie. Harried and too thin, she resembled a disillusioned refugee from an EST training camp. Too agitated to devise a smooth way to broach the subject, he simply said, "George wants to play Damon. But only if you play Holly Relish."

He waited.

A flame of excitement ignited in her eyes, quickly extinguished. "David would freak. It would end our marriage."

"Not necessarily. Give him a chance."

Maddie heaved a disgruntled sigh.

Jake patted her shoulder. "Give it some thought."

He rejoined the circle of friends and family. What was taking Chiara and Arnold so long? He checked his watch, surprised to find that only fifty minutes had passed. It felt like a fortnight. How long did it take to walk a mile? They must be having an epic argument. Recalling the gypsy story, he tried not to freak out as he sprinted over to where David and Joe were throwing knives at the target. After David's fist shot in the air to celebrate a bull's eye, Jake laid a hand on his shoulder. "Bro, will you humor me?"

David turned, and his joy fizzled. "Yeah?"

"They've been gone too long, and Chiara told me something today that …. I would feel better if we checked on them."

"Say no more," David told him.

Joe dragged a hand through his hair. "Do you want me to come along?"

Jake shook his head. "I think it's simpler with the two of us."

No need to spell it out.

They hightailed it to Jake's BMW and drove as fast as the gravel road would allow. Seeing that Arnold's car was gone, Jake instinctively turned toward town. Five minutes later they ran across the car, smoking in a ditch.

Jake braked suddenly, and they made a mad dash toward the wrecked car. A quick scan of the area alerted them to the dead deer, catapulted to the other side of the road by the impact. The windshield was shattered, the front end crushed, and the airbags deployed. He detected no movement in the car.

David swung open the passenger door to find Chiara's immobile form, her hair soaked in blood. "I can get her out!" he yelled to Jake. "They're not trapped or anything."

Jake's heart almost stopped as he absorbed the gory scene. Arnold hadn't been wearing a seatbelt, but Chiara had. David released the buckle now. The airbags had kept them in place, though Chiara's head had collided with the side window. *Shades of Rory* …. Jake couldn't afford to fall apart. He could have kissed his brother for making her a priority. That meant Arnold was Jake's responsibility. He'd do what he could for the guy, asshole or not.

David pulled Chiara clear of the car and carried her to the side of the road. Jake did the same for Arnold. You weren't supposed to move an accident victim in case of neck or back injuries, but knowing David's abilities, Jake wasn't worried. He was more concerned that the car might catch fire and the engine, explode.

Jake watched as David held Chiara's bloody head in his hands. What if her brains were spilling out? *Stop it. Concentrate.* He called 911, sounding like a zombie to his own ears as he gave the operator their location. Arnold still had a pulse. Other than a nasty cut across his forehead, he looked fine. There was no blood on his clothing. There might be contusions under his shirt or pants. No point in having a look-see. What could Jake do about bruises or internal injuries? No limbs were twisted in unnatural positions. Arnold didn't require CPR, thank God. Since Rory's death, Jake had taken a refresher course but had no wish to test his skills. The seconds ticked by with excruciating slowness.

Startled from his trance, Jake heard David say in a low voice, "She'll be fine. Go talk to her." Then he took over for Jake, running his hands over Arnold's chest.

Chiara lay still, her hair matted with blood. So much blood. "Sweetheart," he whispered. David had crumpled his own shirt into a ball to cradle her head.

She opened her eyes and grabbed his hand. "Jake? Where am I?"

"You're safe," he said, choking back a sob.

"*Ti amo.*" She spoke so softly, the words almost escaped him.

The car engine exploded. Though they were well out of the way, David staggered back. Did he have PTSD? One more reason to give up on Africa and the medical profession. Then, as if resisting a demonic force, David returned to where Arnold lay and pressed his hands on his chest once more.

The ambulance drove up and the emergency technicians took over. Jake and David stood together next to Jake's BMW.

"How is he?" Jake asked in a low voice.

"I got to him in time," David remarked, grim-faced. "He'll recover from this, though the future is uncertain. I mitigated the internal injuries, but the guy has heart issues I didn't address. He's in decent shape physically so I'm thinking it's a congenital defect."

A police car joined them, and they spent the next half hour talking to the officers as the ambulance drove away with Chiara and Arnold. The dead deer told a straightforward story.

"Where will they take them?" Jake asked.

"They'll have to be airlifted to Seattle," the young officer replied. "Can you notify their next of kin?"

"We'll do our best. They're our houseguests, but we're not well acquainted. Are you *positive* they need to be airlifted?"

That had to constitute an abundance of caution, given David's ministrations.

"Well, no," the officer said. "My assumption is based on the condition of the car and the amount of blood. The emergency technicians will assess their injuries. If it's determined they aren't in immediate danger, they'll be transported to the full-service hospital in Port Angeles."

After the police car drove away, David gave Jake a hug and said, "Relax, Bro. Chiara will call you herself when the dust settles." He threw open the passenger side door of the BMW and fell into the seat. Seeing his distress, Jake rushed to start the car. "Now comes the headache," David said in a strained voice. "It's gonna be a bad one." He lay back and closed his eyes, his mouth a rictus of pain.

As Jake drove like the devil on speed back to the compound, he continued to hope for a "word" from Rory. Nothing.

Jake felt terrible about putting David in this position. He looked like death warmed over. Maddie immediately put him to bed.

Finding the others pacing the terrace like caged animals, Jake told them, "Everything's going to be okay. At least with Arnold and Chiara. David doesn't look so good."

They collapsed simultaneously onto the deck furniture, as if the music had stopped in a macabre game of Musical Chairs.

Only Jake remained standing. "They hit a deer," he explained. "The airbags deployed. Arnold wasn't wearing a seatbelt. Chiara's head collided with the side window."

"David ..." Ali began.

"Did what he could," Jake said. "Hopefully, it was enough."

Liam made a beeline for the bar and picked up a bottle of Scotch. "Drink?"

"Yes, definitely," the men said in unison.

Around ten, Chiara called. "We are both well," she said. "We'll return in a day or two. I have to go now." She hung up before he could respond. No more declarations of love.

Jake stayed over in one of the cabins. Midmorning the next day, he found David snoozing peacefully on the gargantuan black couch in the Log Palace, Maddie's lap as his pillow. Her head thrown back, she snored softly.

The millstone lifted from his shoulders, Jake returned to his cabin and fell into a deep, dreamless, Rory-free sleep.

In the late afternoon, Jake and David wandered over to the safari tent.

"She was in bad shape," David told him.

"Would she have died?"

David weighed his words. "It didn't look good. She might have lived … but her head injury …." He didn't finish.

Jake wondered what he meant by "look." Did David's hands "see"? Did he visualize the damage and heal it by reassembling the parts? Or was it more mystical than that? He didn't suppose his brother could explain his gift any more than Jake could explain Rory—who he was more determined than ever to summon. Had the young gypsy's prediction been fulfilled? Even if it had power only because Chiara believed in it, she might now rest easy that her fate had been altered.

"Uh, Jake?" David peered into his face. "You're the color of pea soup."

"I'm okay," Jake insisted. Should he tell his brother about the gypsy? Nope. Enough weirdness for one day. Enough weirdness, period.

David clamped a broad, warm mitt on his shoulder. "You know, there are always unintended consequences, right? It's never a free ride when you fuck with fate."

Jake gave him a long look. *No kidding.* Damn it, when was Jake going to tell David about the movie offer? *Hey, Bro, sorry about the headache, and thanks for saving my girlfriend's life. Now, how about you let your wife go off, strip, and have pretend sex with a sleazy womanizer so she can have a career?*

When *was* the right time to broach a subject like that?

CHAPTER 29

———————

JULY FOURTH WAS A QUIET affair for Teresa and the others. They gathered as a family and held their ears at the cracks and booms of their neighbors' mostly illegal fireworks.

According to Ali, Chiara was waiting on Arnold hand and foot, though she'd insisted he recuperate in his own cabin. She had totally recovered. A home-grown miracle, courtesy of David. Her larger-than-life brother claimed nothing good came of his healings and that they weren't reliable. Not that Teresa had noticed. Joe's wonky vocal cords had been good as new, allowing him to complete another successful tour before they crapped out again. Then, David worked his magic again. If David hadn't healed Maddie's busted ankle, she wouldn't have gone to Hollywood to make that movie, *Insanity*. Granted, the fallout of that healing was to be determined. That particular bill would come due at the movie's premiere around Thanksgiving Day. Thanks to David, George had survived being gored by a mountain goat, which meant the O'Connells could not be held responsible for depriving the world of a prime candidate for *People* Magazine's "Sexiest Man Alive."

Now, again, David had come to the rescue by saving Chiara. Arnold was alive, though diagnosed with congestive heart failure. David hadn't fixed that. On purpose? He claimed not. Something about a valve that needed replacing. Couldn't his magic hands "heal" a leaky valve?

Chiara and Arnold had kissed and made up. Minus the kissing, as far as anyone could tell. When the two of them joined the family, and he moved to hold her hand, she rebuffed him as if he were some pervy uncle. Certainly, healing Arnold hadn't benefited *Jake*. Though on the lookout, Teresa hadn't seen him emerge from the B&B. She peered through the window several times a day. Maybe he hadn't noticed. She stopped short of knocking or ringing the doorbell.

Jake must have realized the risks of an adulterous affair. Teresa had never made *that* particular mistake. She thought of Kilo, who had tried to lure her away. Liam had observed them through the window of a hotel bar and assumed the worst, not buying her explanation that it was a chance encounter and totally harmless. He preferred to believe the misleading account of the female bartender who was crushing on him.

Teresa sat in the front yard, now surrounded by a deer-proof fence, enjoying the late-morning sun. Liam was off buying supplies for the backyard trellis, the interior of "his" house now completed to his satisfaction. Furniture with clean lines, abstract art plus a few landscapes, no clutter. Didn't Teresa get one room that reflected *her* personality, *her* tastes? He hadn't offered. Her one request—a grand piano. A baby grand would do. Liam insisted there wasn't room in the parlor. Couldn't she make do with an upright grand?

"Buy your own place," Jake had advised her. Ali's suggestion would be easier to justify: buy a building you can use as an office and a retreat. A parlor big enough for a grand piano. She rubbed the baby bump. "Will you love your father more than me?" she asked the fetus. "You won't always take his side, right?" It stirred but didn't kick.

She closed her eyes, picturing Liam in all his glory as he'd slept beside her this morning, naked, the sheets kicked away in the hot, sun-drenched room. She'd rolled up the shades to let in the fresh air then stood, mesmerized. Despite the shrapnel scars, he looked like a young god. Sensing her admiring gaze, he opened his eyes to half-mast and reached for her. She let him reel her in, as she always did, glad for this proof that, even if he no longer trusted her, he'd never stopped wanting her. Their lovemaking was more rushed than usual, but her body was ready for him. She suspected his mind was elsewhere, perhaps compiling a list of items needed from the building supply store.

The sun shone on the new rose garden she had planted. A cool sea breeze wafted in from the bay.

The rented goats had made quick work of the blackberry vines and scruffy "volunteer" trees, shrubs, and invasive weeds that had taken over the front yard while the house was vacant. They'd had to isolate the rhododendron in a plywood cage, because those goats would eat *anything*, even a tarp. And rhodies were toxic to animals.

His house, not hers. Her hand still rested on her belly. The fetus wasn't very active, not like an athlete, anyway. Perhaps it was too early in the pregnancy. Maybe this child, unlike her or Liam, would be sedate and calm. Would Liam get the boy he wanted? Would a child bring them closer together or tear them further apart?

Through the fence, she saw a station wagon drive up and went to greet Martha. The realtor rolled down the window, exuding steely competence. Teresa wondered if she'd been in the military.

"You ready? I think I've found you the perfect place."

* * *

Jake was enthroned on the overstuffed chair in the attic room, looking out at the sailboats in the bay and resolving to rent one as soon as possible. He'd take one of his brothers, or Liam, along. The chair was comfortable … for an antique. No wonder it was the only piece of furniture that showed significant wear. Jake imagined it was the perfect vantage point of the ghost George had seen, the young man.

"Why don't *you* talk to me?" Jake asked the apparition. "Okay, fine. I'll do the talking." He took a sip of water. "I hope you don't mind my sleeping in your room. It's the only bed I never shared with Chiara. This room has great juju. Although George would beg to differ." His chuckle sounded vaguely demented. "I wish I could stop thinking about Chiara. David sends email updates, insisting Arnold is a 'good guy.' He'll be leaving soon with Chiara to get an aortic valve replacement. Does that mean it's over? I'm getting radio silence from Chiara. Some kind of closure would be nice. Should I believe *anything* she told me? It would be easier not to. Is she still convinced she's going to die young?"

As if the ghost was going to answer …. Jake hadn't heard from Rory, either. Several times, usually at night when he couldn't sleep, he'd driven around the block, knowing his dead friend wouldn't talk to him in the house. Finally, he'd given up. He hadn't been outside in three days, other than for his morning run. What day was it, anyway? A calendar hung on the wall in the kitchen. For something to do, he headed down the stairs to consult it. Hadn't he heard church bells yesterday? Ah, that meant today was Monday, July twelfth. The start of a new week. He had ample food and supplies. No need to venture out.

He resumed his attic vigil. Outside the window, he saw what amounted to a flotilla of small boats—Sunfish, with colorful sails. A class? Once the twins were old enough, he'd teach them to sail. And Lorenzo, of course. He could be the "fun uncle" when Joe was on tour. Not that he had any insight into Joe's plans. For all he knew, "Joe Bob Blade" was done touring forever.

There had been no brotherly bonding. David and Liam more than made up for Joe's cold shoulder, but Jake hoped his rock-star brother would eventually come around. "You could be the one to wave the white flag," he said aloud.

Jake wasn't a moper. He blocked out looming depression with hard work and strenuous exercise. A draft of Book Three, *Zwap*, was complete. Such as it was. Nothing to dance a jig over. So what? His first drafts were often flat-footed.

"So, Mr. Ghost, got any advice? You died young, or so it seems, but people packed a lot into their young lives in your day. Did you have tuberculosis, like Chopin? Look what he accomplished in his time on Earth? You were a masterful artist if these landscapes are any indication." He went over to admire the paintings at close range. "Are there more like these around? I'll have to check out the galleries in town. I think I'd recognize your style by now."

It wouldn't take much imagination to jump right into these paintings, Mary Poppins style. Time for Jake to move on? How had he managed to foul his nest so quickly? He'd always assumed Rory was well intentioned. Why was that? Wouldn't Earth-bound ghosts envy the living? Jake would learn to love again. Once Chiara was truly gone. Long gone.

His cell phone chirped its merry tune. He snapped it open. "Hi, William. Before you say anything, no, I still haven't gotten a decision from Maddie."

"She told us no," William said with no preliminaries. "That rules out George Reed Masters. Back to the drawing board."

"Okay," Jake said, "thanks for telling me."

But William wasn't done. "Listen, didn't you tell me your brother the doctor likes thrillers?"

"Yeah."

"We have a script that isn't working. The hero travels with Doctors Without Borders. I thought David might want to take a look. It needs more than a fact check; it needs a script doctor." Jake heard dry laughter as William appreciated his own "doctor" humor. "What they're willing to pay depends on whether they like his work. I trust them to be fair. Besides, I can judge for myself if David's changes make it viable. Him being at loose ends, he might welcome a challenge."

"What a great idea," Jake said in an even voice, not at all sure it was. Being a voracious reader didn't mean you could write your own books or that you understood anything about pacing, especially in a screenplay. As far as Jake knew, no one in his family watched much TV. They all liked movies, but they seemed to prefer the classics. How could David judge what made a movie work for a contemporary audience?

"Uh, Jake?"

"Yeah. I'll run it past him."

"Good. I'm overnighting it to you."

Shit, he thought. *That means I have to bring it by the compound.*

The screenplay arrived two days later. Jake found it sitting on his porch when he returned from his run. As he stood there, staring at the envelope, Teresa appeared behind him as if emerging from another dimension. Knowing his sister liked to sleep in, he'd been running at first light to avoid such encounters. *She's been watching for me,* he thought.

Breathing hard, she said, "Oh, good! I caught you."

"Funny, you don't look like you've been jogging," he joked. She was wearing sandals and a sundress with an Empire waist to accommodate her growing baby bump.

"I'm glad to see you're alive," she said cheerily. "What's that? More proofs?"

He flashed her a toothy smile. "You're looking lovely. Come on in. I was just about to head over to the compound."

Once inside, Teresa lowered herself onto the couch, hand on her belly. "You think that's wise?"

He shot her a reproachful look. "I'm not going to kidnap Chiara. I'll deliver this to David and be out of there lickety-split." He tapped on the envelope. "My agent thinks David might be just the man to fix this screenplay. It's about Doctors Without Borders."

She clapped her hands, delighted. "The perfect distraction! I hope he goes for it."

Jake fetched two glasses of water and sat down beside her. "What about you? How are *you* staying distracted?"

"I bought a house."

He kept his reaction lowkey. "Oh? That's great. Does Liam like it?"

"Liam doesn't know about it."

"Oh." Realizing his mouth still formed a surprised O, he closed it. When he'd advised Teresa to buy a house, he hadn't meant for her to do it behind Liam's back. "You're not leaving him, are you? Because if so," he pointed at her barely visible belly, "that's going to make things *really* complicated."

She blew out an exasperated breath. "I'm not leaving him. It's on Lawrence Street—a house that's been converted to offices. Ergo, I'll hang my shingle there." She paused. "And I'll use it as a practice studio—once I buy a grand piano."

"Ah. I wondered why your house had no piano."

"*Liam's* house. The parlor is too small. He said there might be room for a concert upright."

"*Might* be?"

Lips pursed, she nodded.

"Shame on him." He stood. "I'm going to shower. I'll just be a few minutes. Come with me to the compound? I could use the company. David's expecting me. Then I'd love a tour of your new office-cum-studio." He leaned down to pat her hand. "I won't stay long, won't even try to see Chiara. I promise."

"You seem fine," she said, surprised.

"I will be." He spread his arms. "This house is like an ashram. Spiritually healing, somehow." He smiled. "My new goal is to commune with the ghost in the attic." Seeing her alarm, he added, "Only if I can do it on this side of the veil. I'm planning to live a long life, even if I have to do it alone."

"You'll always have us." She pointed at the ceiling. "I thought I saw a light on up there. I'm glad to hear it wasn't a glowing entity." She slumped backward and closed her eyes, waving him toward the staircase. "Shoo! Go on, get ready. I'll grab a catnap. Let's get David started on *his* distraction."

While the steaming hot water soothed his aching muscles, Jake smiled at the thought of Teresa's worry for his safety. It was nice to have his family back.

* * *

Hearing a car drive up, Chiara peered through the cabin window and saw Jake's BMW. As she stood rooted to the spot, she imagined running toward him. Then the scene devolved into an old-movie cliché of a man and woman running toward each other in slow motion, the love theme from Tchaikovsky's *Romeo and Juliet* playing in the background.

No. No romantic *deus ex machina* for her. Instead, she wiped away a tear with the back of her hand and turned toward her recumbent husband. They slept apart, but she was the one who tended to him by day.

The night of the accident …. Chiara couldn't explain why she'd been so abrupt with Jake. Had she spoiled everything with one brief sentence? She'd been confused and upset, had felt so stupid for getting in the car with Arnold and so terrible for putting Jake and his family, especially David, in this impossible position. What was her responsibility to her pitiful husband? The family wouldn't have understood if she'd washed her hands of him and rushed to be with Jake. And now … was it too late?

Arnold was propped up on pillows, reading *Time* magazine. He had more energy, now that he was on the right drugs, and they would soon be leaving for the scheduled surgery to replace his aortic valve. His behavior toward her had been … *solicitous*, that was the word. He frequently asked after her health, praising her new wardrobe, calling her "honey" and "darling." It was all talk. She was the one catering to his every whim. He resisted socializing with the others, which had the added advantage—for him—of leaving them with their first impression: that he was a nice guy, a "good" man. He'd been playing that part with her as well. He was as poor an excuse for an actor as he was for a husband.

Once a day, at Chiara's insistence, she and Arnold would go to the basement to spend time with Lorenzo, who had taken to ignoring the former father-figure lying on the couch, preferring to converse with Chiara in Italian. Arnold was overplaying the invalid role. One time Ali left the twins with them while she ran an errand. Josie pointed at Arnold with a pout and said, "Bad!" Chiara burst out laughing. Arnold told her to "shut up," which elicited a chorus of "Bad, bad, bad!" Lorenzo, emboldened by Chiara's new courage, gave Arnold a withering glance but didn't join in. Her husband stormed out and refused to speak to her for the rest of the day except to bark orders when she came in at mealtime or to check on him. She was fine with that. The spirit of defiance was now fully awakened.

She sat on the bed until Arnold put the magazine down.

"What were you going to say to me when the car crashed?" She was never so blunt.

His hand covered hers, giving it a fervent squeeze. "That I wanted you back. That I wanted us to try again."

She recoiled, folding both hands in her lap. "For heaven's sake, why?"

He looked hurt. The expression reminded her of Lorenzo when she called him on his fibs, which mostly concerned sneaking cookies or not washing his hands before meals.

She continued, "Why this change of heart? Did your girlfriend break up with you?"

"I don't have a girlfriend," he said, aggrieved.

"Oh, she gave you your marching orders then." She rose and left the cabin. Jake's car was already gone. He hadn't sought her out.

It was low tide, and Chiara went to fetch Lorenzo for a walk on the beach. With or without Jake, she would not return to her old life. After the operation, Arnold would be on his own.

CHAPTER 30

———◆———

David was sitting with Jake and Liam at a tall table in a trendy bar near Century City. The August heat and haze of vehicle exhaust made dining inside the more comfortable option. It was the first chance they'd had to meet collectively since arriving at LAX four days ago. The production company for *Kapow* had been treating the three of them like royalty. As surreal as life in Port Townsend sometimes seemed, this experience had that beat in spades.

"Like an episode of *The Twilight Zone*," David remarked after the waitress brought their drinks.

What made the situation doubly unsettling was how they'd left things with the women. David didn't have the lowdown on Liam and Teresa and hoped to hear it now. As for him and Maddie, for the first time since returning from their honeymoon, he saw a way out of the doldrums. Jake was simply glad for the change of air—even if Port Townsend's was a lot cleaner. Chiara had presumably returned to Portland with Arnold. At least Jake had been spared the ordeal of seeing her off. Joe had reluctantly opted out of their great escape, having no business here. Besides, he was overseeing a project with Matthew in the recording studio.

He doesn't want to step on Jake's toes, David thought. If Joe had tagged along, someone would have pitched an acting project to him, and his musician brother's life was complicated enough. Not to mention that Ali needed him, having been diagnosed with gestational diabetes. Teresa, after the first-trimester morning sickness, was sailing through a made-for-TV pregnancy. She looked pregnant like Elizabeth Taylor looked old in *Giant*.

All Teresa lacked was a more solicitous husband.

"So, Liam," David said, sipping his whiskey, "how did the screentest go?"

Liam grunted. "Ridiculous. They had me strut around half naked for the camera. I read with so many actresses, I couldn't keep them straight. Not one I've heard of. They look weirdly similar, all frighteningly skinny with suspiciously large and buoyant breasts." He grinned. "That part was fun."

"Models," Jake cut in. "Models who want to be actresses."

Liam took a long pull of his IPA. "Obviously. I'm no Lawrence Olivier, but I could give them a lesson or two."

"Now you see why they're so nuts about Maddie," Jake said, sneaking a peek at David. "She's brainy and funny, and she's not the typical body type. Her breasts are real."

David glowered. "Let's leave Maddie's breasts out of this."

"Get used to it," Liam said with a smirk. "*Everyone's* talking about Maddie's breasts. If *my* audition experience is any indication." He gave Jake a sidelong glance. "You're one sneaky bastard. I had no idea you'd proposed that I play Damon. I thought that by inviting me along you were just giving me a chance to cool off."

David set his glass down with a clunk. "Truth time, me hearties. Liam, what the hell happened with Teresa?"

Liam looked warily from brother to brother. "Huh. You two are about to read me the riot act."

"Someone has to," Jake said calmly. "As long as you're tossing around blame, start with me. I'm the one who advised her to buy the house."

Liam, who'd been slouching, straightened up and got in his face. "*What?*"

Jake wasn't intimidated. "Turnabout is fair play. You bought that ramshackle Victorian without consulting her." He raised a palm to silence Liam's knee-jerk response. "Hang on. I know you were on a break, and I know you needed to escape from the compound. You also needed a compelling project to keep you from brooding. I get that."

"I *really* get that," David chimed in.

"But then, when Teresa moved in, you still acted like it was *your* house."

"She helped me decorate it," Liam protested.

"According to *your* taste," Jake persisted, "like you were a client. She kept expecting you to let her have a room or something. At least allow her to put a piano in the main parlor."

"It's too goddamn small," Liam said through gritted teeth.

"*I* know that. But given the circumstances, no one but you blames her for finding a place to spread her wings a little, especially now that she's going to be tethered in a new way."

"To a child," David offered helpfully.

"Listen," Liam said in a gruff voice, shoulders tense. "She was calling all the shots. It was stifling."

David wanted to slap him silly. "How was she supposed to know that? Did you tell her?"

"She didn't let me get a word in edgewise."

"So buying the Victorian was payback, and when she bought a house, she unbalanced the scales again."

Liam was flushed. David would bet a pile of cash that if Liam's chair had an eject button, he would have used it.

David spoke softly to lower the emotional volume. "No one's ganging up on you. We're her brothers, and we hate to see her unhappy."

"You think my doing a movie is going to help?" Liam said more calmly. "A movie where I have to pretend to seduce a smorgasbord of starlets?"

"Teresa trusts you to behave," Jake said. "More than you trust her. You can have an adventure and give her breathing space at the same time. It's hard being pregnant *and* walking on eggshells."

Liam sighed, defeated. "Is that what she's doing? We make love—"

Jake cleared his throat. "We know. *I* do, anyway. Why do you think I was in such a hurry to move out?" Liam reddened even more, if possible. "Wanting her isn't enough. She needs to feel loved."

Liam's shrug was oddly helpless. "I love her."

"You have a funny way of showing it," David said. He thought of Maddie, realizing he'd ignored her needs too. Not exactly ignored them, more like tried to wish them away.

There was a challenge in Liam's eyes. "How are *you* going to deal with me making love to Maddie on screen? That is, if they give me the part."

"Oh, they'll give you the part," Jake said.

The waitress, who'd arrived with their next round of drinks, batted her eyes at Liam. She was cute, but not Teresa.

"Thanks, Darlin'," he said, toasting her.

After she floated away, David said, "That's why you're a shoo-in. They love ya, baby."

Liam wasn't convinced. "Yeah, I'm pleasant to look at and all—other than the scars—but I've only ever acted in a few lame high-school plays. When has anyone like that ever been cast as a lead character in a major studio movie?"

"*On Her Majesty's Secret Service*," David said.

"Huh?"

"George Lazenby was a used car salesman and an underwear model. Got the part through sheer hutzpah. Did his own stunts. Most popular James Bond, ever."

Liam made a face. David wanted to laugh. His brother-in-law was incapable of looking anything other than gorgeous. Not that he minded his own rough-hewn features, but it didn't seem fair that a man should be blessed with so much beauty, skill, and talent. Yet Liam wasn't a natural showman. Mostly he preferred to keep to himself. He was accustomed to working alone or with one other person. Could he really handle a career move as drastic as this? Could David? From medical doctor to script doctor. Yet both men had been desperate for a change. They were stuck in ruts, like the residents of Moss Manor, who never ventured beyond their comfort zone. Children would find that reassuring. Adults needed more. He and Liam had been forced to take this leap into the void, if only to save their marriages.

"If Lazenby was so popular," Liam said, "how come he was a one-time Bond?"

"They tried to rope him into a multi-film contract," David said, "but he didn't want to be typecast. When he refused to sign, they blacklisted him."

Liam's sneer was somehow elegant. "Nice. You haven't answered my question. About Maddie."

"Maddie won't be your lover," Jake said. "She'll be your nemesis."

"Explain."

"David and I revised the screenplay, and the producers approved the changes. Damon's nemesis is a woman named Lorelei. Damon will have multiple lovers, disposable ones. There's chemistry with Lorelei, but no physical contact. It doesn't much resemble the book, but I don't care about that. They'll probably change the title, say it's 'inspired by characters created by Dirk Fartherly.' The main question is, who will play Mickey, Damon's best friend? That part is way juicier than it was before."

Liam's brow furrowed. "Isn't Mickey based on your buddy Rory?"

The conversation came to a spontaneous pause, a moment of silence in memory of Rory.

Jake spoke first. "He doesn't talk to me anymore, which is just as well. He was telling me about the future—stuff I didn't want to hear."

David stared at him and saw that Liam was fully alert too.

Jake crossed his legs awkwardly. "Nothing that concerns either of you."

David didn't believe him. "Tell us. We're going to imagine way worse."

"Nothing earth-shattering," Jake insisted. "Only that Ali will have a boy, and Teresa a girl." He cast an apologetic glance at Liam. "I know you'd prefer a boy. Sorry about that."

Liam was smiling from ear to ear. "I don't care as long as they're healthy. Did he say whether Ali will be all right? I'm more worried about her." He looked at David. "Can't you *do* something?"

David loosened his tie. *Damn it.* As if he could just make everything right the minute any of them had a medical issue. Next they'd be asking him to cure a hangnail or clear up a pimple. "Listen, Joe already approached me about that. *Maybe* I could fix her issues with the pregnancy. So far the baby is healthy, and she'll be okay too. If things take a turn for the worse, I'll *try* to intervene. But don't you guys get it? Some things happen for a reason. I can't force Ali to eat right or get the bed rest she needs. Not that she's gorging on banana splits or anything .... For the sake of argument, let's say I fix this pregnancy. Does that mean Joe will expect Ali to keep getting pregnant— make me intervene every time? That's not what Ali wants."

"Joe will keep hounding you," Jake predicted, sympathetic.

David sighed heavily. He knew.

Liam asked, "If they do cast me, what's the time line?"

"The project is still in development," Jake replied. "They hope to get to the pre-production phase by February and start filming in April. They're aiming for a Christmas release date—the Christmas *after* next. Shooting might take three months. As the star, your presence will be required more than most. You'll need to talk it over with Teresa ... sensitively."

David noted the hard set of Liam's jaw. If the baby were born on time, it might be only two months old when he was called to the set.

"Teresa won't stand in your way," he said.

Liam rubbed his forehead. "But will she come with me? I can't be separated from her and the baby for so much time."

"Part of the time, for sure," Jake said. "None of the locations will be in the jungle or a third-world country. Some of those European doctors are better than ours. For your marriage to survive, you'll have to work a lot harder to make her feel secure ... and loved. Are you willing to do that?" David and Jake locked eyes. "Teresa's brothers want to know."

Liam replied with conviction, "I'll do everything I can."

"What about George Reed Masters?" David asked.

"He already passed on playing Damon," Jake said. "At the moment, he's not even in Los Angeles."

David scowled. "I wonder if he's heard that Maddie's in the movie."

"I hope not." Jake downed the rest of his gin and tonic. "Shall we call it a night? The natives are restless."

David was suddenly aware of the women—and men—who hovered as close as they dared in the crowded bar. Hardly a surprise: they were three strapping male specimens. No matter that David and Liam wore wedding rings. He gave Jake a playful kick in the shin. "The men are for you," he said with a snicker.

Jake laughed and dropped some bills on the table. "Come on. Let's stage an escape worthy of Damon Morehouse. At least they're after our bodies, not our photos or autographs."

"Our John Han*cocks*," Liam joked. They all grinned.

"You're the only one who'll be fighting off fans and paparazzi," David said to Liam. "No one cares about script doctors or novelists."

"They do if they look like you guys," Liam said as he rose to his feet, tossing his motorcycle jacket over his shoulder like a matador. The crowd fell back, all aflutter, like startled pigeons. Taking advantage of Liam's wide wake, they made their escape.

* * *

On his last day in Los Angeles, Jake received a call from George Reed Masters.

"Hey, bro!" the famous voice said.

Not your bro, Jake thought, bracing for the inevitable.

"I hear Maddie's going to be in your movie after all." When Jake didn't speak, he added, "Liam's gonna play Damon."

"That's the plan." Jake wasn't going to make things easy for George. Everyone knew that if he wanted the part, he could have it.

"I'm gonna be Mickey," George said.

Jake almost dropped the phone. "Really? That's what you want?"

George laughed. "That's what Rory wants. Great opportunity for me to 'expand my horizons,' as he puts it. He says hi, by the way. He also wants you to know that he meant well. But apparently even ghosts aren't entirely selfless."

When Jake hung up, he sat down heavily, struggling to regain his equilibrium.

"You son of a gun," he said out loud.

Rory didn't answer.

CHAPTER 31

During the two flights back—a jet from Los Angeles to Seattle then a charter from Seattle to the miniature but grandly named William R. Fairchild International Airport in Port Angeles—Liam brooded. It had been a while since he'd indulged in a good brood, not since Teresa had agreed to marry him, putting him on cloud 9. He'd floated there until the Kilo Incident sent him crashing to the ground. Why had he let that slimeball get under his skin? He'd tried the friend route, thinking to keep his enemy close. Wrong move. Kilo was a scorpion—like in the fable. He couldn't resist stinging his ride, even if they both drowned.

For Kilo, there had been no hell to pay. Hollywood buzzed with excitement over his TV series and his future prospects. However ... no role for Kilo in *Kapow. Hurrah.* Kilo had asked Teresa to run off with him to Oahu while he shot the pilot of *Hawaiian Eye*, which had been picked up by CBS and would premiere in September. Why had Liam assumed Teresa was tempted, just because she'd been married to the yoga instructor/dancer/ actor for a nanosecond when they were teenagers? Why had he believed the bartender's account of their friendly drink? The woman had been panting after him for months.

Teresa had stripped away his defenses like no woman before her. He sifted through recent memories. *Had* he meant to punish Teresa with *his* house? Had he treated her like she was on permanent probation, waiting for that one false move that would prove his suspicions were justified and shove their marriage over a cliff? The screentests with all the cookie-cutter cuties just drove home how lucky he was to have found this incredible woman. He hoped it wasn't too late. He'd find space for a concert grand piano even if it meant knocking down a wall. Or two.

During the trip to Los Angeles, Teresa and Ali had been in Seattle getting sonograms. Joe had been tied up in a recording session, and Jake had already convinced Liam to come along. Didn't men usually accompany their wives to sonograms? The women claimed to be fine on their own. What idiots Joe and Liam had been to take them at their word. Especially after Ali reported her diagnosis of gestational diabetes to Joe. Since then Liam had heard nothing from Teresa, confirming the sex of his own child secondhand, from Joe.

Damn but he was a selfish bastard.

Rory's prediction had come true: Teresa was having a daughter. Ali, a son. Well, in each case the odds were 50/50 he'd be right. A daughter …. Liam was over the moon.

It was four in the afternoon when Jake dropped him off at his—no, *their*—house. No sign of Teresa. He had wheedled the address of the new place out of the realtor after learning from Joe that his pregnant wife had purchased her *own* Victorian. He'd confronted Teresa in a self-righteous fury—as if she'd hired a gigolo rather than following in his own ill-considered footsteps. The way she looked at him, Liam might have been an ape beating his breast at the zoo. He stormed out and headed to Kelpies to get drunk. Slept in the guest bedroom that night. So mature.

Liam ran the few blocks to Lawrence Street, where more townies than tourists shopped and hung out. Teresa's Victorian was located on the edge of the business district. With his builder's eye, Liam did a quick assessment. It needed a new roof, and most of the cedar siding was unsalvageable. If Teresa had asked him … but she hadn't. Maybe the interior was in better shape.

The shingle read,

TERESA O'CONNELL RYAN, INTERIOR DESIGN
OFFICE HOURS: 9-11 & 1-3—OR BY APPOINTMENT

Finding the front door locked, he peered through the window, but the light made it difficult to see inside. He could hear piano music and recognized one of Grieg's *Lyric Pieces*.

The door was opened by Xenia, a FOSSP woman who sometimes watched the children. Older than the others—at least twenty-five—she was a looker and a standout, especially in lily-white Port Townsend where olive skin marked you as exotic. He should know. North African, he guessed, with her tilted dark eyes and masses of black hair piled into a loose bun. She wore a frayed jean skirt, knee-high boots, and a long-sleeved T-shirt—an outfit pulled together from a thrift store. That meant Teresa hadn't commenced "Project Xenia" yet. Like her brother Jake, his wife loved to dress her friends and family. Liam was proud of not needing her help, despite a fashion-deprived upbringing. Another lead-footed move on his part. He could have asked for her input, just to be nice.

The room was sparsely furnished, just a massive desk that might have belonged to a Victorian banker and a couple of heavy wooden chairs stacked with oversized books.

"Hi, Mr. Ryan. Please excuse the mess. Come in." With a tight smile, Xenia stepped back for him to enter.

"Hey, Xenia," he said. *Mr. Ryan?* he thought. Her tone was decidedly cool. He wondered if his wife had used her as a sounding board for her all-too-justified complaints against him.

"Teresa's in the back room. Follow the music." She went back to poring over a book. "I'm learning about Persian rugs."

At his signature knock—"Shave and a Haircut" without the "two bits"— the music ended abruptly with a few sour notes. He braced for the worst, fearing that nothing could heal the wounds he'd inflicted on their relationship.

Teresa sat at the piano, unsmiling, a rosy glow on her cheeks. Her heart-shaped face was framed in wild strawberry-blonde curls. "Hello, Liam."

No "sweetie" or "darling."

"Or should I call you Damon." Distinct tone of sarcasm.

What could he say? He'd drawn a blank. He felt like an imposter. A pauper masquerading as a prince like in that Mark Twain novel. Even when he'd read it at age nine, he hadn't believed an abused street urchin could ever pass for coddled royalty.

There was a chair next to the piano bench, waiting for a page turner. "May I?" She still stared at him, expression guarded. He sat anyway. "Nice place. Are there offices upstairs, too?"

"I turned them back into bedrooms."

"For you?" he asked lightly.

For a moment she seemed to weigh whether he deserved a response. "One is for Xenia. I might move another apprentice in here too."

"That's what Xenia is?"

"Yes, she's got quite an eye. She aced Fine China 101."

His shoulders relaxed at the news that the bedroom wasn't for Teresa. "Can I kiss you?" he felt compelled to ask. Her body language wasn't promising.

She cocked her head, as if the question was strange. Strange as in "how dare you" or strange as in "of course"? Then she leaned over and touched her lips to his. The message of the kiss was unclear. Her cool lips didn't part. It might have been a stage kiss.

"You know," he said, arms stealing around her, "this piano would totally fit in our other house." She wriggled out of his grasp with the ease of a cat and stood with the piano between them. "If I knocked down a wall," he added.

* * *

Teresa couldn't believe her ears. Perhaps Hollywood had sent back a Beta-male version of Liam. "Who needs a separate living and dining area?" Beta Liam continued, his seductive tone triggering an automatic sensual response. "And if you don't want me to take the role, I won't."

She refused to melt into his arms. The lonely sonogram appointment had driven home a hard truth. Perhaps it was the glint of disapproval in the doctor's eyes when she explained that her husband was traveling and couldn't accompany her. She was in this by herself. Liam claimed to look forward to being a father, but it would be *her* project. His priorities were *his* house, *his* career.

"I would never tell you what to do," she said. *Because it wouldn't do any good*, she added silently.

Liam had dialed his usual cockiness way down. This was quite an about-face. Could she trust it? "I don't want to lose you," he said. "I love you. I screwed up."

How much do you love me? she thought. *Very much? How about "very very much"?* She recalled an old Peanuts comic strip. How many "verys" until Liam said, "Whoa. Not *that* much."

"Teresa?" he said in a small voice after the silence spun out. He was pleading now. He looked about ten.

She stared at the piano keys. "I want to believe you love me. But you haven't acted like a man in love. I don't need all the verys." His brow furrowed. "Never mind. I don't want the words. Show me. And this isn't about sex."

Tears welled from Liam's eyes. *Oh my God*. He was crying! She had *never* seen him cry. She thought about was what he'd braved in Israel, how he'd been robbed of a childhood and never known any love but his sister's. And Teresa's.

Sighing in defeat, she went over and draped her arms around his neck, nuzzling, and breathing in his warm, clean scent. His shoulders were heaving.

"Sweetie," she whispered, "you know I love you. You *know* it. I will never want anyone else. And if I know you love me, *know* it to the marrow of my bones, I won't care where you are, how many beautiful women you have to kiss onscreen."

His shoulders heaved again. Her heart breaking for him, Teresa pressed him closer. That's when she realized he was laughing. Laughing *and* crying.

"Don't be mad," he said, wiping away the tears. "Those women … they can't hold a candle to you. In every screentest, every so-called actress was more impossible than the last. I'm a poor excuse for an actor, and it took everything I've got to pretend to want them."

No newly minted saint could appear humbler or more penitent. "All right. You had me at hello. Oh, that's right, you never said 'hello.' You had me the moment you came in looking like a whipped puppy."

She was leading him up the winding staircase. *Five-four-three-two ....* He caught her in his arms and carried her the rest of the way.

"Teresa? Which way is the guest bedroom?"

She pointed.

He laid her gently on the bed and pressed an ear to her belly, listening. "Ah! I felt something."

"She isn't as active as Ali's baby, but Ali's is a boy." He looked up at her, then, his face radiant with happiness.

Then he kissed her—deeply—and the rest of the world disappeared. There was only them, this moment, in this cozy room. She rather liked the way it had turned out. The stenciled wallpaper, the canopy bed, the landscape paintings picked up at a local gallery.

Not Liam's taste. Not *his* house. A place of her own.

No need to spell that out for her handsome husband.

CHAPTER 32

———◆———

JAKE WATCHED LIAM DASH INSIDE his house. Should he have warned his brother-in-law he wouldn't find Teresa there?

On the plane ride, the guy had been like a coiled spring. If it meant he could have arrived home sooner, he would have leapt from the plane and run back to Port Townsend. As it was, Liam slumped in the back of the chartered plane, scowling, as if plotting an enemy's demise, while Jake and David shot the breeze upfront. Liam didn't even offer his two cents during the James Bond debate. They agreed that George Lazenby was among the best. As for the others, Jake argued that Roger Moore was underappreciated, though he still preferred Timothy Dalton. David insisted no one did it better than Sean Connery.

Had Teresa left Liam because of Jake's advice? He felt a pang of guilt. He'd meant to help the man find his footing, not push him into quicksand. Teresa had confessed that she planned to move out while Liam was in Los Angeles. Jake urged her to discuss it with her husband first, because otherwise she was doing to Liam the exact thing he had done to her, and two wrongs didn't make a right. She resurrected another cliché: Liam would get a taste of his own medicine. He'd never seen her so bitter. *What a mess.*

He parked in front of his rental B&B with a new appreciation for its prissy exterior. He'd grown fond of the ol' haunted house.

After hauling his suitcase upstairs, he trotted back down to the parlor, lit the fire, and opened a bottle of wine. The trip had been a success—mostly. Ever since meeting Liam, Jake couldn't see anyone else in the role of Damon. He'd marveled at George Reed Masters' extraordinary screen presence, though the guy didn't have the same impact in person. William had shown him Liam's screentests—every bit as impressive. He got a kick out of how women reacted to his brother-in-law. Now he knew what Teresa meant when she insisted women *literally* threw themselves at Liam. More like fell into his arms. Three of the women had done just that, even though the scene didn't call for it. Jake chuckled at the memory. Liam had been game, but he always had that gleam in his eye Jake associated with Roger Moore—that it was all a lark, the height of absurdity. No matter what he thought of a particular woman, Liam treated her with the utmost politeness and respect. Then there was the knife-throwing screentest. Liam was a total pro, unhesitant, no nonsense.

After Jake and David were done fiddling with the script, little of Jake's original story remained. If they still called it *Kapow*, wouldn't his fans be disappointed? Holly Relish was gone. Maddie/Lorelei's sexiest outfit was a black catsuit. No sex scenes for Lorelei and Mickey. How had Rory convinced George that the role was worth his time? True, in the new version, Micky's part was much larger. It was almost a buddy movie now. Given his inexperience, Liam would benefit from watching a pro in action. And Maddie claimed George was a good colleague, not a scene stealer.

Rory .... If all of this were to be believed, "friendly" ghosts were not only here to help the living, as in *A Christmas Carol*. That whole incident with the Betty Boop girl—Sally was her name—should have been his first clue. Rory had been like one of those small fish—remoras—that hover around sharks to feed off their parasites. They benefited the shark, but mostly, themselves.

Lulled by the heat of the fire and relaxed by the wine, Jake put down his glass and lay back on the couch. A man sat down next to him.

"Hello," he said in a plummy British accent.

Jake blinked several times. "You're the artist."

"Why yes, I am." The man appeared more solid than George had described. Twenty percent transparent, maybe. Wiry, young but old before his time. His large droopy eyes were sunken and watery. He wore a silk dressing gown, trousers, and slippers.

"I love your work," Jake said.

"You are too kind."

"Is there more?"

"Certainly. Some of it hangs in homes around town. Reynard Silvestre owns a few pieces. Two in your sister's new place. Three pieces are displayed in the Frye Museum in Seattle, attributed to P Day Moray. There's another in the Musée d'Orsay in Paris." The ghost was particularly proud of that one. "My silly descendants," he added with a little moue of disgust, "sold them off with false stories of their provenance. Moray came from a wealthy Scottish family. He and I attended the Ruskin School of Fine Art together in London. The man copied my style for the rest of his long, useless life."

"This place …" Jake said. "Did you scare off the owners?"

"*Terrified* them," the ghost said with relish. "So much so, they left everything behind, down to the last stuffed bear. Believed my spirit might reside in one of the objects. A naked shepherdess, perhaps." His smile revealed a set of gnarly teeth. "I didn't wish to frighten *you* away. You're just the sort of chap whose company I enjoy. Allow them to sell you the house, why don't you? They'll let you keep the figurines."

"The naughty ones," Jake said. He tried to rise, but his limbs rebelled. "What is your name?"

"Simon Elliot. Call me Simon." The man reached over to shake Jake's hand.

"Excuse me," Jake said, "I don't mean to be rude, but my hand isn't currently taking orders."

"I understand perfectly," the man said. "Sleep paralysis. That's all right. I'm a spectral presence; physical contact is beyond me." Again, he bared his gnarly teeth. "I have learned a few tricks, however."

"Such as making clocks chime?" Jake tried to clarify.

The doorbell rang, and the image dissolved and dispersed, like mist.

A dream, then. An oddly specific dream.

"It's probably Liam," he said aloud, stretching. He hoped his brother-in-law wasn't bent on using him for target practice. Would Teresa have divulged his role in the breakup of their marriage? He finished off his glass of wine.

* * *

Chiara shuffled restlessly on the stoop, wondering what kind of reception to expect. If Jake turned her away, she would deserve it. A proselytizing religious fanatic might be more welcome. Not that Jake would ever be rude. He would be kind yet firm, tell her it was too late, that she should have responded to at least one of his many phone messages or emails.

She'd been staying at a nearby motel, skulking about the neighborhood, on the lookout for Jake's BMW. She'd feared he was gone for good. She'd decided against knocking on Liam and Teresa's door. She hadn't seen them outside once. Were they separated? In their brief acquaintance, she'd sensed discord. Three weeks had passed since the accident. A lot could happen in that time. A lot could happen in an instant.

The O'Connell family had believed Arnold's "Mr. Nice Guy" act and would condemn Chiara for abandoning him in his moment of need.

The door flew open with such force it might have been stuck. Jake simply stared at her.

"Jake?" Her voice cracked. She sounded pitiful.

"Oh, uh, come in." The air of distraction had returned. He appeared neither surprised nor pleased.

She entered slowly, tentatively, as if expecting him to withdraw the invitation.

"Were you napping? You seem … disoriented."

"As if I've seen a ghost?"

How could he be flippant at a time like this? "If you don't want to see me, please say so."

He scrubbed a hand through his hair, already disheveled as if he'd just risen from bed. "I thought you were back with Arnold."

"Knowing what you know?"

"What do I know? Not much." He rubbed his forehead. "Forgive me. I guess I'm still jetlagged. My point is, I only know what you told me. Anything else is based entirely on a few brief but intense encounters."

"Where have you been?" she said, hoping to defuse the tension. "Europe, the East Coast?"

"Huh? No. Los Angeles."

"You said 'jetlagged.' "

He laughed. "Wrong word. Uh, spooked."

"Spooked?"

"What do you say when you've seen a ghost?"

"You're the native English speaker."

"Yes, well, 'spooked,' then. Although it might have been a dream. Please, have a seat."

She sat, but her posture remained rigid. "*Your* ghost, Rory?"

"No, Rory has moved on."

"Then what ghost?"

"The one who resides here. Come." He walked her over to the portrait of the young man.

She nodded. "I assumed he'd talk to you sooner or later."

Jake's stance was defensive—his arms crossed. "Chiara, why are you here?"

She hadn't fully considered what it might mean to show up on his doorstep without warning. Until divorce arrangements could be made, she had little to live on. Six hundred fifty dollars cash and a credit card she fully expected Arnold to cancel. She'd paid in advance for two weeks at the motel just in case. She would have called Jake immediately if she hadn't been so afraid of what he might say. "I should have called first," she said in a small voice. "The accident was so … unexpected. Neither of us died. They said it was a miracle. Was it?"

"You think I have the answer?"

"Yes, I think you do."

"It wasn't me."

"David, then."

"Yes." A pause. "He saved your life."

She hadn't dared believe it.

Jake went on, his tone bitter, "I'd say that's the final prediction done with, right? Whether or not you choose to believe in gypsies or fortune telling. Although, if you're willing to buy the existence of ghosts and the possibility of spontaneous healing, that's not much more of a stretch. Whatever … you shouldn't waste another minute of your life on a man like Arnold."

She gave a broad shrug. "I agree."

His manner toward her softened. "How *is* ol' Arnold?"

"Recovering. His girlfriend is caring for him."

"His *girlfriend*?"

She spoke in a rush. "When she found out his heart condition was treatable, she decided not to leave him after all. He'd only wanted to try again with me because he needed a nurse. My past behavior led him to assume I'd roll over at his command. He put on quite an act for your family. After the accident, I didn't see how I could abandon him. I don't give a dried fig for the money! I will find a way to pull forward. But I … first, I had to come here. Because …." She stopped. *Because I love you* was on the tip of her tongue. He was supposed to believe that? Or would he think she was here because her husband had left her penniless and alone?

He made no move to put her at ease.

She sighed. "Jake, I know how this looks. I shouldn't expect you to believe I'm here simply because I love you."

He raised an eyebrow. "Do you?"

"Love you? Yes."

"It's as simple as that?" He wasn't convinced.

"No, it's not simple. None of it is simple." She was on the verge of tears, gesturing like a madwoman. "It will be a messy divorce. I haven't worked for money in years. You will think I'm here because I have nowhere else to go. Not because I want to be with you."

"*Do* you want to be with me?" He was cool and clinical, as if expecting to catch her in a lie.

She clasped her hands in her lap, forcing them to be still. Almost resentfully, she said, "Yes."

He shrugged. "Then stay. I won't make any promises … if that's all right. We'll get to know each other. You can sleep in a separate bedroom. As it happens, you have several choices. If it suits you."

"It doesn't." She allowed herself a small smile.

He came over to sit beside her, took her hand and kissed it. Waited. Neither spoke. She leaned over and touched her lips to his. He kissed her back.

Finally, he pulled away and studied her face as if still searching for the lie. "Are you certain, Chiara? You could stay at the compound. Ali will give you an advance. The children's book you wrote together will be published in time for Christmas. Your cabin is still vacant."

"Whatever you say. I don't want to be a burden."

He pulled her onto his lap.

A laugh in her voice, she said, "You must not want me to think clearly." She squirmed a little. "At least *part* of you is trying to distract me. Would you prefer that I live at the compound?"

"Of course not," he said as he adjusted her position on his lap to his best advantage. "This way I have you at my mercy." He bounced her a few times and closed his eyes as if struggling for control.

"Ah," she said with a chuckle, "you think you'll get your fill then cast me out. That's a chance I'm willing to take."

* * *

As Maddie and David's limo approached the larger-than-life Mann's Chinese Theatre, David said, "What a gaudy mess."

"I think it's grand," Maddie proclaimed, momentarily forgetting her jitters. *The Dance of the Seven Veils* would look tame compared to her cinematic unveiling. Strolling around naked was the furthest thing from acting, but here she was at the premiere of *Insanity*. No turning back.

David claimed to be prepared for the worst. "At least we'll get that part over with at the beginning." At her look of dismay, he added, "That came out wrong. I meant I'm glad I won't have to hold my breath for most of the film waiting for your grand entrance."

She chuckled. "I'm sure George's performance will be riveting, or so he tells me. Anyway, I'm sorry, sweetie, but it's not going to be 'over with.' If

George is to be believed, they've inserted flashbacks throughout the movie."

David groaned. "I know, I know. I only meant that the initial shock will be over with. I'm hoping to forget it's you up there." He cleared his throat. "Why did they rename it, anyway? Wasn't it Grauman's Chinese Theatre for the longest time?"

"Mr. Mann must have donated a lot of money," Maddie said. "Isn't that the way these things work?" She squeezed his hand. "You look so handsome."

"It's the same tux I wore at our wedding. I'm glad you like it. You look … scrumptious. Like the goddess Aphrodite."

Maddie's gown, on loan from a famous designer, was a one-shouldered lavender-satin full-length sheath with a chiffon overlay. It skimmed her curves with the merest hint of cleavage. Her curly blonde hair, now shoulder length, was caught up in an artfully messy updo. In Hollywood, you didn't hide your body—or so said William, Jake's agent. Maddie was still agent-free herself, though many had wooed her in the week since they'd arrived. Also attending the premiere were Jake and Chiara and Teresa and Liam. Ali had stayed behind with Joe to oversee the preparations for Thursday's blowout Thanksgiving dinner at the compound. *Insanity* would open at the Rose in Port Townsend on Thanksgiving Day. It was Tuesday, November twenty-third, and tomorrow they'd head for home.

On the red carpet, Maddie and David held hands for courage. One newscaster, after asking her to describe her gown, said, "What's next, Maddie? We're all waiting with bated breath."

Looking at the woman's name tag, Maddie replied, "Uh, Linnie, I'm sorry, but I've been told not to discuss the future."

"We hear it's a family venture."

"Then you know more than I do," Maddie said brightly. She forged ahead, pulling a surprised David after her. "They told me the news about *Kapow* hadn't leaked," she grumbled.

A dry laugh from David. "How naïve of you! I've already seen tabloid stories about you and George."

"Oh, no! Really?" Maddie said in a furious whisper.

"Don't worry. I know he's an incorrigible flirt. Also a twerp. I don't consider him a threat."

Wait till you see us onscreen, Maddie thought, taking in the sea of gold and red—the velvet seats and the curtain.

They were seated in a block with the rest of the cast—George directly behind her, breathing down her neck. His date was a predictably breathtaking blue-eyed blonde with deep cleavage. His greeting had been an enthusiastic hug. David's brow furrowed, but rather than protesting, he shook George's hand with enough force to break bones. George, to his credit, winced but didn't make a point of flexing his fingers back to life.

The speeches went on interminably, but eventually the lights dimmed and the curtains parted. When David laid a reassuring hand on Maddie's arm, she relaxed her shoulders and concentrated on her breathing. She had expected her part to last ten minutes, maybe fifteen. But the opening sequence dragged on and on, reviving the memory of filming in all too vivid detail. George's attempts to seduce her, the awful producer who had threatened to blacklist her if she didn't let him have his way. George swinging her around, holding her close on the dance floor, all but screwing her in the cab.

There was no denying that the camera loved George. He looked more substantial on the screen, the blue of his eyes diamond bright, his features more interesting than sharp.

Painful as it was to watch, Maddie had to admit that her performance wasn't bad. The actual sex scene was less revealing than Maddie had feared, and when Sadie took her final steps toward the main door, she fairly glowed with infatuation and hope for the future. Enough that you might almost miss the provocative glimpses of Maddie's breasts from the opening of the man's shirt. Almost. Sadie's misplaced ebullience made the rain of bullets that ended her life all the more devastating.

Maddie sighed. *There*, she thought, *I'm gone. That wasn't so bad.*

David kissed her hand, gave her a thumbs up.

As the movie continued, her shoulders began to rise again. They seemed to have used every frame they'd filmed of her. Laughing, kissing George, appearing to go down on him. *Yikes.* George fondling her breasts. *No.*

She could feel David's tension too. So much for being able to relax once her character was killed.

Still, at the end of the day, it was a good movie. If she hadn't read the script, she'd never have guessed who killed her character and why. George definitely lived up to his hype.

As the curtain fell, the cast was ushered onstage to take a bow. She returned to find her husband on his feet, clapping and grinning. Was the smile genuine? She couldn't tell. He gave her a passionate kiss and a full-body hug, much to the delight of the photographers.

"Thank God you're the villain in our movie," he whispered into her neck. "That was—bar none—the most harrowing experience of my life."

She was relieved to hear the laughter in his voice.

EPILOGUE

———◆———

JAKE STOOD AT THE EDGE of the bluff, basking in the sea breeze and the silence. It was early in the morning on Thanksgiving Day. He'd wanted an early start, to talk to David about the screenplay he was currently revising, but Lorenzo had dragged his father down to the beach to take advantage of low tide. When David returned, Jake and he would resume their discussion.

Jake still missed Rory—the man he'd known in life, anyway. *All's well that ends well*, he thought, *and it certainly ended well for me.*

He would have felt sorrier about saddling George with Rory if the actor hadn't made such a pest of himself in Port Townsend. He assumed his dead buddy would eventually move on, find the light, or whatever it was wandering spirits did when they were ready to go to the great beyond. He'd never doubted that Rory was one of the good guys, despite his reluctance to leave this wonderful world behind. *Who can blame him when goddesses like Chiara walk among us?* he thought.

A string of loud obscenities called his attention to Joe, standing next to the vegetable garden.

"Hey," Jake called out, striding over, "can I help?"

Joe was rubbing his hand and muttering to himself. "The chain link fence got damaged in the storm last night. That big branch there ripped open a two-inch gash." He pointed. "Sorry about the F-bombs. I jabbed my palm with the pliers. Went right through the glove."

Jake took a look at the nasty red spot. "Shall I get David?"

"Hah, hah, very funny. I'll live."

Jake almost said, "But will you play guitar again?" *Enough teasing*, he thought. "May I?"

Joe handed over the gloves and the pliers, and Jake set about completing the fix. The brothers conferred frequently over the next half hour. Finally they stepped back to admire their handiwork.

"How'd you learn to do that?" Joe asked, impressed.

"Sensei Liam," Jake said. "Master of all masters."

Joe started to laugh, and Jake joined in. They kept on laughing, stopping just short of rolling on the ground. Not that Jake's reply had been *that* hilarious. It was cathartic laughter. Attracted by the commotion, the dogs gamboled joyfully around them, almost like sheep.

"Do you remember that time you fell off your bike—how I just *knew* you'd been injured?" Joe asked, still chuckling as he rubbed Harry's back with his good hand.

Jake scratched Coogan under the chin. "Mom gave you this lecture about ESP not being real. We showed her!"

"Even when it turned out I was right," Joe said, still grinning like a fool, "she kept insisting it was a coincidence."

Jake grinned too. "I guess that rules out enlightening her about the strange goings-on of the past year."

Joe's smile faded. "How are you doing?" he asked with genuine concern.

"Better, thanks. Uh, have I missed my window?"

Joe cocked his head, waiting for the punchline.

"My apology window. For being such an asshole."

Joe raised his eyebrows. "As long as I can still apologize for being a shit brother in high school and college."

"Done," Jake said. They automatically high-fived.

"Shit!" Joe swore, cradling his hurt hand again.

"Oh, d-damn, sorry," Jake sputtered.

" 'Love means never having to say you're sorry,' " Joe quoted with a sly smile, still rubbing his palm.

Jake snickered. "Talk about literary trash. How old were we when we found Mom's dog-eared copy of *Love Story* in her desk? Ten? She must have liked it. When she discovered us reading the most egregiously bad passages aloud, she was *not* amused."

"Good times," Joe said.

"Could we read that well at ten?" Jake asked. "More like twelve or thirteen."

"I need to get some ice for my hand," Joe said.

"I'll come with you."

Shoulder to shoulder, the brothers headed toward the Log Palace.

* * *

Holiday season at the O'Connell Compound had begun. Was it Thanksgiving already? Ali missed those early small-scale celebrations. With every event, the guest list and territory covered ballooned. At Matthew's request, they'd included several of his new local friends—the ones with no partners or family. *Give it time*, Ali thought, *and our numbers will rival Malcolm Forbes' wedding*. Still, much as she disliked crowds, she was off the hook. She could simply step aside and let the others take over. An unlimited number of FOSSP kids would handle any hitches, and Jean-Louis always provided the most sumptuous feasts. Not that Ali was totally on board with the wild game concept …. Mostly she was grateful for any excuse to spend time with Becca. Holidays also drew the full contingent of family to their little haven. Carrie, Rostand, and … a surprise guest. Not quite the Stone Guest from *Don Giovanni*, but close. It wasn't as if Edward was going to drag them all to hell, much as he might like to. Their sins were hardly on a par with Don Giovanni's. But then, the self-righteousness of Carrie O'Connell's firstborn was legendary.

Then there was her pregnancy … worse than last time. The aches and pains, the embarrassing body noises, the bloating and swelling. Why did her body turn against her like this? The relentless nausea had finally, *finally* abated. Now, gestational diabetes. Did Joe blame her for eating the wrong things? The doctors wanted to focus on how she could eat "healthier." She had never been one to binge on chocolate or potato chips. At least now, with insulin shots, she felt better, and she wasn't anywhere near as large as she had been with the twins. Just one baby this time. A boy. A little Joe! They were both thrilled. Would Joe be willing to stop now? You could take the boy out of the Catholic Church but not the Church out of the boy. Or something like that. He wanted a large family. She wasn't cut out to be a baby-making machine. How ironic that Teresa, so fine-boned and aristocratic, was a walking advertisement for pregnancy. After some initial stomach upset, she glowed with health and carried the baby like a fashionably chunky accessory.

And now, with two of Joe's songs climbing the charts and his vocal cords clear, he was planning a tour. Even though other singers had made those songs hits.

"What's going on in that gorgeous noggin of yours?" Joe asked, leaning down for a kiss. "You seem sad."

"I'm a little overwhelmed, I guess."

Joe looked exactly the same as he had when they were first married—the gold-flecked brown eyes still clear and fathomless, the cleft chin firm, the thick chestnut-brown hair free of gray threads, the body lean and muscular. She clutched her swollen belly.

He was scrutinizing her in that unnerving way of his. "Are you being hard on yourself again? You must know that you're more beautiful than ever. You need only look in the mirror."

She gazed past him, toward the ocean, willing him to stop reading her mind. "Let's not talk about that. I'll just be grateful when this is over." *It's hard on me, can't you see?* she wanted to ask. *I can't spend the next ten years feeling unwell, waiting for the next baby to be born and hoping I'm doing enough for the others.*

"Shall we take a minute to discuss the future? *Our* future."

She was filled with dread. He seemed so solemn.

"It's time to let other people have the babies."

A weight lifted from her shoulders.

"We have other options, don't you think?"

"Foster children," she said, smiling.

He laughed. "Why not? We're already fostering young adults. Lorenzo could use some playmates his age. We have endless childcare resources. But let's hold off until this one is up and toddling."

She rose awkwardly to her feet and threw her arms around the neck of her dearest, sweetest husband. He hugged her tight enough that she felt him stir.

"Really?" she said. "You want this … this wide load?"

"When you put it that way …." He drew back, his expression full of wonder. "Do you know what I see when I look at you? I see blazing blue eyes deep enough to drown in, a heart large enough to love, accept, and forgive a crowd that could fill a stadium. But I also see a woman I will never stop loving or desiring. I can hardly believe what you've been willing to do for us, but mostly for me. I wish I could assume the physical burden for you. Since I can't, I can do better when it comes to other things. Give you more of my time, for instance—"

She wondered how long he would keep groveling before she stopped him. With a smile, she broke in, "Sweetie, I don't need you to become a house husband. I want you to be happy. God knows I'm happy … most of the time. Yes, the pregnancies have been difficult, and yes, I think three's all I can manage, at least for now. But you … there's no need to make any more sacrifices for me." She trailed a finger down the front of his T-shirt. "And now, isn't there something else we can do besides talk?"

He pouted adorably. "You didn't like my little speech?"

"I loved it," she whispered against his lips.

* * *

Chiara stood at the buffet, helping herself to a slice of turkey. If anyone could make a skinny wild turkey taste more delicious than the most gently raised capon, it was Jean-Louis. The secret was slow cooking, he explained, and the perfect marinade. Though tougher than the farm-raised variety, they were far more flavorful.

How strange and wonderful, she thought. The day she arrived, the only bright spot in her life had been Lorenzo. She'd been certain they meant to steal him away. Instead, they'd welcomed her into their lives. She'd fallen in love with a knight out of King Arthur's court, co-written a children's book, and liberated herself from her shard-of-ice husband. Four-year-old Lorenzo was thriving like a rose uprooted from a dark backlot and planted in a sun-filled garden.

They were all bundled up in turtleneck sweaters and down vests. The safari tent was drafty, and no number of portable heaters or warm bodies could change that. Still, the general mood was euphoric. Ali had placed a pile of blankets, scarves, and vests at the entrance, and they could add or discard layers at will.

"What do you think?" Jake whispered into her hair, his hand grazing her shoulder in a light caress.

"I love your family," she said, stealing a quick kiss.

He laughed. "Even Edward?"

She looked around to see who might be listening. In a low voice, she said, "Ali called him the Stone Guest."

"Ouch. You think he's here to drag us down to hell?"

"Not at all," Chiara said. "More like a statue who struggles to come to life."

Jake seemed to consider this as he filled his plate. "It's not fair to judge him based on his past behavior. Speaking from experience, I believe he's a man with a secret. You'll notice he's not wearing his clerical collar."

"Priests don't always wear the collar, do they?"

Jake led her away from the buffet. "I believe they do, at least in public. It might even be clerical law." He pointed toward the two free seats next to David, Maddie, and Lorenzo. "They're saving those for us."

* * *

Jake still couldn't get over Edward's presence at the compound. When Jake himself first arrived, he'd bent over backward to put them all at ease, knowing the kind of trouble his presence might stir up. His working theory was that Carrie had dragged Edward here. His oldest brother had just turned thirty-eight. His auburn hair was silvered at the sides. His skin was weathered, but the too-pretty face benefited from the additional character. Not a lot of laugh lines. Edward, with his almost ethereal beauty, had once eclipsed them all. He had Carrie's fine features and long-lashed blue eyes combined with their father's strong jaw and cleft chin. At six-three, he was only two inches shy of David, but even more daunting, if possible. He had an "air" about him. Hard to get a read on the man. As Jake watched him now from his vantage point halfway down the long table, his older brother appeared relaxed enough. He chatted easily with Carrie and Rostand. Interesting that Rostand was acting more like a guest than a manservant. No doubt Ali had gone out of her way to convince him his help wasn't required.

"Jake?" He swiveled about at David's voice. "Everyone wants to know about Los Angeles. You'd better listen in case I omit key details."

Seeing Maddie bristle, Jake said, "As long as your wife approves. Not that she has anything to be embarrassed about." *Damn*, why had he added that? Maddie was giving him the stink-eye.

David arched an eyebrow. "I was only saying that Maddie was swarmed at the after-party. *Everyone* wants to represent her. Plus she got hit on by some major stars. That's got to be a trip."

"Who?" Ali asked, goggle-eyed.

"Let's see." He ticked them off his fingers, naming two actors in their forties, three in their thirties, and one twenty-two-year-old.

All were household names. Jake had been too interested in checking out the historic estate where the party took place and chatting with the few people who weren't putting on airs to notice Maddie's A-list fan club.

"No kidding," Joe said. "They flirted with her in front of you?"

"It was subtle," David admitted. "You know, complimenting her on her performance and generally ingratiating themselves."

Maddie laughed. "Most were intimidated by the sparks shooting out of David's eyes."

"What was it like seeing yourself up there?" Ali asked.

Maddie shuddered. "Uncomfortable. The opening was not unexpected, although nothing quite prepares you for that kind of, er, exposure. My photo double lying in a pool of blood was supposed to be the end of my character's … contribution. But it was like George said: they kept showing flashbacks throughout the film, and some of them were more, uh, R-rated than I recalled."

"What's R-rated?" Lorenzo asked.

"It means they aren't for children," Joe explained.

"Why not?" he persisted.

"They show things that wouldn't interest children," Chiara improvised. "Boring things."

"Like shopping?"

"Yes, like that," Chiara said with a straight face.

"I've never heard it called that," Jake said with a smile.

"Adults wearing strange things it would embarrass children to see them in," Chiara went on.

"Like when you wore those ugly dresses?" Lorenzo asked her.

She tensed but quickly regained her composure. "Yes, like that."

"Okay," Lorenzo said. "What's for dessert?"

"You have several choices. May and Susan, can you take Lorenzo to the kitchen for dessert?" Chiara checked her watch. "It's getting late, and he's been patient."

His departure was met with a collective sigh of relief.

"I can see you need to watch your Ps and Qs around that one," Edward said in his resonant baritone voice. Jake was amused by their reactions to Edward's comment, as if surprised to discover he spoke English. That plummy voice went a long way toward humanizing the daunting stranger.

"No kidding," Ali said, a little too brightly. "Part of the charm of the children's book Chiara and I wrote together comes from Lorenzo's responses."

"Chiara, how did you meet Jake?" Edward asked, a seemingly innocuous question. Surely their mother had filled him in.

Chiara's eyes darted from Edward to Jake. "I am … Lorenzo's aunt."

"You're engaged?"

"Uh, no," Chiara said. "My divorce is not final."

They all froze.

"Ah," Edward said in a convincing show of heartfelt sympathy, "that sounds complicated."

Later that night, back at the house, Jake lay next to Chiara, admiring the gentle curves of her ivory-silk body. They were both naked, his leg draped over hers. Embers still glowed in the bedroom fireplace. Ever since Chiara had moved into the attic room with him, Jake had experienced no more dreams of his resident ghost—if that's what he was. He still hadn't verified if Simon's landscapes were displayed in Teresa's new place. He was in no hurry to find out. He *wanted* to believe Simon was real.

"Did you mean to tell Edward you were getting divorced?" he asked, brushing a wisp of hair from her eyes.

"No," she said. He loved the worshipful way her eyes swept over him. No other woman had ever looked at him like that. "They don't call them 'father confessors' for nothing. I felt almost compelled, like he'd given me a truth serum."

Jake chuckled. "Edward has that effect on people."

"I expected him to disapprove, or worse—stand up and denounce us."

He leaned over to kiss her breasts then trailed his tongue down to her navel.

She giggled. "That tickles!"

He traveled lower.

She sighed with pleasure. "Perhaps he won't object to our being together after all," she said when she was back in his arms.

"Ah, but would he marry us, do you think?"

She didn't answer, her soft brown eyes round with surprise.

"Never mind about Edward," he said. "Will you marry me? When it's possible, of course."

"What do you think?" She rolled on top of him. "*Si, mio bello.* Do I need to translate?"

He grinned. "I know some basic Italian. I look forward to learning the R-rated stuff."

"You can start with *orribile vestito.*"

He looked puzzled. "I thought it was *vestito brutto.*"

The phrase earned him a lovely peal of laughter. " 'Horrible dress' or 'ugly dress,' your choice."

"What if I told you I don't care *what* you wear? Still, once we're married …" he paused, "will you let me dress you?"

She kissed him on the nose. "I thought you'd never ask."

AUTHOR'S NOTE

Washington's Olympic Peninsula has been my happy place ever since my family first vacationed in that area early in my childhood. When I decided to set a romance novel series there, I considered fictionalizing all the place names, hoping to avoid complaints about accuracy. The O'Connell Compound couldn't exist in the setting I've described. There aren't a lot of megabucks mansions near Port Townsend, and none that overlooks the Strait of Juan de Fuca and has beach access. Maybe in Sequim. That's for starters. If you're bothered by such liberties, I apologize. If not for the pandemic, my husband's health issues, and his strong preference for Arizona, I might have gotten closer to reality. I still visit the Olympic Peninsula whenever I can and have done my best to capture the spirit of this magical place.

I have never seen a ghost, but I've had a few experiences that left me with an open mind. I occasionally know who is going to call or what will be in the mail before it happens. Once, back when I was a soloist at a Christian Science church, I heard a voice in my head telling me the cash was being stolen out of my wallet. This happened during the 15 minutes I sat in my assigned seat waiting for the service to begin. *That's nonsense*, I told it. My purse was in the staff area, which had no public access, and I'd been doing that job for twenty years without mishaps. After the service was over—I obsessed about "the message" the entire hour—I found that the cash (nothing else) was indeed gone. A homeless man had barreled through and departed so quickly, everyone assumed nothing had been taken. Me? I was thrilled to have received what I saw as proof of a great beyond. My husband rolls his eyes at this story.

My daughter-in-law Laura is a licensed therapist who I've always believed to be psychically gifted. Years after this first incident, she held my dead mother's earrings and basically channeled her for over an hour. Laura referred to matters she could not possibly have known.

I loved the TV show *The Ghost Whisperer* and like the idea that ghosts, under the right circumstances, might comfort the living and take pride in their life's accomplishments, even if fate hooked them off the stage of life too soon.

Many thanks to my sister Laura and dear friends Karin and Tina for their continued feedback and encouragement in this series. Romance novels are not my husband Jeff's thing, but he is a huge inspiration. He did read *The Silent Woodsman* and pronounced it "a good book." Aspects of Jeff's personality, humor, and can-do spirit are present in Liam and all the O'Connell brothers.

Book 5, *The Fallen Man*, ushers Edward into the fold and brings my family saga to—I hope—a satisfying conclusion. Not for my charming but amoral mischief makers, of course, who will be back to wreak more havoc in Book 5. But who knows? They might redeem themselves yet. Kilo, Reynard, and George are already complaining to me about being grossly misunderstood.

If you're a fan of this series, thank you!! I would be thrilled if you'd post ratings and reviews where you can and spread the word on social media. I hope to launch a newsletter soon, and if you join, I promise not to flood your inbox. For updates, please "like" my FB page and follow me on my BookBub and Amazon author pages. All links can be found on www.CatTreadgold.com.

Photo by Claudia Meyer-Newman

CAT TREADGOLD HAS BEEN A publisher and editor, a classical singer, an Equity actress, a coordinator in Newsweek's External Relations Department, a secretary at Siemens AG, a voice teacher at Shoreline Community College, a receptionist at a major recording studio, a cater-waiter with Glorious Foods, a restaurant hostess, and a coat-check girl at a fancy New York nightclub.

Cat has an AB *cum laude* in German Literature from Princeton University, a Master of Music in Vocal Performance from the University of Washington, and a certificate in Technical Writing and Editing from the University of Washington.

She was once semi-fluent in French, German, and Italian and occasionally attempts to revive those languages.

Thank goodness she's good with computers (for a digital immigrant) and learned to touch type in high school.

Two of her unpublished novels made it to the finals in their categories (mystery and romance) in the Pacific Northwest Writers Association Annual Contest.

Three of her one-hour adaptations of operas (original translations and dialogue) were performed by Shoreline students while she was a teacher there.

She and her husband Jeff reside in Washington during its drier months and Arizona during its cooler ones.

Cat loves to hike and walk, ride her bike, hula hoop, golf, listen to audiobooks, cook dishes with lots of leftovers, play piano (she used to be good at it), and play accordion (she will never be good at it). She sings in the occasional concert with Ladies Musical Club, but never in the shower. Her favorite classical composers are Ravel, Debussy, and Brahms. She prefers pop music from the '60s and '70s, particularly Steely Dan and the Rolling Stones.

One hot, humid summer in Ohio, while playing a Shawnee Indian in an outdoor drama during the week and Anne in the musical *Shenandoah* on the weekends, she became certified in stage fighting. That skill later helped her win the role of a broadsword-wielding Maid Marian in a Theater for Young Audiences musical titled *Maid Marian (and Robin Too)*. She always wanted to sing the role of *Carmen*, but only did it in Seattle Opera previews. She has played Edwin Drood in *The Mystery of Edwin Drood*, Maria in *The Sound of Music*, Julie Jordan in *Carousel*, Cherubino in *The Marriage of Figaro*, Prince Orlofsky in *Die Fledermaus*, Maddalena in *Rigoletto*, Julius Caesar in *Julius Caesar in Egypt*, and Rosina in *The Barber of Seville*. Along with other fun gigs (a few at Port Townsend's UpStage), her opera quartet, the Operatic Four Players, performed most Friday nights for about a year at an Italian restaurant. For three years, she toured with NOISE (Northwest Opera in Schools Etcetera).

Videos of her vocal performances can be found on the Cattread Channel on YouTube.

* 9 7 9 8 9 8 7 7 3 6 3 4 0 *